"A BOOK THAT SHOULD BE WIDELY READ BY PARENTS AND CHILDREN ALIKE—MOST DEFINITELY AS FEMALE—OF DATING AGE."
—*Atlanta Journal & Constitution*

"A TIMELY, INTELLIGENT BOOK."
—*Houston Chronicle*

"[CORMAN] MAKES YOU FEEL THE MORAL OUTRAGE AT THE HEART OF THIS BOOK."
—*Los Angeles Times*

"A TRUE-TO-LIFE ACCOUNT... [OF] A CRISIS THAT WILL LINGER AND RESONATE FOR QUITE SOME TIME."—*Washington Post*

# PRAISE FOR AVERY CORMAN
## New York Times bestselling author of Kramer vs. Kramer

"A keen observer, his novels
cut close to the bone of
middle-class life."
—Washington Post

## . . . AND FOR HIS DRAMATIC AND POWERFUL NEW NOVEL PRIZED POSSESSIONS

"The story is as current as the headlines."
—Detroit Free Press

"In previous novels, Corman has examined
families in crisis. In his latest book, he tackles the
subject again, exploring [a] highly charged
issue . . . In lean prose, Corman captures Liz's
vulnerability . . ."
—Publishers Weekly

"Painstakingly realistic . . . Corman has
established himself as among the few successful
male writers who writes successfully about
contemporary family and social issues."
—San Francisco Examiner

(continued)

"Corman imbues his novels with a special brand of . . . sensitivity and skill."
—Worcester [MA] Telegram

"Timely and compelling . . . a commentary on a society that is becoming increasingly aware and intolerant of an all-too-common crime."
—San Francisco Chronicle

"Provocative . . . [A] bold, searing story . . . Just as he did in Kramer vs. Kramer . . . [Corman] has responded to the times once more in Prized Possessions . . . Besides writing about a burning issue on campuses today, Corman delves into what it means to become aware, to open one's eyes, to mature, to evolve . . . The author takes us behind the statistics and the polls to the individuals and their hidden tempests, and to the crossroads where compassion and humanity confront violence . . . and defeat it."
—Fort Worth Star-Telegram

"Corman chronicles the family's life with spare but graceful language . . . With sure, broad strokes, Corman gives a complete portrait of . . . seeking justice and healing from the events of one night."
—Washington Post

"A suspenseful story that goes from campus to courtroom."
—St. Louis Post-Dispatch

"Written with a cool hand steering a story of perhaps one of the most explosive issues of our society today."
—Express News

"Avery Corman has a gift for dialogue and predicament."
—Time

# PRIZED POSSESSIONS

## AVERY CORMAN

19735

FIC
COR

BERKLEY BOOKS, NEW YORK

*This book is a work of fiction. Names, characters, places, and incidents are either the product of the author's imagination or are used fictitiously. Any resemblance to actual events or locales or persons, living or dead, is entirely coincidental.*

This Berkley book contains the complete
text of the original hardcover edition. It
has been completely reset in a typeface
designed for easy reading, and was printed
from new film.

PRIZED POSSESSIONS

A Berkley Book / published by arrangement with
Simon & Schuster

PRINTING HISTORY
Simon & Schuster edition published 1991
Berkley edition / May 1992

All rights reserved.
Copyright © 1991 by Avery Corman, Inc.
This book may not be reproduced in whole or in part,
by mimeograph or any other means, without permission.
For information address: Simon & Schuster,
Simon & Schuster Building, Rockefeller Center,
1230 Avenue of the Americas, New York, New York 10020.

ISBN: 0-425-13263-3

A BERKLEY BOOK ® TM 757,375
Berkley Books are published by The Berkley Publishing Group,
200 Madison Avenue, New York, New York 10016.
The name "BERKLEY" and the "B" logo
are trademarks belonging to Berkley Publishing Corporation.

PRINTED IN THE UNITED STATES OF AMERICA

10  9  8  7  6  5  4  3

# PRIZED POSSESSIONS

# CHAPTER
# 1

THE GIRL IS about seven years old and is wearing a blue velvet dress with a white lace collar. Her straight blond hair is cut short and parted in the middle. She is gazing straight ahead, with a look of composure characteristic of so many renderings of children in nineteenth-century folk art. At her feet is a small brown dog of incalculable breed, a folk art dog. She stands on a flowered rug, her hand resting languidly on a small, round Victorian table with a vase containing delicate roses. She is a perfect child in a serene and comfortable world.

The painting hung in the foyer of Laura and Ben Mason's apartment. They would tell visitors they loved the work because it was a classic rendering of the style and period. In fact, the perfection of the child and her surroundings was the way they wanted to think of their own lives and of their own family.

WHEN LAURA AND BEN Mason's daughter, Elizabeth, was five and their son, Josh, was one, the Masons had been included in a *New York* magazine article on families in the city. A full-page color photograph showed them in their living room, surrounded by their folk art collection.

"You have to use the article for the interviews," their friend Phil Stern advised them. "Schools love this kind of stuff."

The Masons were going through the process of finding the correct private school in Manhattan for Elizabeth. The Sterns' daughter was enrolled at the Hargrove School, a prestigious all-girl preparatory school. The Masons favored the Chase School, coeducational and equally prestigious.

"You can't come right out and say: 'Did you see us in *New York* magazine?'" Laura responded.

"You find a way."

The Sterns lived in the same building as the Masons, at Lexington Avenue and Seventy-fifth Street. Phil was an investment banker, Jane a caterer. Frequently, in their quest to extract the best out of Manhattan living—the best Italian restaurant, the best sale on linens, the best children's mattress—the Sterns made the right choices. So if they were advising that to get Elizabeth into the best school the Masons should mention an article in *New York* magazine, the Masons were prepared to take the advice.

LAURA AND BEN were interviewed by the Chase admissions director, who had already observed Elizabeth in a play situation with other children and in a session with a teacher. In his attempt to follow through on Phil Stern's suggestion, Ben made a transition as grinding as the sound of a New York sanitation truck early in the morning. He went from talking about how vital and alive were the children brought up in the city to saying abruptly:

"Laura and I have made a real commitment to the city. Perhaps you saw us in *New York* magazine last month. The piece about New York couples. The couple with the folk art collection."

"Oh, that was you. Yes, I did see it. Very nice. Very nice, indeed."

• • •

Elizabeth was accepted at the Chase School. The Masons were ecstatic. They thought the only Jews who managed to get their children into the school were Wall Street types. Laura was a magazine editor, Ben a folk art dealer. They surmised that they succeeded in getting Elizabeth accepted because they sounded interesting, and of course, the full-page picture in *New York* certified them as interesting. For Ben Mason, who had gone to De Witt Clinton High School in the Bronx, and for Laura Mason, who had gone to Samuel J. Tilden High School in Brooklyn, having a child at Chase was an enormous step up in social class.

The Chase School population was sixty percent WASP, thirty percent Jewish, and ten percent "others." To some of the old-liners, the idea of Jews and "others," or of Jews, who were by definition "others," at Chase was like an unfortunate sociological oil spill.

Ben Mason, thirty-four, was a stocky man of five feet eleven, with light-brown eyes and hair, and a jaw that was so solid it was nearly a caricature of a manly profile. He looked as if he could have been a construction worker instead of the owner of a gallery. Laura Mason, thirty-two, was five feet six and slender, with blue eyes, a narrow, elegant face, and auburn hair. She might have passed for a model, and in her early days at *Home Furnishings* magazine, she filled in as a model on some of the magazine's page layouts. Laura had entered the magazine field when she found that as an art history major from Brooklyn College, she couldn't compete with students from more prestigious schools for the handful of jobs in the art field. Ben was a graduate of Cooper Union and began his career as a commercial designer. They had met when he made a sales call at *Home Furnishings*.

While working as a designer, he became a collector of old advertising marginalia, and this led him to collect folk art. The folk art became his passion. When he began to spend more time on the acquisition and trading of pieces than on his design business, Ben Mason opened his own gallery, at First Avenue and Eighty-ninth Street. He became a dealer well regarded for having a good, small gallery.

ELIZABETH MASON WAS A CHEERFUL GIRL with reddish-to-auburn hair, blue eyes, and a pug nose. She embarked upon a successful career at Chase. She was popular; as she grew older she had an increasing number of play dates, and she was invited to her classmates' birthday parties. Some of these were modest affairs, such as lunch at McDonald's, but some were galas. One Chase parent, a motion picture producer, invited thirty children to a showing of *Pinocchio* in a screening room, followed by an elaborate buffet. There were ice-skating birthday parties, roller-skating birthday parties, parties where a professional storyteller or a magician came to the house. Having attempted to save money for her previous birthdays by running their own parties, with games and prizes, in the apartment, the Masons opted for the magician at Elizabeth's eighth birthday.

"Wasn't it fun?" she said, as they were putting her to sleep. "Thank you so much for making me such a nice party."

They were happy about having a child thoughtful enough to thank them for their effort, and they were satisfied with the event. However, if they counted in the extra money spent on having their weekday housekeeper come in on a Saturday, the party for an eight-year-old cost three hundred dollars.

THE MASON'S HOUSEKEEPER, Mrs. O'Reilly, was a rotund woman from Ireland, who kept the rooms in the Mason apartment as dust-free as was humanly possible. A compulsive housekeeper was a fantasy for working parents. However, Mrs. O'Reilly's idea of raising children under hospital-level conditions collided with the subject of pets, which she deemed unsanitary. Mrs. O'Reilly could not mount a persuasive argument against tropical fish, and the Masons started there. Fish died; there were burials at sea, fish ceremoniously deposited into the East River. The Masons moved on to hamsters. They lived, they died, they were buried in Central Park, a succession of little furry creatures whose running on the treadmill and gnawing on the cage came too close to being a metaphor for New York living for the comfort of the parents.

Over Mrs. O'Reilly's objections, the Masons acquired a part–golden retriever, part–German shepherd puppy at the ASPCA, a lively brown dog that the children named Queenie. Growing rapidly, Queenie skittered all over the street when taken out for a walk, and with no one other than Ben able to walk the dog easily, Queenie went to obedience school. After weeks of training, everyone in the family attending the sessions, Queenie graduated with honors. The Masons now had a dog who could obey the commands "Heel" and "Sit."

This is urban life, Ben said to himself one morning while walking the dog. It cost me three hundred and fifty dollars to train a dog to walk around the block and sit in a New York City elevator.

THE MASONS' NEIGHBORS the Sterns were on the cutting edge of parental overcontrol. Melanie Stern, a year older than Elizabeth, had experienced so many after-school "enrichment" programs that the child was nearly burned out at nine. Phil Stern was a tall, lanky man, vain about his trim middle. He worked out in a gym a couple of days a week and played tennis once a week with Ben. Jane Stern, at five feet four, had a tendency to be pudgy and changed exercise classes as often as her daughter was moved in and out of new activities. The Sterns tried to sell the Masons on the idea of after-school dance classes for Elizabeth, to teach her grace and poise. Melanie, who was chunky and fairly clumsy, was already enrolled in such a class. Elizabeth refused, saying she was simply not interested. She was already a veteran of preschool arts-and-crafts classes, tumbling classes, most recently a Saturday morning art appreciation course, and swimming lessons prompted by Mrs. O'Reilly to make sure the child didn't drown one day.

THE FOLLOWING YEAR, Ben was asked by the New York State Tourism Department to be a guest curator for a traveling exhibit of folk art by New York artists. The project was noted in the art collectors' magazines and in a piece in the *New York Times*. He enjoyed a run of new business and felt encouraged to expand the size of his gallery to larger quarters, at Lexington Avenue and Eighty-first Street.

He told the children at dinner that the Mason Folk Art Gallery was moving.

"Since this is what I do, I'd like to do it bigger."

"I know what I want to do when I grow up," Josh, age five, declared.

The Masons had talked with friends about how fashions change on the subject. When Laura and Ben were children, little girls wanted to be ballerinas and little boys policemen and firemen. Laura remarked at one dinner party that if gender-neutral thinking had truly filtered down, little boys would want to be ballet dancers and little girls policepersons and firepersons. The last time they checked, Josh wanted to be an astronaut and Elizabeth wanted to be an animal doctor.

"What would you like to be?" Ben asked Josh.

"Kung Fu," Josh said.

"Why?" Laura asked.

"Kung Fus are tougher than everybody."

"There goes years of anti-macho rhetoric down the drain," Ben remarked.

"Elizabeth?" Laura inquired of her nine-year-old.

"TV weatherwoman," she answered.

The parents sat, amused, bewildered. Where did these ideas come from?

"Why that particularly?" Ben said.

"Because Connie Brooks, she's on Channel Five and she

came to school to talk to us and she's very pretty and nice, and she wore a beautiful dress, and that's what I'd like to be."

"Well, they get a lot of attention," Laura said. "Everybody watches them."

After the children went to sleep, Laura said to Ben: "I just hope, after all the talking and the marching, that the pendulum doesn't swing all the way back for her generation of women."

"She did say TV weatherwoman. She didn't say TV weatherman's wife."

BEN OPENED THE DOORS of his new gallery with a wine and cheese party. With his background in design, he organized the space meticulously. The pieces were illuminated with well-placed lighting. He wrote descriptive material, which he set in type and mounted adjacent to the objects. His design sense extended to his selection of the folk art pieces themselves, each an outstanding example of a genre. He had created a folk art gallery with the ambience of a small folk art museum.

The guest list included friends, customers, school parents, and Ben's and Laura's own parents, who stood to the side trying to make sense of his business. Laura's parents lived in downtown Brooklyn. Her father, Sol Goodman, was the proprietor of a newsstand in an office building near the Brooklyn County Courthouse. A small, wiry man with wisps of red hair on his balding head, he was fidgety in his demeanor and used the stub of a cigar to underline his opinions, which were largely uninformed. Her mother, Jean, was a thin, quiet woman, whose main activity had always been keeping house and deferring to Sol. Laura's view of her parents was that she had been stuck with a broken radio that could get only one station.

Ben's father, Henry Mason, was six feet tall, stocky, with dark-brown eyes constantly on the alert for weakness in the other fellow. He presided over a ladies' handbag company, with a plant in the South Bronx, to which he drove every day from Riverdale in his black Chrysler. Ben's mother, Belle, was the company's office manager, a slender woman with hazel eyes and light-brown hair that she kept blond. They were fond of saying about themselves, in their joke about the business, that they were "tough as leather." Ben had a younger brother, David, a lawyer in Chicago, the one with "a head for business," unlike the dreamy older son. The parents were mystified that Ben, a boy they never would have allowed to be part of the business, could persist in selling knickknacks and old paintings.

"From these *tchotchkes* he still tries to make a living?" Ben's mother said to her counterparts.

"If you hit it right, you can sell some of this for plenty," Laura's father, Sol, declared.

"How do you know?" Ben's father said sharply. After years of children's birthday parties and holiday events, he had heard enough of the man's opinions, listening to this newsstand dealer rattle on. "To sell this stuff for plenty you have to find plenty of morons."

"These things always looked nice in the apartment," Laura's mother offered weakly.

Ben's father examined an antique, hand-carved miniature Ferris wheel.

"Four hundred dollars he expects to get for this," and they nodded in agreement about the dire straits.

HOME FURNISHINGS, under Laura's guidance as editor in chief, had been in the process of changing from a trade publication to a magazine that also attracted consumer readership. In the three years of Laura's regime, circulation had risen from 70,000 to 100,000. She had worked first as an assistant art director for the magazine, eventually becoming art director. But she always had skills in developing ideas for articles and was a skilled writer. Everything came together for her when she became editor in chief. She raised the level of the publication in terms of its writing, its editorial coverage, and its layout, which she redesigned. She also imbued her staff with a sense of mission; they were going to take yet another trade magazine and make it into a respected forum for design ideas. In her tailored suits, which she wore with a model's flair, she was a stylish cheerleader for her staff and the magazine.

*Home Furnishings* was one of six magazines owned by the publisher, Peter Miller. An absentee owner, he had given Laura freedom to run the magazine. One day, he made a rare appearance in Laura's office.

"Laura, you've done a fantastic job here. I'll always be grateful to you."

"That sounds like an ending," she said warily.

"I'm selling the company. A Japanese group, Oiako, has made a great offer."

"What does this mean?"

"They're moving the company to San Francisco."

"But we've all got our lives here."

"They're not taking any of our people. They've been running some special-interest magazines in the West. They're going to run the book from out there."

"We have twenty people on staff!"

"Everyone will get ten weeks' severance. That's probably an industry record. I think it's more than fair."

"Fair? We thought we were creating something, and now we're going to be out of work."

"You have nothing to worry about, Laura. You've got another four months on your contract. You should have another job in four minutes."

"There are people who define themselves by what they do here. You've just taken that away from them."

"It's a once-in-a-lifetime opportunity."

"For you."

"I'm sorry, Laura. It's, as they say, business."

Miller circulated a memo to all employees. People milled around in shock, and Laura had the task of calming them and reassuring them of their worth and viability in the marketplace.

SHE TOLD BEN the news that night, and he didn't say anything for a moment; too long a moment, she thought.

"It'll be all right," he said. "We'll be all right. It's a self-improvement opportunity for you. I read that somewhere. Some article when I was at a checkout counter."

"I was thinking more along the lines of how do we pay tuition, rent, and taxes."

"We're a little ahead."

"What about day camps for the kids this summer? They can't be home all day."

"We have the money for that. Europeans have been into the gallery. I'm talking Europeans in expensive leather. We're going to be fine."

"Living from European to European."

LAURA TRIED OUT an idea at lunch with two of her friends, both of whom she had met in a consciousness-raising group years before. Molly Switzer was a free-lance writer on women's issues, a tall, thin brunette in her thirties, and Karen Hart, a real estate broker, a stout blonde in her forties. Laura told them she wanted to take advantage of the growing second-home market and begin a new magazine, *Second Home.* She would develop a plan, a format, seek investors, and hire her staff from people she worked with at *Home Furnishings.* The two women were enthusiastic, but with the same concern. Laura and Ben were the standard two-income family. How were they going to live during the months—and it had to be at least months—that would be required to seek financing?

"I'll free-lance. I can do articles."

"What if Ben doesn't go along?" Karen Hart asked.

"*He* went into business and I supported him in doing it."

"Money brings out odd things in married couples," Karen said.

• • •

"I THINK IT'S GREAT," Ben responded when Laura presented the idea to him. "I don't know about where the financing would come from. Or how something like this gets set up."

"I'll find out how you do it. Ben, in your heart of hearts do you prefer that I don't try this?"

"In my heart of hearts, yes. I prefer you had a job and we wouldn't have to worry. Would I ever say to you not to try? No."

"I'll give it three months. That should tell us something."

EIGHT MONTHS LATER, after working with her former art director and sales manager on a sample issue and creating a business proposal with Phil Stern's help, Laura earned the interest of several investor groups. None made a commitment. The magazine she envisioned would cover subjects the other shelter magazines featured: decor, architecture, design. Also included would be articles of specific interest to owners and prospective owners of second homes, vacation homes: such as dealing with architects and contractors. Despite favorable reactions, the investment money was not forthcoming. Laura wrote a couple of magazine articles to supplement the family income. For the bulk of their expenses, the Masons were living literally from purchase to purchase of items in Ben's gallery.

THE FIRST PARENTS' meeting of the new fall term at Chase was interminable for the Masons. The conversation, the way people were dressed, seemed to be personal advertising: Aren't we doing wonderfully?

"And where did you go this summer?" a woman in a cashmere sweater-and-skirt combination asked Laura.

"We couldn't get away. We were both working very hard," Laura answered.

"Well, the fall is a wonderful time to travel," the woman said. "Europe especially."

Laura nodded acknowledgment for the information, thinking they would be lucky if they could take a taxi in the fall.

LAURA MADE AN INQUIRY to the president of the parents' association, a smartly tailored woman whose husband was a lawyer. Elizabeth and the woman's daughter were in the same class. Laura asked about the scholarship program at Chase. The Masons were dealing with two tuitions, now that Josh was enrolled in Chase too.

"Are you asking *for yourself*?" the woman said.

"Yes."

"Oh, my. You live in a lovely apartment. I saw it in a magazine."

"This is true, but we're both entrepreneurs. My husband is the only one with income at the moment."

"Oh, my. I really don't know what to say to you. I don't think this comes up too often," the woman said, using the appearance in the room of someone she knew as a reason to withdraw.

Financial difficulties. You'd think I said my children had head lice.

LAURA MET WITH representatives of a Japanese conglomerate seeking to invest in American magazines; an investor group that Phil Stern assembled, who were exploring various business proposals; existing corporations with magazine holdings; and a syndicate owned by Scott Pierce, known in the press as "the Canadian Rupert Murdoch."

The idea for the magazine seemed too good to abandon, but the Masons had been struggling financially for over a year. The Pierce Canadian syndicate seemed interested. However, Laura had been dangling in meetings with them for six months. She had never met Pierce but dealt with his staff people, who alternately told her they were close to a deal for the magazine and then not. She finally met the man himself. He was so busy, Laura was obliged to have a limousine meeting with him. The limo picked her up in front of the Sherry Netherland Hotel, and they drove to La Guardia Airport for his next flight. Pierce, corpulent and red-faced, was abrupt with her and occupied himself by reading her proposal and a report on it prepared by his staff. Occasionally he looked up to study her face. He asked several pointed questions, which she answered to her own satisfaction. Pierce made a few phone calls on other matters. They arrived at the terminal, and Laura was certain she was going to be dismissed.

"It's been recommended that we proceed. Everything seems to be in order. Congratulations, Ms. Mason. *Second Home* is in business."

"It is?"

"Shouldn't it be?" he said, smiling for the first time.

"Yes!"

"Good. My driver will take you back."

LAURA FILLED THE living room with balloons to announce her news. Ben threw his arms around his wife, and they embraced like ballplayers on a championship team. After fifteen months, their financial crisis was over. The proposal called for Laura, as publisher, and her colleagues the art director and sales manager, to earn salaries of sixty thousand dollars for each of the first two years. They would receive increases if possible after that, and each would also participate in future profits.

The staff she assembled included a core of people she had worked with before. Laura was a demanding editor. She frequently asked for several drafts from her writers, and she required photographers to reshoot when she was dissatisfied. She ran her editorial meetings for the new magazine with authority. Laura had a vision and intended to see it through. She introduced a feature, "Architect of the Month," and this became a sought-after showcase in the field. She prevailed over the objections of her editorial staff and allowed people whose homes were being highlighted in the magazine, amateurs as writers, to write their own articles about the homes. Because of its personal quality, the monthly feature was not only well read; home owners were clamoring to get into print. She instituted *Second Home* house tours across the country. The proceeds were given to the United Way. The publicity accrued to the magazine. The magazine earned high praise in business columns, and from advertising agencies. After ten months as a bimonthly, the publication met circulation and advertising projections. During the second year, according to the plan, it was published monthly.

IN HIS GALLERY, Ben was enjoying steadily increasing sales. He dealt with other dealers for acquisitions but still liked to find pieces himself. When rummaging through the items at an estate auction held in a large Victorian house in Stroudsburg, Pennsylvania, he was drawn to a naive painting standing on the floor in a corner, a rural family flying a kite, a joyful work with exquisite colors. Ben outbid several other dealers for the painting, which he bought for five thousand dollars. When he returned to New York he removed the frame and discovered it had covered the artist's signature, that of a highly regarded folk artist from the early nineteenth century. Ben immediately placed it in a prominent position in the gallery, priced at one hundred thousand dollars.

The *New York Times* ran an article on folk art available for sale in the New York area and used a photograph of the kite-flying painting. Within the week the painting was purchased by the National Gallery in Washington. The story of Ben Mason's find, a classic story of a bargain found in an estate sale of old pieces, was covered in *Time* and *Newsweek,* and a wire service story carried the coverage to Europe via the international edition of the *Herald Tribune.* "This isn't exactly dumb luck," Ben was quoted as saying. "It is, after all, what I do."

The Mason Folk Art Gallery had become a major resource in the field. Customers who had purchased pieces from Ben before wanted the cachet of dealing with him in his celebrityhood. New collectors appeared, as did the Europeans in leather and Japanese traveling in small groups. The Masons went house shopping in the Hamptons and upstate New York to rectify the anomaly of the editor of *Second Home*'s not owning one. They found a place they liked in Sag Harbor on eastern Long Island and decorated it with folk art. In increments, they expanded their domain. With the second home came the need for an automobile, and they bought a Volvo station wagon. Then came the second set of dishes, the second set of silverware, the second stereo system, the second television set. Ben continually rotated folk art pieces from city apartment to country house to gallery. The joke among their friends was that anything of the Masons you sat on or looked at was for sale. He had been known to take something a guest admired and sell it right off the floor. There were a couple of items he would not part with: a copper horse weather vane, Ben's first folk art purchase; and the painting of the little girl and her dog, recently acquired, which Laura and Ben treasured.

Laura and Ben Mason had the two beautiful children, the country house, the station wagon, the dog, the successful two-career marriage. Ben may have said to a reporter that it was not "dumb luck" to find a valuable painting in an estate sale. He knew, though, as did Laura, that they were lucky the way everything had fallen into place for them: the magazine being funded, the gallery becoming established. They chose not to question their good fortune but to expand on it. Ben moved his gallery once again, this time to space on Madison Avenue in the Nineties. They threw a lawn party with a tent in the rear of their Sag Harbor house and raffled off several quilts from the gallery, the proceeds of the raffle going to CARE. They were named in *Newsday* in an article titled "Who's Who in the Hamptons."

The dark period when Ben's success in his business was far from assured and when the creation of Laura's magazine was in doubt receded in their minds. The way their children lived was the way "rich kids" lived when Laura and Ben were growing up. The idea that the children would not continue to be serene and comfortable and go from a fine private school like Chase to fine colleges one day was unthinkable. Their life-style had taken on its own inevitable progression.

DURING THE PREVIOUS summers, Elizabeth and Josh had been attending day camps in the city. Many of Elizabeth's classmates were now going to the best sleepaway camps. Elizabeth wanted to go to a sleepaway camp also and asked to go with her closet friend, Sarah Clemens, a classmate at Chase. Elizabeth at age eleven was a tallish, loose-limbed girl with haphazardly flowing hair. Physically, she and Sarah were an unmatched pair, Sarah a tiny, small-boned brunette who wore her hair short, with bangs.

Sarah took piano lessons faithfully, and Elizabeth sometimes went over to her apartment after school, Sarah playing while the girls sang pop songs. Sarah's parents, both doctors, sought high achievement for their daughter. They thought she would be wasting her time if she didn't attend a music specialty camp.

"Do you know what I heard my parents saying to each other?" Sarah told Elizabeth. "The Asians and the Russians are getting ahead of me. If I don't go to music camp, I'll never be able to keep up with them."

"Should I learn piano?" Elizabeth said. "The Asians and the Russians are getting ahead of me too."

While the parents were making phone calls to other parents for camp recommendations, the girls made their own inquiries and decided that the camp should be coed and in no way were they going to a specialty camp—no camp specializing in music, sailing, crafts, tennis, computers, dance, art.

"We don't want to go to a place where at the end of the summer you're ready to vomit from what you signed up for," Elizabeth informed her parents.

Camp Lakeside in the Adirondacks offered a mixture of

sports, crafts, theater, and music in an atmosphere that seemed to be relaxed and pleasant, and the decision was made that the girls would go there. They spent a happy summer, but for the second day of camp, when Sarah was embarrassed by the appearance of her parents, who came to check on the camp piano and, finding it wanting, arranged to rent a Yamaha for the recreation hall so that Sarah could practice properly over the summer.

ELIZABETH WAS ENROLLED in Hebrew school two afternoons a week after classes at Chase in training for her bat mitzvah. During the months of preparation for the ritual, the cantor praised Elizabeth's musicality, and everything was proceeding toward a wonderful day. Then two weeks before the ceremony Josh brought flu into the house, and the Masons were ravaged with fevers and coughing. Elizabeth's fever passed, but she could not chant her portions of the ritual all the way without coughing. Laura and Ben were trying to figure out contingency plans. The lunch at Tavern on the Green was already arranged. Elizabeth rallied somewhat and insisted she was going to get through it.

"Sarah said I'm going to be memorable, that it's going to be like Mimi in *La Bohème*."

She performed her ritual with technical accuracy, chanting very softly in Hebrew in a throaty voice. Part of the ceremony included the parents making a brief, celebratory speech to the child, and they praised her for her courage, as did the rabbi.

"And now everyone can eat," she whispered to Laura and Ben as the service concluded.

THE SUMMER WHEN Elizabeth was fourteen and Josh ten, they both attended Camp Lakeside. Sarah was back in the same bunk with Elizabeth. Laura and Ben came up during the midpoint of the summer, on parents' visiting day, and they followed the children through their activities. The night's activity was the camp show, the children doing a production of *Guys and Dolls*. Elizabeth was eager for them to see it and told them Sarah was the accompanist.

"By the way," she said, beaming about her surprise. "*I'm* in it."

Elizabeth played Adelaide, and when she sang "Adelaide's Lament" she stopped the show. Willowy, poised, her long auburn hair loose and free, she not only had a stage presence that was breathtaking to her parents, her sense of timing and comedy was stunning. Laura and Ben were moved and astonished. They had always been involved parents. They had watched carefully over every step of their daughter's development since she was an infant, and yet suddenly she had grown into a unique person of her own—overnight, it seemed, when they weren't looking.

# CHAPTER 2

LAURA AND BEN researched every after-school performing arts program in New York. If Elizabeth was a potentially talented athlete or dancer, they reasoned, they would make certain her talents were properly channeled. From her earliest years they had seen that she was involved in activities that could help her to flower; first the preschool programs, then as she grew older they took her to art galleries, theater, museums. They wanted their daughter to have all the opportunities to succeed that were available to males in the culture. This talent of hers was something to build on. They were thinking of her self-esteem, but they were also looking ahead to colleges.

Coming from Chase, she had an opportunity to get into an excellent college and go on to become someone of importance. They knew that college admissions people looked for diverse interests in applicants. If Elizabeth studied in a good theater program, she would have a definite advantage. They accumulated information on the programs for young performers available in New York and presented the material to her when she returned from camp.

"You're so talented. You have to do something with it," Laura said.

"I'm really not interested. The school week is busy enough."

"It will look very good for college," Ben said, getting right to the main point.

"I'm on the paper. That's something."

Her main extracurricular activity was working as a staff member on the school newspaper, writing reviews of movies and plays. Laura and Ben were persistent, though, and persuaded her to look in on a few of the programs in New York.

"To see *Little Women* actually performed by little women is to see true purity in the theater," suggested the pretentious director of one children's performing group.

Elizabeth had been to Broadway shows. The level of work in the young people's performing groups did not captivate her. She also found the performers "too arrogant," "a bunch of little stars," as she reported to her parents and to Sarah. Over the objections of Laura and Ben, she insisted she would continue to do her performing in plays at camp.

THE SUCCEEDING SUMMER, she was Eliza Doolittle in *My Fair Lady*. Laura and Ben had seen Julie Andrews on stage in the original and Audrey Hepburn dubbed in the movie, but for them this was the best *My Fair Lady* ever, even with a fifteen-year-old Henry Higgins. On the way back to New York, Laura said to Ben:

"She's got to do something with it."

"It's a waste. You can't put a camp show on a college application."

"I don't only mean that. She's very good, Ben."

ELIZABETH BEGAN HER junior year of high school, and at the beginning of the term Laura and Ben attended an orientation meeting for parents. The main subject was the college admissions process. The anxiety in the room was palpable, some of the parents taking deep breaths, the asthmatics present giving themselves booster sprays, others talking loudly out of tension. A few, the experienced ones with older children, who had gone through the procedure before, sat with detached expressions, but even they betrayed a pinching around the eyes, not certain of what they could honestly predict for their younger children. The parents were extraordinarily attentive, fearful that any small piece of information overlooked here might cause their child to plunge down the long slope from acceptance by a prestigious college to disc jockey school.

LAURA AND BEN confronted Elizabeth yet again about her musical talent. She still declined to enroll in a performing program. She did not tell them she was working on an idea of her own. Elizabeth and Sarah organized secret tape recording sessions in Sarah's apartment, Elizabeth singing to Sarah's accompaniment in a variety of songs that they rehearsed and rerehearsed, then critiqued. Through Sarah's music teacher, they had the name of a highly respected vocal coach and made an appointment, teenage conspirators. Elizabeth preferred not to let her parents know about this. She didn't want to deal with their expectations, and if she turned out to be a flop, she didn't want them to be disappointed in her.

Elizabeth was petrified. Singing at camp was one thing, but this was real; the woman coached opera singers, musical theater singers. Her name was Olga Bavanne, and she worked in her apartment on West End Avenue. A diminutive woman in her fifties, with a stern face and piercing eyes, she wore black leotards and flamboyant silver earrings.

"You brought your personal accompanist, I see," Olga said, obviously charmed by the age of the pianist.

"Yes; we're friends."

"Do you study?" she asked Sarah.

"With Emma Rausch."

"Oh? That's impressive. Well, ladies . . ."

As they had planned, Elizabeth sang a song by the Lili character in the musical *Carnival!* and Jerome Kern's "All the Things You Are." She waited for the verdict. *If I don't breathe, if I just stand here and don't breathe, it won't be so bad. Then it will be over fast, she'll tell me I'm terrible, I can go home, and that will be that.*

"Elizabeth, people come to me at different levels. Many are professionals, some would like to be. But all my students share the same quality. They *love* to sing. And that's what you have to ask yourself. Do you love to sing?"

"Yes, I really do."

"Well, you have a lovely voice and considerable charm. And I would be delighted to take you on." Spontaneously, teenagers that they were, the girls leapt into each other's arms. "I presume you are not her agent," she said to Sarah. "You have parents, or someone whom I can talk to about this?"

"My parents."

"Have them call me. Tell them Olga Bavanne wants you as her student."

When they got outside the building, the girls, unable to contain themselves, ran three blocks to the bus stop.

LAURA AND BEN were thrilled about Elizabeth's decision to study voice. *Voice.* This was important for Elizabeth, culturally enriching, prestigious. And a definite plus for the college applications.

When told Elizabeth was going to begin serious vocal training, Phil and Jane Stern greeted the news morosely. They were processing everything they heard about other children through comparisons with their daughter, Melanie. Now a senior at the Hargrove School, she was lumbering through the college admissions process. Her main salable extracurricular activity was field hockey. A stocky girl of five feet three, she had a pretty face that was partially hidden by the combination of her bangs and her dark-rimmed glasses.

Throughout Melanie's junior and senior years, a series of tutors marched through the Stern household to help lift her grades on tests and term papers, an array of private instruction that could have rivaled the education of Alexander the Great.

"I'm just an average student," Melanie said to Elizabeth one evening when they went to the movies together. "Why can't my parents get that? I want to go to a big, sprawling school where I can bury myself in an English major, go to parties, have a boyfriend, and get laid."

"Melanie, you're great."

"But I'm not Ivy League."

WITH COLDNESS AND PRECISION, Elizabeth Mason was measured for her verbal and math skills on her first official SAT test: 1220. Laura and Ben had talked to other parents; they owned every available book published on the college admissions process. With the increased competition in recent years for the better schools, they regarded 1300 as the required score for their daughter. The way to get it was to buy it, through private tutoring. They explained to Elizabeth that other students with whom she was competing, some in her school, were using private tutors, and she would be placing herself at a distinct disadvantage if she failed to do likewise.

"It's such a stupid system," Elizabeth said. "You think they ask Madonna or Gloria Steinem what their SAT scores were?"

Elizabeth was beginning to be caught up in the College Sweepstakes herself. She consented to a tutor coming to the house once a week. He was Sawyer Brears, an introverted young man of twenty-three, who worked as a computer programmer by day and had the probing, intense look of someone who could fix your TV, your toaster, your scores.

MELANIE STERN WAS accepted at Wisconsin and chose to go there. She was delighted, and the Sterns managed to rise above her rejections by the Ivy League schools on her list, schools she never wanted to apply to in the first place. They armed themselves with information about prominent graduates of Wisconsin, which they presented to people when they told them about Melanie's choice.

Melanie Stern was the first person Elizabeth knew well who had sex. In her senior year of high school, Melanie began going with a tackle on the Boston University football team, a grinning, affable bear of a kid, who patted Phil Stern on the back and appreciatively consumed meals catered by Jane Stern.

"The question is," Laura asked during dinner at the Sterns', "is Melanie sleeping with him?"

"I really don't think so," Phil said.

"I don't think so, either," Jane Stern said. "He's so cuddly. I think they're sort of chums in a puppy-love kind of way."

"WE'VE DONE IT in bathtubs, standing up in closets, behind staircases, on the floor in my parents' living room while they were at a dinner party," Melanie reported to Elizabeth.

"Did it hurt at first?"

"A little at first. Until things worked out."

"Does he use condoms?"

"When we first did it. But I'm on the pill now. It's more intimate, I feel."

"Right," Elizabeth said, solemnly agreeing.

"I think it's important not to go off to college a virgin," Melanie said to her. "Because then you're a target for fraternity jerks looking to score and boast about it. That's what I heard from my cousin who's at Bucknell."

"The whole thing sounds overwhelming—sex, condoms, the pill, college."

"You have to take it step by step," said Melanie, the elder.

"Then I can't think about sex for a while," Elizabeth joked. "I have to get through my SATs."

• • •

LIKE A LABRADOR retriever puppy whose paws are too big for his body, Elizabeth with her wiry frame had been ungainly through her early teenage years. At seventeen she was beginning to settle into herself. Five feet seven, slender, with a narrow face, high cheekbones, long, nimble legs: at first glance she looked as if she could have been a ballet dancer. This was belied by her face, which lacked the severity affected by many young dancers. It was a sunny, freckled face with a quick smile.

The spring musical production at Chase was *Oliver!* Elizabeth, a junior, won the part of the female lead over several seniors, and gave a sparkling performance. Ben videotaped it for use with her college applications.

After visits to a dozen schools, a list was evolving of the colleges where Elizabeth was considering making applications: Amherst, Smith, Wesleyan, and Layton College. Layton had recently received a number one ranking on *U.S. News & World Report*'s survey of liberal arts colleges. In a second category in degree of difficulty for acceptance, Elizabeth listed Oberlin, Vassar, and Wisconsin.

She would have been overjoyed to be accepted in any of the colleges in the first category and said she would be "comfortable" with any of the schools in the second. But the message was clear to her that her parents wanted her to get into Layton, which they brought up most frequently in their conversations about colleges.

On her next SAT test she scored 1280. The college adviser at Chase said it was excellent and in combination with her B+ average was high enough for most of the schools on her list. Her parents congratulated her for the increase in her scores. However, she could see they were not yet happy. Elizabeth may have shown some independence of spirit in the past: she refused the theatrical training her parents first offered; she found an important vocal coach and worked with her diligently. But by accepting the need to keep raising her scores, she had accepted her parents' goals.

She did math drills and studied vocabulary words on flash
cards. She continued to work with Sawyer Brears as her
tutor. She was pushing to reach that magical 1300 mark. Her
parents' first choice, Layton College, came to be her first
choice. She wanted to be a good little girl and give her
parents what they needed.

DURING THE SUMMER before her senior year of high school,
Elizabeth took a job as a junior counselor at a day camp in
New Jersey. On weekends she joined her parents in Sag
Harbor. Josh, who was becoming a muscular, athletic boy
with his father's solid jaw, was at a baseball specialty camp,
barnstorming his way through the camp baseball circuit.
Sarah Clemens was with a student chamber music ensemble, touring Europe as part of a State Department cultural
exchange program, and Elizabeth spent some time after
work and on weekends with Melanie Stern.

Elizabeth captured the interest of Ned Horwit, a nineteen-
year-old counselor at the day camp, who went to Penn and
whose parents owned a home in East Hampton. Six feet one,
vain and muscular, he tried to convince her it wasn't healthy
for her body, hormonally, not to have sex with him. Elizabeth and Ned saw each other on the weekends and engaged
in an elaborate ritual, Ned pushing her to go further
sexually, Elizabeth going as far as intense necking and
petting but not ready to give up her virginity, or at least not
to Ned.

"I just don't think I'm ready," she confided to Melanie.
"I mean, I'm ready physically but not in my head."

"Technically, you're not even in your senior year yet, so
I wouldn't consider you abnormal. But I just think it's a
good policy to get it over with before you leave for
college," Melanie told her saucily, smiling.

"You're such a pioneer woman," Elizabeth teased.

THE FALL TERM BEGAN, and she went to parties, had dates here
and there, her sexual activity similar to her experience with

Ned Horwit. She was selected to play the part of Guinevere in the Chase production of *Camelot*, giving another sparkling performance. Ben videotaped that show, as well, and edited a presentation of her starring roles for inclusion with her college applications. On her next and final try at the SAT, she achieved a 1310 score. She had surpassed the mark her parents had set for her.

FOR A WHILE the family preoccupation with college was diverted by plans for Josh's bar mitzvah. He performed admirably, the reception was flawless. But within days of the event, college was again dominating the family conversations.

SARAH'S COLLEGE CHOICE was settled; she had already been accepted by Juilliard. Her main concern was whether to pursue a career as a soloist or concentrate on being a chamber music player. Sarah sometimes showed up at a party and brought along the people in her ensemble. One of them, Barney Green, reminded Elizabeth of Schroeder from the *Peanuts* comic strip, because he was cute, devoted to his music, and aloof. Slim, five feet eight, with dark, intense eyes, he was a gifted violinist who went to the High School of Performing Arts. He was headed for Yale in the fall. Elizabeth wondered what it might be like to arouse him. They would make love. Then he would leap out of bed to play his violin. And she would sing. Then music could not contain their passion, and they would make love again. Elizabeth was always catching him looking at her at a party, and then he would turn away to be Schroeder.

AN AUDITION WAS REQUIRED of students applying for a music major at Layton College. On a Friday afternoon in February, Ben drove Elizabeth and Sarah up to Layton. Sarah had volunteered to accompany her friend on the piano. With ivy-covered Georgian buildings curled around a lake adjacent to a forest reserve in Caldwell, New York, near Albany,

it was the most exquisite-looking of the colleges Elizabeth
had visited, a place that seemed to call for the *Pastoral*
Symphony to be playing in the background. They went to
the building that housed the music department and waited in
a reception area with six other candidates—four girls and
two boys—and assorted parents. Elizabeth was the last to be
called. The secretary said that Ben would have to remain in
the anteroom during the audition. Elizabeth and Sarah were
directed to the stage of a theater. A piano stood on stage,
and a committee of three faculty members sat in the front
row, two women and a man.

"Given the importance and the solemnity of the occasion," Elizabeth said, "I'd like to sing 'Adelaide's Lament'
from *Guys and Dolls*."

She delivered a witty, lively reading of the song. The
committee people, after a long day of auditions, began to
relax in their seats, smiling.

"We have time for another," a woman called out, and
Elizabeth performed a lyrical "Out of My Dreams" from
*Oklahoma!*

A LETTER OF ACCEPTANCE arrived from Layton College. When
Elizabeth's parents came home from work, they all embraced, jumping up and down. Ben went out and bought an
ice cream cake that said "Congratulations," and Laura and
Ben opened a bottle of champagne for themselves. They had
raised their daughter for excellence. They had placed her in
a fine private school. They had willingly paid for the vocal
lessons. They had hired a tutor when needed. They had
encouraged her and supported her. Now she was going to a
college far beyond their own aspirations when they were her
age. Elizabeth, their firstborn, represented their dreams of
moving up, of not being kids from Brooklyn and the Bronx
any longer. And she had fulfilled their expectations.

A FLURRY OF PARTIES took place for the seniors at Chase as the
semester wound down. Sarah took Barney Green to one

of these parties, and he and Elizabeth danced together. As the evening ended, Barney asked her to go with him on a Saturday afternoon to the Metropolitan Museum of Art, a bona fide date. They wandered through the exhibits and then sat on the grass behind the museum.

"What are you going to do for the summer?" he asked.

"I'll be a counselor again."

"We're going to Europe again."

"Sarah didn't say."

"She doesn't know. My father found out this morning from someone he knows. We're getting picked for another tour."

"You are?"

"I'm going to miss you. I mean, I shouldn't presume to say that, because we're not boyfriend and girlfriend, in a specific sense. But I always imagined what it would be like to spend time alone with you like this, and now we *are* alone, and this summer we could be alone more, but we won't. I'm not making sense," he said, embarrassed.

"I understand perfectly."

"If I had my violin I could say it better."

"That's my fantasy moment! You play one of the great romantic concertos just for me."

"Anytime," he said. "For now, maybe I could kiss you instead."

They kissed, and she placed her head on his shoulder, and when the awkwardness passed he kissed her again and they moved their bodies down on the grass so that they were lying next to each other, kissing.

"This is very romantic even without the violin," she said.

"I like you very much, you know. I mean, I always have. I can't believe I'm saying this. I can't believe I'm here. And I can just kiss you and you'll let me."

"And vice versa," she said.

• • •

ELIZABETH AND BARNEY started "going together," which
translated into a few formal dates and being with each other
at parties. She was working on a paper on the women's
movement for an independent study course, and the immediate effect was that she insisted upon paying her own way.
Sarah knew they were seeing each other, but their status as
a defined couple was not generally known. So when Laura
and Ben told Elizabeth they were going to the house in the
country for the weekend and she told them she wanted to
remain in the city and work on her paper, the parents
assumed nothing beyond what they were told. Keeping faith
with her word, she did work on the paper all Saturday, and
then Barney came over on Saturday night.

He brought a videocassette he wanted to share with her,
*From Mao to Mozart*, with Isaac Stern. They watched it,
snuggled together, and when it was over they started to kiss.
Slowly, his hands trembling, he began to remove her
clothes, and she helped him along. He slid out of his clothes
and they were on the floor, moving inexpertly but eagerly.
It took a while to line themselves up properly, and for him
to slip on a condom and find her, and then he was inside her.
The pain was greater than she thought it would be, and there
was some bleeding, but they were intent on getting it right
and they tried again and it was much better. She lay in his
arms afterward, happy that the first time wasn't with
someone vain like Ned Horwit, it was with Barney.

They managed to be alone a few more times over the next
weeks, and in terms of performance, matters improved.

"Are you *going* with Barney?" Laura asked, his name
having come up often in her daughter's conversation.

"More or less. He's going to Europe in the summer and
then college in the fall. I'm going away to college. It's for
now."

"You will be careful."

"Yes."

"If it comes to that, there are certain . . . precautions.
What with AIDS and the way people get pregnant when

they don't mean to. The film they showed in school that talked about condoms—it was good advice.''

"Don't worry, Mother, we know what we're doing.'' And to herself, Elizabeth added, At least we do *now*.

THE CHASE PROM was held in the school gymnasium, decorated with balloons and crepe paper, a disc jockey presiding over the music. Elizabeth asked Barney to go with her. They danced very little and sat holding hands for much of the evening. Events were rushing along rapidly: the end of their high school years, Barney departing within days for Europe. He was going to be back in New York only briefly before leaving for school. Elizabeth was going off to college. Other, larger priorities were sweeping in on them.

The disc jockey played the last song of the prom, "Good Night'' by the Beatles.

"We'll see each other as soon as I get home,'' he said.

"I'll be faithful to you,'' Elizabeth said.

"And I will be to you,'' he said fervently.

ELIZABETH WORKED in the New Jersey day camp for the summer, Melanie was a salesperson in a tennis shop, and they met a couple of times a week for dinner and movies. One night, sitting in the sidewalk café portion of an East Side singles bar, Melanie asked:

"Okay, would you go to bed with a cute guy you met in a place like this?''

"On the first date?'' Elizabeth asked.

"It's not a first date. It's a bar pickup.''

"I doubt it.''

"Well, I could, but I wouldn't. Okay, next. Would you go to bed with a cute guy *on* the first date?''

"No. Much too soon.''

"The second date?''

"Still too soon.''

"When?''

"I don't know.''

"Liz, that's what you need, a working estimate."

"Every girl should be prepared, condoms in her pocketbook and a working estimate?"

"Absolutely."

"I thought that if I was seeing somebody I'd go on the pill. But I don't have an estimate for dating."

"So come up with one."

Elizabeth thought for a moment.

"Twelve. Twelve dates," she told Melanie.

"You're tough!"

"Ten. We'll make it ten dates. Look at that—I'm already compromised."

Two of the male counselors had been flitting around her, but they were, as she described them to Melanie, "silly and overbearing."

"That's what a lot of guys are," Melanie said. "If you start disqualifying for that, you'll never go out."

She met no one she wanted to see and was not overly concerned. She would be with Barney whenever they could be together, and she would be going to college soon. At Layton, one could hope to find men with character. That was her fantasy during these summer nights.

Sarah wrote that she had fallen in love with a pianist from a Boston teenage ensemble. "We made love. Yes, me. And we did it to Mahler."

In August, Barney sent a letter saying that she would always have a place in his heart, but at the moment he was going with Monica Frees, also from the Boston ensemble. Elizabeth cried, surprising herself that she could feel so rejected.

Elizabeth's summer job was over; Josh was back from camp. Laura and Ben arranged to take a couple of weeks at their Sag Harbor house. The parents attempted to recapture the days when the children were small and they all went kite flying, bicycle riding. They made an elaborate sand castle at the beach. The castle was gone when they returned the next day, no more sufficient in withstanding the tide than was Laura and Ben's attempt to cheat time and keep their daughter with them a little while longer. The family returned to New York a week before Elizabeth was to leave; she and Laura went clothes shopping to fill in items she needed to take with her. Ben, forlorn, needed something *he* could do with Elizabeth, and they went together to buy a couple of pieces of luggage for her. Ben enlarged the experience by comparison shopping, and finally they made a purchase.

"I'm glad we did that carefully," Ben said, desperate to have helped. "You don't want to take the wrong luggage."

ELIZABETH ENTERED Josh's room, where he was busy with baseball card buying guides. An important show was coming up at the Hilton Hotel, and he was doing research to guide the allocation of his eighty-four dollars, which he had saved from various gifts. The tension in the household over Elizabeth's leaving had not appeared to affect him. His immediate concern was comparative batting averages and Hall of Fame potential.

"Hi, slugger."

"What do you think, Liz—should I go for a Tony Gwynn rookie card if I can get one?" he said jokingly.

"Tony Gwynn?"

"He's about three thirty, lifetime, in case anybody asks you that at college."

"I'd like to think I can call you if something like that comes up," she said, tousling his hair. "Can I?"

"Sure."

"You going to take good care of old Queenie when I'm away?"

"I bet she misses you. I bet she'll look for you at night."

"I cleaned out a lot of stuff from my room. I've got a couple of empty shelves in my bookcase you can use for your baseball card stuff."

"Really?"

"Only the shelves, kiddo. I don't want to come home to see any baseball posters on my wall."

"Thanks!"

They looked at each other, contemplating the next stage of their lives as brother and sister.

"It's going to be pretty quiet around here without you," he said.

SARAH CAME HOME from Europe and Elizabeth went to her apartment, where they filed their reports on the summer.

"We're going to be college women. And not virgins. Not even me," Sarah said.

"College women. And not virgins. Amazing."

"I'm happy about Juilliard, all in all. But I envy you to be going away."

"I missed you this summer. I'm going to miss you."

"We'll always be friends, won't we?"

"Of course we will. What are you talking about?"

"My mother said she isn't friendly with one person she went to high school with. And my father said the same thing."

"They are not us," Elizabeth responded.

They were silent for a moment over the impending separation.

"Liz, good luck at school."

"Good luck to you too. But you're so gifted, you don't need luck."

"You are forgetting perhaps the Asians and the Russians?"

"I love you, Sarah."

"I love you, Liz."

They hugged, but the physical gesture was insufficient to express their feelings for each other. They went to the piano, Sarah accompanying Elizabeth in the singing of "No One Is Alone" from *Into the Woods*, and that seemed to be a better goodbye.

# CHAPTER

# 3

THE GOODBYE SPEECHES. Compared with picnics on the Fourth of July, this was a ritual underreported yet just as American, parents entering their children's rooms on the night before the children went off to college, the parents attempting to deliver the final, inspirational words.

Ben went first, entering the room when Elizabeth's lights were out, kneeling at her bed.

"This is it, darling. I keep feeling like there's something I forgot to tell you or teach you and if I could just remember it, everything will be perfect. It's like I'm on a dock and the boat is leaving and I want to yell out, 'Wait! Don't forget—' But I don't know what I should tell you. I guess I've said it all and it's all been done. I can only say, I love you so much. I'm so proud of you. You're the best of me and Mom and your grandparents. And you have enriched every day of my life by being alive."

"Thank you, Dad, for everything."

They embraced, and he walked out of the room and motioned to Laura, who was sitting in their bedroom, waiting to go in.

Laura sat on the bed and touched her daughter's hair.

"It all happened so fast. I feel like someone miscounted. You can't take little girls at Layton. She's only ten. But it's time. You're ready to leave here, and I know you're going to be great. You're smart and talented and beautiful, and my best wish for you is to just keep going the way you have been. Because you're already a success. If you love somebody, love him very much, but don't lose yourself in him. Remember that you're special. Have fun with it, darling. I'm always here for whatever you need. I'm very proud of you, and I love you beyond anything I could have ever imagined in my life."

They kissed each other, Laura took a last look around the darkened room and closed the door. Elizabeth lay awake for a long time, anxious about what was coming next, while in the next room her parents were awake with what had happened in the past. What might they have done as her parents that they didn't do? What did they do that they shouldn't have done? Both parents finally settled on the same conclusion, that they had done their best. Eventually, they all fell asleep, to drift in and out of each other's dreams.

THE NEXT MORNING WAS DOMINATED by logistics: getting Elizabeth's belongings packed up and into their station wagon. The baseball card show that Josh had been researching was scheduled for that afternoon at the Hilton, and he was not going up to the college. He and Elizabeth said their goodbyes after breakfast. His place in the car was absorbed by a carton containing a dictionary, a thesaurus, and audiocassettes. Ben was driving and needed to rely on the side-view mirrors, since the rearview mirror was blocked. The cargo area was filled with Elizabeth's clothing, computer, printer, television set, stereo system. They set out for the college, modern Okies.

Three blocks from the house, Laura shouted in a panic, "We forgot a thermometer."

"Honey, I'm sure she can get one at the school. They have a drugstore," Ben said.

"What if she begins to run a temperature and there's no thermometer, and all because we couldn't stop now."

"I'll take care of it," Elizabeth told her mother. "That's what I have to be doing for myself now."

"There's something new going around," Laura said. "A strain of a new virus. I read about it. Sore throats, high fever. Dangerous."

"All right. We'll stop," Ben said.

Laura went into a drugstore and returned with the thermometer. She placed it in Elizabeth's cosmetics bag, relieved, as if order had been restored.

MATERIAL SENT TO ELIZABETH from the college suggested that the students arrive in the early afternoon to get settled in their dorms. A reception was scheduled for parents of freshmen at five P.M. At seven-thirty, students were to attend a freshman orientation meeting in the main theater.

The Masons reached the campus at about two and located Elizabeth's dorm, Brewster House, a three-story ivy-covered red-brick building. The dorm was coed. En route to Elizabeth's room, on the second floor, the Masons passed a student lounge, with a fireplace, sofas, a television set. Young men and women who had already settled in were sitting around chatting, at ease with one another. The Masons located Elizabeth's room, painted yellow with white ceilings; a bay window overlooked a quad formed by other dormitory buildings. Single beds were placed on either side of the room, with a desk and chair adjacent to each bed. Elizabeth's roommate was sitting in a chair reading a Layton brochure when they entered. A very tall, thin girl with milk-white skin and long blond hair, she was wearing dungarees and a sweatshirt.

"I'm Liz Mason."

"Holly Robertson."

They shook hands. Elizabeth gestured toward her parents.

"This is my father, Ben Mason; my mother, Laura Mason."

"Pleased to meet you. I came up early with my parents. They left a while ago. I didn't want to claim anything until you got here," she said to Elizabeth. Holly's unpacked belongings sat in the middle of the room.

"That was very nice of you. Suppose I take that bed," Elizabeth said.

"Okay, good. I'll be on this side of the room."

"Where are you from, Holly?" Laura asked.

"Westport. You folks?"

"Manhattan," Laura replied.

"Nervous?" Elizabeth asked Holly.

"Yes."

"Me, too."

Laura and Ben helped Elizabeth transfer her belongings from the car. Their instinct was to help Elizabeth get unpacked and organized, and they started to do so. But they noticed that Holly was managing on her own, and they saw they were embarrassing Elizabeth by their presence.

"Why don't we wait outside?" Laura responded.

"I can set up the stereo," Ben said.

"We'll be outside."

Elizabeth unpacked, and Laura and Ben wandered through the grounds. Layton looked beautiful. A light rain that had been falling stopped. A sweet, clean smell was in the air. In an expanse in the center of campus, the college green, a few boys were tossing a Frisbee around. Elizabeth came out after a while and they took a walk together, watching the other students moving their belongings into the dorms. The older ones kidded with one another; some were coupled off and strolled arm in arm. One couple, oblivious to everyone, kissed as they leaned against a wall. Elizabeth stared at them for a moment. Will that happen for me?

THE INSIDER'S GUIDE TO THE COLLEGES described Layton in terms of "Strong academics, solid tradition, and an idyllic setting. People label it Williams II. As difficult to get into as Williams these days, Layton is a hot school for its size (not too big, not too small) and its excellent faculty-student ratio. Layton justly deserves its high ranking. The students also rank high on the economic scale. Don't let the casual clothes and musician types fool you.''

The incoming freshman class numbered eight hundred, and over a thousand parents were present at the reception held on a lawn in front of the Administration Building. The adults looked as though they were selected by computer: about 25 percent black, Hispanic, and Asian; about 25 percent non-WASP (Italian, Jewish, Greek); and about 50 percent WASP. Half the WASPs looked, by virtue of their blazers with golf shirts, their wash-and-wear dresses, as if they'd just come from a cocktail party at the golf club.

''You're surely in the minority here,'' Laura said to Ben.

''Which of the many possible categories are you referring to?''

''Golf.''

They were standing near the punch bowl not talking to anyone. A man and woman approached them. The father was a short, wiry man with curly black hair. The mother had long black hair and wore a loose-fitting black cotton dress with leather sandals, the only sandals on the premises.

''Jerry Epstein,'' he said, extending his hand. ''And this is my wife, Hedy.''

''Ben and Laura Mason,'' Ben said, and they shook hands all around.

''Quite a place. We can't get over it, to have your kid go to a school like this. It's everything you dream of, isn't it?''

''It's very beautiful,'' Laura answered.

''We're from the Bronx. We live in New Rochelle now. That was supposed to be the big move up. But this is really it. I went to City. Hedy went to Hunter. And we have a boy at Layton.''

''I went to Brooklyn. Ben went to Cooper Union.''

"Cooper Union was bohemian to my family," Hedy Epstein said cheerfully.

"To mine too," Ben said.

"So who is your child?" Hedy Epstein asked.

"Elizabeth Mason."

"And where did she go to high school?"

"Chase."

"Seth went to Bronx Science," Hedy Epstein said. "I hope he'll be all right here. He's not the most sociable of kids."

"He's a computer wiz," Jerry Epstein said. "He makes up computer games. Companies pay him."

"That's impressive," Laura said.

"I don't know zilch about them," Jerry Epstein said. "I own a carpet business, and we use them in the business, but I don't know zilch. He can sit in front of a computer for hours."

"You worry, is he going to keep too much to himself here," his mother said.

"There's supposed to be a lot of activities," Ben offered.

"Still, you worry. And there's the other thing," Hedy said.

"What other thing?" Ben asked.

"We're Jewish."

"So are we," Ben said.

"I presumed," Hedy responded. "Well, then you understand. This used to be a very WASPy place, back when they had fraternities. Are our kids going to be welcome?"

"I haven't heard anything about that," Ben said.

"I really haven't, either. It's just that I'm feeling like we're outsiders in this place," Hedy explained.

"Come to think of it, so am I," Ben said, surveying the parent group. "If they were casting a Ralph Lauren ad out of the people here, I don't think I'd make it."

MOMENTS LATER they were directed to enter Layton Hall, an amphitheater with a glass dome, which had been a lecture hall when the college was established in 1780. The college president, Dr. Hudson Baker, a special envoy to Latin America in the Nixon administration, rose to address the parents. Shiningly bald, a tall, stocky man in his early sixties, he had an easy smile and a soft, lilting voice. He welcomed the parents to the Layton family, recounted the history of the college, and pledged that Layton would uphold its virtues and standards.

"Your children," he said in closing, "will take their place with those who preceded them in the long—two hundred years long—history of excellence of mind and spirit that is Layton College."

"He got me at the end," Laura said to Ben as they left the hall.

"Right. There's a lot of history in this place."

The audience walked back out through a corridor that contained portraits of past college presidents, a heavily carpeted area with plush velvet draperies, which called for hushed voices. Laura and Ben, city kids, quietly filed out with the rest, holding hands, feeling some degree of reverence.

THEY OFFERED to take Elizabeth's roommate out to dinner, but she declined, saying that she had chores she wanted to do. So the three of them went to an Italian restaurant near campus. It turned into a difficult experience: the service was slow; Elizabeth wanted to be with them, but not exactly. They were lame-duck parents. As soon as they were gone, she would actually be on her own, which was exciting, and not.

They walked back to her dorm, and her eyes kept darting, taking everything in, the students, the buildings. A few minutes more and she would be set adrift here. Will I belong? Am I smart enough? Pretty enough? Am I too gawky? Too forward? Are my breasts too small? Am I talented enough? What if they're snobs? What if I get homesick? I'm already homesick.

In the dorm room, Ben noticed a utility closet in a corner.

"Is there maid service here?" Ben asked.

"No."

"Then how is this place going to get cleaned, with no supplies?"

"We'll buy some," Elizabeth answered.

"We better do it now," he said.

"Now?" Elizabeth responded.

"We passed a store on the way in. They'll have cleaning things."

"Dad, I can get it. That's something you do—you get what you need."

"The first week, with so much going on, you might not remember. If you don't clean, dust balls can accumulate. You can breathe it in and get sick."

"Daddy, you should have brought Mrs. O'Reilly along."

"It'll just take a few minutes. It was right down the road."

"She can take care of it," Laura said.

"I'm not leaving here until she has the proper cleaning supplies!"

They humored him. He purchased the cleaning supplies, and Elizabeth put everything away in the utility closet. Laura had her crisis over a thermometer, Ben had his over a dustpan. Now nothing was left to do, no more tasks, or crises.

"Goodbye, my darling," Laura said.

"You have nothing to worry about," Ben said. Then he added, smiling, "And anyway, we'll be back in the morning."

"I love you," Elizabeth told them. "What else can I say? You can't beat the old favorites."

THE FRESHMAN ORIENTATION SESSION in Layton Hall opened with a message of greeting from the college president. As with the parents, he invoked history and tradition. The president was followed by the dean of freshmen, with a spirited speech about student activities. The dean was so exuberant, the atmosphere was like a pep rally. People went back to their dorms for the first night infused with positive feelings about their new school. Elizabeth, exceedingly eager to participate, was thinking that she would definitely try out for musicals, and if that didn't work, she would write for the college newspaper, or run cross-country, or play dorm volleyball, or possibly all of these.

"What are you going to go out for?" she said to Holly when they were back in the room.

"Basketball. It's expected of me. I played for my high school. But I'm getting tired of it. It always calls attention to my being so tall."

"Did you ever dance? I bet you'd be a wonderful dancer."

"Think so?"

"You're an athlete. Dancers are athletes."

"It's a thought."

"I'm ready to sign up for everything," Elizabeth said.

"I know people who just cruise through here, majoring in drinking and sex."

"Oh."

Elizabeth needed to go to sleep immediately. The day had been long, and she didn't want to start factoring in drinking and sex among the many levels of achievement she had to worry about.

Before she left New York she had made a last-minute decision to take an old teddy bear with her. Elizabeth took her bear out of a drawer and placed it on a bookshelf over her desk. When she saw this, Holly removed from her drawer a stuffed tiger and placed it on the windowsill near her bed. It reminded Elizabeth of an episode in one of the picture books from when she was small, *Ira Sleeps Over*. A child goes on a sleepover date with a friend and, resisting possible humiliation, brings his teddy, only to discover the friend also sleeps with a teddy. The two roommates went to sleep, watched over by icons from their childhood.

• • •

THE DINING ROOMS WERE OPEN and represented the first test for
new students. Would they be able to make friends quickly
enough to avoid eating their meals alone? Freshmen could
not rely on eating with their roommates, since people
attended different orientation sessions at different hours.
Across the hall from Elizabeth and Holly's room were two
women who made a rapid adjustment to campus life.
Shannon Harnett, a striking, lanky brunette who wore her
long hair across the side of her face, was from Denver.
Allison Dobbins from Philadelphia was a petite, bosomy
blonde with pigtails that bounced whenever she walked. In
the dining room, boys buzzed by them like flies. The two
girls alternately flirted with them and deflected them, a
game they were apparently accustomed to playing. Because
Elizabeth lived across the hall and already had a slight
acquaintanceship with them, she sat at the same table as
these stars. Shannon and Allison didn't go out of their way
to include Elizabeth, rarely introducing her to any of the
table-hoppers, but they didn't completely ignore her and
Elizabeth assumed this was better than eating meals alone.

IN THE EVENING of their first day, Elizabeth and Holly were in
their room, reading some of the printed material they had
accumulated during the orientation sessions. A young man
knocked on the door and poked his head inside the room. He
was rather small, with wild, curly brown hair, thick glasses,
and a tomato-sauce-stained T-shirt, worn with Bermuda
shorts, black dress socks, and leather shoes.

"Elizabeth Mason?" he said.

"Yes?"

"I'm Seth Epstein. My parents met your parents at the
parents' meeting. My mother said your parents were nice
and that you must be too."

"Yes, Seth?"

He was having difficulty bringing himself to speak his
next thought.

"Want to go to the barbecue together? I can pick you up and we can spend it together," he said quickly.

"You want to go on a *date* to the get-acquainted barbecue? The idea, as I understand it, is for everyone to get acquainted."

"Yes, but what if you don't?"

"Don't what?"

"Get acquainted."

"Seth, I'll see you there. Why don't we just let natural forces operate?"

"Was this too forward of me? I get nervous . . . and get nervous."

"I'll see you at the barbecue."

"Good. I'll be looking for you."

THE ANNUAL FRESHMAN BARBECUE had been held for over one hundred years. People received stick-on name tags from the dean of freshmen as they entered the area of the lake. Several grills were set up, where members of the kitchen staff were preparing hot dogs and hamburgers; condiments were available at buffet tables. Student volunteers tended three nonalcoholic bars. Elizabeth came to the event with Holly, who stopped to talk to someone she knew from high school. The roommates became separated in the crowd.

"Hi, how are you doing?" a young man said to her. He was wearing a Duke sweatshirt, and his name tag said "Joe Wallace."

"Hi, Joe."

"Where are you from?" he asked.

"New York City."

"No kidding. Do people still live there?"

"Where are you from?" she asked.

"Shaker Heights. Cleveland."

"Why the Duke sweatshirt?"

"I bought it when I got into Duke. I got in everywhere I applied—Duke, Amherst, Williams, Penn."

At some point this ends, doesn't it? she said to herself. Where you got in, and your grades and your scores.

"Where did *you* apply?" he asked.

"I can't remember anymore. It was in another life."

"I hear they've got a limit of the people they'll take from New York. You must be pretty smart."

"I'm a music major. I think they allow us to be stupider than the rest."

"What kind of music—rock and roll?" he said, to be clever.

"I sing. Carmen in *Aïda*," she said, quoting a line from the musical *Carnival!*, which he did not respond to on any level.

He lost interest in her at that point and moved on. Elizabeth was intercepted by Seth Epstein. He was wearing clean clothes for the event, a clean white T-shirt, dungarees, and sneakers.

"There you are," he said. "I'm happy to see you. I haven't talked to one person. I was the first one here, and still I haven't talked to anyone."

"Have you been waiting for me?"

"Sort of."

"You shouldn't put all your eggs in one basket."

"It's just that I feel like I know you. You rejected me for a date here, but that rejection is a deeper bond than I have with the people who haven't rejected me yet," he said whimsically.

"That is very complicated," Elizabeth responded, chuckling.

"I knew what was going to happen at this party. I wouldn't talk to anybody, and nobody would talk to me. That's why I wanted to take you. So somebody would talk to me."

"Just relax a little. Try not to be so hyper, and maybe you'd mix better with people."

"This party is my worst fear: I'll be at this college for four years, and nobody will *ever* talk to me."

He was extremely awkward, but Elizabeth found his self-deprecating manner appealing.

"I'll talk to you. I was worried about this party too."

Elizabeth noticed Holly standing at one of the bars, speaking to a student bartender, a very good-looking, broad-shouldered young man. She waved in Holly's direction.

"There's my roommate." Elizabeth took Seth by the hand. As they made their way through the crowd, Elizabeth saw Donna Winter at the outer edge of the assemblage. She was a girl Elizabeth had met at the orientation session on rules and regulations. Each had been aware that the other was finding it tedious, and Donna mumbled drolly under her breath, "They say the rules are about tradition. They're really about potential lawsuits." They had chatted for a while after the session. Donna lived in an adjacent dorm and was going to be taking courses in the newly formed film program. She had thanked Elizabeth for talking to her, admitting the she was worried about making friends at school. A tiny brunette with a pretty face and large, dark brown eyes, she was standing alone at the barbecue. Elizabeth saw the opportunity to be a matchmaker and introduce these two people.

"I'm going to introduce you to somebody," Elizabeth said to Seth. "Now be calm. And ask her a lot of questions about herself. Let the woman talk. She'll be pleasantly surprised.

"Donna, this is Seth. He's feeling a little awkward. Are you?" she asked Donna.

"Yes. Is this event a test? I thought I passed all my tests to get in here."

"Where did you go to school, Donna?" Seth asked, following Elizabeth's instructions.

"Excuse me," Elizabeth said. "I was on my way to somebody.

She worked her way toward the bar and to Holly. The student bartender Elizabeth had noticed was six feet tall, with dark hair cut short, thick eyebrows, and deep-blue eyes.

"Liz Mason, Jimmy Andrews," Holly said. "Liz is my roommate."

"Your roommate? An outstanding room."

"Jimmy's a senior," Holly told her.

"I was just telling Holly—it's kind of hectic for the first few days. They want so much for the freshmen to get acclimated, they pile too much on you."

"I'm already ready for winter break, and I haven't even registered," Elizabeth remarked.

He laughed. Unlike Joe Wallace, he got what she said.

"Suppose, just for a change of pace, you ladies skip the evening session on 'The Junior Year Abroad,' which is all about—"

"Junior year," Elizabeth said, in tune with him.

"And you let me take you two to the movies. *Lawrence of Arabia,* anybody?"

Elizabeth and Holly nodded their heads enthusiastically. People were lined up at the bar; he was obliged to serve drinks and said he would pick them up at seven. As they walked on, Holly told her Jimmy was a history major and on the Layton tennis team. In high school, she and several of her friends had had crushes on him.

THE MOVIE THEATER WAS walking distance from the campus, and Jimmy was brotherly to them, taking each by the arm while escorting them. In the theater, big-bear fashion, he put his arms around both of them. Afterward he took them to an ice-cream parlor near campus.

"I love that movie," Elizabeth said.

"I never saw it before," Holly said.

"Lawrence is an amazing character," Elizabeth said.

"There's no equivalent person in American history," Jimmy said. "I've read a lot about him."

He talked about Lawrence, and Elizabeth was animated in responding to what he had to say. The subject shifted to

Layton College, and she was working at being interested in him, asking him questions in a variation of her advice to Seth Epstein. Jimmy Andrews was attractive and intelligent, and she considered herself to be in a little competition with her roommate for him. To capture the interest of a desirable senior at Layton when they had barely unpacked would have been a small triumph. As the evening proceeded, he was paying more attention to Elizabeth, and Holly became quiet.

He returned them to the dorm room with friendly pecks on their cheeks. After he left, Holly said:

"It wouldn't be me. He's known me too long to be interested in me."

"Let's see what happens."

"I'm sure you'll hear from him. It's not like he's going with anybody. That's why he volunteered to bartend. He said, 'You get to meet the new personnel.' "

LAURA AND BEN PHONED a couple of times during the first few days to see how Elizabeth was getting along, and she gave them a positive report. She had met some nice people; she didn't need anything. And she was registering for classes: a course in twentieth-century American literature, a Shakespeare course, American foreign policy since World War II, sociology, vocal music.

When she went to register, she was able to find a place in all but the foreign policy course, which was oversubscribed, and she opted for a course in American political movements instead. She returned to her room to find a note from Holly:

"It's you. Jimmy called. He'll call you later."

Before getting the note, she had planned to do a few chores, but now she decided to remain in the room and read, essentially waiting for him to call. She didn't wait long.

"Hello there," he said, when she picked up the phone. "Busy?"

"Just reading some things."

"You all registered?"

"I am."

"Great. Listen—my housemates are having a party, sort of the first Saturday night party of the year, and I was wondering if you'd like to grab a bite to eat and then go back to the house."

"Sounds good."

"I'll pick you up tomorrow at seven-thirty, then."

"Seven-thirty."

I can't believe it, she thought to herself. The first Saturday night of the year and I have a date, and he's cute and nice.

"I was never in the running," Holly said about Jimmy having chosen Elizabeth. "He thinks of me as a little kid."

Holly was even-tempered about the matter, and when Elizabeth asked advice on what to wear she was helpful, Elizabeth choosing a skirt and a sweater rather than jeans. The next night, Jimmy came to call wearing loafers, khaki slacks, and a yellow Shetland sweater over a white dress shirt.

"You look lovely," he said.

"I like your look too."

"This is about as dressed up as I get. But I figured, your first date at Layton I'd go all out. It is, isn't it? You haven't been out every night, have you?"

"Hardly."

"Well, we should go to The Babbling Brook. Initiate you."

THE NIGHT WAS WARM. People were lounging outside on the steps of buildings and on the benches that were scattered throughout the campus. They walked to a street just outside the campus area, where several service stores were located, including The Babbling Brook Restaurant and Bar. The place was filled with college students, seated at tables and two deep at the bar. Students had carved their names into the beams and oak walls, and that represented the principal decor. Rock music was playing loudly on the sound system.

"What do you think?" he asked.

"Fun. I don't imagine they play Mozart here."

"No, but after seeing *Amadeus*, I'd say Mozart might have liked a place like this."

They were approached by the maître d', who looked to be a college student, a man in his early twenties who rapidly but completely appraised the newcomer down to her ankles.

"How you doing, Jimbo?"

"Got a table for me?"

"Give me five minutes."

Jimmy guided Elizabeth toward the bar, where he made eye contact with the bartender.

"What would you like to drink?" Jimmy asked her.

"Diet Coke is all right."

"Do you drink?"

"Not usually. And I wouldn't get served in public. I'm only eighteen."

"You don't have false ID?"

"Is it required?"

"You might want to consider it."

He ordered a draft beer for himself and the soft drink for Elizabeth, and they sipped their drinks. Their table was ready, and they were seated in a booth toward the rear, away from the noise of the bar, one of the better tables in the house. Elizabeth ordered a salad, Jimmy a hamburger, and he asked about the courses she had chosen for the semester.

"It's a good balance," he declared. "What you have to watch out for, and I'd say you're okay on this, is not to load yourself up with heavy reading courses where you don't have time to do the work."

"That didn't occur to me," she said, concerned.

"You're okay. In general, it's something to watch out for. You don't want to take, say, all English courses with a lot of reading and essays and never spend a minute outside your room and the library."

"I'm a music major, so that wouldn't happen."

"In what?"

"Vocal music."

"I'm very impressed. The music department here is great. Am I going to get to hear you sing?"

"If I get accepted for something. Mostly I'm interested in musical theater. They don't do as many shows on Broadway as they used to, but I'm very interested in the form."

Pretentious. You're talking too much.

"They do productions here," he said. "Good ones. I've gone to them."

"It was a decision I had to make, if I wanted to go to college or have a career in the theater."

"Really? You must be very good."

I can't stand myself. I'm just like that guy boasting about the colleges he got into.

"Holly said you're majoring in history," she said to him.

"My big question is what to do when I get out. I'm a pretty good tennis player. I never really gave it my all. Which would have meant not going to college. Like you said about college or the theater. It's the same thing."

"Did you play in tournaments?"

"I'm number one at Layton, probably in the top ten, collegiate, in our division."

"*I'm* very impressed."

"So do I go into the business world, into teaching? Do I give professional tennis a shot and try to make a go of it on the circuit?"

Their food arrived. Jimmy ordered another beer and another Diet Coke.

"Being a pro might be fun. For a while," he said.

"What do your parents say?" she asked.

"My father would like to see me turn pro. You can make serious money on the circuit."

He began to talk about his own freshman year: how nervous he was; how it turned around for him the second week, when his history professor, since retired, fell asleep on himself while delivering his own lecture; how one of his dormmates made so many crib notes to cheat on his Spanish final—tiny, nearly microscopic cards that he pasted to his wrists, ankles, inside of his shirt—that he had spent as much time preparing his cheating for the exam as it would have taken him to study for it.

When the check came, she insisted on splitting it. As they left the place he extended his hand to hers, she took it, and they walked along, hand in hand, Elizabeth worrying that her palm was too sweaty.

JIMMY LIVED WITH SEVERAL other seniors in a rambling three-story Victorian house with a porch, in a row of similar houses a block outside the main campus. The house had a sign in front that said: "The Big Leagues." Residence in the dormitories was required for the first two years at Layton; by senior year, many of the students chose unsupervised off-campus housing.

When they arrived at the house, the party was under way. About forty people were drinking beer, talking, dancing. The men were all upperclassmen. Elizabeth recognized several of the women as freshmen. Shannon and Allison were there, talking to senior men, and when they saw Elizabeth they came over to say hello. Elizabeth earned their respect by being at the same party.

"We're in the big time," Shannon said excitedly.

"Who *is* he?" Allison asked, looking in Jimmy's direction. He had gone to a table for drinks.

"Jimmy Andrews. He knows Holly."

"Merely gorgeous," Allison declared.

Jimmy arrived with a bottle of beer for himself and one for Elizabeth. Shannon and Allison were drinking beer out of the bottle, as were most of the people. He handed the beer to Elizabeth, and she took it from him.

"Jimmy, this is Shannon, Allison. We're in the same dorm."

"A quality dorm," he said.

The young men Shannon and Allison had been talking to were impatient, and they signaled for them to return.

"Nice meeting you," Shannon said to Jimmy in a sultry voice that indicated her possible availability.

"Ditto," Allison said with a pert smile, delivering the same message. The girls were a one-two punch.

A rugged young man with unkempt, long brown hair came by. He wore a Layton athletic department T-shirt, jeans, and sneakers and was holding a bottle of beer.

"This is my roommate," Jimmy said. "John Hatcher, Liz Mason."

"Very lithe," John said, studying her anatomy. "Very lithe indeed."

"Are you in personnel?" Elizabeth said.

"Very sharp. Very sharp and very lithe," John said, moving away.

Jimmy took Elizabeth through the house and introduced her to his housemates. They were on various varsity teams at Layton. Jimmy's friends were scattered through the downstairs level, talking or dancing with girls. When introduced, they blatantly looked her up and down, apparently the house custom. The ground-floor level consisted of a living room, a dining room, a parlor with a billiards table, a kitchen, and a sun porch. Jimmy brought her upstairs to see the bedrooms, four on the second floor and three on the third. The bedrooms were linked by disorder, a common decorating theme. John Hatcher and a young woman were sitting on the floor of the room he shared with Jimmy. They looked to have been involved in an intense conversation.

"Excuse us," Elizabeth said. "We're on the house tour."

"Jimmy's friend, this is Carrie," John said.

Carrie, a buxom young woman in a madras dress, with her dark hair loose around her shoulders, nodded in Elizabeth's direction. Elizabeth looked the room over. Tennis trophies stood on a shelf, and there were several books about T. E. Lawrence in with the school texts and reference books.

They went back downstairs and joined a group sitting in the living room, largely senior boys and freshman girls.

Shannon and Allison claimed the interest of about six men between them. The boys were telling war stories about life at Layton. One time an important baseball game with Amherst was interrupted when a dance major choreographing an exercise brought her dancers through the outfield. "Game delayed because of fairies," a young man told the group. They joked about the campus scandal, when an Italian professor, female, and a history professor, male, both married to others, slipped away for an interlude. They had to be rescued by the state police when the car was trapped by a sudden snowfall. "Speculation arose if they would be teaching a course in Assignations," one of the seniors commented. There was the episode when women's panties began appearing draped on the doorknob at the Women's Center. People exchanged stories for an hour. The tales of Layton were reassuring to Elizabeth, a demythification of the institution, which made it less forbidding.

As the party proceeded, people drifted in and out. Nearly everyone was drinking beer; a few couples were scattered about, necking. It became a dancing party in the living room, and Elizabeth and Jimmy danced. She finished a second bottle of beer, took a third, and discarded it after a few sips, thinking she had had enough. She was feeling light-headed and free. This is the best party ever, she thought.

Performing, she did an imitation of Madonna. Suddenly, Jimmy took her in his arms and kissed her. "I just had to do that," he said. "I'm glad you did," she responded, and he kissed her again. The music was playing, three other couples were moving to the rhythm, and Elizabeth and Jimmy stood in the middle of the floor, kissing. John passed through, on his way to the kitchen.

"Hey, over there in Smoocher City—you want a beer?"

"While you're at it," Jimmy said.

"Not me, thanks," Elizabeth said. "I'm way over."

They started to dance again and then stopped to kiss again. As he held her close, she could feel he was hard as he moved himself to position his erection against her. As if he had overstepped the ground rules, he moved back and resumed dancing. John passed through the room with a beer for Jimmy, and they continued to dance. Jimmy kissed her, pressing himself against her once more, and she did not pull away. It felt too good to have him holding her and to know she was exciting him. They danced awhile, then they sat down on a couch in the living room, listening to the music, her head on his shoulder. He kissed her, playing his tongue inside her mouth, and she moved her tongue to play with his. He asked if she wanted to dance again.

They were the last dancers on the floor. People had been leaving for other parties, and this one was dissolving. No one else was in the living room; a couple of people were in the kitchen.

"You're fabulous," he said.

"A lovely night. Thank you for taking me."

"We're not just a bunch of jocks here. We have our elegant side. Let me show you."

He took her by the hand and led her out of the living room, through a corridor, and down a flight of stairs into an unfinished basement, which contained the working equipment for the house. On one side of the basement was a Sheetrock wall with a door. He opened the door and they entered a carpeted room, sixteen feet by twenty, with a stereo system and large speakers on either side of the room, soundproofing material on the walls. There was a record and cassette library, a couple of easy chairs and a sofa positioned in front of the speakers.

"A few years ago, one of the guys who lived here was deeply into heavy metal. He was bombing everybody out. Nobody could think straight. So he had this room made. He graduated, and we all chipped in for the stereo system. The music just accumulates."

She looked through the albums: rock, classical.

"Pick whatever you'd like," he said.

She chose a tape of Handel concerti grossi, he turned on

the system, and they sat on the sofa, his arm around her, listening to the music. She was tired, and after the couple of beers she felt as if she could drift into sleep right there. He moved his hand along her arm, working it up and down, then he pulled her toward him and kissed her. He moved his hand across her breasts as she responded dreamily to his kiss. They were lying on the sofa on their sides, and he ran his hand slowly down. She grabbed his wrist.

"Please," she said. "It's late. I'm tired. This is too fast for me."

"Too fast? Did you bring a calculator with you?"

"This has been a truly lovely night, but now I have to go." She said this holding his wrist. He had not moved his hand away.

"How about a good night kiss, then?"

"One," she said, smiling.

"A good one," he responded.

They were still side by side, and as they kissed, he rolled on top of her. Quickly, so quickly and with such force she could not stop him, he moved his hand up under her skirt and inside her panties, his fingers pushing against her pubic hair, his middle finger inside her.

"No, Jimmy!"

She squirmed to get free of him, of his body, of his finger, but he had her pinned by the weight of his body, and she didn't have the arm strength to push him away from her.

"You're wet. You're hot and wet for me."

"Jimmy, no! Please!"

He had moved his left arm across her chest to hold her down; his right hand worked at her vagina. She grabbed his wrist and tried to pull his hand away.

"You want it so bad."

"I beg of you—let me up."

"You want it."

"I don't! Stop!"

"You're going to love it. Don't fight it."

He continued to work at her with his finger.

She screamed, "Help! Somebody help!"

He went to kiss her and she bit his lip.

"You bitch! You hurt me!"

Angrily, he grabbed her throat.

"Help!" she screamed, but he pushed harder against her throat.

"Please, don't hurt my throat."

She started to tremble and cry, and in so doing, lost her grip on his wrist, and he took the opportunity to slip his finger inside her again, while keeping the pressure on her throat.

"Don't hurt my throat. Please, Jimmy, my throat!" she called out to him, desperately.

He had the key. As long as he held her throat, she was defenseless. She went rigid with fear.

"You're so wet and hot for me," he murmured as he rubbed her inside and out. "You want it so much."

"No, no, stop. Please!"

While holding her down by the throat, with his free hand he expertly undid his pants and pulled them down.

"Help!" she screamed again.

She tried to punch his face, but she could not get leverage with his weight on her, and he applied more pressure to her throat.

"No. Jimmy, no, please."

"Please make love to me, you're saying."

"Don't!" she gasped.

"I know you really want it."

He pulled down her panties. Wedging his knees between her legs, he pushed them apart, continuing to hold her down by the throat. He was in her.

"You got a good rider here. Best in the west." Slowly he plunged inside her and pulled back and did it again. "In and out. And in and out." She was trembling, tears running down her face. "I'm a top stick man around these parts. How's that, baby? And that! And that! And that! And that!"

She remembered the time—she must have been seven;

her brother was in a stroller—when her mother and father took her to the carousel in the park. She was wearing a party dress. She had been to a birthday party, and they came for her at the end of the party and walked through the park. Her father lifted her and placed her on the horse, and every time it came around they were standing there, waving, smiles on their faces, warm, loving smiles, and everyone was so happy.

"And that! And that, baby."

He kept pumping at her and reached orgasm. Then he lay quietly, his body pressing down on her. She did not move at first, swimming in the humiliation. He relaxed in self-satisfaction, and she slid out from under him.

"You know what they say on the pizza boxes," he told her. "'You've had the rest, now try the best'? Well, you've had the best."

Insanely, the Handel was still playing. She noticed it, playing along from another world.

"Sexually speaking, you're not a freshman anymore."

She rose slowly, making pathetic adjustments to her clothing to tidy herself. She shuddered as she felt his semen trickling out of her. She walked unsteadily toward the door, opened it, and ascended the stairs. Everyone from the party was gone. She headed for the front door and he came up behind her, a pleased smile on his face.

"I'll walk you back."

"You'll walk me back?"

"It's late."

"Why did you rape me?" she screamed, her eyes tearing with rage and despair, her entire body shaking.

"Bullshit!" he said. "I didn't rape you. You wanted it."

# CHAPTER
## 4

ELIZABETH VOMITED IN THE STREET—the dinner, the beer, the taste of him, his saliva. She threw up twice more before she reached the dorm, fluids and food particles spilling out of her. The few people who were out did not approach her. She looked like any coed on a Saturday night who had had too much to drink.

*I am meat. I am disgusting, violated meat.*

She made her way into the lavatory on the first floor of the dorm to wash before entering her room. Looking into the mirror above the sink, she saw herself, ravaged, debased, her hair matted. Vomit was on her dress, legs, shoes. The sight of herself made her ill all over again, and she crouched over the bowl, retching.

Holly was asleep when Elizabeth came into the room. She undressed and rolled her clothing and shoes into a ball. They were smelly and repugnant to her. She took a trash bag out of a box in the utility closet, and as she stuffed her belongings into the bag and tied it closed, she started to cry. *Dad bought this so the room would be clean.*

She applied a douche to expunge the fact of him and showered, washing every inch of her body several times over, shuddering in memory as she worked to cleanse herself. She was in the shower for half an hour and still did not feel clean. Wearing a nightgown and bathrobe, she took the trash bag and threw it into a garbage bin behind the dorm. Then she returned to the room, got into bed, and wept on and off for hours, reliving every moment of the evening. She concluded that she was a stupid, naive, ignorant fool: to have had too much beer, to have been so trusting, to have wanted so much for him to like her because he was a senior and so poised and good-looking. It was all thought out, the room downstairs, out of hearing range. He was going to nail a freshman.

The humiliation, the degradation, clung to her all night like sweat on her skin.

Holly stirred in her sleep and heard Elizabeth crying around four in the morning.

"Are you all right?" Holly asked.

"I'm sorry I woke you."

"What is it?"

Elizabeth was too humiliated and ashamed to tell her.

"Homesick. Somebody I broke up with."

"Oh? Do you want to talk about it?"

"It's okay. I'll try to be quiet."

Elizabeth lay still and fell asleep about six in the morning. When Holly left after nine, Elizabeth was still in a deep sleep. She stayed in bed all day, alternately sleeping and crying. Holly returned to the room in the afternoon and found Elizabeth in bed.

"What's wrong?"

This was the moment to deal with it. She could tell Holly and report Jimmy Andrews, or she could remain silent. After a night and most of a day agonizing over the episode, she was convinced of her own culpability. She shouldn't have been in that situation, the way she kissed him, pressed her body against his when they were kissing. She brought it on herself.

"Oh, standard soap opera stuff. Someone I like went

away to school, and now I'm up here, and last night didn't work out too well, and I'm a little hung over.''

''You didn't hit it off with Jimmy?''

''It was . . . a disappointment.''

''Why?''

''He's all show. He's not the kind of man you think.''

''Really? In what way?''

''He's shallow and crude.''

''He could have fooled me.''

''Me, too.''

''He's so charming.''

''At first.''

''What did you do?''

''Went out for a hamburger, went to a party in his house. He's all about looking to make it with you and not one thing more.''

''For some people that might be enough,'' Holly said.

''Not for me. But I have to put everything behind me. Maybe I should start with getting out of bed,'' and she summoned a false, strained smile.

Elizabeth had closed it off. This was a nightmare, but like a nightmare, it had happened in the night and it was over. Classes began the next day. She wanted to melt into the crowd, be anonymous.

*He* was around, though. A senior, he wouldn't be in any of her classes, but she might see him. And he might be bragging. She couldn't bear that, Jimmy Andrews telling buddies how she was a notch on his belt.

When Holly asked if she wanted to go to dinner, Elizabeth declined. After Holly left, she located his number through information and called.

''Hello,'' he said.

''This is Liz.''

''Well, hi.''

''Maybe I should have you arrested—''

''What?''

''Listen carefully to what I have to say. Don't you dare

tell anybody you know that you 'made it' with me. I don't want you bragging. If I hear anything, if I see any of your wonderful pals looking at me with knowing glances, I'll have your balls on a barbecue.''

"Liz, look, it didn't go so smoothly. Maybe we should try again. Get a better rhythm with each other.''

"I can't believe how disgusting you are. Don't you ever look at me or speak to me again.''

THE EFFORT OF TALKING strained her voice, which was husky at the end of the phone call. Her stomach collapsed at the thought that he had injured her vocal cords when he held her by the throat. She curled up on her bed, hugging the teddy bear, rocking it and herself.

Someone knocked on the door.

"Yes?''

"It's Seth.''

"Not now, Seth.''

"Holly said you were sort of hung over.''

"I'm alive.''

"I wanted to thank you for introducing me to Donna. We like each other. A pretty girl likes *me*. This is highly unusual.''

"I'm glad.''

"You going to dinner?''

"I can't handle dinner.''

"You should eat something.''

"Right.''

HER MOTHER CALLED, wanting to check in with her the night before classes. She told her she was fine. No, there was nothing wrong with her voice; it was probably the connection. Her father came on the line. Everything was fine. She was looking forward to classes. She would call later in the week. It was nice talking to them. She chose not to say: Oh, by the way, I was raped. It's true I had a couple of beers and necked with him, but I said no, I pleaded with him, I screamed, and he grabbed my throat and jammed my legs open, and he pushed himself into me again and again. And how have you been, Mom and Dad?

A WHILE LATER, Seth was back, knocking on the door.

"I brought you something to eat."

"I don't want anything."

"You have to eat."

"Oh, come in."

He was carrying a brown paper bag. "Chicken soup!" he announced. He tendered it to her, and she opened the container, tasting it with a plastic spoon.

"It's terrible."

"What do you expect around here?"

"Well, it's warm. This was kind of you, Seth."

"I'd still be out there, right at this minute, standing where the party was, waiting for somebody to talk to me."

"Sometimes the wrong people can talk to you."

"Donna is shy. But we understand each other. I didn't think I'd meet a friend, least of all a girl, and now she's going to be my friend, and I hope you'll be my friend too."

For an instant she thought it would be possible to tell him, that it would be in his nature to be able to sympathize. And he would be outraged, and comfort her. She didn't tell him. She did say:

"Yes, that would be good, Seth. I could use a male friend just now."

IN A COLLEGE of three thousand students, it might have been possible for Elizabeth not to encounter Jimmy Andrews for weeks, or so she hoped. But she saw him the second day of classes. She was coming out of the English department building and he was on his way in, walking with one of his housemates, whom she recognized from the night of the party. Before he saw her, Jimmy was chuckling over something or other. As they passed each other, the humor disappeared from his face. Whatever she had meant when she told him she would have his balls on a barbecue, apparently he was concerned about her threat.

It wasn't much of a victory. Seeing him upset her all over again. She felt short of breath, and her throat began to hurt. She thought this was either from his pressure on her throat or from the vomiting. After lunch she was scheduled for her first class in vocal music. She skipped it, worried that if they were going to sing she would be risking damage to her voice. The college administered a clinic for students, but she wanted to avoid dealing with questions on campus about the origin of her problem. In the orientation brochure, under "Medical Facilities," a medical center was listed in the town of Caldwell and was said to have a full range of services. She called a throat specialist. The doctor was available the following day, and she made an appointment.

DR. THOMAS PHELAN was a small, prim-looking man with white hair. She sat on an examining table in his office, and he stood opposite her.

"You're at the college?"

"Yes, I am."

"What seems to be the problem, young lady?"

"We have a chinning bar in our closet, and you tighten it against the sides of the door. It must have slipped down, and I went into the closet for something. I had a couple of beers, and I was a little . . . unsteady. And I literally walked right into the bar. It caught me across the throat."

He examined her throat carefully, internally and externally, and when he was finished he looked at her dubiously.

"You walked into a chinning bar, you say?"

"It was stupid of me."

"You have minor contusions, which are not consistent with the point of impact that would occur if you had the accident you describe."

"That's what happened."

"What do you want from me, young lady?" he said curtly.

"I'm a voice major. And I was concerned if singing would put a strain on my voice."

"Did someone choke you? Were you in a fight with someone, a boyfriend? Were you mugged?"

"No! I drank too much beer—"

"Yes, I heard you say that." He looked at her with annoyance, while making notes in a file. "All right. I would advise against singing for two weeks. No shouting. No long conversations. Give your voice a rest, and you should be back to normal."

"Thank you very much, Doctor."

"I see that they're not giving courses in candor over there, are they?"

A SLIGHT VOCAL HUSKINESS persisted for a few days. She changed the chinning bar story. In the new version, which she told her parents and the teacher in the music class, she had been walking across the lawn and received a direct hit to her throat from an errant softball. Laura and Ben were worried, ready to have her see a doctor in New York. She assured them she would be all right in a little while.

Though it was a few days late, her next period came. She did not experience any symptoms of sexually transmitted diseases. She was beyond the safety zone the throat specialist had advised, but Elizabeth was still attending vocal music as an "auditor." She had stopped singing.

SHE WENT HOME for Yom Kippur, a hurried visit. She told her parents that her voice was fine and she was fine.

Elizabeth's hopes for Layton—to be in musicals, write for the newspaper, run cross-country, play volleyball— vanished. She became a drone, rushing from class back to her room in order to work, studying until late at night.

She did not see much of her roommate. Holly Robertson was busy with the girls' basketball team, practice and games, and in addition, she began to go with a senior, an engineering major who was on the men's basketball team; he lived off campus with two of his teammates.

"I need a favor," Holly said one night in the dorm room. "I don't want to tell my parents that I'm practically living with a guy off campus. If they call and I'm not here, tell them I'm in the library and take a message. Then call me at Pete's house. Would you do that? Would you cover for me?"

"Sure. Is he nice?" Elizabeth asked.

"Very. He's kind of quiet. But he's six four, which is a good height for me," she added lightheartedly.

"You're happy?" Elizabeth asked, as if that were a distant concept.

"Pretty much. I kind of went for security. I settled in with one guy right away. And I stayed with basketball because it's familiar."

"Sounds okay. You have somebody who cares for you, and you're doing something you're good at."

"Still, it was an interesting suggestion you made, that I try dance. Maybe one day. What's going on with you?"

"Mostly studying. I have to work hard to keep up," she said as an explanation for her monastic behavior.

ELIZABETH NOW HAD the room to herself, to study as late as she wished. While Shannon and Allison ran through several boyfriends between them, Elizabeth had little to do with them or the other people in her dorm. Apart from Holly, with whom she would exchange small talk when they saw each other, and Seth and Donna, whom she occasionally joined in the dining room, she didn't talk to anyone on campus.

HER FACULTY ADVISER was Cynthia Moss, from the music department, a woman who had been present at her audition when Elizabeth applied to Layton. She requested a meeting with Elizabeth in her office. She was a serious-looking woman in her forties, who used her reading glasses to punctuate her remarks.

"Elizabeth, how are you finding life here at Layton?"

"I'm keeping busy with studies."

"I understand you have not been participating in vocal music," she said, looking at her over the glasses.

"I had an unfortunate accident."

"Yes; you were hit by a ball," she said, examining a paper on her desk. "Did you go to the clinic?"

"I saw a throat specialist at the medical center. He said I shouldn't sing for a while."

"For how long?"

"A couple of weeks."

"It's more than a couple of weeks. Are you in pain?"

"Not really. My voice is all right now."

"Then why aren't you participating in class?"

"Frankly, I did quite a bit of singing while I was in high school, and I took serious vocal lessons—"

"I know this. I observed your audition. I urged that we accept you at Layton."

"Not singing for a while gave me time to think about things. And I just don't feel like performing. I guess I've done too much. I'm burned out."

Cynthia Moss peered at Elizabeth and then looked at the paper on her desk.

"You were supposed to be a music major. A music major takes music."

"I'm rethinking things. I'm working hard in my other subjects. My understanding was that we're supposed to be well rounded here at Layton, and I'm trying to be."

"I'm hard pressed to know what the point is in continuing to attend vocal classes without singing."

"Then I should drop the course."

"Is that what you want?"

"Definitely."

"I trust that you'll resume in the spring." She used her glasses to punctuate the remark.

"I can't say."

"Adjustments are often difficult for new students. We have a college psychologist. I'd like you to see her."

"Is she going to tell me, 'Sing out, Louise'?"

"What?"

What? What do you want to hear? That I'm damaged goods and the thought of standing up in front of people and presenting myself cute and perky, and singing, *singing* of all things, as though I were a cheery little bird, is so ridiculous that I can't even bear to think about it. Is that what I should say to you?

"I'll take an incomplete and play it by ear, so to speak," she said curtly.

"We'll talk again in the beginning of the spring semester," the adviser said, squinting at her, trying to reconcile the exuberant, vivacious girl who auditioned for her with this unpleasant person.

LAURA AND BEN came up to spend a few hours with Elizabeth and brought Josh so he could see the school. He loved the grounds, the field house, the playing fields.

"I hope I'm smart enough to go to a school like this," he said.

"Maybe you'll go here," Laura said.

Don't bother, Elizabeth thought. But she smiled, acting.

She showed them the lounges and the buildings where she attended classes, and they went to a Layton-Wesleyan football game. Layton, a traditional loser in football, lost again.

The "softball injury" Elizabeth sustained had healed; her voice was normal. She was somewhat drawn-looking, but she said the work was difficult and she was studying long hours. They laughed about Ben's insistence that they go immediately to buy One-A-Day vitamins: there was not one day, not one minute to waste.

A WEEK LATER, she dealt with Sarah and her parents, telling them in successive phone calls that she was officially dropping music. Sarah was bewildered. She couldn't accept Elizabeth's explanation that she was "burned out."

"It's not like you've been on the road with *Phantom* for three years."

"Don't you ever feel that it gets too much?"

"Career decisions, yes. What I'm going to do *in* music. But not *music*. I wouldn't just drop it. I can't believe this. You're not going out for any plays or anything?"

"The pressure's off, and it's great."

"I don't understand it."

"I've done that, and now there are other things I want to do." And she moved off the subject.

Laura and Ben were aware of complications for young people when they went to college. Some became homesick, had difficulty with their work, with social life; some had nutritional problems, or contracted mononucleosis. They knew something could go awry. They never imagined Elizabeth would tell them this. Without the previous suggestion of a problem at school, knowing Elizabeth was always truthful, they were obliged to accept her explanation, that she needed to get away from music.

"What I'm not sure of is whether you're dropping it temporarily," Laura told her.

"I'm through with vocal music."

"Really?" Ben remarked on the extension.

"Olga Bavanne said not everyone goes for a performing career, and a college education is important to have. I'll be getting an education at Layton."

"This is such a big decision. I feel we should talk about it more," Laura told her.

"I'm a big girl now," she said, with a darkness they did not detect.

"What would you study?" Ben asked.

"English."

They probed for more information; little was forthcoming. She was taking an incomplete for the course and would substitute an English course for music in the spring semester. In the meantime they would see each other when she came home in a few weeks for the Thanksgiving weekend.

"I guess you have to know what's best for yourself," Ben said.

"I do."

"I just can't imagine that you're not going to sing anymore," Laura added.

"I'll sing. I'll sing in the rain. I suppose."


BEWILDERED, Laura and Ben assumed guilt. Perhaps they had loaded her down with too many of their expectations. But she had seemed to love singing. They couldn't fit that component into the explanation. Looking to make sense of the situation, Laura called Olga Bavanne and recounted the conversation with Elizabeth. As it turned out, Elizabeth had called Olga and told her essentially what she said to her parents.

"I was, frankly, surprised," Olga said. "She seems very definite, though."

"We've been handed the decision."

"It is possible she feels that she was being tracked into music and didn't like the feeling," Olga offered. "She might be saying, I am more than music."

"So you think she could be burned out, as she says?"

"Elizabeth might not like us all watching her that way and wants to be her own person."

"Then Ben and I turned out to be just another couple of pushy parents."

"Hardly. And as her teacher, I would be more responsible in this than you."

"Would you ever have predicted it?" Ben asked.

"Never. She was always so enthusiastic."

"Maybe in time she'll change her mind," Laura offered. "Did you hear that? Obviously I'm still overinvolved and I think what she decided isn't right."

"I can't blame you. This *is* a waste. And there's nothing we can do."


INTELLECTUALLY, Elizabeth consigned the rape to the category of nightmares in order to distance herself from it. This did not stop it from violating her sleep in real nightmares. In her dreams a figure hovered over her and she couldn't breathe. She would violently throw herself out of sleep, sweating, gasping for breath. The bad images came in the day too, flickering across her consciousness during her waking hours, triggered by random suggestions of sexuality: a boy in one of her classes who looked at her with interest, a girl on a lawn sitting with a boy, flirting with him. These occurrences would provoke the event to return like a hideous rodent that kept darting across her path.

SHE PASSED a group of students, men and women, gathered around the piano in the first-floor lounge of the dorm, singing songs from a Billy Joel songbook. The accompanist was one of the men who lived in the dorm, a sophomore and a member of a jazz quintet. Elizabeth paused at the doorway and observed. The moment called out for her to join the group, to begin singing along with the others. As she sang they would turn in her direction because of her voice. She would raise the musical level of the group. The pianist would pay special attention to her. Then he would play one of the more wistful of the Billy Joel songs, "Piano Man," and one by one the others would drop out, leaving Elizabeth to sing it solo. She knew it could happen just that way, but it would require singing, relating to other people in an amiable way. She watched them a minute or two more, then withdrew to her room to be alone and lose herself in studies.

SHE NEVER SPOKE OUT in any of her classes and barely spoke to her classmates, apart from the most rudimentary exchanges of greetings. Attracted by her looks, men approached her with a variety of opening remarks. She adopted "I'm sorry; I'm busy," or "I've got a paper I have to write," to fend off overtures. Women in the dorm received the message too. She was so private it was as though she had a quarantine sign on her door.

• • •

HOLLY HAD DRIFTED into the orbit of her boyfriend and was never in the room. One afternoon, Holly was standing with her boyfriend and several of his friends when Elizabeth passed by. She introduced Elizabeth to them. Elizabeth was brusque, "on my way to the library," and she hurried along. The next week, Holly came to the room, which she used primarily for storage, and picked up a pair of boots she had left in her closet.

"Pete's house is having a party Saturday night. Why don't you come by?"

"I'm a little behind on my reading."

"There are some cute guys in the crowd."

"I appreciate it, but I can't."

"They're nice. Most of them are on the basketball team."

"Then they'd be too tall for me," she said flippantly.

"Some of them play the backcourt," Holly responded in kind.

"I'm really off athletes for the moment."

"Liz, this is the Layton basketball team. They're not that *good*."

"Thanks for asking, Holly. It's not what I want to do."

ELIZABETH COULD GO for days without talking to anyone but for phone calls from her parents, or from Melanie and Sarah. With her friends she tried to keep the focus of the conversations off herself. When they asked about her, she performed set pieces: She was working hard and finding the work challenging, the men not. The men at Layton were vain and not too interesting so far, but maybe Mr. Not Quite Right but Acceptable would come along. Melanie, never one to be timid, said, "Seven weeks. Have you gotten laid yet?" Elizabeth paused for a breath and said, "No." She ate her breakfasts and lunches alone, usually standing at a snack bar. Saturdays and Sundays, the long days without classes, she studied and napped off and on. Several times Seth and Donna invited her to join them for dinner or the movies. She declined for reasons of study and ate her dinners in her room, watching the nightly news. Elizabeth was living college life like a shut-in.

ON A FRIDAY EVENING, she was settling in for her standard dinner fare, a tuna sandwich, a diet soda, and the news, when Seth and Donna poked their noses into her room.

"You should be getting out more," Seth said.

"Come to the movies and dinner with us. We want to celebrate that we're still together. And you're the one who introduced us."

"That's very sweet. But I have so much work this weekend—"

"Liz, we're all in the same school," Donna said. "We know how much work you have or don't have. You can take time out. They're showing *The Red Shoes*."

"I can't."

"Even my mother says you should get out more," Seth said.

"Your mother? You discuss me with your mother?"

"Her need for information is insatiable." Elizabeth smiled. "Really, Liz. You were walking into the dorm and I was sitting across the way and there were a few kids there. And one of the guys said, 'Nice-looking,' as you went by. And one of the other people, who lives in your dorm, said, 'She's a goddamn hermit.'"

"Well, that's one kind of reputation to have," she said to them. "Not the worst kind."

A goddamn hermit. That's what I am.

"Liz, come out with us," Donna said.

She thought about it. She wasn't being asked to deal with men at a party. These people were being very generous, and she told them, "Okay, I will. Thanks."

As she gathered herself together to join them, she said, "There will be a ballet of *The Red Shoes* tonight."

THE MOVIE, attended by some one hundred fifty students, was shown in the auditorium of the arts center. Two film series ran throughout the school year at Layton. One consisted of two-time-a-week showings of conventional films. The second was a Friday-night series of art films. Elizabeth had never attended any of the showings. According to Donna, the Friday series attracted an ''artier crowd'' than the regular movies. They looked like interesting people to Elizabeth. Taking everything in, the familiarity with one another of people in the audience, their obvious pleasure in being there, Elizabeth squinted as if, after being in darkness, she had suddenly come into the light.

This was the fourth time Elizabeth had seen *The Red Shoes*, and she knew many of the speeches, as did people in the crowd, the cognoscenti applauding lines and scenes.

''It was like being at a ball game,'' Elizabeth said afterward at a hamburger place near the campus.

''They were incredible filmmakers, Powell and Pressburger,'' Donna said. ''They did these florid, wonderful movies, but then they also did something as simple as *I Know Where I'm Going*.''

''I never saw that,'' Elizabeth said.

''I'm on the film committee. Next term I'll get them to show it.''

''You know a lot about movies.''

''Donna's mother and father are film editors,'' Seth volunteered.

''I'd like to be a director,'' Donna said. ''Next year we start making films. Maybe you'll act for me,'' she said to Elizabeth.

''I want to star in a western,'' Seth said.

''You? A person who thinks *High Noon* is better than *Red River*? It's how it holds up today that counts,'' Donna said. ''Not what people thought of it *then*.''

''Look, I concede that you know British films of the forties and fifties—''

''British? Only British?''

''But you don't know beans about westerns,'' he said. ''*High Noon* has all the classic elements.''

For Elizabeth, sitting with Seth and Donna was like watching a movie, with teasing, banter. Nothing like that seemed remotely possible for her.

Seth and Donna wanted to know Elizabeth's sense of the school thus far, and she said her main concern was being able to handle the work, so she stayed pretty much to herself. She gave them her standard explanation for dropping vocal music. Donna found Layton much preppier and closed off than she had expected. Seth agreed and thought the men were snobs and the women ignored him, "but then women have always ignored me." Donna had not, though, and they were obviously sleeping together. As they talked about the school, Elizabeth's mind drifted, and she imagined what it would be like to sleep with Seth. Would he take off his socks? Would he bump you with his bony knees and elbows? Then suddenly she wasn't thinking of Seth, and she saw Jimmy coming at her again. She couldn't have a playful sexual fantasy any longer that was not intruded upon by the rape.

They paused to say good night in front of Elizabeth's dorm.

"I appreciate your taking me for an airing. Please tell your mother I got out," she said to Seth.

"She'll know in minutes. We have fax machines so she can keep in touch with campus activities," he joked.

"Next Friday night, *Open City*," Donna announced. "Would you like to come with us?"

"I'd like that very much."

She returned to the room and lay on her bed, thinking about the evening. Life was going on outside her room, people were seeing movies, falling in love. The next time I have sex with anyone, I'd have to have been married to him for three years. She amused herself only slightly with her joke. Being in the company of a man, going through the social rituals, seemed unfathomable. She tried to summon the memory of Barney, sweet Barney from another time, but the image of the hideous rodent kept darting into the room.

# CHAPTER
# 5

THE FATEFUL PARTY, the only party Elizabeth had attended at Layton, became merely a blip on Jimmy Andrews' radar screen as he went to other parties, scanning the campus for "new personnel." Two months into the semester, he now had the bedroom to himself on weekends. His roommate, John Hatcher, was conducting a traveling relationship with his girlfriend, a junior at Hamilton College. She had a room of her own in a house off the Hamilton campus. John visited her every weekend, taking his books with him for school-work, leaving the room free.

John Hatcher was a straight-A student, a philosophy major, the kind of scholar-athlete prestigious schools valued. Both of his parents were professors; his father taught political science at Georgetown, his mother history at George Washington University. He tried to balance himself between academic pursuits and being a regular guy. A catcher on the Layton baseball team, when he tended bar at house parties, he displayed a card that said, whimsically, "The Catcher in the Rye." He was usually respected by his housemates for his intelligence and ethical point of view, except for those times when he became too judgmental for their tastes and they dismissed him as being "tight-assed."

John had joined "The Big Leagues" out of his desire to be one of the guys. The members of the house drew names out of a hat for roommates, and John Hatcher and Jimmy Andrews ended up sharing a room. They did not have much to do with each other. John was either in the library at nights or with his girlfriend on weekends. John could not understand his roommate's relentless pursuit of women. Jimmy's hunting seemed to John both amoral and humorless.

"Are you making the party scene again?" John said to Jimmy as another weekend approached.

"And if I am?"

"You go about your social life as if you were studying for a final."

"Yes, Father John, tell me about it. *You* get laid every weekend."

"With my significant other. Where's that redheaded one, the freshman? She seemed nice."

"We didn't get along."

"You told me you screwed her."

"I didn't know we didn't get along *until* I screwed her."

"Jimmy 'Bop 'em and Drop 'em' Andrews."

"You took yourself out of circulation. Your opinions don't count."

"Where are the parties this time?"

"I happen to be going home. There's a father-son tournament at my parents' club."

"The other guys are going to get ahead of you," he teased.

"I doubt it," he responded.

"You guys are like errant knights in search of the Unholy Grail."

"Who can be as literary as you? We call it pussy."

Jimmy Andrews said goodbye to his housemates. He joked with them about exactly the point John Hatcher had teased him about: while he was home in Westport, they would be getting ahead of him in scoring with women.

Back in the room, John Hatcher gathered several books from his desk and packed them into his book bag. Jimmy Andrews' intellectual credentials, which he had flashed so conspicuously for Elizabeth, were purloined. Lawrence of Arabia was a subject of interest for *John Hatcher*. The books in the room were for a paper Hatcher was writing on T. E. Lawrence.

JIMMY ANDREWS HAD been playing in father-son tennis tournaments at the Sweetbriar Country Club in Westport, Connecticut, for the past eleven years. The Andrewses were regularly defeated in those early tournaments, and the boy was given tennis lessons. He spent part of every summer at a tennis camp and began competing in junior tournaments. He had not played in any noncollegiate tennis tournaments since his freshman year of college, and he held no national computer ranking. He was, though, the number one player at Sweetbriar. He and his father, Malcolm Andrews, an undistinguished B tennis player, had won the annual father-son tournament for the past three years.

The tournament was held to coincide with the annual raising of the bubble over the tennis courts, which permitted club members to play during the cold-weather months. The club was the major social outlet for Malcolm and Penny Andrews. Her father had been a charter member of Sweetbriar. Penny and her two sisters grew up playing at the club. Eaton Fisk was a commander of a submarine during World War II and became the founder of Fisk Electronics, which manufactured communications equipment for naval vessels. At the time of his death, the Captain, as he was always called, was also chairman of the state Republican committee. When Penny Fisk married Malcolm Andrews after her graduation from Vassar, the young couple received a house in Westport and their membership at Sweetbriar as wedding gifts. The club was restricted in those years and still retained that character; less than five percent of the current membership were Jews and blacks.

On the first Saturday of every month, a dance was held at the club, and except for times when they were away on holiday, Penny Fisk Andrews, chairperson of the Sweetbriar social committee, and her husband, Malcolm, attended, danced, smiled, and mingled. Andrews was an insurance man who specialized in corporate and personal pension plans, so the club, a stocked pond of the affluent, was at the core of his business-social life. He had been the only child of a postal employee in Reading, Pennsylvania, and his dressmaker wife. His parents had carefully saved money over the years so that their boy would one day go to college. He was accepted at Lehigh and after an unexceptional college career decided to become an insurance broker. He achieved moderate success and maintained offices in Manhattan and in Westport.

Penny was the last of the three Fisk sisters to marry. Her older sister married a man who was taken into the firm by the Captain, as was the youngest sister's husband. No position was available for Malcolm Andrews, who had to settle for the large colonial house, membership at Sweetbriar, and Fisk Electronics as a pension fund account. Penny kept herself busy with volunteer activities that befitted a member of Sweetbriar. Socially, the Andrewses lived a cut above their income. Their home and membership in the club could never have been achieved by virtue of Malcolm Andrews' earnings. Over the years he exerted self-discipline and restricted his drinking to no more than two vodka martinis a night, even at a public event. Beyond that limit, he was given to brooding and would conclude that his only discernible virtues were his looks and his fox-trot.

THEY HAD MET at New York Republican headquarters during the Goldwater campaign for the presidency in 1964. "In your heart, you know he's right" was a main theme of the Goldwater campaign. Andrews' heart went out to Goldwater because he learned from one of his co-workers at New

York Life that working as a volunteer was a good way to meet wealthy girls.

Penny Fisk was thin, with a pageboy in need of maintenance, and she had inherited the Captain's flat, masculine nose. Her social life in New York had been nonexistent. Malcolm Andrews was nearly six feet tall, with thick black hair, bushy eyebrows, and blue eyes. He was the kind of good-looking Republican she had hoped to meet at campaign headquarters.

On election night, when Goldwater was trounced by the uncouth Lyndon Johnson, Penny Fisk wept. Malcolm Andrews consoled her by taking her to his apartment, where she spent the night. He was her second, the first being a boy from Yale during her senior year. Penny Fisk and Malcolm Andrews were married ten months later, at the club. The story of how she wept when Goldwater lost was repeated over the years by her husband. She asked him not to tell it anymore; she felt embarrassed by it. Ignoring her, he still insisted on recounting the episode at times when people sat around and reminisced about their early days. He thought the story was a nostalgic and charming testament to how loyal a Republican his wife had been, and in his circles the story was a selling point.

LESS BENEFICIAL WAS the story of their son Mitch, six years older than Jimmy. Much had been expected of him, the Captain's first male grandchild, Penny and Malcolm's first-born. Aided by extensive tutoring, and thanks to the Captain's contacts, he was accepted at Princeton. He lasted for one year and dropped out. He came back home and said that he wanted to take time off to work and travel. He would try a small college somewhere in the Midwest later, away from the family and their expectations. With Penny's passive approval, Malcolm Andrews gave his son an ultimatum. Mitch was to reapply to colleges immediately. In response, Mitch Andrews moved to California. He worked at odd jobs, eventually enrolling at the University of California at

Riverside. After his graduation he became a personnel
manager for an electronics firm. He never returned to the
East.

When Mitch went to California, it strained Malcolm
Andrews' social skills. He would say to people: "Mitch is
off finding himself on the West Coast. But Jimmy got into
Layton." He always made a rapid transition away from
Mitch to Jimmy. Jimmy was the pride. Jimmy was the
family treasure. Jimmy was good for business.

HE WAS DRIVING home in the Toyota he had been given as a
getting-into-Layton gift. As Jimmy neared the house, he
anticipated that his father would want to go over to the
courts that evening to sharpen their strokes for the tournament, which began in the morning. His mother would be
ready with an elaborate dinner to celebrate his coming home
for the weekend. He would be expected to satisfy both,
which meant he would end up hitting balls with his father on
a full stomach. They would ask about school and his friends.
How were the boys in the house, his roommate; was he
going out with anyone special? He would give them
serviceable answers, as he always did. They were not really
asking how it was going in his senior year, because they
wouldn't want to hear the real answers—I'm scared shitless
about what to do when I graduate; to be good enough for the
circuit, I should have been destroying everybody I played
against in college, and I didn't. And even though I nailed
four girls already, which puts me in the lead in the house,
you don't want to hear that one of them, the first one, played
so hard to get that I had to force the issue a bit, and then she
told me I raped her, which is stretching it because what was
she doing rubbing up against me? But I don't need her to
hassle me. I've got enough hassles in front of me when I
graduate, and what the hell am I going to do if I don't go on
the circuit? Go into business like Dad and spend my life
kissing ass?

"Great. Everything's going great."

"Your classes?"

"Just great, Mom."

"And at the house, your roommate and everybody?"

"Everybody's terrific. John went to see his girlfriend. The guys are having a party."

"Well, I made a nice turkey for tonight."

"You made an entire turkey for the three of us?"

"You can always have sandwiches over the weekend."

"We play at ten tomorrow," Malcolm said. "Art Schultz and his son. The kid's no more than eleven."

"That's a first-round bye," Jimmy declared.

"They're giving people court time this evening to tune up. I'd feel more comfortable if we hit awhile. We'll go over after dinner, okay?"

"Great."

MALCOLM ANDREWS WAS fifty-three and still fit. He played tennis year-round at the club, but he had torn a muscle in his calf during the previous summer and he was favoring the leg slightly, not running hard for balls that were wide.

"Come on, Dad," Jimmy shouted across the net.

"I'm warming up," Malcolm Andrews responded.

"You've got to pull your weight."

AT THIRTEEN, Jimmy Andrews defeated his father for the first time. He had been given instructional lessons at the club every week, refining his strokes on Saturdays and Sundays with hitting lessons. Although the lessons cost two hundred dollars a week, Malcolm Andrews considered it an investment for the future. Penny Andrews became her son's personal chauffeur, bringing him to his lessons, waiting for him to be finished, taking him home. Her afternoons revolved around him.

Jimmy started competing in regional junior tournaments when he was fourteen. He was already as tall as his older brother. As the proprietor of his own company, Malcolm was able to attend some of the tournaments, and Penny made certain to be there for the others. Her chauffeuring activities became more extensive as they traveled to tournaments throughout New England, New York, and Pennsylvania. Some were so modest they were held in nothing more than local public park facilities, on cement surfaces. Some were first-class events at country clubs or tennis clubs, featuring referees and linesmen.

At the tournaments, a few of the girls cried after losses; the boys tended to turn dark and remote. Nearly all the boys, including Jimmy by the time he was fifteen, adopted the Strut. They walked with an ambling, shoulder-rocking gait and a smug look on their faces. They had been so catered to by their parents, so much energy and money had been focused on their ability to hit a ball over the net, that they were convinced of their own superiority.

Cheating was rampant. In the lower-level tournaments, where the players themselves called the balls in or out, players often called close balls in their favor. At a tournament in a public part in Philadelphia, three close calls had gone against Jimmy. Having never seen such behavior, Penny sought out the official in charge of the tournament.

"How can you allow cheating like that?" she demanded to know.

"There's an awful lot of pressure on these kids," he explained. "My opinion is, some of them are outright cheaters. But some of them, with all the pressure, they really want to believe a ball that's really in is out. They 'see' it out when it isn't. What can you do?"

Jimmy Andrews adopted the Strut and cheated along with the rest. When Penny and Malcolm observed the overall pattern of behavior at junior tournaments, they did not counsel their son not to cheat. There were always justifications: a call that went against him earlier in the match, or in a previous match. Eventually, they, too, began to see it out when it wasn't.

• • •

WHEN HE WAS SIXTEEN, Jimmy Andrews added tactical complaints to his gamesmanship and began to protest regularly to referees about bad calls. Here, Malcolm Andrews had John McEnroe, Sr., as his parental model. John senior allowed John junior to get away with that kind of behavior all those years, and it didn't seem to hold the boy back.

During his senior year of high school, Jimmy led his school team to a district championship, while competing in several eighteen-and-under tournaments. He reached 10 regionally, his highest ranking. A client of Malcolm Andrews', a member of Sweetbriar, was on the board of trustees at Layton College, and he sent a note to the admissions office in Jimmy's behalf, pointing out that he was a fine lad. On his visit to the school, Jimmy met with the tennis coach, who told him that Layton did not offer athletic scholarships, but he was aware of Jimmy's potential as a member of the team and he would send a recommendation to Admissions. Jimmy Andrews was not on the professional circuit, but his family did recoup part of the time and money they had given over to his tennis playing when he was accepted at Layton with grades and SAT scores that never could have qualified him academically.

TO WIN THE father-son tournament at Sweetbriar, a doubles team had to win four matches. The Andrewses won their first three matches easily and were in the final. The Sunday final, preceded by a drinking lunch in the main clubhouse, was a social event at the club and usually attracted at least a hundred people. A bartender with a rolling bar for the diners moved in and out among the tables of the clubhouse dining room. By the time of the match, many of the people who strolled over to the bubble were weaving along.

The Andrewses were going to be playing the Thompsons. Reg Thompson, an investment banker, was a man in his early forties, who played at the same level as Malcolm. His son, Donny, was sixteen. Jimmy had never seen Donny play; the Thompsons were divorced, and Donny lived with his mother in New York. He had heard Donny had competed in a few tournaments.

The players warmed up for about ten minutes before the match. Jimmy sensed the adults were about even in their strokes. Trained to make appraisals of an opponent during a warm-up, he judged the boy to have excellent ground strokes. He had a two-handed backhand, as did Jimmy, and he bent close to the ground on his strokes.

As they began to play the match, it was evident that Donny Thompson was a whippet. Lobs were totally ineffective against the Thompsons. Donny had outstanding anticipation and could race back from the net to reach lobs on his or his father's side. Although he was not a heavy hitter, he hit the ball unerringly. Jimmy began scowling and ordering his father around. Weekend tennis players in the crowd, drunk and sober, applauded how hard Jimmy hit some of this serves and ground strokes. Meanwhile Malcolm Andrews and Reg Thompson were engaged in a middle-aged men's struggle over their bellies and their opponents. Most of the points were decided on their errors rather than the sons'. Playing a strategic, off-speed game, the Thompsons won the first set, 6–3. In the second set, Jimmy continued to scowl and mutter, grumbling about calls but hitting the ball hard. Despite Jimmy's intensity and hard hitting, the Thompsons were good enough to keep balls away from him, and Malcolm's game was not steady enough. At 5–4, the serve was Donny Thompson's. The game went on for a while, and finally, at match point, the boy hit a ball that Malcolm mis-hit at the net, to give the victory to the Thompsons, 6–3, 6–4.

They shook hands, and Jimmy walked off quickly. He would not shower. He rushed to the car and sat there, avoiding the spectators, Malcolm and Penny following a few minutes later.

"You played very well," Penny said.

He had played fine tennis and made few errors. The

fathers were not equal; Reg Thompson was steadier than Malcolm.

"You did play very well," Malcolm Andrews added, but it was not said in a convincing tone of voice. Jimmy knew what his father was really saying: You knew how much this meant to me. This is my personal prestige at the club, and now other people took over, new people, and it wouldn't have happened if you played even better.

ELEVEN WEEKS INTO the term, the freshmen were settled in. The first anxious times were over; fear of terrible room-mates, fear of oppressive work loads, fear of not being able to belong, were subsiding. For Elizabeth, her entire social life consisted of the times she went to the movies with Seth and Donna. They attended a showing of *The 400 Blows*.

"The freeze-frame at the end is one of the most stunning images in the history of modern film," Donna declared as they were leaving.

"It's a haunting movie," Elizabeth said.

"Did you ever see *The Wild Child*?" Donna asked.

"I don't think I ever heard of it," Elizabeth answered.

"Tomorrow. Lunch in my room. *The Wild Child*. Discussion to follow."

"I have a history paper—"

"Liz, this is Truffaut. More important than any history paper."

"To a film major."

"To anyone. This is required," Donna said.

THE NEXT DAY, Elizabeth brought a few bags of popcorn to Donna's room, a section of which was given over to a film library of videocassettes brought from home. Donna's roommate was Sterling May, a striking black girl with a long, limber body.

"Haven't seen you around," she said to Elizabeth when they were introduced. "Did you just enroll?" she asked teasingly.

"I've managed to convert my first five weeks at school into independent study."

"Uh, here comes Prince Charming," Sterling remarked as Seth entered the room, dressed exceedingly Seth in a rumpled dress shirt with the sleeves rolled up unevenly, creased khaki pants that were far too short, revealing black socks falling down, and food-stained sneakers. "Get your clothes in the L. L. Scream catalogue?"

"Sterling, why don't you go somewhere and run?"

"Your wish is my command, O prince of fashion."

"Sterling runs track," Donna explained.

"Do you work out?" she asked Elizabeth.

"I used to jog. I seem to have given it up," she said.

"I'll catch the end of this little film festival," Sterling said.

They ordered a pie from a nearby pizzeria and watched the movie. Sterling returned from her run and sat on the floor for the last half hour. When it was over, Donna, who had said, "Discussion to follow," raised the issue of the purity of the savage spirit presented by Truffaut in the story.

Sterling was a drama major, playwriting specifically, and proceeded to compare *The Wild Child* with the play *Equus*. Seth talked about schizophrenia, which surprised Elizabeth, who had assumed he was solely a computer/math wiz. Elizabeth was dazzled by them. Her contribution to the discussion was to say that the slow, deliberate way Truffaut ended his scenes in *The Wild Child* suggested to her a silent movie or pages turning in a book. That was credible enough so that she didn't feel like a total dumbbell with the others. She thanked them and returned to her room.

That is what college is supposed to be, Elizabeth thought, and she was filled with warm feelings toward them for including her. Suddenly, she started to cry over how lonely she had been—and why. That filthy, disgusting bastard!

# CHAPTER
# 6

ELIZABETH WELCOMED Monday mornings, when she could get back into the routine of classes without any large blocks of time to pass. Rainy weather was best for her. Everyone rushed along, and her pattern of scurrying, eyes down, was indistinguishable in the rain.

Walking quickly, averting her eyes, she had managed to avoid seeing Jimmy Andrews since that first time. But one day she went to the bookstore to buy paper for her computer printer, and as she approached the store, there, right in her way, leaning against the side of the building wall, was Jimmy, his arm around a blonde. Elizabeth kept her eyes down and walked past them into the store. They were still there when she emerged, and the girl turned in Eliazabeth's direction to size her up. Elizabeth noticed this. He told her something! He's been talking about me!

Back in her dorm room, she began calling him every fifteen minutes, and close to seven that evening, he picked up the phone.

"Hi!"

"It's Liz Mason. What did you tell that girl?"

"Are you crazy?"

"She turned to look at me. To look me over. Why would she do that, unless she knew something about me?"

"You're nuts."

"What did you tell her—that you nailed me? Did you brag to make yourself look like a big man on campus?"

"I *am* a big man on campus."

"I warned you about this. What did you tell her?"

"We were playing a game, checking out people walking by and trying to guess if they were good in bed. I didn't say I laid you. It was a game. *She* said you looked like a lousy lay."

"And you agreed, right? You rape me and then tell people I'm a lousy lay."

"I didn't say anything about you."

"I don't believe you. I don't want you talking about me to anybody! If I get any sign you are, I swear to you I'll go straight to the police!"

She knew he was bragging to people that he had had her. She wanted to take a baseball bat, go over to his house, and smash him in the balls. The violent stories in the tabloids of rage-inspired crimes had come to have a logic to her. She was, however, a well-bred young lady. She tried to beat down the rage by running out of it. She put on her jogging shoes, shorts, and a T-shirt, and ran over to the field house, which had a quarter-mile indoor track outlined on the hardwood floor. She ran at a fast pace for about two miles and then lay on a mat, sweating, looking up at the ceiling, feeling slightly better. At least she had avoided being arrested on assault charges. As she lay there, a muscular young man in shorts and a T-shirt, who had been working out on the parallel bars, came over to her.

"Hi," he said, narcissistically kneading his arm muscles for maximum effect. He gave her what was probably his best come-on smile. "I haven't seen you around here. Are you new?"

I can't go through this, she thought, looking up at his stupid, toothy grin.

"No, I'm old," and she rolled over on her stomach to block him out.

SOME OF THE football players who lived off campus were having a party and Jimmy stopped by. A video of a Monty Python movie was being shown on a big-screen TV in the living room. He passed through, went to the kitchen, and took a beer. A petite brunette with a pretty, nearly sculptured face was leaning against a wall, looking uncomfortable to be there.

"I'm Jimmy Andrews."

"Janna Willis."

"I haven't run into you. Are you a freshman?"

"Yes."

"What are you majoring in?"

"Psychology. Are you on the football team, too?" she said.

He read that as disapproving.

"Tennis."

"Really?"

"Do you play tennis?"

"Not college level."

"Maybe we can hit balls sometime, for fun."

"Maybe."

Loud, boozy laughter came from the living room.

"Not the most tasteful of movies," he commented.

"I'll say."

"They showed *Lawrence of Arabia* around here not long ago, the new version. Have you seen it?"

"I like that movie a lot."

"He was fascinating, wasn't he? There's no equivalent person in American life," he said, and launched into his Lawrence of Arabia routine.

JANNA WILLIS WAS from a small town in Illinois, the first in her family to attend college. She was committed to working hard and doing well at school. She restricted her social life to Saturday nights, with an occasional Friday night or Sunday night off. On Saturday mornings she was a volunteer at a day care center in Caldwell. She and Jimmy began to see each other, and he told John Hatcher, "I found myself a nun who screws."

She loved to dance, and Jimmy was perfect for her; he always knew of a party around campus. She was perfect for Jimmy: he had the rest of the nights of the week to try to score with other women. He enjoyed taking her to parties and watching the other guys scrambling around, when his sex for the night was guaranteed.

"You go out with somebody like Janna, from the Midwest, it makes you see how difficult East Coast girls are," he said to some of his housemates one evening.

"Maybe it's just the girl," someone suggested.

"No, I'm onto something important here. Midwestern girls are easier to be with than East Coast girls."

"It's good you're not a sociology major," John Hatcher said. "The idea of you being turned loose out there as a theorist . . ."

SETH WAS BUSY with various entrepreneurial activities, selling students software games he created on the computer. Donna was running through the entire catalogue of the video store. The two of them were together most nights of the week as a couple, but they extended an open invitation to Elizabeth to join them for dinner, movies, anything she wanted.

In passing, she would see Donna's roommate, Sterling, who was cordial but remote in her own way. Sterling adorned her wall with Spike Lee and Miles Davis posters. She usually sat with other black students in the school lounges and dining areas. One day, she surprised Elizabeth in the library and asked her to go jogging.

"I'm not a pro."

"I didn't ask you that. Three miles, seven-thirty A.M. tomorrow?"

"Okay. You're on."

They ran with similar long strides, but Elizabeth, less experienced a runner, was pressed to keep the pace. Their conversation while running was about Seth and Donna and how good it was that they had found each other. They arranged to meet again and began to jog together a couple of times a week, talking about schoolwork and events outside school. Elizabeth, as usual, kept the conversation away from herself. Sterling confronted her about this one morning.

"You're real good at *asking* questions. 'What got you interested in playwriting?' 'Where do you think the civil rights movement stands today?' "

"Did I ask those? Pretty good questions."

"Where are *you*?"

She didn't answer for a moment or two as they ran along in silence.

"I'm in here somewhere," she said quietly.

THE LARGEST CLASS Elizabeth attended was Twentieth Century American Literature. There were two hundred students in her section. The professor was Randolph Billings, a self-consciously handsome man in his forties, fond of running his fingers through his hair. Coeds usually occupied the first few rows, several vamping him shamelessly. Donna was in the class also, and she and Elizabeth sat next to each other.

Billings was theatrical, delivering his lectures with broad arm and body gestures, playing to the front rows. He had assigned *Miss Lonelyhearts* and was acting out various parts of the book, to the delight of his people in the front, who giggled intensely.

"He's about as subtle as Olivier if he was drunk," Donna said to Elizabeth.

Elizabeth covered her face with her hands to smother her laughter.

"Did I put you to sleep, young lady?" Billings asked, pointing at Elizabeth.

"No. I'm sorry."

"Now that I have your attention, perhaps I could ask you a question. Why do we read *Miss Lonelyhearts*?"

Two hundred people in the room turned to look at her. Elizabeth's face became flushed.

"Have you read it?"

"Yes."

"Speak up. I can't hear you."

"Yes!"

"And—why do we read it?"

Elizabeth was frozen. Once she had played Eliza Doolittle, and now she could not bring herself to raise her voice to speak in a lecture hall.

"It's—uh—"

"It's uh, it's uh?" he mimicked. His admirers were laughing. "Yes? Why do we read it?"

She sat unable to speak.

"You might have said, 'We read *Miss Lonelyhearts* because it's short.'" More laughter. "It *is* short, isn't it?"

"It is," she answered.

"You might have said, 'because it's required.'" He was playing to the crowd. "You might have said, 'because the professor told us to.' All those are correct answers. What else might you have said? Can you tell us? You *do* speak?"

The moment felt like an hour, everyone looking at her, Elizabeth rigid with silence.

"As a rule of thumb for this class," he said to the group at large, "if teacher asks if you've read something, don't say you have when you haven't."

"I did read it," she protested, raising her voice slightly.

"Did you? Can you name three characters?" he said, still playing a game.

"Miss Lonelyhearts and Shrike and Doyle," she said, pushing herself to speak up. "And we read it because it's chilling. And brilliant. And even though it was written sixty years ago, it reads like headlines from hell. Or the daily newspapers. Whichever comes first for you."

Billings was so stunned that for an instant *he* couldn't
speak.

"Indeed. Aptly put. And your name is . . ."

"Liz Mason."

"Welcome to the class," and he moved back toward his
lectern with a broad look for his fans that said, Imagine that!

WOMEN'S AWARENESS WEEK was scheduled by Jean Philips,
the psychologist who served as the director of the Women's
Center. Various issues of relevance to women were going to
be discussed in seminars and lectures. Elizabeth did not plan
to attend any of the events, except for two that were
mandatory for freshman women, Sexually Transmitted
Diseases and Rape Awareness. Laura and Ben wanted to
know which sessions she was going to, and she knew from
their inquiry that they were conscientiously following the
school calendar in the literature the college sent to parents.

"I'm not into it," she said to them.

"Really? Some of the sessions sounded interesting,"
Laura said.

"I'll make a couple of seminars. It's mandatory atten-
dance. Sexual awareness. Birds and bees kind of thing."

"And everything's going all right?" Ben said, so eager
for her happiness that she couldn't bear to speak to him.

"Fine. How's Josh? Is he around? I haven't talked to him
lately."

"I'll get him," Laura said. "Take care, study well, have
fun."

"Right, darling," her father added. "Be well."

Josh came on the line.

"Hey, Lizzie!"

"How's everything?"

"Queenie's not good. She walks very slowly."

"She's getting old. How's school?"

"Okay. We'll see you soon, right?"

"Thanksgiving."

"Mom is so excited. Everybody's coming, all the grand-parents, the whole deal."

"To see the darling girl," she said.

She wondered how she would possibly get through Thanksgiving. Jimmy Andrews, she presumed, was going to have a fine Thanksgiving. His parents, whoever they were, would look adoringly at him, serve him his dinner, and he would sit there puffed up, telling them Big Man on Campus stories. She imagined his all-American family giving thanks for their splendid lad.

ELIZABETH MADE HER way through the first seminar, on sexually transmitted diseases. Attending the one on rape was so onerous an idea that she called the Women's Center to see how serious they were about the mandatory atten-dance requirement. She was told that it was strict university policy for freshman women to attend these events, and if she was unable to, she would have to attend a makeup session later. She decided that she might as well get it over with and took a couple of aspirin for the vicious headache that came over her as the time approached. *What are they going to tell* me *about rape?* When she arrived, Donna and Sterling were already seated in a row that was fully occupied, and she took an end seat about three-quarters of the way toward the back of the auditorium.

Jean Philips came out on stage with rapid, purposeful strides. In her early thirties, she was a slim brunette who looked as if she might have been a student herself, but her voice defined her maturity; it was resonant, poised. She began by saying, "Rape is one of the most unreported crimes in America. Last year here at Layton, three incidents were brought to my attention involving Layton women raped on dates. Right here, with Layton men. None of the women chose to press charges, for reasons of their own. They felt they were partially to blame. They had been drinking. One of them had broken up with the boy and had slept with him before, but these women *were* raped. You don't read about date rapes in your college literature. Well, this is the night where we get it out in the open. We're going to learn why rapes happen. And what you can do to prevent rape.''

Elizabeth slumped into her seat. The famous locking-the-barn-after-the-cow-has-been-stolen. She felt the headache reemerging.

Jean Philips brought out a guest speaker, a woman who had written extensively about rape. She discussed rape from a historic perspective, the manner in which rape was treated in the media, and the incidences of rape on college campuses. People shifted nervously in their seats as the speaker talked about cultural attitudes toward women that make "the unthinkable both thinkable *and* doable."

Elizabeth thought about Professor Billings and how he would fit the pattern, the way he patronized women students with his theatrics, treating them as bimbos. Then she imagined what Jimmy Andrews and his pals would make of this rape awareness session. They would be checking out the women in the audience, joking around and imagining who would be good in bed.

THE NEXT PORTION of the program featured a troupe of professional actors, three men and three women in their twenties, wearing casual clothing and looking as if they belonged on campus. Jean Philips introduced them and said they were going to dramatize some of the most common situations that can lead to rape. In the first vignette they presented, a couple was on a couch drinking beer, talking about school, and then he started to flatter her about the way she looked. They began to kiss, and then they reclined on the couch, necking heavily, the man running his hands over her body. Some laughter passed through the audience. Then the male actor suddenly slid his hand under her dress. The action froze at that point.

"I'd like to ask you to consider where we are in this situation," Jean Philips said.

"Horny," someone called out, producing loud laughter.

"I grant you that. But the question is, Does this situation have to lead to sexual intercourse? If you neck with a man, if you allow him to fondle you, is the next step automatically intercourse?"

She gestured for an answer from the person who had called out.

"They're pretty far along the line there."

"Are they? Does that mean necking *must* lead to intercourse?"

"You'd like to have a choice," someone else said. "You'd like to be able to express affection without necessarily going all the way."

"Then you have to think about what you're doing. Not place yourself in vulnerable situations. And you have to feel empowered. We're going to do a little assertiveness training. I want all of you to shout loudly, decisively, *No!*"

She encouraged the audience to yell *No*, louder and louder. Elizabeth, in her row, weakly shouted *No*, while thinking, It doesn't help if no one is listening to you.

Now two other performers came on stage, took a position on the couch, and started necking. After a while, the woman tried to stop. The man pushed her down, grabbing her arms and twisting them, pushing his body down on her. She shouted *No*, trying to squirm away and fight back. As this was occurring, Philips said to the audience, "We, as women, have to send out our message, loud and clear. *No* means *no!*"

The man continued to force himself on the woman, and as he did, Philips called for the audience to yell, *"No!"* She exhorted them, "Louder. You have to make them hear that *no* means *no.*"

The scene on stage was so vivid, it was borderline prurient. The audience was rooting for the woman to fight off the man. The man attempted to mount her, as Philips led the onlookers to shout *No*, over and over.

Elizabeth was calling out with the others. But it was no

longer the couple on the stage that she was seeing. Jimmy Andrews was on top of her, holding her down, pressing her throat, entering her again and again. The audience was shouting, *"No!"* The woman on stage was fighting with the man. Elizabeth saw only what had happened to her, that bastard inside her, holding her down. She jumped and raced out of the auditorium, her head aching, her throat burning with remembered pain.

Donna saw Elizabeth rushing from the hall in tears. She and Sterling ran after her down the steps and out of the building, as Elizabeth took off across the green, running at full speed into the night, crying.

Sterling ran with her long strides, while Donna fell behind. "Liz!" Sterling called out. "Liz! Wait for me!" Elizabeth turned and saw them behind her, and she ran faster.

"Wait, please!" Sterling shouted as Elizabeth burst out of the campus entranceway and into the streets beyond. "Wait!"

Elizabeth kept running until, gasping, she finally stopped and leaned against a tree.

Sterling caught up with her.

"What's wrong?" Sterling said. Elizabeth didn't answer. She was shaking her head and crying.

Donna reached them. "Liz! What's going on?"

"I was raped. I screamed, I tried to fight back, but he held me by the throat and he pushed me down and he raped me." She started moaning.

"Easy, girl," Sterling said. "When did this happen?"

"The first weekend."

"Who did this?" Sterling asked, trying to put her arms around Elizabeth to comfort her.

"Jimmy Andrews." And then she started crying again.

Donna smoothed the hair away from Elizabeth's eyes, and Sterling held Elizabeth in her arms.

# CHAPTER
# 7

ELIZABETH SLEPT POORLY that night, reexperiencing the incident. Bedeviling her sleep was the knowledge that Jimmy Andrews was probably sleeping like a happy baby. He hadn't become a hermit, he hadn't been afraid to talk to people.

Donna and Sterling had brought her back to their room. In the morning they suggested she seek out guidance, not try to handle this by herself. They thought she should see Jean Philips at the Women's Center. She agreed to go, and the three were waiting outside the office when Philips arrived.

"Good morning."

"I'd like to talk to you about a rape," Elizabeth said, and Philips' face became grim.

"Please come in."

"Can my friends come?"

"By all means."

Philips led the girls into her office, asking them to be seated. The office contained shelves with books on women's issues, and on the walls were various posters and fliers advocating women's rights.

"Are you freshmen?" They nodded affirmatively. "And you were at the event last night?"

"Yes," Elizabeth said.

"Please start from the very beginning. Tell me exactly what happened."

"I'm Liz Mason. Jimmy Andrews is a senior. He knew my roommate, and we went to the movies, the three of us. He asked me out. And then it happened, the Saturday night before registration, September second."

"Before registration?"

"Yes."

"You'd just arrived?"

Elizabeth described the incident, speaking slowly, trying to get the facts straight and not break down in the telling.

"So if I have this accurately," Philips said after hearing the account, "afterward you douched, showered, and threw away all your clothes?"

"Yes."

"And the doctor you saw didn't make a complete examination?"

"Just my throat."

"It's very brave of you to come in here. Not enough people do."

"It never would have happened if I hadn't been so stupid." She banged her fist against her leg. "I shouldn't have been drinking beer. I shouldn't have led him on. I shouldn't have gone downstairs with him. You said it, how you're supposed to think about what you're doing. I wasn't thinking. I'm a stupid fool!"

"You are not a stupid fool. You are a victim of a crime. You didn't bring this on yourself. You were in a situation that happens all the time and *doesn't* lead to rape. You were raped because somebody raped you! He did it, not you. You're not bad and you're not wrong—and you're not guilty of anything!" She had become agitated, frustrated by this kind of incident.

She turned to Donna and Sterling. "Ladies, could I speak to Liz alone a moment?"

"You okay?" Sterling asked, and Elizabeth nodded. "We'll be right outside."

"Have you told anyone about this?"

"Nobody. Last night I told Donna and Sterling, and now you."

"You've been keeping this to yourself? You haven't spoken to your parents?"

"My parents! God, this is going to break their hearts!"

Jean Philips crossed to her and took Elizabeth's hands in hers.

"We're going to get you through this. It happens to people, and they get over it. You have friends here who seem really nice, and your family—what kind of terms are you on with them?"

"They love me. They love me, and I let them down."

"That's not true. They can help you. You don't want to cut yourself off from them. You don't want to keep all this inside. We should let your parents know."

"I'm going to see them Thanksgiving."

"You must tell them. And between now and then I want you to come to see me. It's called counseling. But what we'll do is talk. We'll talk this out. Can you come in every evening at six?"

"*Every* evening? I'm that far gone?" she quipped.

"No, you're not. Not if you can say that and make me smile."

JEAN PHILIPS TRIED to move Elizabeth from the position of blaming herself to recognizing that a crime had been committed and she was not the criminal. She sought to reinforce Elizabeth's positive feelings about herself by praising her attempt to carry on in spite of the rape. Philips also attempted to reestablish healthy attitudes about the opposite sex, encouraging Elizabeth to realize that Jimmy Andrews was not all men, that all men didn't do this. Philips also tried exercises in which Elizabeth fantasized walking through the dining room or across the campus, unashamed, head up, making eye contact with people. Elizabeth was to work on it outside the sessions, and she willed herself to practice while walking outside.

Donna had told Seth about the rape, and he came to Elizabeth's room to tell her how sorry he was. What could he do for her? he asked. She said he should just continue to be her friend.

As she began to experience more positive feelings about herself, in counterweight, the rage toward her assailant grew.

"When do I reach the point in this therapy where I'm healthy enough to walk out of this office and kill him?"

"There are steps we can take for the anger. It's okay to be angry at him, so long as you don't turn it in on yourself."

Elizabeth never brought up the fact that she had stopped singing since the attack. Lacking that information, Jean Philips couldn't confront it. The therapy appeared outwardly to be working, but the injury to Elizabeth's spirit was so deep that singing, performing, being vital and outgoing, was something she no longer associated with herself.

JANNA WILLIS AND JIMMY ANDREWS were still seeing each other. After her hard work during the week, she emerged on Saturday nights eager to have fun. She saw the best in Jimmy—his affability, his ease in moving confidently on campus. He was pleasant to her, he liked her. She assumed, because of the cordial nature of their times together and because she saw him on Saturday nights, that their relationship was exclusive. She was mistaken.

Some of the football players told people they were bringing in "imported merchandise," girls from the State University at Albany. Jimmy went to their party, had quite a bit to drink, and ended up having sex upright in a clothing closet with a girl who was drunk and whose name he couldn't retain.

Janna had expected to see Jimmy that evening, a Saturday

night, and learned from someone who was at the party that Jimmy was there and was seen going off with a girl. She came to his house the next morning.

"Why did you go to that party last night?" she said. "We were supposed to be together."

"It wasn't definite."

"Yes, it was. Jimmy, you hurt me."

She started to cry, which startled him.

"I like you very much," she said. "I thought you liked me."

"I do."

"So why do you have to go running to meet other people?"

"I don't know."

He asked her to spend the day with him. They went out for breakfast, and afterward she picked up her book bag from her room and they returned to his house, where she worked on a reading assignment for one of her classes. Under her influence, he also studied. She was immersed in a volume on medical ethics. He knew that he wouldn't have gone near a book like that.

In the afternoon they hit tennis balls on a campus court. This was something they had talked about doing together. Jimmy assumed she would be unexceptional. She was a good player. He liked that she was not as boastful as some girls were and then turned out to be quietly competent. Back at his house, they showered together and he took her into the room and they made love. She felt soft and clean to him. The night before, in the clothing closet with the girl whose name he didn't remember, there was the smell of beer and tobacco on her breath and on her clothes.

ONE DAY, Elizabeth was emerging from her English class, walking head up, as she had practiced, when she saw Jimmy Andrews with Janna Willis, leaning against the building. They were smiling, and she assumed Jimmy was playing his Who's Good in Bed? game. Elizabeth stopped to observe

Jimmy Andrews in the light of her recent counseling sessions. Jean Philips had suggested that he was typical of a group of spoiled young men who think they have everything coming to them, who have been so indulged they expect to get their own way. She wanted to look at him in that context, and nothing in his demeanor negated that view. He was looking superior, with his latest girl next to him.

"Majoring in smirking, are you?"

"Excuse me. Was I talking to you?"

"Right, you don't talk. You're a man of action," and Elizabeth walked on.

His face became tense, and he shrugged his shoulders for Janna's benefit.

"Jimmy?" Janna asked.

"I went out with her one time, I didn't want to see her anymore, and she's not taking it very well."

"No, she's not."

"She really mental."

"Am I dealing with a major heartbreaker?"

"That's not me anymore. But I wasn't a virgin when I met you," he said, trying to be charming, and the matter was dropped; she was charmed.

At their next session, Jean Philips suggested that sniping at Jimmy Andrews on the phone or every time she saw him in public was not going to have long-term benefits.

"There was a rape, a crime. If you don't make any formal complaint, you're spared going through procedures. On the minus side, you feel that no justice was ever done."

She explained the options available to Elizabeth. The first was to do nothing and leave it at that. Or she could go to the police. Even though the event had taken place weeks before, she could still file a complaint. If she chose this route, she had to understand that police procedures were blunt and a jury trial was a public ordeal. An option was to bypass police procedures and ask for an administrative hearing by the college. The college grievance board had been established to hold hearings on a variety of complaints by students against other students or against members of the faculty. Jean Philips told Elizabeth that she had been given assurances that the college grievance board would be a viable alternative to police involvement. Rape complaints were going to be handled with speed and thoroughness. If the complaint was found to be valid, the penalty for rape would be immediate expulsion for the rapist.

"What do you think I should do?"

"Speaking as your counselor, I'd want you to do what makes you feel good about yourself. But I think we have to start bringing these men to justice."

"I don't know. I can't bear him walking around like a big stud. But the idea of a trial . . ."

"It's a difficult decision. Except we have to make these men hear *No*," Philips said, losing her objectivity. "They have to realize that if they don't listen, it's rape. And it's a crime. And they'll be punished."

"Maybe the hearing would be best, then. If they kick him out of school, that would be some kind of justice."

Elizabeth organized a hearing of her own with Seth, Donna, and Sterling, in her room. They went over the pros and cons of the options. The discussion itself was helpful to her, confirming that she had friends who supported her and were concerned about her.

"I'm not for your doing nothing. That doesn't end matters for you," Sterling said.

"It's like I'm a victim, and then I'm a victim again because I'm so passive."

"If you press charges and you have a trial, it can go on and on," Donna said. "With newspapers, all that."

"I know. I'm leaning toward the hearing. And then when I go home I can tell my parents that this thing happened but an action is being taken."

"Have we completely ruled out having him killed?" Seth said.

"I thought of doing that myself," Elizabeth said.

"Don Corleone would only have the guy beaten up.

'We're not murderers, in spite of what this undertaker thinks,'" Donna quoted, in a truly terrible Brando impersonation, which made them laugh.

TWO DAYS BEFORE the Thanksgiving break, Elizabeth was escorted by Jean Philips to the dean of students' office in the Administration Building, to file a formal complaint with the Layton College grievance board. The dean was William Harlan, who administered student activities at Layton and was Philips' supervisor. Elizabeth and Philips entered an office overlooking the college green. Harlan, a fair-complexioned man in his forties, wore the uniform of academia, a button-down shirt with striped tie, a tweed sports jacket with suede elbow patches.

"Jean," he said in greeting.

"This is Elizabeth Mason."

"Elizabeth. Please sit." He motioned the two women to a leather couch, and he sat opposite them in a chair.

"I've told Elizabeth about the grievance board, and she'd like to file a complaint. This is a rape case. You and I have talked about this kind of situation."

"Yes. This involves a claim against one of our students, of course, or you wouldn't be here."

"A senior. Jimmy Andrews," Elizabeth replied.

"And when did this take place?"

"Orientation week. Saturday, September second."

"Before we even had the rape awareness session on the calendar," Philips said, lobbying for a better priority.

"Elizabeth, let me explain the procedures here. We are not a court of law, but we do attempt to maintain the same protections as would be provided in a court of law. We are a three-person board. In your case, it would be myself, as the dean of students, Mr. Frank Teller, who is the counsel, the lawyer, for the college, and Dr. Madelyn Stone, who is a vice president of the college. Obviously, a board on this high level doesn't sit on cases involving, say, the alleged theft of a Walkman from a dorm room. Other people do that.

But this is an alleged rape. We want to give your complaint the proper weight.''

"Good.''

"You realize that if we decide against the defendant, it means immediate expulsion from Layton College?''

"Yes. That's why I'm here.''

"I'm obliged to tell you that we have a responsibility to protect our students from unwarranted claims. We can't have our procedures abused for reasons of spite or any number of emotions. In the course of the hearing, if the panel finds your claim was frivolous, they can rule that you are suspended.''

"I don't understand," Elizabeth said.

"This is no different from normal legal procedures, where perjury is a crime or where a suit can be answered by a countersuit. Last semester, an allegation of theft was made that revealed itself to have been born out of malice. We have to watch out for those kinds of claims.''

"Her claim is not frivolous. Her intent is to have the person who raped her punished. There has to be a proper mechanism.''

"There is. We are committed to handling these matters properly, with justice for all concerned. Otherwise we wouldn't have these procedures.''

He handed Elizabeth a binder. The title read: "Procedures in a Grievance Board Hearing.''

"When will you schedule it?" Philips asked.

He consulted his book.

"We don't want to delay too long, do we?" he said.

"No, we don't," Philips answered.

"We'll hold the hearing two weeks from Saturday. Elizabeth, you'll see in the folder that we need a signed letter of complaint from you. Drop that off with my secretary before the Thanksgiving recess. Have a nice holiday. I'm sorry we met under these circumstances.''

He stood and extended his hand to Elizabeth.

"Good to meet you," she said. As they shook hands, he

looked into her eyes. Elizabeth felt as if he was taking her measure.

Elizabeth and Philips wished each other the best for the holiday, and for Philips' benefit, Elizabeth made a broad comic gesture, tossing her head up and holding it high as she walked back to the dorm. That's called kidding around, she said to herself. Not a lot of that lately.

ELIZABETH CONVENED HER CABINET, Seth, Donna, and Sterling, and they went over the procedures material.

"I need witnesses, people who saw us at the party."

"Maybe somebody in the house heard you," Donna suggested.

"You think they're going to come forward?" Seth said. "'Oh, yes, I heard a cry for help, but I was busy.' Those guys are going to stick together."

"She can't know what anyone saw or heard until she gets into this," Donna said.

"You need some proof, Liz," Sterling told her.

"I did go to that doctor. He's probably got a record that there were bruises to my throat."

"That's good," Sterling said.

She wrote the doctor's name on a piece of paper and began to compile a list of people who were at the party. The others tried to help in identifying by name students Elizabeth described.

Elizabeth was given an appointment to see the doctor on the following day. He browsed through her file and did recall her.

"What did you walk into this time, young lady?"

"Doctor, when I came to you last time, I didn't tell you the truth."

"Is that a fact?"

"The bruises, they were from a rape. The person held me down by the throat."

"I see." He ran his fingers gently across her throat. "Have you any pain here?"

"No."

"Any huskiness to your voice? Do you consider your voice normal?"

"It's normal."

"Who raped you, young lady?"

"A boy at the college. We were on a date."

"Have you reported it to the police?"

"I reported it to the college authorities. There's going to be a hearing at school."

"Why did you lie to me?"

She took a moment to answer. "I was ashamed."

"What are you doing for yourself in the aftermath?"

"I'm seeing somebody at the college for counseling. And then there's the hearing. That's why I'm here. I wondered if you could give me a copy of your records. Could you say that you examined me—"

"I only examined your throat."

"Could you say what you found? The date and the bruises and how you thought somebody choked me."

He thought for a moment and said, "All right, young lady. I'll give it to you."

"Thank you so much."

"Why does this happen?" he asked philosophically. "Were there drugs? Were you drunk?"

"I had a couple of beers. No more than that. Not nearly enough to justify a rape," she answered, the therapy helping her there.

ELIZABETH WENT HOME for Thanksgiving. Mrs. O'Reilly had helped prepare the meal. The grandparents were there. Her uncle, David, had come from Chicago with his wife and children, a boy of seven and a girl of five. Elizabeth bluffed her way through a report about Layton, wanting to keep a pleasant Thanksgiving dinner intact. In the morning, when her brother was still asleep, she asked her parents if they would come into the kitchen. She was anxious; she read the anxiety in their faces reading the anxiety in hers.

"First of all, I'm not pregnant and I don't have any sexual diseases," she said. The anxiety in their faces remained. Why was she talking about sex? "I'm sort of okay now. I've been seeing a counselor, and I have a little support group in the people I told you about, Donna and Sterling and Seth. The thing is . . . I was . . . raped." As their faces fell in anguish, she stumbled forward into their arms. They caught her. Laura held her, trying to breathe; Ben pressed her hands to his lips.

"How did it happen?" Laura asked.

"It was on a date. The first week. He was very smooth, Jimmy Andrews, a senior. My roommate knew him from home, and he took us to the movies, and then he asked me out. I had a couple of beers at a house party. Nothing more than that. We danced, we kissed. I didn't know where it was leading. He took me to a room they had in the basement. I thought it was just to listen to music. And we did, at first. I kissed him again, and then I wanted to stop. He started to force me. He held me by the throat. And that was my weak spot, that he'd hurt my throat. And he raped me."

"My poor darling."

"I'll kill him," Ben said.

She looked up at her father through tears, smiled, and touched his face affectionately. "We've already considered that. What we're going to do is get him thrown out of school."

"This happened when you first got up there? And you didn't say anything to us?" Laura told her. "We saw you, you came home, we were up to visit, and you never said a word?"

"I couldn't bring myself to tell. I was so ashamed. We had an event. Rape Awareness. It was ridiculous. They were giving us tips to avoid rape, and I'd already *been* raped. The girls, Donna and Sterling, helped me. And I went to the women's counselor. She's been helping me, too. I wasn't a virgin. You should know that. Barney and I—"

"Let's get him behind bars. Has he come near you again?" Ben said.

"We're not enamored of each other."

Laura was trying to piece everything together.

"The ball hitting you in the throat—that was made up. And the business with not singing, dropping music—that was related."

"I saw a throat doctor and he said not to use my voice for a while, and then I couldn't bring myself to sing."

"And you still haven't?"

"No."

"My God, what he did to you . . . ," Laura said.

Elizabeth gave them the home phone number of Jean Philips, who was expecting their call. Philips told them that without minimizing the pain, with time and help Elizabeth could get over the incident. Philips seemed astute and sympathetic, and they were grateful for her involvement.

Elizabeth showed them the folder for the grievance board procedures, a copy of the letter she had submitted to initiate the action, and a copy of the doctor's report, which indicated injuries consistent with a physical struggle. Ben called his brother for legal advice. He was staying at the Plaza Hotel for the weekend and came over in half an hour. David Mason was three years younger than Ben, taller and slimmer than his older brother. After consoling his niece, he moved into a lawyer's mode.

"My specialty isn't criminal law, you understand. But you have to tell me about evidence."

Elizabeth told him that she had thrown away all her clothing that night. He looked over the procedures folder and said:

"It's impossible to know what a college hearing board is going to respond to."

"You think we should go through with a hearing or go to the police?" Ben asked.

"Or leave it alone?" Laura said. "There's an argument for Elizabeth getting back into a normal life. She can see this therapist, who seems sensitive. And not get herself dragged into public.''

"That's ridiculous. She was raped. You have to do something," Ben said.

"Frankly, you can take this as far as you have the stomach for," David told them. "The most dramatic result you can get is to send the rapist to jail. That also carries the greatest burden. Police, prosecutors, lawyers, a trial. A trial is a mess; people obsess over trials.''

"Why would we put Elizabeth through that?" Laura said.

"A college hearing might not be much fun, either," David said, "which is Laura's point.''

"Exactly my point.''

"Whether you can win in either case, I don't know. People judging rape cases prefer to have somebody captured in the act, preferably by two policemen. There is an argument for leaving it alone.''

"Could I say something? If it's left alone, then I'm a victim twice. I get raped and he's not even inconvenienced.''

"The hearing might be a way to proceed. It's faster," David suggested.

"I'd like to do that. Have this hearing. Get him thrown out of school—in his senior year. That would be fine with me.''

"If that's the way you go, you should have a criminal lawyer advising you.''

"Thank you, Uncle David.''

He put his arms around her and hugged her.

"You're the same sweet, lovely girl," he said.

ELIZABETH HAD TOLD her brother she would spend some time with him when she was home. He had asked if she would go with him to a new baseball card shop, and later in the day they went off together. Trying to show her parents that she was going to be all right, Elizabeth left smiling, wearing a Mets hat backward. Alone in the apartment, Laura and Ben

were distraught. Ben called Martin Reed, the lawyer David
had recommended, and they arranged for a meeting.

Laura and Ben were unable to sleep that night, visited by
images of Elizabeth, the little girl at birthday parties, the
teenager beginning to emerge at camp, the young singer.
"He took away her innocence . . . and he took away her
voice," Laura cried out in bed suddenly. Both were trembling.

ELIZABETH MET SARAH the next morning in front of the
Metropolitan Museum. The day was warm for November,
so they took a long walk through the park. Sarah did the
talking first; Elizabeth had established that pattern in their
phone conversations. She answered Elizabeth's questions
about her first few months at Juilliard.

"I have some news," Elizabeth said, and began to speak.

"Oh, no," Sarah kept repeating, holding her arms in front
of her, and when Elizabeth was finished, Sarah slumped
onto a park bench, holding her stomach.

"Why didn't you tell me? I would have come up. I would
have been there right away."

"I know. I couldn't face it myself."

Elizabeth talked about the counseling and why she had
made the decision for the hearing and how that was going to
proceed. They had walked back to their starting place at the
steps in front of the museum, where a string quartet was
playing for a crowd.

"How are *you* playing?" Elizabeth asked.

"Pretty well."

"That's good."

"Do you want to go back to the apartment and we'll do
some songs?" Sarah said.

"No, it's all right."

"You can't just stop singing."

She tousled the hair across Sarah's forehead. "My
true-blue friend. I just don't feel much like singing."

They kissed each other on the cheek and said they would

talk by phone the next week. Elizabeth would keep Sarah informed, and Sarah would come up to Layton if Elizabeth wanted her to. They began to walk home in opposite directions, and as soon as Elizabeth was out of sight, Sarah slumped back onto a park bench.

# CHAPTER
# 8

Jimmy Andrews received a letter from the dean of students on the Monday after the Thanksgiving weekend, informing him that he was to appear before a grievance board panel to answer charges by Elizabeth Mason that he raped her. The letter urged him to contact his parents immediately and advised that his family secure the services of a lawyer. A determination of his guilt would result in his expulsion from Layton College. Enclosed with the letter was a copy of the grievance board procedures. Jimmy started to sweat and feel faint; this time, it was he who threw up.

He dreaded dealing with his parents and getting them involved, though he knew they had to be: a lawyer was needed. His father would be at work, his mother probably at the club. He didn't know how to proceed, what to tell them. He went over the procedures folder. Witnesses would be called, his friends dragged into it, Janna too. Would they line up all the girls he had ever slept with? His distress turned to rage. I should have known she was trouble. Goddamn her!

She necked with him, danced close, pushed up against him, went downstairs into the music room voluntarily, necked with him again. What the hell had she expected, an anti-sex lecture?

He tried to organize his thoughts, his defense.

All right, she was coming on to me and I took her into the music room and we had sex and when I didn't want to see her after that she tried to get back at me. She's nuts. She started calling me up, saying crazy things in public. And when I still wouldn't see her again, she says I raped her, which is her crazy way of getting even.

His mind was racing. He tried to think how it would sound to people if he admitted that he had sex with her. Maybe it was better to deny that anything happened.

We were necking, that's all. She was coming on to me, and we kissed a few times while we were dancing. Nothing more than that. I didn't much like her. She talked too much, one of these verbal New York girls who talk everything to death. I wasn't interested in her, and when she realized it, she freaked. She's nuts. She started harassing me to take her out again, and when I didn't, she concocts this story to get me.

JIMMY WANTED to establish this premise with John Hatcher. However, there was a significant problem: Jimmy had bragged about it. He had told people, including John, that he had scored. He thought it might be smarter now to admit he was just bragging then to admit to the sex.

"Take a look at this," Jimmy said when John returned to the room from class.

He showed John the letter from the dean.

"She says you raped her?"

"She's crazy."

"Rape? You said you made it with her."

"I really didn't. That's the thing. You remember that night, how she was coming on to me? Well, I figured I was going to score anyway, so I counted it. It was heading that way."

"What were you doing, betting on futures?"

"Something like that. But when I got to thinking about it, how much trouble she was, the way she talked . . . You know that kind of New York girl, talks everything to death. I punted. I didn't call her again, and she freaked."

"This is really freaking," John said, handing him back the letter.

"She's crazy. She calls me up, she stops me on campus. 'When am I going to see you? I thought we had something important.' I didn't rape her. She concocted this whole crazy story because I wouldn't make it with her."

"What are you going to do?"

"I'm going to fight it. I'm not going to let her drag me down. *You* didn't see a rape, did you?"

"I didn't see anything. I was upstairs. And then we went out."

"Nobody saw a rape. There wasn't any. Just some sexually screwed-up lunatic making up stories."

He took the story to Westport that evening, calling ahead to tell his mother he was coming, not to be alarmed but he needed to see them about something. She *was* alarmed; he had just been home for Thanksgiving.

While Jimmy spoke, Penny Andrews sat motionless, with her hands to the sides of her face. Malcolm tapped his foot nervously. Jimmy provided his parents with a detailed version, from the time when he and Elizabeth first met, right through to their last exchange, in front of Janna.

"I should have known from the beginning there was something wrong with her. She wore me down with her talking, like I was in some grueling match. I just didn't want to play in her game. And she couldn't take it. She freaked."

"Terrible," Malcolm said.

"I mean, this is totally insane. This is a girl I didn't even have sex with, and she works it into this lunatic fantasy about rape."

"She must be seriously disturbed," Malcolm said.

"She is," Jimmy said.

"We'll get the best lawyer money can buy," Malcolm said. "She can't get away with this."

"Thanks, Dad."

Malcolm rose and patted his son on the back. "I'll make some calls right now. Get the ball rolling. Guess you'd better not go back to classes until we've seen somebody."

"Whatever you think best."

"It took a lot of fortitude for you to come here right away and look this thing right in the face and tell your parents what's going on."

"I knew you'd understand."

Penny had not moved, still had not taken her hands from her face. She was stricken with dread. While Malcolm made phone calls in the study, she went to her bedroom and lay down. Jimmy brought her a glass of warm milk.

Malcolm reached his friend Clark Dunne, a successful lawyer in Greenwich. Dunne owned a substantial amount of real estate in Connecticut. He liked to sail, and he played golf and tennis at Sweetbriar. Malcolm, who had to work hard for his income, resented the invitations from Dunne to go out on his boat or play tennis with him at the club, since many of these were for weekdays. But because Dunne steered business to him, he seldom declined. He considered it a waste of time when it turned out to be just the two of them.

Dunne was bald, with small, beady eyes and a hawk-beaked nose. When he was feeling his most envious of Dunne, Malcolm consoled himself that he was far better-looking. But no matter how many clients Dunne steered his way, Malcolm knew he couldn't match the man's life-style, which troubled him greatly. Malcolm had married into the Connecticut club culture. He never felt he owned his acceptance there. This latest development wasn't going to increase his prestige.

"Dreadful, Malcolm, dreadful," Dunne said, on hearing the injustice perpetrated on Jimmy by an unstable girl.

"Well, you need two things," he told him. "A top criminal lawyer and discretion."

"Exactly. I can't have this become common gossip at the club."

"Discretion is my middle name. I personally know of four affairs at the club and two criminal investigations under way involving a couple of our Wall Street club members, and I haven't breathed a word."

"We have to protect Jimmy."

"I have the man for you. Brett MacNeil. I'll call him myself. Brett's the tops. He's done major criminal trials in New York and Connecticut, so I'm sure he can handle a college hearing."

"I appreciate this very much."

"Now, I don't know how you feel about this, but I'm told he also represents some of the people from the crime families. I don't hold it against him. Everyone is entitled to representation under the law."

"It's a plus, I think. Those are very demanding people."

THE MEETING was held in MacNeil's office the following morning at eleven. Penny, unable to get out of bed, did not attend. The lawyer was in his early fifties and had the physique of a lightweight boxer. He examined the procedures folder and made notes.

"Young man, it's extremely important for you to be totally honest with me. As your lawyer, I can't defend you properly unless I know the facts of a case. The first question I have for you is: Did you rape her?"

"No."

"Rape is nonconsensual sexual intercourse by forcible compulsion."

"We didn't have that."

"What did you have? Sex?"

"No."

"Did you have any sexual contact with her?"

"I kissed her a few times, that's all."

"Suppose you tell me what happened."

Jimmy gave his version of the evening in detail. The lawyer took notes, while a tape recorder ran. When he finished, MacNeil asked:

"How much did you have to drink that night, Jimmy?"

"Very little. I'm not a big drinker."

"How much?"

"A couple of beers, tops."

"And the girl?"

"She had a few. Three, four."

"This kissing you refer to, it took place only in the living room?"

"That's right."

"While you were dancing, you say?"

"Yes."

"Did you initiate that?"

"She did, actually. I wasn't that interested in her."

"How so?"

"She was one of these big talkers, you know, who has to talk everything out—your interests, your future career, all that kind of stuff. She did that through dinner and then through the party. It was wearing me down."

"Why did you kiss her?"

"Because it was there."

"How many times did you kiss her?"

"I didn't keep count."

"Three, eight?"

"About four times."

"Standing, lying down?"

"Just during the time we were dancing."

"Be explicit. Mouths open? Tongues?"

"Maybe after the first couple of times."

"When you kissed, were your bodies touching?"

"When we kissed."

"And you stopped and ended the evening? Why?"

"She was getting boring. She was going on about love and relationships, and I said the party was about over and

I'd see her back to the dorm. I was thinking if I got her home, maybe I could go to some other party. She started saying how she thought we were onto a meaningful relationship. And I told her she shouldn't make too much of us—it was nice, but nothing more—and she got crazy mad.''

''And that's when she left by herself?''

''She left, and I went to bed. I wasn't in the mood anymore for anything.''

''Was anyone nearby who heard this conversation between you, or did anyone see her leave?''

''I don't know. The party was about over by then.''

''You said that after that night she started bothering you?''

''Calling me, stopping me in public, saying things.''

''What things?''

''How we could have had something important, a meaningful relationship. Why don't I take her out again? When could we get together? And because I didn't want to see her again, because I wasn't interested in her, she does this. She says I raped her.''

''Why didn't you like her, Jimmy?''

''The constant talking. I could see it wasn't going to be worth it, all that maintenance.''

''It didn't stop you from sticking your tongue in her mouth. It didn't stop you from pressing your body up against hers. It didn't stop you from dancing and kissing until a party was over.''

''Mr. MacNeil, Jimmy's been very honest about this. You can neck with a girl without having any other motives than that,'' Malcolm said.

''Can you? I'm speaking to Jimmy. Why did you neck with her, Jimmy, if you were so incompatible?''

''It was just kissing. Somebody comes on to you, you go along with it. And I didn't know right away she wasn't for me. It took a while.''

''So a full-blooded male with a girl coming on to him,

kissing, with bodies against each other, decides this isn't the girl for him and stops right there and says he'll take her home. That's your story, Jimmy. Plus the idea that a girl who wasn't raped and with whom you didn't even have sex is charging you with rape because you rejected her and *didn't* have sex with her."

"I didn't rape her. That's all that happened between us."

"Well, the panel is going to be speculating about it. Of course, they can speculate all they'd like. What this is going to turn on is evidence. I don't know what they have on you."

"I'm sure they don't have anything. They couldn't."

"We'll be given the opportunity before the hearing to discover what the other side has. What do *you* have, Jimmy? Anything else you care to say?"

"I've told you everytning."

"Ever been in trouble? Ever been in a similar circumstance?"

"Jimmy doesn't even have a record of a traffic violation," Malcolm said. "He's a fine young man, on the Layton tennis team."

"If we decide to go that route, do you have character witnesses we can call?"

"Any of the people I know at school."

"What do you know about Elizabeth Mason?"

"Just that she's a head case."

"I'm sure she'll have witnesses to say she's not. Jimmy, Mr. Andrews, a hearing at the college level doesn't preclude the possibility of criminal charges in the courts. You're dealing with someone willing to step forward and make an accusation. Even if you win this hearing, it's possible an attempt might be made to press criminal charges against Jimmy at a later date."

"That's ridiculous. She's unstable," Malcolm protested.

"I'm explaining the ramifications. In your favor is the fact that it's very difficult to get a rape conviction on a date rape in the courts, or even bring it to trial. If the situation was as Jimmy describes it, we should prevail. The college hearing is a different matter. It's quasi-legal, a pretend trial. Let's get through that first, with our options intact for any further problems down the line.''

"Fine," Malcolm said.

"Jimmy, make sure you behave yourself until we can get this out of the way,'' the lawyer advised.

JIMMY RETURNED to Layton and took Janna to The Babbling Brook for dinner. He placed the hearing in the context of Elizabeth Mason's emotional problems, reminding Janna that Elizabeth was the hostile girl who came up to them outside the English department building.

"She's stuck with this bizarre story,'' he said. "I mean, we never even had sex. She's probably told it to a bunch of people and can't get out of it.''

"If she's so sick, she might do something violent,'' Janna said.

"She's looking to make trouble for someone who didn't want her, that's all.''

"Let's hope that's all it is.''

"More important, if I need a character witness, would you vouch for me?''

"I'll embarrass you by telling everyone how great you are.''

As they were leaving, Janna gave him a warm embrace of reassurance. She could not possibly reconcile the crime of rape with her bonny Jimmy.

ON THE MONDAY AFTERNOON following Thanksgiving, Elizabeth went with her parents to see the lawyer Martin Reed. He was in his sixties, heavyset, a well-tailored man with a suntan in November. His elegant midtown office had a fireplace and was furnished with antiques.

"I have a granddaughter who's a junior at Amherst, so I'm very sensitive to this situation,'' he said.

"We appreciate your talking to us,'' Laura told him.

Elizabeth was asked to tell about the incident, and like his counterpart, the lawyer recorded the statement on a tape recorder as he made notes. He asked several questions to clarify details, paying particular attention to her behavior following the rape, discarding the evidence, visiting the doctor, delaying reporting the crime.

"Nobody saw the act. You drank beer. Underage, Elizabeth. You went to the room with him. We have no physical evidence. I could give the boy's defense to somebody one week out of law school, and my lawyer would have a hard job losing this case."

"Oh?" Elizabeth said, deflated.

"A college panel, if they follow the most rudimentary procedures, is going to have as much difficulty with the weakness of your position as a jury."

"David said it's difficult to get a conviction in a rape case short of the rapist captured in the act," Laura said.

"People are convicted of rape. But not with this kind of evidence. There's a lawyer on the panel. I don't know how you can get this past him."

"Is this your technique, to paint a dark picture so that we don't expect too much?" Ben said.

"No, you shouldn't expect too much. What you might have in your favor—and I stress *might*—is that it's not a jury trial. College disciplinary hearings are legal amalgams. There's flexibility. You have the doctor's visit, you have people to place the couple at the party together. If they believe Elizabeth, if she's overwhelmingly convincing, and they don't believe this Jimmy Andrews, they *might* find him guilty. Might."

"Can we get this rapist tested for AIDS?" Ben asked.

"I don't know of a legal way to compel that," the lawyer answered.

"Why would we possibly pursue this hearing?" Laura said.

"I can't answer that for you. I'm trying to give you a reading from a defense attorney's perspective."

"We pursue it because Elizabeth was raped. We either make use of the hearing or we go to the police," Ben said.

"But if we have such a weak case," Laura said, "what is Elizabeth getting out of it? He's going to deny everything, won't he? And we can't prove it."

"Technically, he doesn't have to say a thing," Martin Reed told them. "His lawyer is going to know your choosing the hearing doesn't preclude going to the police. If I were defending the boy, I'd be keeping my eye on self-incrimination and any future legal proceedings. If he gets a good lawyer, he'll probably elect to not have him testify at all, and given the circumstances and the lack of evidence, leave it to you to make the case."

"He raped me," Elizabeth said angrily. "I don't understand why he doesn't even have to sit through a hearing. He doesn't have to do anything."

"There it is," Ben said. "That's the reason to go ahead."

"But our case is weak," Laura told him.

"Mr. Reed just said if they don't believe the rapist and they do believe Elizabeth, they might find him guilty."

"Might," Laura said.

"They'll believe Elizabeth because she's believable," Ben responded.

"I want to have the hearing," Elizabeth said. "I want him to have to get a lawyer, worry about it, sit there while he hears me tell people what he did to me."

"Then it's decided," Ben said.

CONCERNED THAT THEY were invading Elizabeth's privacy, yet needing support from friends, Laura and Ben told a selected few people about the incident. Laura had lunch with Molly Switzer and Karen Hart, who were shocked when she told them.

"Don't take this the wrong way, but with some of the things you hear about, it could have been worse," Molly said.

"That's why I think this is like a hit-and-run accident,

and she walked away from it alive, and she should just try to go on,'' Laura said.

"For all the progress we've made, women still get raped. And this is the new generation of males, no less,'' Molly added.

"Don't you think we should just leave this alone?'' Laura asked them. "Why are we dragging her into a situation with a criminal lawyer and legal proceedings that probably won't work out?''

"To try to get justice,'' Molly answered.

"There's never going to be any justice,'' Laura responded. "I want her to get back to a normal life as quickly as she can, to be a college girl.''

"That may just be wishful thinking on your part,'' Karen said. "It may take her a while to get back to normal.''

"Or it may be my best judgment, that not getting entangled is the fastest way to *be* normal again.''

THE STERNS WERE STUNNED.

"We're going to use a panel they have at Layton to get the kid. But something tells me we should go right to the police,'' Ben said to them.

"And have her interrogated, and have her personal life examined under a microscope, and keep her in that situation for months on end, and go through a trial, so that she's not a college girl anymore but a crime victim?'' Laura said in a rush.

"You see where Laura stands on it,'' Ben said.

"What does Elizabeth want?'' Jane Stern said.

"To have the hearing,'' Ben responded.

"Then that's what you should do,'' Phil Stern said.

"If this were Melanie, wouldn't you just want her to return to a normal life as quickly as possible?'' Laura asked.

"We're talking about a couple of weeks,'' Ben said.

"Yes, and what if we lose? The lawyer isn't the least bit optimistic. What are we bothering for?''

"So she doesn't give up. What kind of courage is it, if she gives up?"

"Ben, are you General Patton? Courage is not to immerse yourself in it but to go past it."

BEN AND ELIZABETH'S sentiments prevailed, and they were proceeding with the hearing at the college. Martin Reed spoke to Elizabeth about possible witnesses. The lawyer then followed up with phone calls to the people involved.

In the Mason home, when Josh entered a room, Laura and Ben cut conversations short. He seemed to be aware of something. Their friends, Elizabeth's friends, a lawyer knew about the incident, and they were becoming devious to keep their own son ignorant. This was the central issue in their family.

"I guess you've noticed a lot of whispering around here lately," Laura finally said.

"Are you getting a divorce?" Josh asked, a child of his time.

"No. Nothing like that," Ben said.

"It's about Elizabeth," Laura continued. "Early in the school year, when she first went up to Layton, something bad happened to her. She was on a date, and the boy she was out with raped her."

"She's going to be all right," Ben said. "She's been going to classes and making friends in school."

"Elizabeth tried everything she could to fight him off, but he was too strong for her," Laura said. "We want to see that he's punished. If we have a trial, it will get drawn out and Elizabeth has to keep living with it through all the proceedings."

"What we're going to do," Ben explained, "and that's why there's been so much conversation going on in the house, is have a hearing at the college. They have a committee set up for this kind of thing. A lawyer is helping us, and we want to have that boy thrown out of school."

"Why would anybody do that to her?"

"Because he's a terrible person," Laura said.

Later, before he went to sleep, Josh took the old dog, Queenie, into his room for solace, and they could hear him talking softly to the dog.

PENNY PUSHED HERSELF to leave her bed. She was running a charity dinner at the club for the Red Cross; she was needed for the flowers, the seating. When the evening came, she and Malcolm attended. It went well. They danced and smiled, and neither of them told anybody about the unhappiness raging through their family.

The lawyer said a subtle part of the defense would be for the panel members to see the stability of Jimmy's family. But Penny knew that sitting there with her son being judged would make her think her parents had been right; she had married beneath them, and this was what it had come to. She would think of Malcolm's striving and pushing and wonder if it had been a good model for his boys. She would think of Jimmy's behavior on the tennis courts. It was vulgar, but Malcolm and Jimmy needed it, that it was good for his game. She was sure she would start to think about these things during the hearing, and weep, and prejudice the panel.

When she told Malcolm that she would rather not attend the hearing, he became furious. Malcolm demanded that she pull herself together for Jimmy's sake. The lawyer advised that they both be there. Eventually, Penny agreed. Malcolm wanted to know what she intended to wear, to make certain she had her clothing picked out ahead of time so there would be no last-minute tension. They would take a room at the inn the night before, and they would be on time and look impressive for Jimmy. The black knit suit with pearls, she decided, and the black bag, no hat, tasteful and yet not inexpensive. What would her father have thought? She was using her schooling, and her years of ballet lessons and riding lessons and social events at the club, she was using her breeding to help defend her son from rape charges.

• • •

FOR MALCOLM, the following day, a Saturday, would be a
test of Clark Dunne's discretion. He was scheduled to play
in a mixed double game with three clients for whom he
had created pension plans: Zack Warren, a real estate
developer; Sondra Grayson, a management consultant; and
Patty Dambroise, wife of Bob Dambroise, the owner of a
Bridgeport paper manufacturing company. They played two
sets and then sat in a patio area and sipped drinks. No one
mentioned Jimmy. Dunne had respected the Andrews family's privacy.

Malcolm directed the conversation to a safe area, a
discussion of the appropriate jail sentences for Wall Street
buccaneers like Ivan Boesky and Michael Milken.

"Many people think Milken was a genius," Malcolm
offered.

"An evil genius," Patty Dambroise said.

"He did figure something out," Zack Warren said.
"Everybody's looking for an edge."

Malcolm Andrews wondered what his edge was, how he
could ever reach parity with these people. He seemed
always to be riding on Penny's status. Several of the club
members had increased their assets considerably during the
1980s, principally the Wall Street people. When Michael
Milken was first in trouble, his friends took a large ad in the
*New York Times* to say they supported him. Milken had
made millions of dollars for some of his friends. Through
his friends Malcolm had only earned a living.

He was convinced that if Jimmy would only push himself
a little more, the boy could be a competitive player on the
professional tennis circuit, and that would change Malcolm's status automatically. Malcolm would have the prestige of being the father. He had seen them sitting courtside
at the matches, the fathers of people like McEnroe and
Capriati. The position the fathers occupied was prestigious,
beyond money. And it had to help them in whatever their
businesses were. Jimmy was not likely to be a tennis player

on the highest level. He was good enough, though, Malcolm believed, to make a substantial living and to be known within the sport. Jimmy could be his asset, a chip for Malcolm to match the inherited assets of the goddamn people at the club.

He shared these thoughts with no one. His friends were club friends, business friends, not people you talk to about your most intimate concerns. He was sure they wanted their business to be handled by someone in control, not someone with frailties, with longings.

Once, back in college, he had friends he could talk to. They would sit around the fraternity house and drink and talk into the night about love and life and their futures. That was gone. In adulthood, with his personal and business worlds so interconnected, he felt he could never reveal himself to the people he knew. On his way out of the club after the match, he waved with false cheerfulness to various club members. Malcolm Andrews was a marooned man.

STUDENTS WERE UNLIKELY to refuse a letter from the dean of students urgently requesting their appearance at a college hearing. Nonstudents were another matter. Reed wanted the throat specialist to appear before the panel; the doctor was reluctant to do so. A prehearing session for the lawyers was scheduled by the college counsel five days before the hearing. During his trip to Caldwell, Reed went to see the doctor and managed to persuade him to appear at the hearing, prevailing upon his sense of justice. Reed would also call Shannon Harnett as a witness, so he could establish that Elizabeth and Jimmy were at the party together. Donna and Sterling would be asked to testify as to Elizabeth's reactions to the rape awareness event. He considered having Holly Robertson testify. When he spoke to her, she talked about Elizabeth's crying after the date with Jimmy Andrews. But Elizabeth never told her about a rape; on the contrary, she gave her a false story. Reed thought Holly's testimony could be damaging under cross-examination. Jean Philips, though, would be a crucial witness, who could attest to Elizabeth's credibility. Finally, Elizabeth would appear to present her version of the events.

THE PREHEARING SESSION was held in the office of the college counsel, Frank Teller. He was a slight man in his forties, with a rumpled look—not a match in tailoring for the big-time lawyers. Teller reviewed the procedures for the hearing. The lawyers would be permitted opening and closing statements and the opportunity to examine and cross-examine witnesses. The panel members would function in the manner of an active judge at a legal proceeding, free to interrogate witnesses themselves. The panel would use the legal cornerstones, presumption of innocence and proof beyond a reasonable doubt, as their standards for a decision.

During the discovery process, Jimmy's lawyer, Brett MacNeil, learned that apart from the written report from the doctor, which did not refer to a gynecological investigation of the girl, there was no evidence. The lawyers thanked Teller for his courteousness and left the office, pausing in the vestibule of the building. They were opposing each other in this matter, but they were both defense attorneys with a professional world in common.

"Mr. Reed, if you were a prosecutor, I'd be curious about why you were bringing this to trial."

"Mr. MacNeil, I'm not a prosecutor; I'm assisting the family. So if you were about to propose a plea bargain," Reed said wryly, "I'm afraid I can't help you."

"Is the idea here to give the girl her day in court? Because she'd never get into a criminal court on this evidence."

"Don't try your case in front of me, Mr. MacNeil," Reed said. "Incidentally, whatever the evidence, the girl was raped. I sincerely believe that, and if she says your client raped her, I believe that too."

JIMMY WAS LYING in his room, listening to rock music, when his lawyer paid him a visit.

"I just want to go over a few things with you. There's something called attorney-client privilege."

"I know what that is."

"So this is between us, for me to put together the best defense for you. Your parents aren't involved. No one will know. Jimmy, directly and honestly, did you have any sexual contact with her other than the necking that went on in the living room?"

"No, I didn't."

"Let me give you a definition of rape again. It means nonconsensual sexual intercourse by forcible compulsion."

"I understand the definition."

"I want everything to be clear."

"It is clear. All I did was kiss her."

"And she's made up this entire story?"

"She did, and she doesn't know how to get out of it."

"All right, then, Jimmy."

"I thank you for all your help, Mr. MacNeil," he said in a sincere tone of voice.

THE EVIDENCE, or lack of it, had been exposed, and Reed was certain from his adversary's reactions that MacNeil had no intention of having Jimmy Andrews testify. Reed chose to spend the next few hours at Layton talking to and coaching the most important witnesses. He met with Jean Philips, Donna, and Sterling, and scheduled a meeting with Elizabeth at three P.M.

Ben appeared suddenly in Elizabeth's room a few minutes after three, startling his daughter and the lawyer.

"Dad?"

"This is important. I should be here," Ben said.

Reed told them that if MacNeil was bold enough, he might choose not only not to call Jimmy as a witness but not to call any witnesses. This was an approach Reed himself might take if it were his client. He asked Elizabeth to give once again her version of the events, and as she spoke he counseled her to keep her head erect and her shoulders back, important for maintaining a sense of poise and credibility. He interrupted her throughout with skeptical, harsh questions.

Because the process was tense and difficult for Elizabeth, Ben felt justified in being there. Several times he cheered his daughter on, telling her she was doing great, and finally Reed asked him to be silent. The lawyer spent two hours working with Elizabeth and complimented her at the end, saying he was pleased with the session. After Reed said goodbye to the Masons, Ben took Elizabeth to dinner at the Italian restaurant. He overflowed with advice, reviewed Reed's coaching tips, added his own refinements. Instructing her never to drop her head or her eyes, to maintain her voice level, he assumed an expertise that could only have been acquired from watching movies with courtroom scenes. He was exhausting her. She was relieved when he left.

MATTERS BROUGHT BEFORE the college grievance board were considered private by the Layton administration. Notices about hearings were not released to the press or to the college newspaper. While Elizabeth's complaint against Jimmy was officially known to very few people on campus, she was experiencing an undercurrent of resentment. Several students looked at her in an unfriendly manner. Shannon and Allison ignored her. Jimmy had successfully launched the idea among some people at the college that Liz Mason was a troubled person who was causing trouble.

People in his house knew about the hearing because John Hatcher had mentioned it. Jimmy's basic position for his housemates, for Janna, and for a couple of the other athletes who were aware of the hearing was that he was totally unconcerned, the hearing was a formality, and the girl was crazy.

"I don't think about it much. It's not like something you can study for," he said offhandedly to a few of his housemates who were sitting around the living room. "I'm not even taking the stand."

When they were alone, Janna asked a question of Jimmy that went to the heart of his denials.

"Honey, what I don't understand is, if this is so unimportant, how come your family had to hire a lawyer to defend you?"

"It's in the guidelines. The college doesn't want anyone to claim they didn't get a fair hearing."

"She must have a very strange imagination."

"Yes."

"It's not right that she gets to do this to you."

"She's not doing anything to me, when you think about it. I'll go in, she'll make her crazy claim, and they'll throw it out."

"They should have her see a psychiatrist. Make it mandatory. This is aberrant behavior."

"You're absolutely right," he said.

THE HEARING WAS SCHEDULED for eleven-thirty on a Saturday morning. The lawyers were arriving by plane early that day. Both sets of parents drove to Caldwell and arrived the night before. Laura and Ben thought it was inappropriate for Josh to attend the hearing and he was staying with Laura's parents. Reed had phoned Elizabeth during the week to review her testimony and remind her about her demeanor. MacNeil, on the other side, had advised the Andrews family to maintain their composure and not react to anything said during the hearing.

Jimmy and his parents went to dinner at The Babbling Brook, and Jimmy brought Janna. He needed this cute and trusting girl not only to reinforce his integrity for his parents but to do so for himself. The hearing was hanging over them, but the conversation was pitched at a small-talk level, since Jimmy's parents were reluctant to discuss the rape charge in front of someone. Janna looked at Jimmy affectionately as they held hands.

"It's too bad Janna can't be a character witness for me," he said.

"What do you think you'll do this summer, dear?" Penny asked Janna, needing to change the subject.

ELIZABETH AND HER PARENTS were at a restaurant nearby. Without an outsider to balance the conversation and with Ben relentlessly analyzing every step of their approach, they talked about nothing other than the hearing. The lawyer had told them that Jean Philips had been a practicing psychologist in Albany. Donna had especially sought Jean Philips' help in combating her shyness so she would be as effective as possible in testifying for Elizabeth. Ben was consumed with these nuances. Laura wanted dinner to be over and for Elizabeth to get a good night's sleep. Ben went so far as to ask Elizabeth to present her testimony at the dinner table, one last time, to see if he could detect any last-minute rough spots.

"Ben! You'll catch the show tomorrow," Laura said.

"I just want to make sure it's right."

"I've been coached enough, Dad. This is like the SATs of rape."

He did not smile. Laura called for a check to get them out of there and Elizabeth back to her dorm.

THE PRINCIPAL LODGING for visitors to the college was the Layton Inn. As the Masons passed the front desk on the way to their room, the Andrewses were standing there.

"Any messages for Andrews?" Malcolm was saying to the clerk.

Laura and Ben paused, and Penny, noticing them, turned in their direction.

"Nothing, sir," the clerk said.

Malcolm turned away from the desk and saw the Masons. Both sets of parents were about the same age. Both couples were dressed similarly, the men with woolen coats and tweed jackets and slacks, their good suits waiting for the main event in the morning. The women wore furs, Laura a long raccoon, Penny a mink. Their children were at the same school. They paid many of the same bills.

"Andrews. So you're this famous boy's parents," Ben said, his anger right at the surface.

"So you're this famous girl's parents," Malcolm retorted in kind.

"It should be a very interesting day tomorrow. We'll get a chance to observe the product of your parenting," Ben said.

"Ben, this is not the hearing," Laura told him.

"Jimmy's a good boy," Penny said.

She looked to Laura. Another mother would understand. You care for them and love them, you do your best. The fear is always there that something can go wrong.

"If you'd done your job as a father," Ben said, "we wouldn't be here."

"Ben . . ."

Laura pulled Ben's arm to draw him away.

"You do your best," Penny said to Laura, pleading.

Laura looked at her, and for a moment there was a flicker of recognition between the two women as they saw themselves in each other. Then they went in opposite directions, separated by the anger.

# CHAPTER 9

IT'S THE EASTER PARADE, Elizabeth thought, observing all the major participants in their smartly tailored outfits. Looks like neatness counts. Everyone stood in an anteroom of the Administration Building, each side avoiding the other. A receptionist informed them the hearing was commencing. The witnesses were to remain until called for testimony.

Behind a long table sat the three members of the panel. William Harlan, dean of students, was in the center of the triad; to his right was Frank Teller, the college counsel; to Harlan's left was Dr. Madelyn Stone, the vice president of curriculum for Layton College. A fair-complexioned, thin woman in her late fifties, she wore a tailored suit; her graying blond hair was pulled back tightly from her face. A single chair facing the table was in place for witnesses. Behind it was a row of chairs, with a space several feet wide in the middle of the row to divide the sides in the dispute. As Elizabeth, her lawyer, Laura, and Ben took their seats, Harlan nodded in acknowledgment in Elizabeth's direction, showing no emotion. Nor did the other panel members.

The Andrews family entered with their lawyer. Jimmy and Malcolm were walking erect and confidently. Penny was clutching her pocketbook as though it were a security blanket, her eyes darting about the room until Malcolm fixed her with a stare, freezing her expression.

Harlan motioned to a secretary, who sat at a desk to the side of the room. She turned on a tape recorder, and Harlan addressed the participants.

"Elizabeth Mason, James Andrews, this hearing is binding under the disciplinary code of Layton College governing nonacademic matters. We will use the same standard that is the cornerstone of the American justice system. We grant the defendant the presumption of innocence. The charge against the defendant must be proven beyond a reasonable doubt. I note that both claimant and defendant are represented by counsel, who, according to the grievance board guidelines, will be permitted to participate in this hearing to examine and cross-examine witnesses. The members of the panel will be free to do the same. Mr. Reed, do you have an opening statement?"

Reed rose and addressed the panel.

"Members of this distinguished panel, we have chosen this forum because Elizabeth Mason and her family feel that the penalty, explusion from Layton College, is sufficient justice. I would point out that it would be a light sentence indeed in the world outside this college campus.

"The defendant looks to be an upstanding, well-dressed young man, accompanied as he is by his parents. His parents were not with him, though, on the night of September second, when he took Elizabeth Mason to a party at his residence. On that night he invited her to go into the basement of the house, where, after playing classical music, which he thought would delight her, he moved the simple, ordinary act of a young couple kissing to the criminal act of rape. James Andrews and Elizabeth Mason were together that night, exclusively in each other's company, and we will prove this. Elizabeth's throat was bruised from being choked, from her being held by the throat, and we will prove this. She attended a rape seminar, and at that event, a

simulation of attempted rape on stage caused such distur-
bances within her that she went fleeing into the night, and
we will prove this. She was given counseling specifically to
help her deal with the fact that she *is* a rape victim, and we
will prove this. Elizabeth Mason's credibility is unassail-
able, and we will prove this. James Andrews, a senior at this
college, willfully took advantage of the naïveté of a freshman girl, so new to the campus that she had not yet attended
one class, and he lured her to a solitary room and by his
greater physical strength, and by pressing down on her
throat, forced her to have sex, without her consent, which is
the crime of rape. On this college campus, in this society,
you cannot do that and get away with it.''

MacNeil stood before the panel.

"Distinguished panel members, my colleague suggests
this forum has been chosen because it would provide justice
in this matter. In fact, this is the only forum available to
them. They would not be able to introduce this matter in the
criminal justice system. They would not get an indictment.
They would not get this matter brought to trial. There is no
case. There are no witnesses to this alleged incident. There
is no evidence. No hair or skin or clothing fragments, no
semen traces, none of the elements customarily sought in
allegations of rape. And yet this teenager makes a very, very
serious charge. So serious that this hearing would not
provide Jimmy Andrews with his constitutional guarantees.
Accordingly, to protect Jimmy's constitutional rights, he
will not take the stand here and risk self-incrimination. Nor
will we call anyone else to testify. We invite this young
woman to prove beyond a reasonable doubt, without any
physical evidence, without witnesses to the alleged event,
that which she would not even be able to bring to trial, and
which she will not be able to prove here. It cannot be
proven.''

● ● ●

ELIZABETH DISLIKED being characterized as a "teenager." She was eighteen. What else was a college but a place where people were still in their teens? Reed leaned over and said to Elizabeth and her parents, "Exactly what I expected. No surprises."

DR. THOMAS PHELAN WAS the first witness Reed called. He testified that the nature of the wounds to Elizabeth's throat was similar to injuries he had observed from physical assaults. Dealing with the fact that Elizabeth did not report a rape to him, he stated that it was not unusual in these circumstances for the victim to deny the reason for the injury out of guilt or humiliation. He suspected she had been assaulted when he first examined her and was not surprised to hear later that she claimed to have been raped.

MacNeil cross-examined him aggressively. He was able to verify that the doctor had not conducted a gynecological examination. And the lawyer asserted that they were not concerned at the hearing with what Phelan "suspected." On rising to leave the chair, Phelan said:

"I've seen those injuries in rape cases. And I've seen the victims deny the circumstances. Somebody injured that girl. You can't lawyer that away."

THE NEXT TO BE CALLED were the students. Reed used Shannon Harnett to establish that Elizabeth and Jimmy Andrews were at the party together, that they were in each other's company on a date. During cross-examination, Shannon testified that she saw nothing unusual between Jimmy Andrews and Elizabeth Mason that night.

Donna and then Sterling testified to Elizabeth's reactions at the rape awareness event, how she had run from the auditorium crying, had told them she was raped. In his cross-examination, MacNeil elicited that they were not present at the party when the rape was alleged to have occurred and were repeating for the panel Elizabeth's version, not their own.

Jean Philips was called and taken through her credentials as a psychologist and an educator. Reed then asked:

"Based on your knowledge of the field, how common on college campuses is a rape of the kind suggested here?"

"Objection," MacNeil said.

"I'll sustain that," Teller ruled.

"I want to make certain that what we're dealing with here is not a crime so unusual it would be unbelievable to think it could happen here," Reed argued.

"The general phenomenon of college rape is simply not probative of this defendant's guilt," MacNeil stated.

"Sustained. Mr. Reed?"

"What about rapes at Layton College? How many have there been?" Reed asked Philips.

"Objection."

"Sustained again."

"As an expert on the behavior of young people—"

"We're not dealing with young people in general," MacNeil argued.

"Sustained."

Reed changed direction. He asked Philips to describe her contacts with Elizabeth and the general extent of the counseling. Then he asked:

"Has Elizabeth Mason's behavior been consistent with someone who was raped?"

"Yes," Philips answered.

"Objection."

"Ms. Philips didn't declare she was raped. It's consistent behavior. I'll allow that," Teller said.

"She didn't report it at first, and she gave a misleading story," Reed said. "Is that common?"

"Yes. It follows the pattern of rape trauma syndrome. Rape victims frequently manifest unusual behavior, denying a rape to themselves and others."

"Have you ever had someone," Harlan interjected, "a student or a patient, come to you with a tale that was very detailed but that was untrue?"

"Yes."

"Is it possible that this is such an occasion?" Harlan continued.

"I have been treating her for rape. The details are so precise, her version has been so consistent, that if it were untrue, you would have to look for other personality aspects to support a tendency to fantasize or dissemble in that manner. I have not found any such signs. What has emerged in her treatment, her thoughts, fears, dreams, is consistent with rape victims."

REED CONCLUDED his questioning of Jean Philips, and Mac-Neil took over, looking at her as if she were a thief turning state's evidence.

"Psychology is not as exact a science as, say, physics, is it?"

"No, but there are patterns that reappear, are documented sufficiently for us to call it a science."

"But you can't be inside Elizabeth Mason's head."

"Yes, in a sense. I can see patterns of behavior."

"Can you know, scientifically, what she is thinking?"

"I'm not a mind reader, if that's what you mean."

"I mean concerning another person's thoughts, or emotions, there will always be a gap between what you suspect, intuit, surmise, and what you actually know."

He stayed with this for fully fifteen minutes, seeking to discredit her ability to state definitively whether or not Elizabeth was telling the truth. Philips matched him on the theoretical arguments but she could not "prove"—Mac-Neil's word—that she knew fully the patient's thoughts or motivations.

"Do freshmen ever experience adjustment problems away from home for the first time?"

"Objection."

"Sustained," Teller said.

"Don't students specifically manifest certain personality problems—"

"Objection."

"Sustained."

"Let's deal with your job, Ms. Philips. Don't you have your job because colleges need psychologists to deal with student stress?"

"Stress is not specific to college students and not germane to this case," Philips said.

"How do you know it's not germane? You're not a mind reader, as you say. Now, you head the Women's Center?"

"Yes."

"Your first obligation is to the women of Layton?"

"I work for the college. My specialty is women's issues."

"You're not appearing for Jimmy Andrews."

"He wasn't raped."

"And we don't know that anyone else was. Isn't your entire outlook colored by your position, that of the women's advocate here at Layton?"

"I am objective."

"How can you be? These are subjective matters. You are not a witness to a rape, you are a witness to the counseling of a teenager at a stressful time."

"I am a professional—"

"No doubt. But with an agenda."

"I would never allow a personal view to interfere with my judgment in a matter such as this."

"Not knowingly. But I leave that to the field of psychology. Thank you, Ms. Philips."

Harlan called for a brief recess, and the Masons convened at their side of the room with the lawyer.

"That was nasty," Laura said.

"She stood up to him well," Reed responded. "She said six different ways that she believes her."

"Do you still want to go through with this? There's no law that says you have to," Laura said to Elizabeth.

"This is our day in court," Ben said, answering for her.

"I was speaking to Elizabeth."

"I want to," she said.

Elizabeth excused herself to go to the ladies' room, and Laura went with her. As they walked down the hall, Laura took Elizabeth's hand in hers, as if trying to bring back a time when Elizabeth was still little.

ELIZABETH OCCUPIED the witness chair, and Reed directed her through a meticulous, precise narrative. She began with the first time she met Jimmy at the barbecue and continued through the events at the party. When Elizabeth reached the part about descending into the basement with Jimmy, the room was so still it was as if everyone had stopped breathing. She described the space in detail, how it was set up to muffle loud music, where the furniture was placed. She told how they settled on the sofa and how, after a couple of kisses, she attempted to leave, how Jimmy forced himself on top of her, held her down and entered her. Penny Andrews began shaking, and Malcolm was unable to get her to stop. Across the room, Laura buried her face in her hands and Ben clenched his fists.

Throughout Elizabeth's prior testimony, the panel members had interjected questions to clarify points, but from the moment when she began to describe the rape itself, they fell silent. With a voice diminished in its strength by the emotional strain, Elizabeth described her response after the rape, throwing up in the street, discarding her clothing and showering in order to expunge the crime. Tying her testimony in with Donna's and Sterling's, Reed asked her to tell about the rape awareness evening and how that caused her to react so strongly and led her finally to confess she was raped. It was Elizabeth who used the word "confess," and Reed took advantage of it, underlining that she had been feeling shame for having been raped. She completed her testimony and dropped her head.

When Elizabeth finished, Penny uttered a soft, audible No, in denial of the testimony. Malcolm grabbed Penny's wrist hard, to silence her. Elizabeth had been prepared for her appearance; she had gone over it several times. She did not realize that by recounting in front of other people these details, which the lawyer said were important to build up credibility, she would be obliged in the process to relive the experience. Elizabeth thought she might become ill right in front of the panel. Reed brought her a glass of water, and she managed to steady herself for the cross-examination that was to follow.

MACNEIL TOOK HIS PLACE, appraising her carefully, knowing that if he came down too heavily on the witness he could cause the panel members to sympathize with her.

"Ms. Mason, you said you went downstairs to an isolated room with Jimmy Andrews, and you described that room in detail. But didn't you also say that Jimmy took you on a little tour of the house?"

"Yes."

"So isn't it possible you saw that room when you went on the tour, and that's how you can describe it to us?"

"No. He didn't take me there in the beginning."

"Do you know of anyone who saw you go down there?"

"No, but I did go there."

"No one saw you. You say you screamed. Did anyone hear you, did anyone come running?"

"It was sort of soundproof. And people had left—"

"No one saw you, no one heard you. Ms. Mason, you waited for a long time before reporting this alleged rape. Were you waiting all that time for Jimmy, to whom you were attracted, to call you again?"

"No."

"And when he didn't call you, did you try to get even with him?"

"No."

"And you methodically destroyed every piece of evidence, so that you have nothing here to confirm your story?"

"I told about that."

"Yes; your description of destroying the evidence is very precise; your entire story is. It's as if it were written out. Was it?"

"No."

I'm not a liar, she thought. He raped me. She glanced over at the panel, scrutinizing her. She felt as though she were the subject of a laboratory experiment.

"You said you were drinking that night. You said you had two beers and a few sips from a third bottle?"

"Yes. Just a few sips."

"Could it have been more than that? Could you have lost count after a couple of beers?"

"No."

"What else do you drink illegally? Hard liquor?"

"No."

"Do you do drugs, smoke pot?"

"No."

"But you were consuming beer? Were you drunk?"

"I wasn't drunk."

"We don't know whether you were or not. We have no test results. It's just one more item amid all this unsubstantiated testimony that we do not have any evidence whatsoever to support. That will be all. Thank you, Ms. Mason."

HARLAN CALLED for a brief recess before closing arguments. Her parents and the lawyer congratulated Elizabeth for the way she had handled herself. She didn't think she was so convincing.

He made me sound like loose change.

"MEMBERS OF THIS distinguished panel, I congratulate you for the care with which you have administered this hearing," MacNeil stated in his closing argument. "The concept of following the principles and procedures of the American system of justice is altogether admirable. And thus, Jimmy Andrews' guilt must be proven beyond a reasonable doubt. Those are the guidelines here. Reasonable doubt. Doubt

permeates the proceedings. We began without evidence.
Witnesses have been called. There is still no evidence. As
for what motivated Elizabeth Mason to say months later that
someone raped her, I don't know. A psychologist cannot
know, either, except to speculate. Speculation is not relevant. *Evidence* is relevant. What we know is that there is not
a shred of proof for these charges. No evidence. The
doctor's report is that of a throat specialist. He never
conducted a gynecological examination. The doctor offers
no evidence of rape. Nobody who appeared before you
offered any evidence of rape. What testimony do we have
about the night of September second? They were seen at a
party together. I'll grant that. Nothing else about that
evening can be substantiated. Nothing. Certainly not the
story of a teenager undergoing the stress of being away from
home for the first time, a period which has caused so many
emotional problems in young people. The claimant must
prove beyond a reasonable doubt that Jimmy Andrews
raped her. What may have been proved is that they went to
a party.

"Without the presumption of innocence and the concept
of reasonable doubt, we would have a chaotic society.
Anyone could bring charges against anyone else for any
reason. Prosecutors in the criminal justice system do not
permit cases to come to trial unless they feel they can prove
a case beyond a reasonable doubt. Jurors do not convict
unless they are convinced beyond a reasonable doubt. Nor
can you. You must use the evidence at this hearing to
support your belief. And there is no evidence. One cannot
simply cry rape and not prove it. You must find Jimmy
Andrews not guilty of this complaint, or it would be a
mockery not only of the traditions of Layton College but of
the traditions of American justice.

"I thank you."

ELIZABETH WAS BITING her lip in nervousness. She turned to
look over at Jimmy Andrews. He sat impassively, properly

coached. I can't believe that bastard was inside me. In me. Would it help if I just got out of my chair and pointed a finger at him and screamed, You did it! You did it no matter what your lawyer says! They'd think I was crazy. She observed Penny Andrews, who was nodding her head yes to the defense attorney's summation. Earlier Elizabeth had noted she was shaking her head no. Now, *she's* crazy.

"DISTINGUISHED PANEL MEMBERS, we thank you for the opportunity to present this case," Reed said in summation. "My colleague's strategy was to call no witnesses. The defendant himself was not called. This protects James Andrews from self-incrimination. It also protects him from scrutiny and cross-examination. The statement that there is no evidence to prove the case is inaccurate. James Andrews and Elizabeth Mason were together on the night of September second. This is documented by Shannon Harnett. Shortly afterward, Elizabeth Mason was treated by a doctor for throat bruises caused by a physical struggle.

"Rape is sexual intercourse without consent, effected by force. No evidence? Elizabeth Mason did not choke herself. She is a rape victim. In her behavior as observed and reported here by her closest friends on campus, Elizabeth Mason is a rape victim. In her behavior as observed and reported by a psychologist trained and experienced in dealing with people of college age, Elizabeth Mason is a rape victim. She has been treated for rape. Her dreams, her patterns of behavior, are those of a rape victim.

"Do not shield yourselves from the truth by assuming it can't happen here. It happens here. It happens at college campuses across the country. You saw Elizabeth Mason. You listened to her. You must ask yourselves why in the world would she go to all this trouble, implicate her parents, friends, have her privacy invaded in this way, go through the emotional strain of this procedure, if she were not telling the truth. A trained psychologist testified that she did not find in her behavior any tendency to lie, to dissemble. She is an honest young woman, who tells the truth. You must ask yourself, was she credible? If you believe her, then she has identified the guilty party. *She* is the eyewitness to the crime.

"Naively, a freshman on a date with a senior, she went to a soundproof room set aside from the general activity in a house. They kissed. She wanted to stop. She said no. And James Andrews would not listen. He took what he wanted by force, without her consent. That constitutes rape. Here or anywhere, rape is unacceptable and must be punished.

"I thank you."

HARLAN INFORMED the participants that when a decision had been reached, they would be contacted by telephone and asked to return to the conference room. The Masons went to Elizabeth's dorm, the Andrewses to Jimmy's house. The lawyers, with other business, went to the inn to make phone calls.

Harlan, Stone, and Teller adjourned to a smaller room, a lounge within the building.

"Well, we have a classic case of acquaintance rape before us, in all its ambiguity," Teller said. "You never have witnesses. There's always a gray area of interpretation. Was there consent or not? Was there force or not? I tend to believe the girl. Whether I would vote to convict is another matter."

"What did she expect would happen?" Madelyn Stone said. "She has too much to drink. She throws herself at the boy. She gives him a sexual opportunity."

"He has to be only human," Harlan contributed.

"The crucial moment is early on," Stone suggested. "The moment she steps into that basement room. Entering that room constitutes consent. Settling on a couch with him, necking with him in that room. All of it is consent in some form. With consent, it isn't rape."

"I agree completely," Harlan said. "Her behavior was definitely provocative all night. Loose behavior. Drinking beer. She can't suddenly, in the middle of sex, and that's where they were, in foreplay, withhold consent. She'd already given it.''

"What you both say is fascinating. Do you realize what you've said?'' Teller asked.

"That the boy is innocent,'' Stone responded.

"Exactly,'' Harlan said.

"You have both accepted her version of the events that night. She has, through raw credibility, convinced you of a sequence of events. You choose to interpret the events in your particular manner. But neither of you says that it didn't happen.''

"I suppose that's true,'' Stone said. "There is an interpretation possible, though.''

"No. If you accept what she's saying to account for part of the evening's progression, why isn't *everything* that she's saying acceptable?''

"I can't accept it,'' Harlan said.

"Why not? You believe her all along, but not about the crucial moment. The crucial moment is not when she enters the room, Madelyn, it's the moment prior to intercourse. If, at that moment, she says no, regardless of what led up to it, and he forces her, it's rape.''

"But how can you know that?'' Harlan said.

"That's why we're here.''

Teller turned on the tape recorder, and they listened to the proceedings at the hearing, skipping over some of the less important moments.

"I don't hear sufficient evidence,'' Harlan said. "I'm persuaded by his lawyer on that.''

"I think it's a lack of communication between them,'' Stone said. "The girl foolishly—and it *was* foolish of her—placed herself in a sexually provocative situation, giving him encouraging signs all night. She says no, I'll grant that, I believe her about that. But he thinks she doesn't really mean it. Not the way she's been acting. He forces the issue. They've both been drinking, and it becomes blurred as to whether she really wants the sex. They have the sex. And he thought she wanted it, even though she was saying no.''

"She wanted to be taken," Harlan said.

"He *thought* she wanted to be taken," Stone responded.

"What about the bruises?" Teller said.

"There's no evidence the bruises occurred during sex," Harlan stated. "Perhaps there was a second rapist. The Second Rapist Theory," Harlan said, trying to be amusing.

"Marvelous, a second rapist," Stone said. "But the bruises could have been caused by the sex being rough, or from that blurred line as to how much he thinks she needs to be pushed to say the yes he thinks she really means. Lack of communication. Not rape."

"Beautifully put, Madelyn, I can stand behind that," Harlan said.

"I happen to disagree with you both. I think everything the girl said is true, up to and including the description of the rape. I can't go along with her account because she's credible and then all of a sudden discount it in the middle. My problem is not with believing her; it's taking the next step—proving my belief. There's reasonable doubt for me because of the lack of evidence."

"They have no evidence," Harlan said.

"Circumstantial evidence. Hearsay. With the guidelines we've established, I can't find the boy guilty," Teller said, with reluctance in his voice.

"Then we're agreed. It's unanimous," Harlan said.

"We're going to have one very unhappy girl on our hands," Teller said. "I believe she was raped."

"Frank, we held the hearing, they had an opportunity to mount their case, they couldn't persuade us in a legal sense," Stone said.

"Do you really think he didn't rape her?" he said, addressing his remark to them both.

"The evidence was circumstantial enough and unsubstantiated enough so that we can honestly say we couldn't find him guilty," Harlan said.

"What about the girl?" Teller said. "According to the guidelines, if we believe her claim was frivolous, we can suspend her."

"I wouldn't go that far," Stone said.

"So is she going to be disciplined, yes or no?" Teller asked. His colleagues both shook their heads no. "All right. The claim was not frivolous and they're both exonerated. Bill, you get to make the happy announcement."

"What exactly am I going to say?" Harlan responded, suddenly at a loss.

"Say that this panel has met and considered the matter and that we found insufficient evidence and therefore we determine him not guilty," Teller replied.

"Insufficient evidence. Excellent, Frank. That says it all," Stone responded.

"I'm sure the girl and her family won't think it's very fair. But who says life is fair?" Teller commented.

ABOUT TWO HOURS after the hearing was adjourned, the phone calls came through, telling the participants to return to the Administration Building for the verdict. The Masons and their lawyer entered the room, taking their positions before the panel, as did the Andrews family with their lawyer. The families were so nervous no one took a seat, the two sets of parents standing on either side of their prized possessions.

"Ms. Mason, Mr. Andrews," Harlan said. "After listening to and evaluating the testimony and after judicious deliberation by the members of this board, we deem there is insufficient evidence to support the charge and find the defendant not guilty."

Jimmy and his parents embraced each other. The Masons stood still.

"We further deem the charge brought by Ms. Mason was not frivolous. The matter has been judged and is hereby deemed closed."

Harlan smiled, a little wrap-up to end the business, a professional kind of smile, a flight attendant's smile. The Masons were the first ones to leave, to get out of that room. Outside, Jean Philips and Elizabeth's friends were waiting to hear the decision. When Elizabeth emerged and made a thumbs-down signal, Jimmy's friends, Janna and a few of his housemates, burst into high fives.

"Insufficient evidence," Elizabeth said to her group.

Jimmy, his parents, and their lawyer came out of the building and were greeted by their supporters. Ben watched them congratulating each other, congratulating somebody for raping his daughter. He walked over to them quickly and with the element of surprise managed to grab both Jimmy and Malcolm by their collars and push them back against the building wall. Penny screamed in fright.

"What kind of people are you?" Ben shouted.

He was pulled away by Jimmy's friends.

"You watch it, or I'll have you arrested," Malcolm said to him, and Laura clutched Ben's arm to pull him back.

The groups separated, and Elizabeth turned to watch Jimmy and his people move on. He gets to smile and walk away.

# CHAPTER
## 10

DEFEATED, THE MASONS RETURNED to Elizabeth's dorm room with their lawyer. Martin Reed told them the lack of physical evidence made it impossible for the college to rule in Elizabeth's favor. He reminded them that the board's decision had no standing beyond the college and no bearing on whether or not Jimmy Andrews could still be brought to trial. If they wished to pursue it further, they could go to the police to file charges. They also could file an action against the college or a civil action against the rapist. Ben was impatient with Reed's legal advice and relieved when he left for the airport.

"The only thing he was right about," Ben said to Laura and Elizabeth, "is that there are other courses of action. We should clear everything out of this room, pack up the car, and get Elizabeth out of this place."

"A while ago you were talking about courage. Now you have her running away," Laura said.

"This is a dreadful place," he responded. "They let a girl get raped, and they let the rapist get away with it."

"I can't leave. It would look like I was leaving in disgrace for making up a story," Elizabeth said, kneading her forehead to drive out her latest headache.

• • •

AFTER EXPRESSING HER SYMPATHIES to the Masons, Jean Philips went into the Administration Building.

"What in the world went on here?" she demanded of the panel members.

"We held a hearing," Harlan replied. "We weighed the evidence and made our decision."

"Did you believe that girl was lying?"

"We weren't obliged to assess whether or not she was lying," Stone told her, "but whether or not we were presented with sufficient evidence to uphold her claim."

"That is a very stuffy response."

"I beg your pardon."

"I told this girl a hearing was a viable option, a place where she could get justice without going to the police."

"We were in that room for two hours, Jean, deliberating, listening back to the testimony," Harlan said. "We were obliged to do that, to hold a proper hearing, and we did."

"If you couldn't find in favor of this innocent girl who was raped here—"

"Who *claims* to have been raped," Harlan hurried to say. "Whose claims were not properly substantiated—"

"Who was raped! Then how the hell will any of my women ever get an honest hearing at this college?"

Teller answered slowly, as if also explaining it to himself. "In a court of law, or in an administrative hearing like ours, you have legal guidelines. In the real world, guilty people sometimes go free because the case against them isn't strong enough. That can happen on a college campus too."

"But it makes me out to be a charlatan, a shill for the college. I tell these women they don't have to go to the police, there's justice here, and there isn't. Why was this procedure set up? It doesn't work."

"They didn't prove their case," Harlan said.

"A crime in an unsupervised student house, a senior raping a freshman who doesn't know which way is up, certainly wouldn't have looked good for Layton. Did that go into your decision?''

"That's an outrageous presumption, Jean. You have no right to impugn our motives, simply because the verdict does not fulfill your requirements,'' Stone said.

"I won't counsel women to go through these hearings anymore. I'm telling you that. I'll send them right to the police.''

"Exposure to those harsh procedures may not be in the best interests of Layton women,'' Harlan said.

"Of course you'd say that. The dean of students doesn't want the police crawling all over the campus.''

"I was thinking of the well-being of our women.''

"What about the well-being of Elizabeth Mason?''

"You're being insubordinate,'' Harlan said.

"No, I'm being upset. Even psychologists can get upset,'' and she walked out of the room.

In her view, she had given a student dreadful advice and she needed to undo that act. Jean Philips hurried to Elizabeth's dorm, where she found the Masons in a frayed state.

"I want to apologize to you, Liz, and to your parents. I really thought the hearing procedure could work.''

"Then you were as naive as anyone,'' Laura said.

"I don't know that it has to be said at this point, but I believe you deeply, Liz.''

"It's too bad you weren't on the panel,'' Ben responded.

"I don't think this should stop here. He shouldn't be allowed to get away with it. I know I didn't encourage you to do it before, but that was a mistake. I think you should report it to the police.''

"Is that psychologically sound?'' Laura said.

Philips paused for a moment. "Yes, I believe it is. For Liz to feel she's taken charge and explored all avenues.''

"I don't know what to do anymore,'' Elizabeth said.

"This was a crime. It should be reported,'' Philips said.

"You made that point,'' Laura told her.

"Jimmy Andrews has no right—" Philips continued.

"We know that," Laura said, cutting her off.

"Well, I'm available if you need me for anything."

"Maybe you could give us directions for the fastest route out of this place," Ben snapped.

BEN PHONED HIS BROTHER, David, in Chicago and told him about the hearing, coloring the account with his opinion that Reed had been completely ineffective. David did not concur. Listening to Ben's account, he felt no lawyer could have won for Elizabeth in a hearing of that nature. As to what they should do next, and whether or not they should go to the police, David advised them to be very certain before taking that path. He was not arguing that justice should not be served, nor was he suggesting they should not press charges. They needed to be aware of the difficult, public nature of a criminal investigation and a trial. He confirmed that the alternative of a civil action could drag on and keep the incident in Elizabeth's life for years.

THE MASONS WENT to dinner in a coffee shop in the Caldwell mall, away from the campus, and debated the issue. Ben was agitated, short-tempered. He wanted to get Elizabeth packed up and out of Layton College. What kind of college was it where they permitted drinking parties and allowed young women to be subject to sexual assaults? Elizabeth contended that leaving Layton would be delivering a victory to the rapist and to the college. Laura was trying to organize the arguments in a rational manner. They went back to Elizabeth's room without having made a decision.

If they reported the rape to the police, Elizabeth's privacy would be invaded, her sexuality made public. Civil lawsuits would keep the anger bubbling in their lives. As she had argued from the beginning, Laura wanted to let the matter end. They had tried to punish the assailant. They didn't have enough evidence. The main issue for her was Elizabeth's well-being, to see her get on with her college years. She agreed with Elizabeth that dropping out of Layton was incorrect. She suggested that Elizabeth try to finish out the year and then transfer if she was uncomfortable about staying there.

Ben was no longer listening. He dialed the college operator and asked to be connected to the president of Layton at his home.

"Dad, this is not a time to call."

"It's Saturday night. What are they going to think of us?" Laura said.

"I don't care."

"Hello?" a woman answered on the line.

"My name is Ben Mason. My daughter has been raped at this college. I need to speak to Dr. Baker right now."

"I'll see if he's available."

"Ben—" Laura said, exasperated.

"This is Dr. Baker," the president of the college said.

"Are you aware that a hearing was held today by your grievance board on the matter of the rape of my daughter, Elizabeth?"

"Yes, I am. It was very thoroughly reviewed, and it's my understanding there was insufficient evidence."

"The decision was insufficient, as far as I am concerned."

"This was a panel convened on the highest level, Mr. Mason."

"We need to talk about the college's responsibility in this matter. I am here on campus with my wife, and we need to talk about it now."

"Perhaps you should speak with our college counsel, Frank Teller. He'll be in his office on Monday."

"I was present for your orientation speech, Dr. Baker. You can't be so lofty in your principles about this school and then handle a sensitive matter like this by pushing me off to your lawyer, whose handiwork I have just observed. I'd like to point out that my wife and I have considerable experience with publicity and its effects. We *know* people in the media."

"Mr. Mason, you are obviously upset. I have a busy calendar tomorrow, a luncheon, a tea. But why don't you come by in the morning with your daughter? We'll have a nice little continental breakfast and talk. Nine-thirty?"

"Nine-thirty it is."

Ben turned to Laura and Elizabeth. "He's going to meet with us."

"For what purpose?" Laura said. "What is he possibly going to say?"

"We get the satisfaction of confronting him. He's giving us the continental breakfast. The matter is important enough for him to see us, but not important enough for them to serve eggs."

DR. HUDSON BAKER greeted them at the door of his house, located on a hill overlooking the campus. He was wearing a navy blazer, white shirt and striped tie, gray flannel slacks. Ben, who had chosen to wear a suit and tie for this breakfast meeting, contemplated the world as divided between people who wear a tie on Sundays and those who don't. Usually, Ben didn't. He was certain Baker usually did. Politenesses were exchanged, and the Masons were guided into the dining room. They sat at the table, and as if to demonstrate his interest and sympathy, Baker asked Elizabeth several questions about her classes, her professors.

"What you might ask me," Elizabeth said to him so bluntly that even the self-assured former diplomat straightened his shoulders, "was whether I was raped by a senior at this college in a house owned by this college. And the answer is yes."

"We conducted a thorough—and legitimate—hearing on this subject," Baker said.

"Did you mean to say legal?" Ben asked. "Or legitimate?"

"Both, in a sense," Baker offered. "We are within our

legal rights to conduct a hearing regarding student discipline. And it was done legitimately.''

"But it wouldn't measure up to objective standards," Ben said. "Whitewashing, stonewalling, are a couple of words that come to mind.''

"I beg to differ. The panel, I understand, was extremely responsible in its decision. The evidence was insufficient," Baker said.

"The hearing was a kangaroo court, and this is a kangaroo breakfast," Ben said. "A kangaroo *continental* breakfast.''

"I do not agree with you," Baker replied.

"Here is what we want. A full four-year scholarship for Elizabeth. With a refund retroactive for this term.''

Startled, Elizabeth and Laura exchanged glances. What was he demanding?

"Really?" Baker said, startled himself.

"As compensation for encouraging an atmosphere where a freshman woman is raped. For allowing the illegal consumption of alcohol by your students. For conducting a hearing that indicates no interest in policing student crime.''

"Dad, they're not going to do that.''

"If you wish to apply for financial aid, that is your choice. I can tell you, though, that nothing in this matter would in the slightest reflect on a favorable decision in your behalf.''

"No? Suppose we fill out a form and under 'Reason for this application' we write, 'Rape'?''

"Please, Dad. They've all made the position of the college very clear.''

Baker turned to look at Elizabeth.

"I'm not sure, young lady, that given the hostility of your father to Layton College, and your difficulties in adjusting here, that you can be happy at this school. We do our best in the admissions process, but every year there are a few students who simply do not fit in.''

"Are you throwing her out?" Laura said.

"On what grounds would we . . . throw her out, as you

put it? I am merely offering my opinion as an educator, as someone experienced in these matters, that she might be happier somewhere else.''

"Do you know the song 'You're Going to Hear from Me'?'' Ben said wildly.

"Ben!'' Laura said.

"No, I'm not familiar with the song.''

"You're going to hear from me. Thank you for the breakfast roll.''

The Masons left the room, unescorted.

"Easy, Ben.''

"I was back in the schoolyard again with a big bully. Except he was a bully with a tie,'' Ben said.

"We should go to the police,'' Elizabeth said. "Now it's as if I'm the one who did something wrong.''

"No, darling,'' Laura said to Elizabeth. "Study, do a term paper, go back to your singing. Don't get trapped in this.''

"You're for letting him get away with it?'' Ben said.

"I don't care about him. I care about Elizabeth.''

"She wants to go to the police.''

"I do, Mom.''

"We never should have had the hearing,'' Laura said. "And now we're getting in even deeper.''

"It's what we have to do,'' Ben said.

They set out for police headquarters. In their family the idea was for the children to live ''culturally enriched'' lives. Police cases were something you read about in the newspapers or saw on the nightly news. It didn't happen to you.

THE POPULATION OF Caldwell was approximately 25,000. A shopping mall on the outskirts of town attracted much of the local traffic. On this Sunday morning, as the Masons drove onto Main Street, the place could not have looked much sleepier. A few cars rolled through, and only two people were walking along. Police headquarters was located in a three-story red-brick municipal building in the center of town. They approached the desk where the sergeant on duty sat.

"We'd like to report a rape," Ben said.

"Who was raped?" he asked.

"I was," Elizabeth said.

"And when did this take place?"

"It was a while ago. September second."

"And you decided to report it now? On a Sunday morning? Well, the people who deal with that are not on duty right this instant. Why don't you have a seat, and I'll see if I can locate them."

They waited forty-five minutes. A lanky man in his forties appeared, introduced himself as Joe Mallory, and summoned them to come inside with him. He was wearing a plaid shirt, corduroy pants, and work shoes. Fair, with thinning light-brown hair and brown eyes, he moved slowly; in his gait and dress he looked as if he could have been a local farmer. He took them through the main room, which was quiet and empty, but for one officer on duty monitoring calls from squad cars. The Masons were brought to a cubicle at the side of the room, a small space with old metal furniture, paint peeling on the ceiling, and various bulletins and memos taped to the partition walls.

"This is Detective Ann Neary."

A woman in her late thirties, wearing a sweater, plaid slacks, and sneakers, was seated there. She had a closed-off, hard expression that announced she would have been more comfortable doing anything other than being in this room on a Sunday morning with these people.

"We've never been in a situation like this before," Laura said. "What are the procedures?"

"We take a statement," Mallory replied. "We investigate. Then, if the district attorney believes there's a case solid enough, it's taken before the grand jury. If they hand down an indictment, the case goes to trial."

"That's what we want," Elizabeth said.

"Then let's proceed with your statement," Mallory told her.

"Tell us your name, date of birth, and address, and then give us your exact recollection of what took place," Neary said.

Elizabeth gave a thirty-minute description of the rape, prodded by questions from the detectives. Ben interrupted several times with his interpretation of the events. The detectives, impatient with him, kept telling him to be quiet.

"Have you had any contact with Jimmy Andrews since September second?" Mallory asked Elizabeth after she finished her statement.

"I've seen him around, and also at the hearing."

"What hearing was that?" Neary asked.

"At the college. They had a grievance board."

"What did this board find?" she asked.

"They said 'insufficient evidence,' but they were protecting the college's reputation," Ben answered.

"Even the lawyer we had said the evidence was meager," Laura contributed.

"Honey, *we're* not trying the case," Ben said angrily.

"You folks can sit here, but *you're* not being questioned," Mallory told them. "Please don't say anything unless we ask you something directly." He turned to Elizabeth. "On the subject of your parents, when exactly did you tell them about the rape?"

"When I went home for Thanksgiving. My counselor at the college, Jean Philips, suggested I tell them about it because I decided to make a complaint through the board."

"And before that, did you talk to your parents, did they ask how things were going at school, and did you say anything about the rape?"

"I didn't. I couldn't bring myself to say anything."

"For two and a half months you had conversations with your parents," Mallory continued, ". . . and did you see them?"

"I went home once, and they came up to school once."

"And you never told them you'd been raped?"

"No."

The phone rang, and Mallory answered it.

"Yes? . . . I think you should. . . . Okay." He hung up the phone.

"Who testified at this college hearing?" Neary asked.

"A psychologist who's been treating me. Dr. Phelan from town, who told about my bruises, how they could only have been caused by a physical struggle. Two friends of mine who vouched for my behavior, Donna Winter and Sterling May. A girl in my dorm who saw me with Jimmy at the party that night, Shannon Harnett."

"Folks, we're going to ask you to sit here for a few minutes. The district attorney is going to join us," Mallory informed them.

Mallory and Neary withdrew.

"I know we're getting into something we shouldn't," Laura said.

"Yes, you made your opinion very clear. Why the hell did you say that about the evidence?"

"Because this is a mistake. We've been here nearly two hours, and we haven't even begun."

"The alternative, which is to let him get away with it, is not right," Elizabeth responded.

"You say that on a Sunday," Laura replied. "What happens when this starts to interfere with school? Your job is supposed to be going to school. That's what we saw when we visited colleges, how wonderful it is for college kids to just have school to be concerned about."

"I'm uneasy too. But it's not for the same reason," Ben said. "You saw this town. It's a Toonerville Trolley stop. And the detectives, they look like dairy farmers. I don't know if these country bumpkins are sophisticated enough for a crime like this."

IN THE HOUR they waited for the detectives to return, Laura's and Ben's positions hardened. The time it was taking confirmed Laura's feelings about being overcommitted. Ben claimed the detectives didn't know how to handle the situation.

The two detectives came in, followed by an exceedingly thin man with an angular face and a protruding Adam's apple, quite tall, with light-brown eyes and brown hair. He was well dressed in a crisply pressed blue suit, white shirt, and bow tie.

"I'm Carl Peters," he said, extending his hand to each of the Masons. "I'm the district attorney. I've just been reviewing your statement with the detectives," he said to Elizabeth. "We have a few things we'd like to clear up."

"Before we continue," Ben said, "could I understand something? Is this a case that must be handled in Caldwell? Albany is nearby, a bigger city, possibly with bigger city resources. . . ."

"A trial, if we get to that, would be conducted in Albany. You're worried whether we can handle the investigation?" he said. "Where are you from, Mr. Mason?"

"New York City."

"And what do you do?"

"I'm a folk art dealer. My wife runs a magazine."

"If a rape occurred in your place of business or at your wife's magazine, would there be any reason why the investigation would be handled by people in New Jersey?"

"No."

"Two years ago, we had a serial murderer at large here, a case that received national attention. The case was broken by Detectives Mallory and Neary. As for me, I worked in the Manhattan District Attorney's office after Columbia Law. My wife is a counsel to the governor in Albany, and so we live here."

"I was merely trying to get the correct information."

"Yes, I understand your prejudices. But disabuse your-self of the notion that a rape case is beyond our capabilities. The only question here is: What are the facts of the case?"

He turned to Elizabeth. "When your parents asked you

how you were, by not telling them, that was a deceit, wasn't it?''

"I wanted to protect them from knowing."

"Still, that was a deceit."

"In a sense."

"That's splitting hairs, isn't it?" Ben said.

"It is. But within those kinds of distinctions, people are found guilty or innocent of crimes. So, other than what Elizabeth reported to you, you have no firsthand knowledge of the crime?"

"None."

"Mr. and Mrs. Mason, could you wait outside for a while? We'd like to speak to Elizabeth privately." Ben and Laura were reluctant to leave Elizabeth. "These are our procedures," Peters insisted, and they left the room. Peters settled into a chair, and Mallory and Neary pulled their chairs forward a bit.

"Elizabeth, you say that you told no one about the rape for two months?" Neary asked her.

"That's right. I was upset."

"During that time you talked to friends, at school, at home possibly. They must have asked you how you were, and you didn't tell them?"

"I didn't. For the same reasons I mentioned."

"You were deceiving your friends, then, just the way you deceived your parents?"

"I didn't mean it as deceit."

"The doctor who examined you, the one who gave you a report for the hearing," Mallory said, taking up the questioning. "Did he state that you were raped?"

"He confirmed that my bruises were from a physical struggle."

"When you first saw him, a few days after the rape, did you tell him you were raped?"

"No."

"What exactly did you tell him?"

"That I walked into a chinning bar."

"You made a false statement to the doctor who examined you?" Peters said, getting up and starting to pace.

"But then I told him the truth, later, when I went back for a copy of his report, and I'm sure he believed me then. I know he did, from his testimony at the hearing."

"Did you tell anyone else the bruises were from a chinning bar?"

"I was trying to keep the incident to myself, and I wasn't in very good control. I also told people that I was hit in the neck by a softball. That's when I dropped out of vocal music, because I was afraid to hurt my voice, and then I just couldn't bring myself to sing."

"Whom did you tell that you were hit in the neck by a softball?" Peters asked.

"My parents. A couple of faculty people at school. My vocal teacher in New York."

"So you lied to all of those people?"

"I was very upset," Elizabeth protested, sweating with nervousness. "The psychologist said at the hearing that there's something called rape trauma syndrome, and I'm sure that's what I was going through."

"Whatever you were going through, you deceived your parents and friends, you lied to the doctor, telling him about a chinning bar, you lied to everyone else, telling them about a softball injury."

"Were you a virgin?" the woman detective said abruptly, and Elizabeth was startled.

"No."

"How much sex have you had? How often do you do it?" she asked.

"I had a boyfriend at the end of senior year of high school, and we made love a few times."

"Is that a few times once, or a few times a few times?"

"On several occasions."

"How many lovers before that?"

"Nobody."

"How many before this incident, since this incident?"

"No one."

"Did your boyfriend ever rape you?" Mallory asked.

"No, he never raped me."

"Did anyone else ever rape you?"

"No."

"All right. Concerning the night of the party," Peters said. "As far as you know, nobody saw you enter the basement with Jimmy Andrews."

"Not into the basement. But we were seen together."

"You were necking with him and willingly went down to the basement with him and necked with him there?"

"But when he wanted to have intercourse with me, I said no. I shouted, I fought back."

"And you were drinking that night? How much?"

"Two beers and a little from a third. I wasn't drunk."

"Were you sober?" Mallory said.

"I wasn't drunk. I was in command of my senses. I knew I was being raped!"

"You weren't seen going into the basement," Neary said. "Were you seen emerging?"

"I don't think so."

"You went back to your dorm and carefully destroyed every possible piece of evidence. You douched, you showered, you took all your clothing, even your shoes, and you threw it all out, into a garbage bin, and now it's gone, three months gone at the bottom of the city dump," Peters said.

"I was in a hysterical state."

"Well, you couldn't have done a more effective job of destroying evidence if you were in a rational state," Peters said sarcastically. "Did you tell anyone in the dorm about the incident after it happened—dormmates, roommates?"

"I was too ashamed."

"Do you have a roommate?" Neary asked.

"Holly Robertson."

"What did you tell her?"

"She heard me crying in the night, and she asked me why, but I made something up. I was too humiliated."

"You've come in here to charge that a senior at Layton College named Jimmy Andrews raped you," Peters said. "You have no physical evidence, you can produce no one who saw the act, you lied repeatedly about the alleged incident, changing your story as needed, you lied to the very doctor whose report you claim supports your story, you've had a hearing at your college where your witnesses offered statements based on opinions and hearsay, and where your accusation was not upheld, you've waited three months to go to the police. What in the world are you offering to encourage us to believe your story and to warrant a further investigation?" Peters said.

Elizabeth was unable to answer. The detectives and the prosecutor, working along lines of evidence and logic that would be pertinent in a court of law, had exposed every weakness in her story.

"My word," she managed to say softly.

"We'll be in touch with you," Peters responded.

Elizabeth walked out of the office to the bench where Laura and Ben were waiting, and they rose apprehensively.

"They're not country bumpkins," Elizabeth said, drained.

THEY RETURNED to the inn to wait for a call from Peters about whether he would conduct an investigation. He called in and said he was going ahead with it.

"You are? Excellent," Ben said.

"You and your wife will not be needed. Your daughter, I presume, will be at school."

"Yes, she's going to be here. When will this begin and how long will everything take?"

"I can't give you an exact timetable. It could be a couple of weeks or more for the investigation, depending upon what we learn. If there isn't enough to charge him, we'll stop at that point. If we decide to proceed, and he's indicted, preparation for the trial and jury selection, under the best circumstances, would bring us to trial in four or five months."

"Oh."

"But we're way ahead of ourselves here. We don't know where the investigation will lead."

"Anything I can possibly do to help . . . ," Ben said, buoyed by the news.

"What could you possibly do to help, Mr. Mason?" Peters responded brusquely.

Ben reported the sequence Peters outlined. Laura was unhappy with the information.

"Well, we've got ourselves a ball game," Ben said, cheerleading.

"This is not a ball game," Laura responded darkly.

DAVID TOLD THEM they should not be too optimistic. An investigation was the minimum the police could do. The key element was how vigorously they pursued it. Ben announced to Elizabeth and Laura that he would stay there to keep on top of the investigation. Laura had to be back in New York to get out an issue of the magazine, but he could remain for as long as necessary. His assistants could run the gallery; he would be able to take care of any important business by phone over the next couple of weeks. For business purposes, he might even go into the surrounding area and look for quilts and the like when he wasn't in the room at the inn, which he was going to maintain as his headquarters. He rambled on about how he could be a fly on the wall, hang around the campus and pick up information the detectives might miss, and he wouldn't be a burden to Elizabeth. She wouldn't be obliged to see him, but he would be at the inn for whatever she might need.

"You're going to be watching over me, so that nothing bad happens to me? It already happened, Dad."

"I know. I know."

Everything came crashing in on him: the strain, the hearing, the bastard and his father, their lawyer, the breakfast, the detectives, the prosecutor, the awfulness, his helplessness to protect her. His head started to spin. She was right; he couldn't watch over her so that nothing bad happened. It had happened. He started to cry. He didn't even know how to cry. He made little gasps. Elizabeth, who had never seen her father cry, tried to comfort him, putting her arms around him as she fought back her own tears.

"They can't do this to us," Ben said as he caught his breath.

"That's why I can't just drop it. Mom, I can't."

"All right, darling," Laura said, near tears.

"But you shouldn't be here all the time, Dad."

"I know. We'll go back to New York," Ben told her. "I wouldn't have done much good here anyway, snooping around. The Crying Detective."

THE NOTION THAT she had lied to people by not telling them about the rape troubled Elizabeth, and she wanted to be forthright with Melanie Stern, whom she had kept completely uninformed. She called Melanie at Wisconsin. She was loving school, studying hard, had broken up with her latest boyfriend, but that was all right because she wanted to take stock, figure out what she was really looking for in a man.

"Melanie, when I first got to school, I was raped on a date."

"Liz! Oh, Liz! Are you okay?"

"Yes and no."

"Who was it, how did it happen?"

"An arrogant, deceiving sonofabitch. He got me into a room in the house where he lived, where nobody could hear me screaming, and he held me down and raped me. We had a hearing with a disciplinary board at school, and it didn't work out. We've just gone to the police."

"I'm so sorry."

"I'm muddling through. I'm a little untested on my estimate just now. He threw off the curve a bit. It was a first date."

"Do you have people around to help?"

"I have friends here. And a psychologist at the Women's Center. My parents were here and just left. The police are going to investigate. And I'm hanging on. The president of the college advised me to leave."

"Fuck him!"

"Melanie, always a straight talker. That's exactly right. Fuck him!"

# CHAPTER

# 11

DETECTIVE JOE MALLORY WAS MARRIED to a woman who worked in the local bank as a teller. They had two children, a boy of twelve and a girl of fourteen. Ann Neary, married to a high school science teacher, had a boy in his freshman year at the State University of New York at Stony Brook. Layton was never a consideration for Ann Neary's son. He wouldn't have received a scholarship, and they couldn't afford the tuition. As the detectives drove through the campus gates, Ann Neary expressed her general feelings about the place to her partner. "Rich brats," she said.

Mallory and Neary checked in with campus security. They were beginning their investigation with Shannon Harnett and Allison Dobbins, since, in the Mason girl's version of the events, they were at the party on the night the rape was supposed to have occurred. The detectives went to the dorm early in the morning and asked the girls to come outside for a few minutes. They were flustered about talking to the police. In the questioning, neither said that she saw anything of consequence that night.

"I'd like you to write down every person you can remember being at that party. Even if they were there for just a couple of minutes.'' Neary handed over a notebook and a pen, and they made a list. After they wrote down the names, Mallory said:

"You went to another party that night?"

"Yes," Shannon said.

"And Elizabeth and Jimmy remained?"

"Yes."

"Were they drinking?" Neary said.

"Everybody was drinking beer," Allison replied.

"Which is illegal under age twenty-one," Neary said with annoyance. "Did you notice how much she and Jimmy had to drink?"

"I didn't."

"But you're sure you saw her drinking?"

"I did. I was sort of checking her out," Allison said. "We had just moved in, Liz lived across the hall, and she was pretty, and I was trying to figure what kind of girl she was, you know, good to be around or competition. A party girl or what."

"What kind of girl is she?" Neary asked.

"Strange."

"In what way?" Neary said.

"The way she keeps to herself. She always keeps her door closed. She never parties or goes out with anybody or never even speaks to anybody, except her odd little group."

"Do you agree?" Mallory asked Shannon.

"She's Remote City," Shannon answered.

THE DETECTIVES ASKED questions of people who were on Allison and Shannon's list of party guests. Then they expanded their inquiry as the names of other people at the party were revealed. These were informal exchanges under trees, over coffee or pizza, leaning against buildings. Nobody who was at the party had noticed the couple go off to another room together. "An iceberg," "a loner," was the way she was described by a couple of people, and others who had noticed her at school characterized her in similar terms. Responding to these observations, Neary said to her partner, "She sounds a little 'off' to me."

ELIZABETH SENSED she was being stared at as she moved about campus. A couple of times she turned quickly and caught people watching her, and then looked away. Exasperated, she said to two women on a walkway:

"What are you looking at?"

"Are you paranoid?" one of them said to her.

"People staring at you can make you paranoid," Elizabeth answered.

WHEN JIMMY LEARNED the police were investigating, he was frightened. They hadn't been able to prove a rape in the college hearing, but the police used different methods. He adopted the public position among his friends that this was more of the girl's craziness and the investigation was meaningless. He tried to protect himself with denial. He did not call his parents or the lawyer, hoping the investigation would never reach him and would be dropped for insufficient evidence, like the grievance board hearing. If the police approached him, then he would make his calls. He would go about his everyday activities, apparently unconcerned.

Janna heard about the detectives asking questions of people and didn't understand why.

"She reported it to the police," Jimmy said. "If somebody reports something to the police, you get police."

"Why is she causing so much trouble?"

"She was shot down at the hearing. It must have made her crazier."

"Evidently she needs notoriety. It must be part of her pathology," the psychology student suggested.

"Definitely," he agreed.

JIMMY HAD NOT restricted his partygoing. Partly this was a manifestation of denial, partly his need to be where the action was at Layton. At a Friday night party, Jimmy drank and danced with a young woman whom he tried unsuccessfully to bring back to his house. She lived on the same floor in the dorm as Janna, and Janna found out about it.

"What do we have between us?" Janna demanded of Jimmy when she saw him the next night.

"A very nice relationship."

"If you really cared for me, you wouldn't want to be with anybody else," she said, still in the thrall of his good looks and self-assurance.

"I like you a lot."

"Well, you're going to have to choose between me and the rest."

"Janna, I'm not seeing anyone else. It's just us."

He thought he was being honest with her, in a fashion. He wasn't seeing anyone else—at the moment.

SINCE JIMMY HAD NOT informed them, Malcolm and Penny were unaware of the police investigation. Penny had chosen not to even bring up the subject of the college hearing again, and that was fine with Malcolm. Apart from Clark Dunne, nobody at the club knew that his son had appeared before a college panel for a rape charge. His principal concern about Jimmy was that he keep his tennis game sharp during the off season. The college made court time available for the tennis team on indoor courts set up on the floor of the field house, and Jimmy worked out with some of his teammates. Malcolm called each week to check if Jimmy was practicing. Over Christmas, the Andrews family was going to Scottsdale, Arizona. Malcolm had arranged for time with the club pro for Jimmy.

"THE POLICE CALLED," John Hatcher told Jimmy. "They want to know what I know about September second."

"Tell them. I'm not worried."

"Should you be worried?"

"John, answer their questions. You didn't see a rape."
"I know what I saw."

JOHN HATCHER WAS ill at ease in the interview. Mallory thought he was on the verge of revealing information, but he did not. For most of the party he was upstairs in the bedroom with his girlfriend. He said they left at some point for hamburgers. He could not even state how many beers Elizabeth and Jimmy drank during the course of the evening.

SANDY MCDERMOTT WAS one of the people who had been at the party. She was the girlfriend of Jimmy's housemate Rod Wyman, also a tennis player. Sandy, a junior, was a petite, lively brunette, an athlete herself and a member of the women's volleyball team. She favored wearing warm-up suits and sneakers. Sandy had assumed a sisterly role with most of the boys in The Big Leagues. The previous year, before she came to know them, she had gone, during a party night of heavy drinking, to the same room where Jimmy Andrews took Elizabeth, and she was nearly raped. The man, Arne Patrick, lived in the house and was an overbearing lout she couldn't get rid of all night. He had told her he was taking her to a place where it was quiet and she could sleep it off, and once there, he tried to force himself on her. She never reported it to the campus authorities because she knew she'd been drunk. She was seen at two parties that night drunk. She felt she could never get anyone to take her claim seriously.

Rod Wyman knew about the incident through Sandy. He told her that if she was questioned, she shouldn't say anything about that night. The police would get the impression The Big Leagues was a rape den, and it might look bad for Jimmy. The jerk who tried to rape Sandy was gone, graduated.

He was joined in the argument by three of his housemates, including Jimmy. They said Sandy owed loyalties to the guys in the house, not this freshman girl, and she shouldn't give the place a reputation for rape. She was confused about what she should say to the detectives. She wanted to be honest, but she did feel loyalties. These were her male pals; she was going with one of them. She decided not to bring up the experience, which she wasn't eager to talk about anyway. When Neary questioned her, Sandy McDermott was visibly nervous, but she added nothing to the detective's knowledge.

MALLORY AND NEARY expanded the investigation to people who were not present at The Big Leagues the night of the party but who might have information. They went to the house where Holly Robertson lived with her boyfriend and interviewed her in the living room.

"You were Liz Mason's roommate at the start of the semester?" Mallory said.

"I still am, technically."

"What did she tell you about the night she had a date with Jimmy Andrews?"

"That it didn't work out. That he was crude and only interested in one thing."

"Did she elaborate?" Neary asked.

"No. I always thought Jimmy was kind of impressive. I'm from Westport, where he comes from. I was surprised when she said that."

"Did she ever tell you that Jimmy Andrews raped her that night?"

"Is *that* what she's saying?"

"Did she ever tell you that?"

"No."

"Did she tell you anything specific about their date?"

"Nothing. She was crying in bed during the night, and it woke me up. The next day I asked her what was wrong, and she said something about love troubles with a guy she was seeing before she came to Layton."

"She cried during the night, so loudly that it woke you up?" Mallory said.

"Yes."

"And you're sure this was the night she had the date with Jimmy? You can pinpoint it in your mind?"

"The first Saturday night. I remember it very clearly. My roommate had a date and I didn't, and it was with someone I would have been very happy to go out with."

"Did you observe her doing anything during the night?" Neary asked.

"No."

"Has she ever told you anything about that night since then?" Neary continued.

"No."

"But you're a hundred percent sure she was crying?" Mallory said.

"I'm positive."

"Did she ever bring up this love she left behind?" Mallory asked.

"She never talked about it again," Holly answered.

"Did she ever cry during the night, during the day, before then, after then?" he said to her.

"I never noticed."

"Odd," Mallory said, looking at Neary. "This one night, the one night she went out with Jimmy Andrews, she's in bed crying, and she tells her roommate it's about a lost love who's never mentioned again."

"I wouldn't know too much. I don't see much of her."

"What is she like as a person?" Neary said.

"I thought she was kind of nice, but she's pretty private. Antisocial even."

Neary looked over at Mallory as if to say, "More of the same."

ELIZABETH COULD NOT walk from place to place on campus without feeling people were whispering about her, staring at her. The next weekend, Seth and Donna went into New

York together, and Sterling was visiting a friend at Cornell. Without friends to cushion her, she was directly exposed to the school population. She was the girl who had brought the police onto the campus, who had filed a complaint against one of the guys, a regular guy. When she sat down to have a juice on Saturday afternoon in one of the student snack bars, a boy who was at the other end of the table got up as soon as she took her seat. She finished and walked out, as several people stared at her coldly. She stayed in her room for the rest of the weekend. The following week she discovered a new development in her notoriety. When she passed groups of athletes standing around, they would stop speaking, and as if by prior agreement, they would focus their attention directly at her, staring in a menacing way.

HOLLY WENT TO SEE Elizabeth in their dorm room. Elizabeth was studying when she entered.

"Liz?"

"Hello."

"The police came by, asking questions. They said you claim Jimmy Andrews raped you."

"It's true, I'm sorry to say. I reported it, and they're conducting an investigation."

"Jimmy? Our Jimmy?"

"Your Jimmy maybe. Not mine."

"What happened?"

"He took me down into a basement room in his house that night. We were kissing. I told him to stop and he wouldn't. I couldn't fight him off, and he raped me."

"I find that very hard to accept."

"Thank you very much."

"You wouldn't think he'd do anything like that."

"He did, though."

"How come you never said anything about it? I was right in the room with you."

"I was in shock."

"Wasn't anyone around?"

"He seemed to have it all worked out. Nobody heard me yell for help."

"He's got a reputation for being a total lady-killer."

"He's also a total rapist."

"I don't know what to say."

"What did you tell the police?"

"I told them I didn't know much, that you never told me Jimmy raped you."

"I wasn't talking about it."

"They were kind of interested when I told them you were crying in the room that night. But I told them you said it was because of someone you once went with."

"You say a lot of things when you're raped, Holly."

"Are you going to be able to prove it?"

"Who knows? Do *you* believe me, Holly?"

"I don't have anything to go on. In some ways, I know Jimmy better than I know you."

"And the Jimmy you know could never rape anyone."

"I'm not saying I don't believe you. I just don't know what to believe."

"He might have taken you out that night and not me. And you're the one who might have been raped."

"Assuming he'd do anything like that."

"Right. And I'd be the one listening to you, saying, 'Why would Jimmy possibly do a thing like that?'"

"I'm sorry."

"I understand. But let me tell you this, Holly: no matter what the police think, no matter what the people on this campus think," she said fiercely, "Jimmy Andrews raped me. It was rape."

DETECTIVE NEARY QUESTIONED Janna Willis, who said Jimmy was a thoughtful, honest person and he wouldn't rape anyone. The detective was unable to learn anything pertinent to the rape accusation.

Convinced his integrity was just as she had presented it to the detective, Janna asked Jimmy to work on a little project.

They could set up a tennis net in a school gymnasium in Caldwell, and on Saturday mornings Jimmy could give tennis lessons to the children from the day care center. He found this open appeal to a positive side of his nature welcome. He also thought it would look good with the police in terms of his character. He gave the children a lesson, and the director of the center asked if he would come back to do it again every week. With Janna standing by smiling, confirmed in her judgment, he said of course, he would be delighted.

DONNA AND STERLING were interviewed. They were passionate in their belief that Jimmy Andrews had raped Elizabeth. In separate meetings with Neary, they were consistent in recalling Elizabeth's response to the rape awareness event. Neither, however, could provide evidence to support Elizabeth's accusation.

Mallory and Neary went to see Jean Philips in her office. She reiterated the testimony she gave before the grievance board. Elizabeth Mason was a rape victim. No pattern in her behavior indicated a tendency to lie. Her dreams, her responses, were those of a rape victim. For all her conviction on the subject, though, Philips could not offer any proof that Jimmy Andrews was the assailant, other than believing her patient's word.

SETH EPSTEIN WATCHED for the detectives and overtook them in the parking lot.

"I know you're conducting an investigation. I don't want you to overlook anything important."

Seth was wearing a stained ski jacket, an old sweatshirt, torn dungarees, soiled sneakers.

"Do you have direct knowledge of something relevant?" Mallory asked, taking in his appearance.

"Not direct. But I've been following this closely. The people you've interviewed. What you're likely to find out."

"You've been following our activities closely?" Neary said.

"Liz Mason's my friend, so I've taken a personal interest in this case."

"You have?" Neary said. "Encyclopedia Brown, are you?"

"Your problem is evidence," Seth stated confidently. "That's what gave the grievance board their opportunity to weasel out of it. That's what's going to be a problem in your investigation."

"Thank you for pointing that out to us," Mallory responded.

"I've been hanging around, mostly at The End Zone, which is right next to The Big Leagues, and I've been in The Big Leagues too."

"Hanging around? What do you mean?" Mallory asked, wondering what a kid like Seth Epstein would possibly do to be welcome by the oldest students on campus. His first thought was drugs.

"I'm a computer wiz. I know that sounds pompous, to call yourself a wiz, but I am. And I make up computer games. I made some up and I sold them to the guys at The End Zone and also a guy at The Big Leagues."

"And?" Mallory said.

"I learned something important about the people who live in those houses. They're big shots. They really think they're hot stuff."

The detectives waited for Seth to go on. He had nothing further to give them.

"That's it?" Mallory asked.

"It shows a frame of mind," Seth said. "Big shots, who think they're above it all."

"Do you have anything else?" Mallory asked.

"No, but I'll keep my eyes and ears open. I'm on the case."

"That's very reassuring," Mallory said.

• • •

THE DETECTIVES WANTED to see the interior of the house where the rape was alleged to have taken place. They chose a time midmorning, when most of the residents would be in class. One of the men was drinking coffee in the living room. The detectives asked if they could look around. He was hesitant, but they convinced him it was in Jimmy's interest. They walked through the rooms on the main floor, looked at the bedrooms, then went downstairs to the basement and the music room. The room was as the Mason girl had described it.

"Would you take someone down here for sex, if you had a bedroom upstairs?" Neary asked.

"If I had a bedroom with a roommate, I might." Mallory turned on the stereo to an FM station. "Give me a minute and start screaming."

He closed the door behind him and ascended the stairs. Standing in the living room, the music playing in the basement, he could barely hear Neary's screams. He moved to the other rooms and couldn't hear her at all. He reported to her back in the music room.

"Right above us, you can hardly hear anything. Nothing from the other parts of the house. Plus he was on top of her. Maybe his body muffled the sound. I should get one of these young boys to jump on your bones and then do a test."

"Cute. But you can hear from the living room?"

"Very slight. There's a stereo there. If that was still on, you wouldn't hear anything."

"The party was over. People left," Neary said.

"The music still might have been playing. Let's try it with music on in both places."

They tested it that way, Neary listening this time from the living room while Mallory called out in the downstairs room. Then she turned off the living room stereo.

"With the music off upstairs," she said, "I could hear you, but it was very faint. With the music on, nothing."

"So depending on where people were, and what was on,

she could have screamed for help and nobody would have heard her,'' Mallory concluded.

JIMMY WAS TAKING Janna to the movies on a Saturday night. A party was being held at The Big Leagues, and he stopped for a beer before he left. Someone seemed interested in him. She was a sophomore from Syracuse, eager to play, he thought, and he was sure he could have had her if he wanted to. But he had come to feel very apprehensive, with the police continuing to investigate. He thought he shouldn't do anything to jeopardize his relationship with Janna. She was important to him now. She gave him respectability.

CARL PETERS RETURNED a phone call from Ben Mason and informed him that they were still investigating. Ben had been calling every few days to check on their progress. He thought about the rape obsessively. Now that he had seen the rapist, he could imagine the attack in detail. Ben sat numbly in his office or at home, seeing Jimmy Andrews ravaging Elizabeth.

THE BIG LEAGUES, where Jimmy lived, and on either side of it, The End Zone and The Sports Complex were sometimes called sports row, because of the number of athletes who lived there. The boys from these houses greeted Elizabeth with hostility whenever they saw her. Others who were at the party and who resented being brought into a police matter were cold to her. Aware of the anger directed toward her, Seth, Donna, and Sterling individually or in combinations made certain that she was never by herself if she wanted company.

One evening, Shannon and Allison approached Elizabeth in the dorm.

''Are you pleased with yourself?'' Allison said to her.

''Meaning?''

''We're living in a dragnet.''

"I tried to keep this within the family. I brought it to the board. It didn't work out."

"You lost," Shannon said. "You had no case."

"Oh? Are you suddenly prelaw?" Elizabeth said.

"They're going to come down on us because of your little-princess complaints," Allison said. "Without parties and a few beers, this place will be a goddamn tomb," Shannon added.

"I'm not a princess. What would you do if you were raped—throw a party?"

"Jimmy says he never raped you. That you made it all up," Shannon said.

"Why would I? You think this is pleasant for me? To have our local sex goddesses tell me how I might mess up their social lives?"

She walked away from them.

THE HOSTILITY DIRECTED toward Elizabeth by some of the people on campus continued, but the more extreme element of men added a vulgar change. At times she heard them behind her, men smacking their lips in a mocking, kissing sound.

THE DETECTIVES CONTINUED their interviews for two weeks. One person they wanted to speak to, Betty Whelan of the women's lacrosse team, was off campus with knee surgery. She was said to have dated Jimmy for a brief period of time in the early part of the semester. She had not been at the party on September 2. Two men who were there and left early were also on a list of less important leads. The students would be leaving for their Christmas break soon, and the detectives were ready to give Peters their report. Mallory and Neary discussed whether to bother with these last interviews. Their commitment to persistent police work prevailed. The interviews with the two men were unproductive. They waited for Betty Whelan to return to campus and questioned her in a student lounge. Betty, a junior, was an athletic-looking blonde with a wholesome appearance.

"Do you know what's going on around here regarding Jimmy Andrews?" Mallory asked.

"I heard."

"On September second, there was a party at The Big Leagues. Were you there?"

"No. I met Jimmy a week or so after that."

"And you dated him?" Neary said.

"You can call it that. We were together for a few weeks."

"Where did you meet him?" Neary asked.

"At a party at The End Zone."

"And you're sure you don't have your parties mixed up, that you might have been at The Big Leagues?" Mallory said.

"No, I know where I come in. Somewhere after Liz Mason and before Janna Willis."

"How do you know where Liz Mason comes in?" Mallory asked, reacting to this opening.

"Jimmy told me."

"When?"

"We were standing around one day, and he was playing some dumb game about who was good in bed. A girl walked by, and he said he knew she wasn't good in bed because he started off the semester with her."

"Did he say that?" Mallory asked.

"Yes."

"Do you know Liz Mason?" Neary asked.

"No."

"How do you know we're talking about the same person?"

"Jimmy mentioned her name. 'Liz Mason. C minus,'" he said.

"Tell me exactly the conversation you had with him about her," Mallory said.

"She walked by, and Jimmy said, 'Liz Mason. C minus,'

and I said, 'How would you know?' And he said, 'I scored with her. I started off the semester with her.'"

"You remember that clearly? Those were his exact words?" Mallory said.

"Yes."

"Did he ever say anything else about her?" Neary asked.

"No."

"You're certain he said, 'I scored with her. I started off the semester with her'? And he identified her to you?" Mallory asked.

"Yes."

"He never said anything else?" Mallory said.

"Nothing."

"Thank you for talking to us, Betty," Neary said.

"I don't think he raped anybody."

"No?" Mallory said.

"He's not that kind of person."


"SO OUR DARLING boy tells somebody that he scored with Elizabeth Mason," Mallory said to Neary as they were driving back toward police headquarters. "That's heavy, Ann."

"He could have just been boasting."

"Or not."

They immediately reported the conversation to Carl Peters, who had an office on a floor above police headquarters in the Caldwell municipal building.

"This is a change in the weather," Peters said. "We've got him actually saying he had sex with her. Was this Betty Whelan credible?"

"Seemed to be," Mallory said.

"I think so," Neary responded.

"All right, give me your rundown."

"At about seven-thirty," Mallory said, reading from notes, "Jimmy Andrews picked up Elizabeth Mason at her dorm, and they walked over to The Babbling Brook for hamburgers. They were seated at seven forty-five and left at nine," Mallory said. "The party was in progress when they arrived at nine-ten, and people were sitting around and talking, drinking, a few were dancing. People began leaving for other parties, and by eleven-forty this one was basically over. Only six people were left in the house, with Andrews and Mason still there. None of them saw anything. The alleged rape would have taken place after eleven-forty."

"Did anyone see her drinking?" Peters asked.

"Several people. No one could recall anything specific about how much she had to drink."

"Anyone see *him* drinking?"

"He was seen with a bottle of beer in his hand all through the party. It could have been one beer or many. We just don't know," Neary answered.

"The doctor who examined her is convinced the contusions on her neck were inflicted by someone, as opposed to her walking into something," Mallory said.

"That's a long way from raped," Peters commented.

"It still leaves us with how her neck got bruised," Mallory said.

"Andrews says to someone he had sex with the girl. Andrews and the girl are together only one night, September second," Peters said. "And that's the night she claims he raped her. I'd love to have a go at him. Let's see if we can get him in here. Innocently, ask him to stop by. That we just have a few questions to help us drop the case."

"Let's do him before these marvelous kids go home to their marvelous Christmases," Neary said.

THE NEXT DAY, Detective Mallory walked up to Jimmy Andrews outside his house. Mallory was as casual as he could be. He said they just wanted to clear up a few details. Jimmy instinctively refused. He said he had to speak to his lawyer. He went upstairs and called MacNeil immediately.

"The police are investigating. They talked to some people around here, and they want to talk to me."

"So the girl reported it. All right, so be it. Don't talk to anybody. I'll handle this. Tell that to your parents."

"Do they have to know?"

"Of course they have to know! Call them!"

JIMMY REACHED HIS father at his office. Malcolm was so upset by Jimmy's call he left work. He was worried that Penny, who had barely held herself together during the hearing, might tell somebody about the investigation. He was considering not saying anything to her until there were other developments, but by the time he came home, she knew. MacNeil had tried to call Malcolm at his office, missed him there, and called the house, informing Penny. She'd had three vodka martinis before Malcolm arrived.

"Police?" she said to Malcolm when he entered the house.

"The girl went to the police. It's nothing to worry about. Formalities. They're not going to come up with anything that didn't come out of the hearing."

"Police!" she shouted.

"Take it easy, Penny. We have to contain this. Nobody knows."

"Why is he being investigated?"

"If she filed a complaint, they're obliged to follow up. MacNeil is on it. We'll take care of it."

"Why are they doing this to Jimmy?" she asked.

MACNEIL EXPLAINED TO Malcolm on the phone that evening that Jimmy had the right not to submit to questioning by the police. The only reason to agree to it was if they felt Jimmy could be so convincing the case would be dropped.

"Then we'd be done with it," Malcolm said.

"Only if he's convincing."

"You spoke to him. He didn't rape that girl. That's what the panel said."

"Let's not lose the thread here, Mr. Andrews. The panel didn't question him. The police will."

"Well, suppose he doesn't talk to them. Would we be done with it any faster?"

"They'll probably keep investigating until they come to some conclusions."

"I've had enough of this girl and her insane charges. If Jimmy talks to them and they believe him, it's over, isn't it?"

"I would say so. But I'd prefer to keep them away from him. Let *them* make the case."

"I don't want a case. It's already caused too many repercussions. I don't want my family to have to deal with this anymore."

"Having Jimmy questioned may not get you there."

"I want out, Mr. MacNeil. Jimmy's a very convincing young man. They'll see that, and we'll be done with it."

"Mr. Andrews, I prefer not to take any risks."

"I'm walking on eggs. My wife could tell somebody about this any minute. My clients could hear. It has to be closed off. Let them talk to Jimmy, and we're done with it."

"I really advise against it."

"I've had enough. Get us out of it!"

"Let me talk to the D.A. Maybe we can work out some kind of deal."

EAGER TO QUESTION Jimmy Andrews, Peters agreed to make an arrangement with MacNeil. Nothing could be used against his client; it was solely for background information, and MacNeil could be present. MacNeil informed Jimmy about the arrangement and asked:

"Is there anything else you have to tell me about this? Now is the time."

"It happened just as I said."

"All right. Give them the exact version of the events that you gave me, not one thing more."

ON THE DAY of the interview with the police, Malcolm walked into Jimmy's room and cuffed Jimmy playfully on the chin. The gesture looked as if he were following an out-of-date manual he'd read on how to be manly with your son in a time of crisis. MacNeil arrived and had Jimmy rehearse his version of the events carefully before they went to police headquarters. The lawyer made Jimmy go over it three times to ensure that his presentation was smooth.

CARL PETERS INTRODUCED everyone in his office. Peters sat behind his desk, Jimmy in a chair facing him. Malcolm and MacNeil were on a sofa on one side of the room, the detectives in chairs on the other.

"You know by now about the investigation," Peters said to Jimmy. "Elizabeth Mason claims you raped her. We'd like to hear your side. Our agreement is that nothing you say here will be used against you in a court of law. This is to help us determine whether or not to drop the case."

"No problem," Jimmy said.

He maintained a nonchalant attitude during the first phase of questioning, as the detectives and the prosecutor questioned him about how and when he first met Elizabeth Mason. Jimmy recalled how they were introduced at the barbecue, the movie evening together with her roommate, and then his invitation to the party. His story was identical to the girl's to this point. The questioning proceeded to the night of their date together.

"Do you remember what time you picked her up?" Peters asked.

"It must have been around seven-thirty, eight."

"And what did you do?"

"We went to The Babbling Brook for hamburgers."

"What did you talk about?" Mallory asked.

"School, the future. She liked to talk a lot."

"And you don't?" Peters said.

"Not the way she was talking. She wanted 'serious' conversation. 'Meaningful' talk," he said sarcastically, "where you're supposed to tell your innermost thoughts on a first date."

"You didn't like that?" Peters said.

"She was making it into real important stuff, how that was the way you're supposed to relate."

"Did it make you angry?" Peters asked.

"Just a little bored. I was happy when we could get to the party."

"And what happened there?" Mallory asked.

"People were standing around, kidding around, some were dancing."

"Drinking?" Neary said.

"Beer."

"Did you drink beer?" Neary asked.

"I had a beer."

"And at the restaurant?"

"I had a beer there."

"Did she drink?" Neary said.

"She had a few beers."

"They served her in the restaurant?" Peters asked.

"Not there. At the house."

"Who served her there?"

"It was an open bar."

"Did you ever get her a beer?" Peters wanted to know.

"Excuse me," MacNeil said. "We're not trying to slip in a charge of serving alcohol to a minor, are we?"

"Now, we wouldn't do that to your client," Peters answered. "We'd like to know how much people had to drink. What we have so far is the girl drank 'a few beers.' Jimmy, you only had two, you say. One at the restaurant and one at the party."

"That's right."

"So she was drinking more than you, was she? And you had one beer, when some of the guys we talked to said they had four and five," Peters said to him.

"That's what I remember."

"All right, what happened then? The evening didn't end on your one beer at the party," Peters remarked.

"People talked, danced, drank beer. The usual party stuff."

"What did you and Elizabeth Mason do?"

"Same as the others."

"People said they saw you kissing her in the living room. Did you kiss her, Jimmy?" Peters asked.

"I must have."

"Do you remember kissing her?"

"Yes."

"How many times?" Peters said.

"Three, I guess."

"So all her talking didn't turn you off to where you wouldn't kiss her?" Neary said.

"She was coming on to me."

"And you kissed her because she was coming on to you, this girl you were bored with. You didn't take her home. You didn't end the evening. You kissed her," Mallory said.

"It was no big deal."

"We'll decide what's a big deal here and what isn't," Peters said.

"Jimmy came in here of his own free will," said Malcolm Andrews, who had sat quietly through the previous questioning. "You don't have to talk to him in this manner."

"Mr. Andrews, this is our investigation, thank you. Jimmy, were you kissing her because you wanted to see where it would lead?" Peters asked.

"It was nothing. Just the way the party was going."

"Was there any other sexual transaction between you?" Neary asked him.

"No."

"This all took place in the living room?" Peters said.

"Yes."

"You just stopped kissing her and then you took her back to her dorm," Peters said.

"I was thinking if I took her back maybe I could make it to one of the other parties."

"Is that what happened?" Neary said.

"I never went anywhere else. I told her that nothing much was happening at our house and I'd see her back to the dorm. And she got angry. She started saying things: I thought you liked me; I thought we were going to have a relationship. I could see we were going nowhere together. And I told her."

"What did you say to her?" Neary asked.

"I tried to be diplomatic. I said people sometimes don't hit it off in every way, but that didn't mean we still couldn't be friendly to each other. And she got really angry and she stormed out. Next thing she's calling me up. When are we going to see each other again? She's stopping me in public and saying crazy things. How she thought we had something important together, a relationship. Crazy. One date, a few kisses. We had no relationship. To get back at me for not seeing her again, she concocts this story that I raped her."

"In the college hearing, she said you took her down to a room in the basement of the house and that's where the rape took place. Did you take her to that room?" Mallory asked.

"I did. When we first got to the party. I showed her around the house. My roommate was in our room with his girlfriend. He could tell you that."

"This girl you can't wait to dump you show around the house?" Mallory asked.

"It was in the beginning of the evening, before she began to get to me."

"How is it that a couple of people who were the last to leave the party don't remember seeing you in the living room?" Neary asked.

"She must have gone home already, and I must have gone upstairs."

"Was your roommate there?"

"He was out."

"And you never took her into the basement room except at the beginning of the evening?" Neary said.

"That's right."

"Nobody else recalls dancing with you that night, Jimmy. Who else did you dance with?" Mallory said.

"I don't remember."

"Who else did you have a conversation with?"

"There were people around. It could have been anybody."

"Nobody remembers talking to you, not for more than a quick few words," Mallory said.

"They don't remember. Neither do I."

"Is the reason they don't remember you dancing with anybody or talking to anybody that you were paying so much attention to this girl you claim you couldn't bear?" Mallory asked.

"I only learned how little I liked her as the evening went on, when she started to wear me down with her talking."

"You didn't do more than kiss her in the living room? You never took her anywhere else in the house to kiss her or do anything else with her?" Peters said.

"That's right."

"Jimmy, do you know a girl named Betty Whelan?" Peters said.

"Yes."

"You went out with her for a while, didn't you?"

"A while."

"Did you tell Betty Whelan that you scored with Elizabeth Mason?"

"I don't know."

"She says you did. She says you told her you scored with Elizabeth Mason."

"I don't remember saying that to her."

"For what possible reason would she tell us that she was positive you said to her you had sex with Elizabeth Mason?" Peters said.

"I can't say. Maybe she can say."

"She's on record as telling us you told her that."

MacNeil could not refrain from biting the inside of his gum in consternation at this piece of information.

"Maybe I said something, sort of like bragging. To impress her."

"With what a cocksman you are?" Mallory said.

"About being kind of a big guy at school, thinking she'd be impressed with that."

"Because you wanted to score with Betty Whelan?" Mallory said. "That's the kind of card you play, your cocksmanship?"

"It was talk, that's all."

"Did you score with Elizabeth Mason?" Peters said.

"No. Absolutely not."

"What you told Betty Whelan was a story. You were conning her?"

"It was a kind of bragging."

"All right, Jimmy, I'll give you your choice," Peters said. "Were you conning Betty Whelan when you told her you scored with Elizabeth Mason, or are you conning us now when you tell us you didn't? Which is the con job, Jimmy?"

MacNeil intervened. "If this were a courtroom, I'd object to your badgering the witness."

"Very well, Mr. MacNeil, you answer it for your client. When is he conning? When he tells somebody he had sex with Elizabeth Mason, which had to be the one night he was with the Mason girl—the night she says he raped her? Or is he conning us now when he says he never had sex with her?"

"He answered the question. He never had sex with the alleged victim. It was bragging."

"Elizabeth Mason has had a vendetta out for you ever since that night. Is that correct, Jimmy?" Peters said.

"Yes. She's weird."

"And on that night, even though she was coming on to you, kissing you—you, a person who uses sexual exploits as a way of trying to impress girls—you decide that you don't like how much she *talks*, and you choose to end the evening without sex?" Peters said.

"I'm sure Jimmy missed a question, if there was one in there, Mr. Peters."

"Simple questions, then. Did you rape Elizabeth Mason?"

"No," Jimmy answered.

"Did you have sex with Elizabeth Mason?"

"No."

"Did you say you had sex with Elizabeth Mason?"

"Yes."

"So in spite of what you *said*, you didn't have sex with Elizabeth Mason; you only said you did."

"He already answered that several times," MacNeil said.

"So he did. We thank you gentlemen for your 'cooperation,'" Peters said, terminating the interrogation.

MacNeil, seething, did not speak for several minutes after they left police headquarters. They walked in silence to his car. He drove to the end of town and parked on a side street.

"Jimmy, this is not some game you're in. You're the subject of a criminal investigation! You could be charged with rape."

"I didn't rape her."

"I'm your lawyer. I'm defending you. Answer me without the bullshit. Nobody has to know but us. Did you have sex with Elizabeth Mason?"

"Yes."

"Jimmy?" Malcolm said, mystified.

"You told me you didn't," MacNeil said.

"I was scared."

"Beautiful. You were scared."

"I got the notice from the dean, and I didn't know what to do. I figured it would be better to not say I scored with her, better if I just said I made that up."

"How many people did you tell you had sex with Elizabeth Mason?"

"Betty Whelan and a couple of the guys at the house. Four people maybe."

"Fabulous."

"I didn't know she was going to turn out to be so crazy. The part about her calling me up and saying things in public, all that is true."

"You can't blame him," Malcolm said, "dealing with an unstable girl."

"She's only doing all this because I rejected her," Jimmy said.

"Is this Psych 101?" MacNeil responded. "Suddenly, she's not so unstable. Suddenly, you're telling me you did have sex with her. The question now is what kind of sex?"

"She was coming on to me. She kept rubbing up against me and I just kept going as far as I could and she never objected and we did it."

"Where did this take place? In the basement room?"

"Yes."

"So she's not making that up. Was it with her full consent?"

"Absolutely."

"Was there force?"

"No."

"And after that night did you have sex with her again?"

"That was it. I was going to walk her back to the dorm, but I didn't say the right thing or something. I didn't tell her I really, really cared for her. And she got crazy."

"Yes, that word again," MacNeil said.

"I decided she wasn't worth the talking. I never called her again, and that must have freaked her out."

"It's terrible what she's done," Malcolm declared.

"Please, Mr. Andrews! We've gone from dealing with someone who's 'crazy'—Jimmy's characterization—to someone who merely has a different interpretation of a sexual act."

"I didn't rape her, Mr. MacNeil."

"Jimmy, from now on you keep your mouth shut about this case. Don't tell anyone your psychological interpretations. Don't tell anyone you slept with her or you didn't sleep with her or that you said you did but you didn't or that you said you didn't but you did. Let them make the case. It's still thin. Don't hand them anything."

"Yes, sir."

"That's almost too long a sentence for you. Keep your mouth shut. We've had enough of your brilliant strategies."

AFTER THE QUESTIONING, the prosecutor and the detectives went over their notes on Jimmy's appearance.

"I can't stand any of these kids," Neary offered.

"I don't believe a word he's saying," Mallory told the others.

"He didn't sell me," Peters said. "But maybe she had too much to drink and got out of control. In the testimony at the college, she said she went into the downstairs room with him. She never claimed he dragged her down there. Is it possible she let him screw her and was feeling guilty or angry afterward and decided to call it rape?"

"No," Mallory said.

"I don't know," Neary offered.

"It is possible she was trying to get back at him when he didn't call again?" Peters asked.

"No way," Mallory said flatly. "The bruises. Where did she get the bruises?"

"Rough sex?" Neary said.

"I think what happened," Mallory suggested, "is this wise guy was figuring, If I just keep going, she'll go all the way. But she didn't. And he kept going anyway. Right up to raping her."

"Well, I don't believe him," Peters said. "But basically all we've got for our time is her word against his. I'm never going to get a conviction on that."

# CHAPTER
# 12

BEN MASON, DETECTIVE, could have cracked the case. He would have hired actors to come up to Jimmy Andrews when he was on the street, the actors saying, "Aren't you the guy who raped Elizabeth Mason?" Everywhere Andrews turned, somebody would be saying that to him. He would get notes in his mail, he would get calls in his room: "Aren't you the guy who raped Elizabeth Mason?" He would become rattled, frightened, lose his arrogance. Under brutal, repetitive interrogation, he would waver, inconsistencies would emerge. They would have him. Or Ben would trail him like vapor, surrounding his every move, using sophisticated sound equipment to catch him saying the wrong thing about the incident. When he realized that wherever he went he would be hounded by the crime he had committed, he would fall apart.

Ben developed these ideas from the crime novels he had begun to read constantly, good ones and bad ones. He was taking long lunch hours, leaving work early, to read his books, studying the cases in the books, marking key sections with a liner as if he were taking a course in school. Laura learned all this from his assistants. At home he would have sweeping mood swings. The grandparents were told about the rape, and they began to call, upset and anxious for information. If Ben answered the phone, he delivered long, tangled discourses on the procedure in investigations and crimes, quoting the detective novels he had read, recommending that they read them.

"Ben, I really think you should see someone," Laura said, "a therapist to help you."

"I don't need a therapist," he replied.

"I'll get the name of somebody. It's a terrible strain, I know."

"I'm perfectly fine. If I'm a little overinvolved with the matter, I think that's altogether understandable."

LAURA WOULD PASS BEN as he sat in the living room, and sometimes he had stopped reading his latest book and would be staring straight ahead, lost in speculations. Often Laura had to repeat questions to him. When they made love now, he was detached.

The weekly tennis game with Phil Stern was modified after Phil developed elbow problems. Phil and Ben now played doubles with two friends of Ben's, Tony Pappas, a commercial art designer, and Roger Mack, another folk art dealer. Laura asked the men if they could encourage Ben to seek help, and each said he would see what he could do. They were getting dressed in the locker room after their latest match, when Phil said:

"This thing has you down, doesn't it?"

"What do you expect?" Ben answered.

"Maybe you should seek some counseling, Ben," Tony said. "It has helped people."

"I don't need a shrink. What I need is a master detective."

Ben launched into a detailed analysis of the case against Jimmy Andrews. He presented this in a precise, controlled manner. The men did not pick up on the obsession; they

only heard what was on the surface and were impressed
with his mastery of the case.

"We brought it up," Phil told Laura on the phone that
night. "He wasn't buying. He's under a strain, but who can
blame him?"

"We're all under a strain," she replied.

"If it were me, I'd be climbing the walls."

Phil turned the phone over to Jane, and after he left the
room, Jane said to Laura:

"What Phil didn't tell you," Jane said, "is that they
came out of this with the titles of detective novels Ben
suggested they read."

"I asked them to help me get Ben into therapy because
he's falling apart, and they end up sharing his detective
novels."

ELIZABETH WENT THROUGH her final exams of the fall semester
and assumed she did well enough to pass her subjects. She
packed her duffel, said goodbye to her friends, and boarded
a bus for New York. Exhausted by everything, she napped
on and off during the ride into the city. She needed to
separate herself from Layton College, to get back into
familiar city modes. She called Melanie Stern, who was in
from Wisconsin for the holidays, and Sarah Clemens.

Wanting to spend a little time alone with her brother, she
took him to lunch in a neighborhood pizza place. They
talked about Josh's school term for a while, but he was
fidgety, tearing his napkin into little pieces. Then he brought
up the subject that was on his mind.

"This person—do you see him at school?"

"He's not in any of my classes."

"He hurt you?"

"I'm okay. I'm buying. The pizza's on me."

"Mom said he's a tennis player."

"He is."

"He plays for Layton?"

"Yes, but I don't imagine I'll be going to see him play."

"An athlete shouldn't do anything like that. He shouldn't have done something so bad."

"The police are involved. Maybe he'll be punished."

"We were studying chivalry in school, and in olden times, I would have avenged your honor. I would have slain him in battle," he said with seriousness.

"You just grow up to be a good man. That'll be honor enough."

ELIZABETH AND MELANIE went to a movie and then to a Third Avenue pasta restaurant.

"You look tired," Melanie said.

"I am. I'd like to sleep for a year. But if I did, I bet I'd wake up and the first thing somebody would say to me is, 'Hey, remember, you were raped.'"

"It's always on your mind?"

"It's never that far away. And with the hearing and then going to the police, it stays alive. Like snakes in your closet. But enough about me. What do *you* think of my rape?"

"Why are there such creeps out there?"

"Funny how your standards change. Forget sensitive, intelligent, and nice-looking. Right now I'd settle for a guy who wouldn't rape me."

SHE WENT WITH SARAH to see *Gypsy* on Broadway. Walking along the street after the performance, Sarah asked:

"Did it inspire you to sing?"

"I haven't even thought of singing," Elizabeth answered. "There's been so much else happening."

"All negative. You have to put positive forces back into your life."

"The Maharishi of Juilliard."

"Truly. It's a waste."

"Not for my public. I have no public."

"I'm your public."

Sarah sang in her small voice, trying to encourage her.
"'Curtain up . . .' Sing it for me."

"I just don't sing anymore, Sarah."

THE GRANDPARENTS ARRIVED for Hanukkah and the traditional
gift competition. Ben's parents gave a CD player to Elizabeth, a shortwave radio to Josh. Laura's parents countered
with a telephone answering machine for Elizabeth and a
Walkman for Josh. Checks came from both sides for Ben
and Laura. The Masons contributed nightgowns, socks,
blouses, shirts for their parents, a sweater for Elizabeth,
baseball cards for Josh, as they all sat around a little lake of
boxes and tissue paper. Ben was cheerful for a time, then
looked at the gifts scattered about the living room, running
a perverse "This is the cat that ate the cheese . . ." ditty
through his mind: "This is the affluence that bought the
life-style that needed the private school that fed into the
college that led to the rape of my daughter."

Ben's mother asked if Elizabeth was okay after "you
know," unable to say the word. Elizabeth told them she was
hoping the prosecutor in Caldwell would bring the case to
trial successfully so she could be vindicated. Ben's father
insisted that to get the rapist behind bars, what was required
was "top dollar," and he was willing to go in with them so
they could hire "one of those big lawyers who handle the
big trials." Ben pointed out to his father that it was the other
side who hired the lawyers, the defendant's side, and
Elizabeth's side was taken by the prosecutor.

Laura struggled to make a transition to Josh, to his school
year, and yet they continued to talk about the crime, the
college hearing, the investigation. She vainly attempted to
introduce what had been the most recent cover story at the
magazine, log cabin housing, not a hot enough subject to
command the floor. Ben drifted into his obsessive pattern,
explaining his principles of police work from detective
novels he had read. Josh excused himself to watch television, while Laura and Elizabeth remained in the room, upset

to see Ben carry on that way. He moderated an aimless, uninformed discussion among the grandparents, correcting them, adding to their remarks. Ben Mason was out of control, working the room as if he were a talk-show host.

THE MASONS HAD made no plans for the Christmas vacation, preoccupied as they were with the crime. Apart from general plans to see Sarah and Melanie again, Elizabeth was not committed to do anything during Christmas week. Laura thought it would be good to have a family vacation. She called a travel agent, hoping to get them on a flight to a warm-weather place, preferably the Caribbean, where they had the best chance for clear skies at that time of year. When she mentioned the idea of getting away to Ben, he started mumbling about ''affluence.'' This was the very reason they needed a vacation, she said to him—he was mumbling to himself. Elizabeth and Josh were excited about the idea. Theirs was a family in desperate need of a vacation. The travel agent said they were too late in making the request; people planned Christmas vacations months in advance, and the flights were booked.

In one of the changes of temperament that characterized his behavior, suddenly Ben was going to save the day. He called a customer of his, an executive at American Airlines, and the Masons were booked for Christmas Day on a flight to St. Thomas, with a return a week later, on New Year's Day; they would stay at a condominium where American Airlines had connections.

On the flight down to St. Thomas, Elizabeth looked out the window at the clouds and the distant landscape below and imagined the plane plunging out of the skies. It would explode on contact. You have to make it happen instantly so nobody suffers. Your parents and your brother don't have to grieve; they're gone too. You don't have to go through the humiliation of the prosecutor deciding *not* to bring it to trial, or the public exposure if it came to trial. You get to be remembered as a nice girl.

She saw it happening, the plane going down and bursting
into flames. Then she saw Jimmy Andrews reading about it
in the newspaper. He knew he shouldn't, it was too indecent
because so many other people had died, but he couldn't hold
back a smile. He was totally free. Exonerated by the college.
Given a gift from heaven. He strolled along, feeling great,
bouncing in his stride. Like hell! She willed the plane to fly
safely, and when it descended, she felt as if she had landed
it by virtue of her own willpower.

AMID THE PALM TREES and the rum drinks, Ben became
slightly subdued on the subject of the police investigation.
He could go for a full day without introducing the matter.

He had brought down a stack of detective novels in a
carrying bag, like a squirrel hoarding nuts. On vacation in
the Caribbean, he was underlining passages. The Masons
played tennis as a foursome, went to different beaches on
the island, sunbathed, snorkeled. Although he had been a
reasonably competent swimmer, Ben was swimming with
furious, choppy strokes. When the children were little,
Laura and Ben would keep them in view when they were in
deep water. Laura now told the children to make sure that
they always kept their father in sight.

Ben had become extremely controlling, planning each
day's schedule at breakfast, suggesting dishes for people to
order at meals, cautioning them to add more skin protection,
to get out of the sun, into the water, out of the water.
Hectoring the waiters and waitresses in restaurants to speed
along the service, he was a jittery New Yorker doomed to
fail in his attempt to change the entire pace of the Caribbean.

On their last day of vacation, while they were snorkeling,
Ben suddenly hurried out of the water, went to a pay booth
in the beach restaurant, and phoned Carl Peters in Caldwell.
Standing in his dripping suit, Ben demanded to know why
more hadn't been made of the throat doctor's findings.
Peters told him they had considered the doctor's report and

the bruises. Everything was on hiatus until the students returned to campus, he explained.

At both airports, leaving St. Thomas and arriving in the city, Ben was overinvolved with making certain that all of their pieces of luggage were in a tight pattern and didn't get lost and that *they* stayed together and didn't become lost. Ben was wearing a Caribbean straw hat, which he wore rakishly at an angle. Nobody would have been able to tell by looking at him. He was a man with a terrific suntan in the middle of the winter who also happened to be having a nervous breakdown.

JIMMY AND HIS PARENTS were in Scottsdale, at a condominium owned by Penny's mother. They went there every Christmas. The complex encircled a gold course and featured tennis as part of the facilities. Malcolm had managed to make clients of several of the condominium owners. Scottsdale expanded Malcolm Andrews' business horizon, and holidays there were working vacations. This Christmas was no different from the others, even though back east a police investigation involving his son was being conducted. He certainly was not going to bring up the subject at the condominium, and the Andrews family did not discuss it among themselves. Penny looked out through the clear, calming liquid of vodka drinks in a chaise lounge. People imbibe more on vacations, she reasoned, as each night she drank herself to sleep.

Jimmy was at the tennis courts for several hours each day, to tune himself up for the spring tennis season, playing with the club pro, as his father had arranged, and with some of the better players in the complex. One evening, Penny had gone to bed, Jimmy was in the living room watching television, and Malcolm was drinking by himself on the terrace. He came into the room and suddenly said to Jimmy in an angry voice:

"Let's hope the police wind up this goddamn thing when you get back to school."

"Sorry it's put you out," Jimmy said, and walked from the room.

Before Jimmy went to sleep he thought about Janna. He reasoned that if a decent person like Janna accepted that he wasn't capable of rape, then he wasn't. As long as the police were still investigating, he felt it was very important to keep her in his corner. Jimmy decided that when he returned to school, he was going to take himself out of the competition.

PENNY SPOKE BRIEFLY with her mother, Elena Fisk, to wish her a happy New Year. Penny presumed her mother was sitting in her favorite white wicker chair, overlooking the pool and gardens in her house by the ocean in Palm Beach, Florida. The Captain had bought the house for her one year as a Valentine's Day present, and she spent her winters there. As she spoke to her mother, Penny could see her wearing her latest face-lift, smoking from a cigarette holder, a Tom Collins at the table to her side. Penny would not dare tell her about Jimmy's problems, and have the grande dame sit in judgment on her life, on her decision to marry Malcolm Andrews, and listen to her talk about "breeding."

When Malcolm had told Penny that Jimmy did have sex with the girl, Penny accepted Jimmy's explanation for not admitting it in the first place: he was scared because this girl was causing such problems. She couldn't begin to think of going into any of this with her mother.

"Everything is hunky-dory," Penny said.

AFTER THE TRIP, during the two weeks that remained of the winter break, Elizabeth wanted to work as a volunteer in a day care center on East 106th Street, where she had helped distribute clothing when she was in high school. She felt that not only would she be doing a good deed with her time, it would help get her out of her own head for a while. Ben was unsympathetic to the idea and worried about her safety traveling back and forth. Elizabeth, however, was adamant. She would be dealing with harmless children. She would take a bus; she would be all right. Ben then announced that Josh, who had been going to school and returning on his own for several years, needed his father to accompany him. "I'm fourteen years old!" Josh protested.

Laura told Ben he was in desperate need of help.

"I beg you to do this. I have the name of somebody eminent from Molly. She did an article about him."

"Look, I got to this point in my life without a shrink. I don't want to be hooked in for the next fifteen years."

"Ben, I'm thinking ahead to next week. You've got to see somebody. You're falling apart."

"Honey, it's so awful," he said. "Elizabeth was raped!"

"Yes, she was. And we have to live with it. You have to see somebody, Ben."

A CONSULTATION WAS ARRANGED with the psychiatrist, Dr. Isaac Fraiman, who conducted his practice from an office at Park Avenue and Eighty-sixth Street. Ben occupied a leather lounge chair, and the psychiatrist sat behind his desk. He was a small man in his seventies, with hunched shoulders, thinning white hair, thick glasses. This guy is too old and frail to do much good, Ben thought when he first saw him. Fraiman spoke with a slight European accent, in a soft voice that Ben had to strain to hear. Ben stated his hesitation about being there. He had avoided being in therapy all his life, and he wasn't thrilled about beginning now. He thought that his behavior in the past weeks was perfectly understandable and began to tell about Elizabeth's rape, the college hearing, and the police investigation. He slipped into a tangled monologue about the failures of the detectives and the shortcomings of the investigation.

"It sounds like the good father would like to solve the case and put everything right. Let me tell you how I operate, Ben. At this stage of my professional career, I don't do long-term therapy. I perform first aid for people who are in specific difficulty. That is you. If you wish to continue therapy with another therapist afterward, I welcome the thought for you. What I can do is help you through this time. Help you work through your rage and your feelings of helplessness in light of this crime. There is rage, is there not?"

"Yes, I suppose."

"And a feeling of helplessness?"

"Probably."

"You're functioning in all aspects of your life? What is your profession?"

"I run a folk art gallery."

"And you have been operating on all cylinders, reaping great business victories?"

"I've been reading a lot of detective novels," Ben responded sheepishly.

"Exactly. I charge one hundred dollars an hour. I would like to see you four times a week. Six-fifteen P.M., Mondays through Thursdays, is available. This therapy won't go on for years. Life is too short for you to be in this mental state."

BEN BEGAN THE SESSIONS. Fraiman worked in swift brush strokes. He would guide Ben to talk, listen to his responses, and then make a concise observation. He encouraged Ben to understand his rage. "A violation of a daughter. This is rage in a father on a classic level. Wars have been fought on such as this."

Fraiman led Ben to see that his surrogate detective work, the crime novels, the intricate, time-consuming speculations about the case, were examples of Ben thrashing around, helpless, unfocused. His controlling behavior with the family was an attempt to be so protective that nothing unfortunate could ever again befall any of them. He was trying to be the perfect father, to make everything right.

In one session, Ben was talking about how their lives had been proceeding so smoothly until this happened.

"What happened, Ben?"

"What do you mean?"

"Something happened that is not in the correct progression. You struggled, you succeeded, and then this. Much of what you are feeling is connected to success."

"I don't know what you're talking about," Ben said.

"You had a fantasy that one day you would be successful. And part of that fantasy was that once you were, you would be successful forever. Then this happened. Your daughter was raped. It says to you that you're not a success. Which is a cockamamy thought."

"If I'm thinking it."

"You are. Success, success, success, then rape. Rape equals failure. Ben, you didn't fail as a father because your daughter was raped. And she didn't fail as a daughter. There is no failure here. There shouldn't be such an emphasis on success, either, but I suggest you take that up later."

"I knew you hook people in," Ben joked.

"It was a terrible deed. And it's done. You can't do anything about it. You want to be a good parent; the best thing you can do is give support to your daughter, and you don't do that by becoming an unreliable, wacky father."

BY THE FOURTH WEEK of Ben's therapy, after sixteen sessions, he was beginning to become steadier, starting to phase out his detective novels, and regaining his concentration at work. Elizabeth had gone back to Layton for the spring term. When Ben spoke to Elizabeth, he did not bring up the case and talked only about her classes.

He stayed in touch with Peters, though. The district attorney kept telling him they did not have enough to prosecute but they were going to talk to some of the students again.

Laura continued to believe that the sooner Elizabeth proceeded with her life the better off she would be. For her to go back to school, start a new term, and still be mired in the progress of the investigation, with a possible trial and publicity, was unhealthy for her.

"Let's get Elizabeth out of it."

"The police are still investigating. *They* haven't dropped the case."

"It drags on. It holds her in place."

"This is best, to see that justice is done."

"For whom?" Laura said.

THE STUDENTS HAD RETURNED to school for the new semester. In Caldwell, a cocktail waitress was beaten one night outside the bar where she worked, the fourth such incident in recent weeks. Because the case was covered widely in the local media, it was assigned to Mallory and Neary and given priority over the campus investigation. Late at night in a Caldwell coffee shop, Mallory commented to Neary how far they were from a resolution of the Mason-Andrews rape case.

"The kid hasn't been accused of raping anyone else," Neary responded.

"What does that mean?"

"He's obviously not a mad rapist on a rampage."

"It was never that. It was a wise-ass pushing a girl as far as he could and going too far."

"So what happens if we don't get him? She's still in school. He's graduating. And it'll be done with," Neary said.

"But he raped her."

"*If* he raped her," Neary retorted. "And if she's really wrecked by this, her rich parents can transfer her out and she'll get right into Williams or some other fancy school and live a beautiful life."

"This isn't about whether *our* kids can get into Layton or not," Mallory asserted.

"Well, they can't, so you're right."

"What if she's just a nice girl who got raped?"

"You mean rich but nice."

"He raped her, Ann. I know what some guys get like when they've got a hard-on. He just kept pushing, and it became rape."

"And she was drinking, under age. It's not open and shut, and I'm not too worked up over it, Joe. No matter how *nice* she is."

NEARLY EVERY NIGHT after Josh went to sleep, Ben and Laura argued about whether or not the complaint should be dropped, a nasty tone simmering between them. Dinners with Josh were little performances, as the parents pretended to be getting along just fine. Ben's therapy was of no help in ameliorating the situation with Laura. Fraiman wanted him to see that they were both caught up in their rage and they had turned the rage upon each other. Ben conceded that might be true, but the case should proceed and they should lock the bastard up.

LAURA AND BEN used dinner in a restaurant with the Sterns as a forum. Phil Stern agreed with Ben and took the proceed-and-lock-him-up position, macho and certain. Jane sided with Laura and Is it best for Elizabeth? The couples stumbled from that into a discussion about the way men see things and women see things, the men insisting they lived in a more realistic, rational world, the women believing they were more practical while being humanistic. Laura went home feeling she had betrayed Elizabeth by allowing her daughter's personal dilemma to be the entertainment for the evening. She expressed those feelings to Ben before they went to bed, and they argued about that.

JOSH OVERHEARD HIS PARENTS arguing. Wanting to be taken seriously in the house, he considered it important to have an opinion. He called his lawyer uncle to learn what he could about whether or not the complaint should be pursued. After David made his explanation, Josh asked:

"What do *you* think?"

"I think it would be better for Liz to call it off. It's so difficult to get a conviction in these kinds of cases, and I wouldn't like to see it go on and on."

"But if they call it off, it's like Liz was a liar."

"That's a valid feeling, Josh. But feeling it may not be enough to win anything."

The next time he heard his parents arguing, Josh came into the bedroom and tried to be mature and responsible.

"I was talking to Uncle David about this—"

"What?" Laura said.

"He explained it to me. I think if the case is dropped, it makes Liz out to be a liar. She shouldn't be made out to be a liar."

"This is not something you should be worrying about," Laura said.

"How can he not be? He's in the house."

"You'd say that. Because he agrees with you."

"He expressed it very well. She shouldn't be made out to be a liar."

"Can we end this, please?" Laura said. "Ben, this has gotten too large. It's taking us over."

THE OPEN-ENDED aspect of the criminal investigation contributed to the acrimony between Laura and Ben. If the police decided further action was useless, the specific point of contention between them would be removed. Peters still regarded the case as current.

"This is begging for us to cut it off," Laura said to Ben. "Once and for all, can we have Elizabeth drop the complaint?"

"No. It's not what she wants, and it hasn't played itself out yet."

"It has for me," she said angrily.

IN HIS WEEKLY TENNIS game, Ben was hitting the ball as hard as he could. It helped ease his anger, at least for the time he was playing. After one match, he confided to Phil that he and Laura could no longer be in a room without arguing. Phil thought Laura and Ben had been coping as well as anyone could have under the circumstances. Their personal problems had not been apparent to him. His advice to a buddy was that women go through cycles, monthly, seasonal. To stay married, you just had to ride out a woman's cycle, he counseled. Ben managed a smile, knowing what Laura would think of that kind of attitude.

LAURA CONFIDED IN MOLLY Switzer and Karen Hart that the arguments with Ben had become incessant.

"Your daughter's been raped and you're both in pain. There has to be a strain on the marriage," Molly said.

"The fact is, when everything was going well for them, they were fine," Karen continued. "What they have, by definition, is a marriage where they fall apart in a crisis."

"I don't know how we can survive this. We can't talk without it being an argument."

"See a marriage counselor," Molly said. "Don't just stand there."

Laura made the proposal to Ben that they consult a therapist together.

"How much therapy can I handle?" he pleaded. "Why don't you simply stop making this into something you have to win?"

"Why don't *you*?"

"Laura, this will end eventually. They'll drop the case, or they'll pursue the case. There'll be a trial, or there won't be a trial. He'll go to jail, or he won't go to jail."

"When? How long do we have to wait? This is ruining our family, it's ruining our marriage."

"Elizabeth wants to see it through and I do and you don't. And you can't stand that."

"She was raped and there's no case against the rapist. That's why the police aren't getting anywhere. The sooner we accept that, the sooner we can get on with our lives."

"I can't accept it, and Elizabeth can't."

"Ben, this waiting for justice is keeping us all victims."

• • •

With the start of the new semester, Elizabeth observed a rush of energy on campus. Many of the people who had gone out of their way to make her feel uncomfortable were too preoccupied to think about her. The first week back, Elizabeth went to the movies and dinner with Seth, Donna, and Sterling. They talked about her belief that there was no vindication for her without a trial. Eventually, though, they drifted to other subjects: the new term, their new courses, other people, events in the news. Even with her friends the rape could not remain the only subject of interest.

A heavy snow fell. In the quadrangle, a group built a snowman that evening. Elizabeth thought of the scene in *Meet Me in St. Louis* where in a frenzy Margaret O'Brien wrecks the snowmen. She could take a broom out there and whack its head off. How dare you people have fun when somebody can get raped in this place and nobody cares? If I did that, they'd really think I'm crazy. Elizabeth looked out her window at the snow falling, covering everything, and it seemed as if the crime was being buried by snow.

# CHAPTER

# 13

JEAN PHILIPS ASKED to serve as Elizabeth's adviser for the
new semester. They met to discuss the courses she was
taking and went over her grades for the previous semester,
two C's and two B's. "Good, considering," Philips said.
She talked about some of the activities planned for the
Women's Center and said she hoped Elizabeth would
attend.

"Would you like to see me for counseling on some kind
of basis? Regular? Now and then?" Philips asked.

"I'd like to manage without it."

"I'm always here. Please remember that. What's going
on now with the police investigation?"

"It's moving slowly."

"We should do another rape awareness event and this
time make it mandatory for *men*. I know of two more rapes
here since yours."

"Two more?"

"The women told me in confidence, but they decided not
to report it."

"I wonder why," Elizabeth said sarcastically.

"One person was raped by someone she used to go with.

219

The other was at a party, drinking pretty heavily, and a guy she knew forced himself on her. Three this year,'' Philips said despairingly.

"We ought to have a scoreboard for this on the college green," Elizabeth responded.

HOLLY ROBERTSON DROPPED by the dorm to see Elizabeth, which was something of a surprise since she usually came by only for belongings she stored in the room.

"How's everything?" Holly said. "Pretty good to end up with a single for freshman year."

"I do have a lot of privacy."

"Liz, we're having a party at the house next Saturday. I know you're not too keen on that kind of thing, but I'd like you to come, and maybe bring the kids you hang out with too.''

"I'm *not* too keen on that kind of thing."

"I realize that. But there are a couple of nice guys in the group, and I think you'd have a good time. It would mean something to me if you came."

"It would?"

"Well, I remembered that first time we were talking, when we first met, and I said something about feeling too tall and wanting to get out of basketball. You said maybe I should look into dance. That always struck me as a very decent thing to say."

"I must have been thinking of Judith Jameson. I saw her on a ballet special. She was tall, very lovely."

"Whatever you were thinking of, you said it. And I told it to Pete and some of the guys, and that I thought you were probably a very decent person and I wanted to invite you to our party. Well, it became a real political issue in the house. Several of the guys absolutely refused to have you set foot in the house, and it made me furious."

"I appreciate that, Holly."

"*They* don't know what happened that night. Why should they automatically take Jimmy's side? It became a male-female thing. And I said they were sexists. And you shouldn't be banned from the party, and if you weren't invited, I wouldn't show up.''

''You said that?''

''I can't stand that they take such a position, that he *has* to be right and you *have* to be wrong. Finally, Pete went along with me, and he got the others to back down. So I'm formally inviting you. I want you to come.''

''It's great that you stood up for me. But I just can't get my head in that place.''

''To go to a party?''

''It's more than that. It's going through all the party talk and everything.''

''Really? For a little while?''

''Thank you very much, Holly. I appreciate it. I just can't get into a party frame of mind.''

SHE DIDN'T WANT parties. She didn't want therapy. She wanted to do something with her anger. Her parents kept calling, constantly taking her emotional temperature. Melanie and Sarah also called often to see how she was coping. She disliked the role she was assuming, the wounded bird. She had once written a paper on activists in the women's movement. Her own mother had started a new magazine. But she couldn't see herself as an activist; she was behaving like a passive woman. People were being raped at Layton; she was one of them. She had reported the rape to the authorities in the hope *they* would do something about it. They weren't accomplishing anything, and she wasn't doing anything on her own.

Elizabeth put on her down jacket, bundled up, and walked out into the cold night. As she walked along, she imagined the scoreboard, a large wooden sign: ''Rapes at Layton This Year: 3.'' It would be a running tally. As others turned up—and she was sure they would—the number could be revised.

She strolled over to sports row and stopped at The Big

Leagues. No parties could be heard; the boys were behaving
themselves quietly inside. In front of the house, a snowman
had been erected during the recent snowfall. Yellow urine
stains were rippled across the surface of his body. She
envisioned the boys, pleased with themselves, urinating on
the snowman. She picked up a loose piece of paper that was
lying on the ground and, with a pen from her jacket pocket,
wrote on it, setting the paper at the bottom of the snowman,
packing it in place with snow. This isn't a big protest, she
thought, but it's a start.

It said, "Frosty the Rapist."

SHE RETURNED THE next day, and the sign was gone. She
started to think about mounting a real protest. Her sense was
that it should not be solely about *her* rape. That was an
invitation for people to dismiss it.

Elizabeth went to tell the Women's Center director that
she wanted to organize a protest against all rape at Layton.

"We certainly can use it," Philips replied.

"I don't think the administration feels that way."

"No college wants rapes, Liz."

"But if they have them, they don't want it known.
Suppose I did put a scoreboard on the green and it said:
'Rapes at Layton This Year: Three.' Do you think they'd let
it stay there?"

"There are rules against structures on the green."

"Of course there are. If I put it somewhere else, then,
don't you think they'd find rules against it, wherever I put
it?"

"They might. What you need is the imprimatur of my
office. If what you're doing is a sanctioned activity and part
of the Women's Center, you should be able to do anything
you please, so long as it's not violent."

"If we have a protest and my friends come in with me, I
wouldn't want them to get in trouble."

"I'll see to it. I can't think of anything more within the
charter of my duties."

• • •

To TEST HER idea, Elizabeth called Holly Robertson, who she thought would give her an objective point of view.

"Hi. How was the party?" Elizabeth asked.

"Fun. I'm sorry you weren't there."

"I may have an invitation for *you*. Suppose I organized a protest against rape. Would you join in?"

"Depends, Liz. What kind of protest?"

"I don't know yet. A statement against rape on campus."

"Anything you do, Liz, is going to be a vote on whether people believe you or Jimmy."

"What if it isn't protesting my rape but it's about rape in general. Would you join in?"

"If it's a protest against rape, I might. Who's *for* rape?"

"A CECIL B. DEMILLE production," said Donna when the girls were together that night. "A cast of thousands."

"We have nearly three thousand people on campus," Sterling suggested.

"So far, what we have are three," Elizabeth responded.

"I can get Seth."

"I think it should be all-girl, like field hockey," Elizabeth quipped.

"Maybe Seth can wear a dress," Sterling said. "Can't be worse than the way he dresses now."

They tossed ideas around for a couple of hours: a scoreboard tallying rapes; a Winter Carnival of Rape, with floats and snow sculptures in protest; a flashlight march, followed by speeches on the college green.

"Holly Robertson told me it's going to end up being a vote on whether people believe Jimmy or me. Well, what if I'm not even identified because I'm wearing a mask? What if all the women wear masks?"

"Masks! I love it," Sterling said. "We could parade through the campus in masks."

"We could also have a float in the shape of a penis, and we all sit on it, carrying banners," Donna said.

"A huge penis?" Sterling said. "What are you trying to say with your penis?"

They all started to laugh.

"I don't think we have it yet," Elizabeth said drolly.

"How's this for a banner?" Sterling asked. "Screw rape!"

"I move for an adjournment," Elizabeth said.

"WHAT WOULD BE GREAT," Sarah said, when Elizabeth told her about the idea, "is if you used music. Let's say you decided to have a march. Behind the marchers you have musicians playing like in jazz funerals. I could write it."

"That would be outstanding."

"Something solemn, funereal. And then," she added, chuckling, "I could hand it in for my composition class."

"Too bad they don't offer a women's study course where I can get credit for being raped," Elizabeth joked.

ELIZABETH TOOK Sarah's suggestion of using music in the procession to Donna and Sterling, and they tossed ideas around again. The thought of a musical procession appealed to their sense of drama, as did the use of masks. The next time they met, Seth was included, and Sterling brought along Candace Clure, a friend from the theater department. A petite black girl with an angelic face, Candace was very enthusiastic. She was studying costume and scenic design, and her knowledge of stagecraft was valuable to them. She suggested a type of mask to be held in front of the face, flat cardboard that could be produced in quantity and attached to a stick, which the participant would hold. They agreed that a reproduction of Edvard Munch's *The Scream* would be effective for the mask.

The concept for the protest evolved to the idea of a long, silent procession of women holding the masks in front of their faces. At points along the march, selected people would strike tableaux in mime of sexual violence. Men were to be depicted by masks of satyr's faces. As the tableaux were struck, the procession would freeze and the marchers would suddenly reverse the masks, which would bear slogans of protest: "Rape Is Criminal," "Date Rape Happens Here," "*No* means *No*," "No More Rapes at Layton." The solemn music would be played as background. The procession would originate at the Women's Center and move through the walkways of the campus, past all the dorms, then out of the campus gates to the off-campus housing, returning to campus and the Administration Building, where the march would come to an end.

ELIZABETH DRAFTED A FLIER announcing the demonstration and brought it to the Women's Center's print shop, where a copy was run off: "Protest Against Rape at Layton. Too many date rapes are happening here. The next could happen to you. Lend your body to the cause. Send the message to Layton men that *no* means *no!* No more rapes at Layton!"

The protest would be held in two weeks, on a Saturday morning. A female student who prepared publicity for activities originating from the Women's Center worked with Elizabeth on wording for a press release to be given to the college newspaper. It referred to "growing concern about the number of rapes at Layton College." This was shown to Jean Philips, who modified it to "alleged rapes."

Philips was required to submit all fliers and press releases prior to their distribution on campus to her immediate superior, William Harlan, the dean of student activities. The submission to Harlan was theoretically to keep him informed of the activities of the Women's Center.

Seconds after reading the flier and the press release, Harlan was on the phone with Philips, demanding that she come in to see him immediately.

"What the hell is going on here, Jean?" he said when she entered his office.

"The Women's Center is sponsoring a rape protest."

"You're going to promote the idea of rape on the Layton campus. Have you taken leave of your senses?"

"I'm not promoting rape—"

"You're promoting the fact of it. We put rape awareness on our calendar to cover ourselves on the subject. We're covered. We don't have to do any more than that."

"Women students want to protest."

"And you say yes? And you want to put an announcement in the paper? The paper is read by news services, by parents, alumni."

"We notify the paper about all Women's Center activities. If we sponsor a talk by a right-to-lifer, we give the paper an announcement."

"Jean, this is an inflammatory protest. You're not here to create negative publicity about the college."

"Two more girls were raped here since Elizabeth Mason—"

"What girls?"

"I'm not at liberty to reveal their names."

"Was it reported?"

"They declined."

"So it's just talk."

"The protest is going to be very tastefully done. Street theater. With masks, music, a procession through the campus and beyond."

"Sounds perfect for a front-page picture in the newspaper."

"You can't close your eyes to this, Bill, no matter how many hearings come up with 'insufficient evidence.' Women are being raped here."

"Allegedly. We have three thousand students at Layton, and among them, simply on the basis of numbers, there are likely to be people of less than commendable conduct. Occasionally, because of miscommunication between people, as in the Mason girl's case, a rape is going to be claimed. Can you understand, Jean, that doesn't mean we advertise Layton as a hotbed of rapists?"

"One rape is too many. And we've had three this year, with an entire semester to go."

"*Alleged* rapes! When there's no evidence of rape on this campus, we shouldn't have people marching up and down publicly, calling attention to a problem that doesn't exist."

"It does, though."

"Jean, many of your ideas have been sound. This is not." He handed the flier and the press release back to her. "I'm going to withhold approval of this protest. You can't go through with it."

"How can you veto a protest?"

"It's against the interests of the college and the women of Layton, in whom it will create unnecessary fears."

"I'm not in control of their lives. These women may still want to do it."

"I charge you to discourage them. Failing that, conduct a small, quiet seminar at the Women's Center."

"A small, quiet seminar?"

"There will be no rape march here. The announcement is not sanctioned for release on the college bulletin boards or to the college newspaper."

"This is a violation of academic principles. You're making a grave mistake."

"No, you are, with this combative attitude. I'm getting a very negative feeling about your attitude about this job. Our discussion is over."

When she stepped outside the office, she leaned back against the wall, admonishing herself. She knew that she had handled the situation poorly; she didn't know what else she could have done. She had promised Elizabeth Mason that any of her friends participating would not get into trouble. Philips could no longer extend the protection of her office. If people did demonstrate on campus when they were banned from doing so, they could be subject to discipline by the administration. The students would have to organize their own protest and march outside the campus grounds.

Jean Philips was engaged to a state assemblyman from Schenectady. She spoke to him by phone that evening, and it was his opinion that she had left herself little leeway in the situation. If she endorsed a protest, having been told that it was not in the interests of the college, she would be rendering herself expendable.

She believed, though, that her mission was to give support to young women. Jean Philips told Elizabeth that the demonstration had not been approved by the dean of students but she would meet with Elizabeth's group in her office to discuss alternatives.

LAURA CALLED ELIZABETH, expecting to hear the usual account of her daughter's ordinary activities at school.

"We were going to have an anti-rape protest on campus. Except the dean—you remember William Harlan—he banned us from holding it."

"Slower, please. Who's behind this?"

"I am. And my friends. It's not just about my rape. That's the key. It's protesting all rape at school."

"And who would be protesting?"

"Everyone we could get. There were at least two other rapes since mine."

Elizabeth told her mother how it was to be organized, describing the masks, the use of mime, the music. Laura at first worried that this was another variation of her daughter's being rooted in the role of victim. But Elizabeth was so animated in the telling, the central idea was so creative, that Laura began to see it differently. In this instance, Elizabeth wasn't being held in place by her rape. This was her way of trying to move beyond it.

"He banned it? How can he do that?" Laura asked.

"By saying we don't have permission to march."

"He says you can't protest rape?"

"We're meeting with Jean Philips to work out a strategy."

"It's amazing. We marched for women's rights. We were going to make sure that as a girl you'd have every advantage boys have. And you grow up and you're raped and you can't protest because some man says you can't," she said emotionally. "If you want to protest, you get to protest!"

"That's what I've been thinking. We should march, regardless of what they say."

"Nobody at that school can stop you from making a protest. They have a parents' council. I'll get them involved."

"Mom, I thank you a lot for this. But I'm going to handle it. And we're going to march."

BEN DID NOT take kindly to the news of Harlan's ban. He resented what he considered yet another offense to his daughter on the part of Layton College. He phoned Elizabeth to tell her he would straighten out the dean, the president of the college, the trustees, or anyone else who counted.

"I'll take care of it, Dad. It's something *I* have to do."

ELIZABETH AND HER GROUP—Donna, Sterling, Candace, and Seth—met at the Women's Center with Jean Philips. Philips explained that they would be violating campus security regulations if they entered campus with their demonstration.

"I absolutely believe we have to march anyway," Elizabeth declared. "What is campus security going to do—beat us up?"

"Right on! To coin a phrase," Sterling said.

"It's not that easy," Philips told them. "If Harlan does call out security, then what you could end up with is not a march but a confrontation with security."

"That wouldn't be bad, in terms of publicity," Seth said.

"You may not get your point across. Here's my suggestion. You begin by marching off campus, around the campus. That way you get pictures taken for the paper. You have an actual march. Then you bring the line of march onto the campus. If Harlan causes trouble, it's at the end, not the beginning, and you've already had your demonstration."

"That makes sense," Sterling said, and the others agreed.

"Get a march permit from the Caldwell police," Philips said. "Clear it with them so you don't have problems."

"Not to worry," Elizabeth joked. "I know people there."

"In terms of the college, you won't be able to use the Women's Center to print fliers for you. You won't be able to post anything on the bulletin boards or in the Women's Center."

"I'll run off fliers on my printer," Seth said, "and we'll just go around to all the dorms and slip them under people's doors."

"And we'll put something in the newspaper," Candace suggested.

"Again, that's something I can't help you with officially."

"Everything gets announced in the paper," Candace said. "They'll run it."

"I'll mention it to students at the center, unofficially. And I'll help with any advice you need, also unofficially," Philips offered.

"I love the underground nature of this," Elizabeth said.

THEY WENT THROUGH the dorms, slipping fliers under people's doors. The college newspaper, the *Layton Journal*, was published on Mondays, Wednesdays, and Fridays. Candace contacted a woman she knew who worked on the paper and gave her a copy of the original press release. A woman reporter was assigned to the protest story. Philips would not offer any comment. Elizabeth told the reporter that she had prepared a press release and a flier announcing the march and was informed that Dean Harlan withheld his approval.

The reporter then spoke to Harlan, who was astonished to learn that the protest, which he thought he had avoided, was alive. He issued a statement: "Rape is not a problem of significance at Layton. These fear-mongering protesters are behaving irresponsibly and with extreme ill will toward this college. They are within their rights to protest, but not on private property. We intend to protect Layton from their irresponsibility and their anarchic need to create a false issue at the expense of our college community."

Harlan called Jean Philips after talking to the editor. He was livid.

"I ordered you not to have a protest, and you organized it anyway."

"I'm not organizing it. The protest has its own people."

"And you had nothing to do with it?"

"I told them I was not involved."

"You didn't tell them *not* to do it. You didn't put together the seminar I suggested. The newspaper called. They're running an article about the entire situation."

"I see."

"Jean, I will recommend strongly that your contract is not extended beyond this semester."

"Is there time to get that into the article?"

"I'm going to see about terminating you, effective immediately."

"The head of the Women's Center is fired at Layton College for advocating the right of women to exercise their rights? Bill, you need a PR person just to help you get through your day."

COLLEGE NEWSPAPERS in America are divided into two important categories, those that are funded by the colleges and those that are independently financed. Newspapers in the first category have always been subject to possible censorship by college officials. The *Layton Journal* had been established as a private organization thirty years earlier, with funds donated by an alumnus who owned a chain of newspapers. The donor's intention was to provide the college newspaper with independence. William Harlan could do nothing to block the article discussing the protest. He could only read the article, along with everyone else. The headline read:

HARLAN SQUELCHES RAPE PROTEST
ORGANIZERS TO PROCEED ANYWAY

Accompanying the story was a picture of Elizabeth,
Donna, Sterling, Candace, and Seth together, playfully
named by Elizabeth the "Layton Five."

The appearance of the article and the possibility of further
publicity caused Dr. Baker to call an emergency meeting of
the Layton College administrative board. The board consisted of Baker; Frank Teller, the college counsel; Madelyn
Stone, the vice president of curriculum; Paul Vernon, the
dean of admissions; Prescott Wane, the vice president in
charge of faculty; and Morgan Warner, director of public
relations. William Harlan, who was also on the board, was
called before his colleagues to explain his position on
banning the protest. He insisted that rape was not an issue at
Layton. The allegations of rape were unproven, and the
situation was exacerbated by a malcontent on the faculty,
Jean Philips. He portrayed her as an ideologue with her own
private agenda, fomenting misguided ideas about women's
rights. Based on the fact that rapes had not been proven to
have occurred, he saw no need to alarm the students, the
alumni, and prospective students. The protest was irrespon-
sible and unfounded, and by banning it, he was denying its
validity.

The board discussed whether to rescind the ban or allow
it to stand. Frank Teller said that Elizabeth Mason might
have been raped as she claimed, and therefore on that basis
alone the protest was well founded. Madelyn Stone argued
that Teller was attempting to retry the case and said the
hearing they held was not able to produce evidence to
support the girl's claim.

They debated the issue for over an hour. Layton was one
of the most highly regarded liberal arts colleges in the
country. Their acceptance of the protest would imply that
rape, this seamy crime, was widespread enough at Layton to
warrant a public demonstration. The protest would be a

challenge to the school's prestige, a prestige that also accrued to them personally.

However, they recognized that banning students from protesting on campus could cause extremely negative publicity. The college would be denying their students the right of free speech. They asked Harlan to abstain and voted unanimously, but regretfully, to reverse the ban and allow the march to proceed.

HAVING BEEN REBUFFED, Harlan informed Philips in a poisonous tone of voice that her students could march as they wished. Elizabeth and her group immediately issued a statement to the college newspaper, which ran a page one article:

## RAPE PROTEST TO PROCEED
## HARLAN SAYS FREE SPEECH PARAMOUNT

"Although rape is not a problem of significance at Layton College," he was quoted as saying, "taking precedence here are the constitutional guarantees to which our students are entitled. Weighing the fear-mongering position of the protesters against the paramount right of free speech, we at Layton come down on the side of freedom."

The reporter alluded to "alleged" rapes at the college. The rest of the piece included quotes from Elizabeth, a call to march.

Several members of the board of trustees, having seen the articles in the school newspaper, phoned President Baker with their concerns. Baker smoothly informed the callers that the original ban was established because the protesters had been manipulated by a malcontent faculty member to organize a protest that had nothing to do with a problem at Layton. In keeping with the rights that the college held dear, the protest would be allowed to proceed. Several of the trustees asked to know the name of the faculty member involved. They were told by Baker, "Jean Philips, who is in charge of the Women's Center, an unfortunate place to have a dogmatic ideologue. Her days at Layton are numbered.''

DEPRIVED OF FUNDING from the Women's Center, Elizabeth and her friends were personally paying for the costs of the march. After the article appeared, Elizabeth received two dozen calls from women at Layton who did not know her but wished to be included in the demonstration. Elizabeth's group could not begin to predict, given a population of approximately fifteen hundred women at the college, how many would show up for the demonstration. Their target was to make one hundred masks. If more than a hundred people arrived, they would distribute the masks at intervals within the ranks.

On the Saturday a week before the demonstration, Sarah came up to Layton with the music she had written, and Elizabeth introduced her to the group. ''This is my Sarah,'' she said with enormous affection. Sarah brought a tape of her composition, which she had recorded in a studio at Juilliard. Played by friends of Sarah's at school, it was a melancholy, haunting piece scored for piano, French horn, and trumpet, overdubbed with a jittery, rhythmic theme played on a synthesizer, which added a tense urgency to the mood. The piece ran for six minutes. When it was over they applauded, Elizabeth embracing Sarah, proud of her friend.

They figured out a way to play the music outdoors. The six minutes would be repeated on a tape to run for thirty-six minutes. They would make a dozen copies, designate people to carry portable tape recorders at intervals in the ranks. At a signal, they would turn on the tape recorders, and the music would be distributed along the line of march.

THREE NIGHTS BEFORE the demonstration, Elizabeth's group was working on assembling masks in her dorm room, when two women students entered the room.

''Is this the famous Layton Five?'' one of them asked. She was a tall, striking woman with a narrow face and high cheekbones, dressed in a souvenir T-shirt from a pro-choice march on Washington.

"I'm Kate Thomas," she said. "This is Maggie Lynch."

Maggie Lynch was a short, stocky blonde, who wore a sweatshirt, dungarees, and sneakers.

"We're with the Women's Action Alliance," Kate Thomas said. "Do you know about us?"

"I've seen things in the paper," Elizabeth replied.

"We deal with women's issues," Maggie Lynch stated. "We get out information, bring in speakers, run demonstrations."

"Naturally, we're interested in what's going on here," Kate said. "What *is* going on here?"

"We're going to march," Elizabeth said. "We have masks, banners, music, people to simulate acts of sexual violence."

"Right now what you have is basically a freshman demonstration," Kate said. "I don't know how many upperclass people are going to throw in with you, when you're not known *and* you're new here."

"Could we get some idea of how this is going to play?" Maggie said, gesturing toward the masks.

"You want us to audition?" Sterling asked.

"This is something Women's Action would be interested in getting involved in," Kate said. "But we'd like to know what it is that we'd be getting into."

Elizabeth and the others exchanged glances and decided to accede to the request. They went out in the hallway and enacted the crucial elements of the march, playing the music, freezing to form the tableaux, flashing the masks. People drifted out of their rooms to watch.

"Dynamite," Kate said at the conclusion of the presentation.

"It's great stuff," Maggie said.

"What if it's big?" Kate asked her colleague. "If we can deliver some big numbers, it becomes a really important protest."

"We can try," Maggie said.

"We're going to see how many people we can deliver," Kate told Elizabeth's group. "In the meantime, you're doing fine. If you're the new generation at Layton, we're going to be all right."

ELIZABETH HAD BEEN keeping Laura and Ben informed about the status of the demonstration. As the day of the march approached, Ben called each evening, hoping to hear Elizabeth tell him she could not possibly manage this enterprise without his help. He mentioned to his therapist that if this were a theatrical performance, he would be expected to attend. The therapist simply said Ben should abide by Elizabeth's decision. Laura was ambivalent, wanting to help Elizabeth, to be there for her, but aware that a march organizer's mother at a student protest would be laughably irrelevant. Elizabeth turned away Ben's overtures, saying she had people to help her on campus. On the night before the march, he called again.

"You sure I shouldn't be there in case you need anything?"

"Dad, I don't know how I'd be able to entertain you," she said, and he understood that one thing she needed was for him *not* to be there.

ELIZABETH AND HER GROUP still did not have any idea of how many people would show up for the protest. They went through all the dorms the night before, reminding people they were needed. They heard nothing further from the Women's Action Alliance. The count they were working with was seventy-five, representing students who told them they would be present. Seth bought a bullhorn, and forty-five minutes before the start of the march it seemed unnecessary. Only a handful of marchers were there. Sarah was present for the event, a reporter and a photographer were covering it for the *Layton Journal*, and Jean Philips was standing to the side as an onlooker. Holly Robertson came, and Elizabeth hurried over to thank her, grateful for her gesture of support.

THEY STARTED ARRIVING in force about a half hour before the march was to begin. Some came alone, others with friends, some in groups, as if an entire wing of a dorm or all the residents of a house turned out together. People kept arriving. Men were showing up also. In addition to Seth, about forty men joined the crowd.

The leaders of the Women's Action Alliance appeared, with a large contingent of women who seemed to know each other; they were bunched together at the rear. Elizabeth went over to Kate Thomas and Maggie Lynch.

"Thank you so much! My God, how many people did you bring?"

Looking at the crowd, Kate said, "About a hundred."

"This is fantastic."

"We got some guys too."

"Who are they?"

"Good guys," Maggie said.

By eleven o'clock, more than three hundred people were there to march. Elizabeth and her group assembled everyone in a line, three across. The masks and tape recorders were distributed among the marchers. Elizabeth gave her final instructions to the group at large. Four groups of four people dressed in black were placed along the line. At signals, the line was to stop, the groups would freeze into tableaux of sexual aggression, and the masks would be suddenly reversed, the slogans shown, everything performed in silence.

Elizabeth dropped her hand, and a dozen portable tape recorders were clicked on by the people designated to carry them. The protesters became still, the music enveloping them in a singleness of purpose. They started to walk slowly, among them one hundred masks of anguished faces. From the first moments when the line began to move, it was apparent to the participants that they formed an emotionally

powerful image: the music, the women behind masks of
anguish, moving in silent protest.

THEY WERE KEEPING to the route Philips had suggested. First
they would march along the streets that bordered the
campus. Twenty of the homes there served as off-campus
housing for Layton students, including the houses of sports
row. Several houses were occupied by women students.
After circling the campus, the marchers were to enter the
main gate, go past the dorms, and stop at the Administration
Building.

In the same way that people will applaud at a parade,
onlookers clapped at the sight of the tableaux and the
shifting of the masks. The marchers attracted attention all
along the route. When they resumed marching after one of
the tableaux, Elizabeth, Sterling, Donna, Seth, and Candace
reached their arms out to one another, touching hands in
celebration. Some of the women students out doing their
Saturday chores applauded, while among the male students,
a few of the smart alecks hooted or whistled.

Elizabeth had read in the *Layton Journal* that Dr. Baker
was hosting a brunch for parents of third world students at
his house. He was in there. She didn't want to stop at the
Administration Building. She wanted to march the protesters right up to his doorstep. Insufficient evidence? What do
you think of this? Three hundred of us. Isn't that evidence
of a rape problem here?

"What if we take it right to Baker?" she said to Sterling.

"Absolutely."

Elizabeth spoke to the marchers through the bullhorn.

"We're going to march right to Baker's door!"

A yell of assent rose from the crowd.

"This is incredible," Sarah told her.

"You've written the Triumphal March from *Aida Two*."

Jean Philips, who had come closer to the front to see what
was happening, was now trying to decide how best to move
her belongings out—should she rent a van or get profes-

sional movers? She didn't see how she would last at the college through the weekend.

The marchers were to pass two more blocks of residential housing before heading on to the campus.

"The infamous scene of the crime," Elizabeth said to Sarah as they came to the block containing The Big Leagues, The End Zone, and The Sports Complex.

A CROWD OF HECKLERS from this row of houses was waiting for the marchers, a dozen young men leaning against parked cars, hanging out windows, standing on the porches, several drinking beer. As the demonstrators approached, the males moved to the curbline. The plan for the march was to stop there for a tableau and a reversal of the signs, a flashing of the protests specifically for the men in these houses. Because the demonstration was silent but for the music, the heckling, loud and organized here, was overpowering the mood of the march. They had a prepared chant: "You don't get drunk and spread your legs/And get to call it rape."

They were laughing uproariously. Jimmy Andrews was with them, standing in the doorway of his house.

"You don't get drunk and spread your legs/And get to call it rape," he chanted along with the rest.

MANY OF THE WOMEN took exception to the heckling and were breaking with the line of march, shouting back at the men. Elizabeth and her friends were trying to get the women in line again, but they couldn't do anything about the heckling from the men or the retorts from these women. Someone from a window on the second floor of The Big Leagues threw a missile. A water bomb made out of a tied condom came splashing onto the street, landing in front of the marchers. The men were doubling up with laughter at what they considered to be a fabulous sight gag. Another missile came out of a window, and then another. They had been set up in advance, and from each of the houses, condom water bombs were hitting the street and some of the marchers. A

couple of water bombs landed without breaking, and women
hurled them back at the men. From the porch of The End
Zone, eggs were tossed into the crowd. These were ballplayers; their aim was true, and marchers were getting hit.
The crowd was being dispersed by the egg and water bomb
throwing. Several women were shouting at the hecklers.
Elizabeth had the bullhorn in her hands, and she called out
to the men:

"You're behaving like animals. Stop it!"

A football player burst out of his group of friends and
grabbed the bullhorn away from her and started chanting
into it:

"You don't get drunk and spread your legs/And get to
call it rape."

All the men were chanting it now, as if it were directed
solely at Elizabeth. Tears in her eyes, but angry, she turned
back to the marchers and tried to remobilize them. She gave
a signal for them to show their signs, to point them at
the hecklers, but the marchers were scattered. Turning to the
men, Elizabeth was hit in the head by an egg, to cheering
from the mob. She picked up a condom water bag that
splattered near her and tossed the dripping remains back.

THE CONFRONTATION lasted for twenty minutes. A local
resident called the Caldwell police. Two squad cars arrived,
and the policemen dispersed the crowds. As a last gesture
for the marchers, Elizabeth raised her fist in the air, and
those who remained did the same, trying to regain some of
their composure and the dignity of their protest by doing so
in silence.

THE CALL FOR squad cars had been heard in the police station
by Detective Mallory. Something was said about a rape
protest at Layton. He phoned Ann Neary and picked her up
at home. They arrived at the scene as the crowd was being
scattered by the uniformed officers. Walking along the

sidewalk to get closer to the action, they saw Elizabeth in the center.

"Now why would she do all this if she wasn't raped?" Mallory said to his partner.

"She would if she was a screwball. If she had a thing against men."

"She'd have to be a real screwball to do all this. Come on, Ann, get off it. Why would she report him to the college and report him to us and get these kids to throw in with her?"

"I suppose you're right," she conceded.

"You heard her story. And you heard his. Ann?"

"He raped her," she said.

"That's right. He raped her. And we've got to nail the sonofabitch."

# CHAPTER

# 14

A PRESS CONFERENCE for campus reporters was conducted by Elizabeth and her friends immediately following the confrontation. People from the *Layton Journal* were present in front of the Administration Building, along with reporters for the Women's Center newsletter and the campus radio station. The march organizers drafted a quick statement, excoriating the men for their behavior and calling the protest a success for the size of the turnout and the visual impact of the march itself.

"The administration is on notice," Elizabeth said in the question period. "Are they for rape? Are they against free speech?"

ELIZABETH ACCOMPANIED Sarah to the bus station, and they waited for her bus back to New York.

"You came through for me tremendously."

"We don't have this kind of campus life at Juilliard."

"I don't fit in here, Sarah."

"Please. You're an asset to this place."

An announcement was made that the bus was ready to leave.

"Whatever you need me for . . . ," Sarah said. "Campus violence is a break from the quiet city."

"I could go either way. Lead another march. Or get on this bus with you and go back to New York."

ELIZABETH REMAINED in the station when Sarah left. The chanting of the boys stayed with her. The taunts were directed primarily at her, it seemed. She wondered what it was like to be a smiling Betty Coed. Shannon and Allison are your closest friends. You smile and dance and drink and screw. Nobody rapes you. Everybody likes you. Cute as a button. You're the Sweetheart of Layton College.

EXPLODING HER OUT of the reverie was the Eyewitness News Team. A tall, slender blond reporter in her thirties, wearing a duffel coat and earmuffs, rushed toward the bench where Elizabeth sat, followed by a technician with a camera that bore an Eyewitness News logo.

"Elizabeth Mason?"

"Yes."

"They told me you came down here. Veronica Warwick. I'd like to ask you a few questions about the incident today."

"Why?"

"We're doing a story on the battle between your marchers and the boys."

"In what context?"

"What are you, my news director? Look, we're tight. I need film. We didn't get the battle. It's talking heads time. You marched, didn't you? You had something to sell. So let's sell it."

Elizabeth imagined herself appearing on television screens throughout the area with the words "Rape Victim" at the bottom of the screen. She was not going to say she was raped and titillate people. She had been protesting rape on campus, not her own rape.

The reporter asked Elizabeth why she was protesting, and

she responded that she had heard about rapes on the Layton campus and felt the college officials were unconcerned. To the direct question "Were you one of those raped?" she answered, "That's irrelevant to my feelings about the issue." The reporter pressed her, but Elizabeth would not give any more than she had offered. Elizabeth talked about date rape being the crime nobody wanted to acknowledge at Layton and spoke about the hostility of the men who broke up the demonstration.

"Good copy," the reporter said to her. "I think we've got a shot at getting on the air."

They jumped into their Eyewitness News van and sped away.


LAURA AND BEN WERE able to find themselves in agreement on a subject. Elizabeth described the march to them, and they were allied in their anger with the Layton College administration for not protecting the marchers, for tolerating rapists and sexists.

"Liz and her friends had a rape protest," Ben told Josh. "Some boys threw eggs and water bombs and broke it up."

"Was she hurt?"

"No," Laura replied. "She's going to talk with her friends about what to do next."

"That's pretty lousy," Josh said. "To throw things."

"It sounds like it was very impressive for a while, before it stopped," Laura said. "With music and street theater."

"Liz did it?"

"She did. With her friends," Laura answered.

"She's great," he said unconditionally.

Laura's and Ben's eyes met for a beat, and they were united in the feeling that their daughter *was* great, brave and creative, and they could be proud of the kind of parents they were together. At the time, the feeling was not one they could sustain.

● ● ●

THE TELEVISION REPORTER WHO interviewed Elizabeth contacted the college for an official statement. The Layton public relations director, Morgan Warner, was a longtime aide of President Baker's, who had worked with him in the State Department. Warner was off campus on a Saturday afternoon, and Baker had also left campus, after his brunch. Unable to reach either of them, the reporter asked the switchboard operator to put her through to someone who could talk about a student demonstration. She was connected with William Harlan. He knew nothing about the incident. He had been in his study when the march took place, having had no intention of watching the demonstration. Harlan called campus security and was informed about the skirmish outside the campus grounds. Irate, he formulated a statement and called it in to the reporter.

ELIZABETH'S GROUP GATHERED in her room to watch the local six o'clock news. Twenty minutes into the show, a teaser announced, "Trouble amid the ivy," with a shot of the main gate at Layton.

After the commercials, the female anchor introduced the reporter.

"At Layton College, a street fight between male and female students. Veronica Warwick has the story."

The reporter was seen standing in front of The End Zone.

"It was billed as a protest against rape on campus. Three hundred women assembled to march."

She held up one of the protester's signs. A close-up revealed the words: "No more rapes at Layton."

"Here, at a row of houses occupied by students largely from athletic teams, the women were confronted by hooting, beer-drinking male students, who threw eggs and water bombs made out of condoms.

"William Harlan, dean of students, spoke to us and said, quote: 'The hecklers behaved irresponsibly, and their behavior cannot be condoned. But I must stress that rape is not a problem at Layton and does not call for protest in the first place.''

Elizabeth's face came on the screen, and her group yelled their approval. She flushed at the sight of herself. I'm on TV. I look terrible.

"The administration has to decide," she said. "Are they *for* rape? Against free speech?" On the bottom of the screen she was identified as "Elizabeth Mason, Rape Protester."

"The Layton men who threw things at us are crude, hostile children with a warped sense of humor, or crude, hostile sexists who think rape is a big joke. Maybe they're both."

She was cheered loudly by her crowd. Next on-screen was a housemate of Jimmy Andrews, identified as "Bill Casley, Layton Student." He was a burly tackle from the football team and had been one of the major egg throwers.

"*This* is their spokesman?" Donna said.

"These girls—what they do is drink too much and they go all the way. They wake up the next day feeling hung over and guilty. So it's us they blame. We're not rapists here. We're college students. And we don't like anybody calling us names. They want to play dirty. We can play dirty too."

"Beautiful," Sterling called out. "Absolutely eloquent."

The reporter reappeared on the screen.

"Eggs and water bombs thrown at protesters. This was a hard educational lesson here for the students who marched against rape. From Layton College, this is Veronica Warwick for Eyewitness News."

ELIZABETH'S FRIENDS were jumping up and down and congratulating each other. Across campus at The Big Leagues, they were also celebrating. To the dozen men gathered around the television set with Bill Casley, he had got his points in, and more than that, their man was on TV! Within minutes, the *Albany Times-Union*, auditing their media competitor, called Harlan for information for a story they were doing on the incident.

• • •

JANNA WILLIS WAS SPENDING her customary Saturday hours at
the Caldwell day care center when the march and skirmish
had occurred. She returned to the campus to hear about it
from women in her dorm. She was told that people from the
house where Jimmy lived had disrupted the protest. She
went directly to see Jimmy and confronted him.

"What happened here?"

"The marchers were very hostile. They came right up to
us as if we were a bunch of rapists. The guys thought they'd
make a joke out of it."

"That didn't sound like a joke."

"You had to be here to know what happened. The guys
were laughing, the girls were yelling. The whole thing sort
of escalated."

"These are your friends. You should have stopped
them."

"I couldn't. The thing just got rolling. But it was only
meant to be some fooling around, nothing more. Don't
make anything of it."

THE SUNDAY *TIMES-UNION* CARRIED a story in the local section,
with a photo supplied by the *Layton Journal* photographer.
The headline was:

## SEXES TANGLE OVER RAPES AT LAYTON
## TEMPERS FLARE
## EGGS, WATER BOMBS FLY

The article described the conflict on the street. In a
statement, Dean Harlan said rape was a nonissue at the
college. Elizabeth was quoted, with her statement about
rape and free speech. The Caldwell police commander said:
"Drinking is at the root. The hecklers were drinking beer.
These college kids engage in a lot of underage drinking that
we can't police effectively and the college isn't doing
enough about."

"Negatives on free speech, rape, *and* drinking," Baker said to Warner. The two were meeting on Sunday morning, with the newspaper in front of them. They had seen the TV report, which was picked up on the late-night news.

Warner was a heavyset man in his fifties, the nonaca-demic on the staff, which he emphasized by wearing bold Turnball & Asser shirts and ties.

"We have to exercise some damage control. Come out for free speech and against rape and drinking," Warner said drolly.

"Harlan is a dunderhead."

"We should get Jean Philips in here. She might be able to tell us something about the rapes we can use in a statement."

"While she's still on the payroll."

"Right. You don't want to fire her before the contract is up. We'll end up with the women marching about *her*."

WARNER FENDED OFF other reporters by saying the campus was calm, the incident was minor, and the president of Layton would speak to this shortly. Symptomatic of the mayhem Baker and Warner were experiencing, the person they hoped might give them some background in order to frame a proper statement was Jean Philips, whom Baker had already committed himself to fire.

AT ELEVEN ON SUNDAY morning, Baker asked Jean Philips to come to his house within the hour for a meeting. She thought the subject under discussion would be the termina-tion of her employment. When she entered, she found it curious that Baker greeted her cordially. Morgan Warner was present, and William Harlan was not. They settled themselves in Baker's living room.

"Have you seen the paper this morning, Jean?" Baker asked.

Although she was a trained psychologist, she did not like

to overdo the business of trying to read people in situations. Still, she knew serious anxiety when she saw it.

"Yes, I did."

"There was a piece on the local news last night at six," Warner said, "and again at eleven."

"I saw it."

"This publicity is the worst kind of attention for a college," Baker said. "Crime on campus, campus unrest. It troubles the students, parents, and alumni. It frightens away the quality students we need."

"Maybe they should be frightened," she said.

"We're thought of with colleges like Williams and Amherst, sylvan settings for the pursuit of academic excellence. So these kinds of incidents go to the very heart of what we are," Baker stated.

"The incident yesterday was caused by the same attitudes about women that lead to rape," she said.

"Bill Harlan points out that we have no record of rapes at Layton in recent years, except for the charge by the Mason girl," Warner offered.

"Six that I'm aware of."

"What?" Baker said.

"The other women didn't file charges, but they told me they were raped."

"What do you think we should be doing?" Baker asked.

"Changing the attitudes about gender on this campus. And for a start, if women protest rape, they should be allowed to do it. This is Layton. This is not Tiananmen Square."

"In a student population that is constantly turning over, with a quarter new each year—" Warner began.

"Yes, I know the argument. But even one rape, one young woman sexually abused, is one too many," she said.

"I wouldn't like to think we have a community of rapists here," Baker said.

"Rapes happen on campuses all the time. We're not immune," she responded.

Baker walked to the window and looked out, thinking.

"Well, we have to defuse this unrest, for the good of the students and the college," he said. "Suppose we have a major schoolwide colloquium on rape. I'll expect you to set it up, Jean. And I'll issue a firm statement to the students that egg throwing and water bomb throwing is totally unacceptable as free speech. They can express themselves in the colloquium. After all, this is Layton College. This is not Tiananmen Square," he said slyly. "Jean, would you like some tea or coffee? I'd like to know how you'd go about 'changing attitudes about gender.'"

When the meeting ended, Baker watched her from the window. She was walking so quickly in her excitement, she was nearly running.

JOHN HATCHER RETURNED to the campus after his customary weekend stay with his girlfriend.

"You missed the fireworks," one of his housemates told him.

A half dozen of the people in the house were sitting around the living room, and they recounted the episode with the women, a triumphant report. Bill Casley, The Big Leagues' own, having appeared on television, was strutting about.

Hatcher read the account in the *Times-Union.*

"Whose idea was it to bombard them?" he asked.

"Mine," Casley said proudly. "We knew they were coming, and I thought it would be funny to take some condoms and load them with water."

"If they cut back funds for football because the team was so bad, what would you think if you got together a protest and a bunch of women started screaming at you and throwing eggs and saying we didn't need football and you were a bunch of dumb jocks?"

"Don't get preachy with us, Hatcher," one of the other football players said. "It was great, and Casley got on television."

"Sounds like you guys confirmed the worst view of us."

"Next time we'll put our objections in a prissy little essay and you can write it for us," Rod Wyman said.

THE MONDAY ISSUE of the *Layton Journal* carried a page one story of the march and the skirmish between students. The leading players were quoted, except for Harlan, who, gagged by Baker, issued a "no comment." Baker's statement appeared in the article, as it did in the local section of the *Albany Times-Union*.

"Date rape on college campuses is an unfortunate fact of American life," Baker stated. "The extent of these acts varies widely from campus to campus. No one can seriously suggest that at Layton, considering the prestige of the college and the high standards of acceptance, date rape even remotely begins to approach the national average. But even one rape is too many. To ensure better communication between Layton men and women and to explore the problem of rape, an important colloquium on rape is being planned for all students.

"As to Layton men heckling rape protesters, such behavior is totally unacceptable and an affront to free speech. Future offenders will be severely disciplined. If men have views on the subject, they are invited to express them at the colloquium."

He concluded by saying, "This is not Tiananmen Square; this is Layton College. Be proud of your college as we in the administration are proud of you."

SETH WAS WORRIED that his acceptance along sports row was threatened now that he had been seen with the women at the protest. Hoping to be an undercover detective and pick up some scuttlebutt to aid the investigation, he had created a new computer game he was going to make available to the athletes. Thus far he had managed only to confirm his original finding, which he had passed on to the police, that the people who lived in those houses were "big shots" who thought they were "above it all." On the Monday evening following the march, he went to The End Zone with what he considered his masterpiece game. He sold the games for twenty-five dollars apiece, but he thought the new one was so good he intended to make it available only by rental, at ten dollars a night. He made this announcement to several of his regulars. One of them, a fullback on the football team, was a major egg thrower during the skirmish. He didn't waste any time confronting Seth about the protest and his allegiances.

"You marched with the girls, didn't you?"

"Circumstances."

"Oh? What's the deal?"

Making his best attempt to talk like the guys, Seth replied:

"When you're getting laid steady, you don't want to give it up."

"*You're* getting laid steady?" one of them said.

"My girlfriend was one of protesters. I couldn't break up with her over this. My penis made me do it."

They thought that was acceptably funny, and it served to reduce the tension. He was able to present his game, which was designed like a Mario Brothers arcade game, the object being to move a figure past various obstacles in order to obtain a goal. The goal in Seth's game was getting laid. This was also the name of the game. The obstacles were members of the faculty, rivals, feminists, campus security, President Baker, Dean Harlan, all of whom appeared suddenly to throw baseballs at a male figure in order to knock him down. The figure pursued various coeds, chasing them into bedrooms for intercourse. The sex was depicted: the man would mount a woman. Sometimes in the middle of sex one of the combatants would enter, throwing baseballs, and sex would not be consummated. When the man was alone in the room long enough having sex with the woman, the screen lit up with flashing letters that spelled out "Orgasm." This counted for one point in the player's

Getting Laid tally. Seth demonstrated the game, and the men thought it was terrific, laughing, pushing each other to try.

Bill Casley was at the house, and he was having a wonderful time playing the game. He didn't want to give it up for the next player.

"Fantastic how you did this," he said to Seth.

"Thanks. Ten dollars a night rental," Seth replied.

"It'll go over great with our guys," he said.

Casley manipulated the male figure into the room with the coed.

"This is like the Fuck Room in our house," Casley said.

"What's the Fuck Room?" Seth asked.

"In the basement. Where we take chicks to get them out of the way when we want to nail them."

"The Fuck Room. That's pretty funny," Seth said. "Maybe I could modify it for you guys and put that in the game."

"Come on, Casley, let someone else play," one of the men complained, and the next player began.

Seth's demonstration was successful, and he collected his ten dollars rental fee. He tried to remain restrained as he concluded his business and walked slowly out of the house. They were involved in playing Getting Laid and paid little attention to him as he left. He rushed back to his room and called police headquarters to reach the detectives. He was told they were unavailable and would be in at eight-thirty the next morning. Seth was there waiting for them when they arrived.

"ENCYCLOPEDIA BROWN IS HERE," Neary said as she saw Seth sitting on the bench.

"I have important information about the rape," he said.

"Come on in," she said, and led him to her cubicle.

Mallory arrived a few minutes later, surprised to see Seth there at that hour of the morning.

"I've been hanging around some of the off-campus

houses," Seth said, "making up computer games. I thought maybe I'd pick up something useful."

"Yes; you found out they were big shots. I remember your previous breakthrough in the case," Mallory said.

"Last night I was at The End Zone, showing them a new game. One of the people there was Bill Casley, who lives in the same house as Jimmy Andrews. The game I made up is called Getting Laid, and the idea is to maneuver a girl into a room and score. And when Casley saw it . . . you might want to tape record this or something . . ."

"Keep going," Mallory responded impatiently.

"He said the game reminded him of the Fuck Room in his house. That's what he called it, and when I asked him what that was, he told me it's a room in the basement of their house—and I'm quoting him exactly—'where we take chicks to get them out of the way when we want to nail them.'"

"Well, what do you know?" Mallory said.

"That's where Jimmy took Liz," Seth said, "and that's why he took her down there, to get her out of the way."

"The Fuck Room," Mallory remarked for his partner's benefit. "And it's set up in the basement for exactly that purpose."

Seth nodded his head.

"Thank you," Neary said to Seth. "You've done very well, Inspector."

# CHAPTER
## 15

THE INVESTIGATION was wide open.

"I'm telling you," Mallory said to Peters and Neary in the district attorney's office, "this kid is a wise-ass who was out to get laid. It got out of hand."

"If somebody's screaming in that room, people upstairs might not hear it," Neary said.

"That's *why* they take them there," Peters said. "Let's pin this thing down."

They decided Bill Casley should be questioned to confirm the name for the basement room. Mallory and Neary waited in a car for Casley to return to his house.

"Bill? Can we speak to you for a minute?" Mallory called out.

Casley was walking with one of his friends. He shrugged and said, "See what happens when you get on TV." He walked over to the car.

"Suppose you get in," Mallory said.

"I already told you everything I know."

"Maybe you didn't," Mallory said firmly. "Get in."

Casley got in the backseat of the car. He was uncomfortable about being there, which was what they intended.

"We'd like a little privacy," Mallory said, and he drove four blocks north to a quiet residential street where no students could be seen passing by. The detectives turned from the front seat to face him.

"On September second, the night when Elizabeth Mason and Jimmy Andrews were at a party together in your house, did you see them go downstairs?" Neary said.

"No. I told you that before. I left early. There was another party that night. A bunch of us went there."

"If you're trying to score and people are still in the house or maybe someone's in your room, where in the house would you take a girl?" Mallory asked.

"I don't know."

"Downstairs? The basement room?"

"I might."

"Did you ever take anybody down there?" Mallory asked.

"Are you after me for something?"

"You're not in any trouble, Bill, if you just answer the questions. Did you ever take anybody down there?" Neary said.

"Maybe."

"As far as you know, did anybody else in the house take anybody down there?"

"They might have. I don't keep track of everybody's business."

"Did Jimmy Andrews ever take anybody down there?" Mallory said.

"Ask *him*."

"The guys in your house, they take girls down there, don't they, when they think they can score and they want some privacy?" Neary said.

"Look, we're not bad guys. We don't do anything the chicks don't want."

"Is the room in the basement where you and your buddies take girls specifically to be private and to score?" Mallory asked.

"If the girl is willing."

"It *is* a room where you take girls? It's known for that in the house, isn't it? A guy going down there is looking specifically to get laid."

"You don't know how it's going to work out every time."

"Did you ever get laid in that room?" Mallory continued.

"I suppose."

"Did anybody else?"

"I suppose."

"Do you call it the Fuck Room?"

"Yes. So?"

"Not everybody would know that, though," Neary said. "You're not going to let that out, so that every girl who's asked to go down there knows that she's going down into the Fuck Room?"

"We don't advertise it in the *Layton Journal*, if that's what you mean."

"That's what we mean."

Satisfied with the information, they drove him back to the house, thanked him, and let him go.

"You're not going to want to hear no from a girl when you've got her in a place that's called the Fuck Room," Mallory said to Neary. "Andrews sure didn't take her down there to listen to music."

BILL CASLEY saw Jimmy Andrews later in the day and told him the detectives had been asking questions about the basement room and that they knew what it was called in the house. Jimmy was casual in his response. But he went immediately to a public phone a block from the house, where he could speak without being overheard, and called Brett MacNeil.

"Some things have been going on I thought you should know about," he said to the lawyer.

"What?"

"A bunch of girls had a rape protest the other day. Some of the guys took offense, and there was a bit of a fight."

"Was there? Was this a big thing?"

"I don't know if you can say it was big."

"Is it known outside campus?"

"Well, there was something about it on TV."

"TV? Wonderful news, Jimmy. That's what we want, publicity about rapes at Layton," he said with annoyance.

"The police have been around."

"Sure they have."

"A guy in the house told them something. I don't think it matters. It's not evidence."

"Please don't tell me what is and isn't evidence."

"Some of the people around here call the room where I had sex with Liz Mason the Fuck Room. Because it's quiet down there and it lends itself to sex."

"The Fuck Room?"

"It's meant to be funny, that's all."

"Who calls it that?"

"Just the guys in our house."

"Because it's a room for sex?"

"Kind of."

"Kind of. Do you see the tone of it, Jimmy, setting a room aside for sex?"

"It's supposed to be a joke."

"What goes on in the Fuck Room, Jimmy? If the girl doesn't fuck, do you let her go upstairs with your blessings? Or if your expectations are so high, do you coerce her so you'll come out of the Fuck Room with a fuck?"

"If she doesn't fuck, she doesn't fuck. Liz Mason *did*. I keep telling you that, goddammit!"

"Listen to me, Jimmy. You can expect them to come after you again. Don't tell them a thing. Tell them to get in touch with me."

"Right. And I'm calling you from a pay phone on the street, so nobody can hear."

"Good thinking," he said sarcastically.

Brett MacNeil was accustomed to clients who were of the criminal element calling him from "safe" phones. Now his college boy was doing it.

FOR JIMMY, the night with Elizabeth was a very long time ago. This was the first week of March. He had met her in September. He had been living responsibly, decently. Jimmy considered it incredibly bad luck to have become involved in any way with her. A girl like Janna, Janna herself, could have been waiting at the next party, at the next house. The year would have been so different if only he had met Janna first.

Why didn't they leave him alone? Elizabeth Mason was walking around, she was organizing protests. This so-called rape victim was doing just fine.

MACNEIL'S READING OF THE SITUATION was that the district attorney still did not have a winnable case. The fact that a room was set aside for sex did not prove Jimmy raped the girl. Still, it was not good news, nor was television coverage of a rape protest on campus. He contacted Malcolm Andrews, who did not know about the protest or the continuing investigation.

"Dear God. Are you saying this could go to trial?"

"Unlikely at this point. They haven't added one shred of evidence. Still, it's becoming a possibility. The D.A. might be encouraged to take it to a grand jury and push for an indictment. I wanted you to be prepared."

"Jimmy's a good boy. He didn't rape that girl. Why would he?"

"Let's hope we don't have to answer that in court." Catching himself, MacNeil quickly added, "But if we have to, we'll win."

MACNEIL REVIEWED THE CASE against Jimmy Andrews with two of his partners, Tom Kelleher, a beefy man in his forties, and Barbara Malley, a trim brunette in her late thirties, a former prosecutor in Stamford. The prevailing opinion was that MacNeil's response to the father was still valid. If they went to trial, given the lack of evidence and the difficulty in obtaining date rape convictions, the defense was solid. Thinking ahead, they agreed that the best strategy if they went to trial would be, as in a grievance board hearing, to keep Jimmy Andrews off the witness stand. As they ended the meeting, Barbara Malley said to her partner:

"What about this kid? Do you think he raped her?"

"I wasn't sure at first. But I think he did," MacNeil said.

BRETT MACNEIL DID NOT VIEW his position as being morally dubious. Everyone was entitled to a fair trial under the law, and it was his job to see that people were accorded that right. When he had come out of law school, he had worked as a public defender in Boston, and many of his clients were guilty of the crimes for which they were charged. He had defended them, and by protecting their rights, he had protected the criminal justice system that would find others, improperly charged, innocent. Jimmy Andrews was entitled to counsel. MacNeil's sympathies were with the parents. He viewed the mother as fragile and bewildered, the father as an intellectual lightweight overwhelmed by the son's predicament. His sense was that if the son had to do time, the parents would go to pieces. The kid did something arrogant and stupid, MacNeil concluded. He probably raped the girl, but he was not inherently a rapist. If he could be kept from going to prison, MacNeil thought that would be a good use of a defense attorney's time. He would be performing a service to the parents, and a soft kid like that, prison would literally eat him up.

TROUBLED, Malcolm Andrews contacted Alice Whitson, a woman with whom he had conducted a two-year affair. He

had not seen her during the past six months. Their affair had
ended when she began a relationship with an unmarried
man. Alice Whitson was an assistant bank manager, a
divorced woman in her forties, a person whom Malcolm
always relied on for stability. This was an emergency, he
told Alice. He had to see her. She was still in her
relationship, she told him, but agreed to meet him for a
drink.

Suffering exquisitely, Malcolm delivered an elaborate
account of Jimmy as the maligned victim. Alice didn't
understand why the police were still pursuing the matter if
Jimmy was above suspicion. She decided that she wasn't
going to allow Malcolm to use his crisis as a way of
maneuvering himself back into her life. She sympathized
and told Malcolm she regretted his troubles but couldn't do
anything for him.

"That's it?" he said. "You mean I just have Penny?"

"I'm sorry. I can't give you what you want anymore."

She could see how profoundly he needed his son to
sustain him. Back there at home was the truth of his
marriage. Malcolm couldn't sell her on the idea that his son
was completely incapable of rape. Lord help this man, she
thought, if they prove that the boy did it.

WITH THE PROSECUTOR'S OFFICE keeping the case open, one of
Laura's strongest objections was undermined. She could no
longer say the investigation was a meaningless activity. In
Caldwell, they were taking Elizabeth's complaint very
seriously. Aided by his therapist's counseling, Ben did not
gloat that his view of the investigation was prevailing. The
climate between Laura and Ben was becoming somewhat
calmer. Contributing to it was the pride they both felt in
Elizabeth.

"I want you to know I've been spending top dollar on
us," Ben said to Laura one evening. "My last few sessions
have been all about us."

"And? Can This Marriage Be Saved?"

"It's like what you said about Elizabeth. We've got to get past it."

Ben was now willing to see a marriage counselor, and his therapist recommended Angela Woodson.

"She's a smart old bird," Fraiman said. "She's seen everyone's crap."

When Ben first came to Fraiman, the therapist had said it would be for first-aid purposes. They were at a good stage, he suggested, for Ben to stop seeing Fraiman and begin family therapy with Laura.

The Masons went to see the marriage counselor, who turned out to be a flamboyant-looking woman in her sixties, tall and silver-haired, dressed in an Armani suit; she wore tinted glasses indoors. Woodson asked them to articulate their problems. Laura went first, and she talked about the rape, the college hearing, the police investigation, the incessant arguments, the rape demonstration. As the therapist listened, her eyes appeared to be closed behind her dark glasses, and both Laura and Ben wondered if she was napping, whether they had put her to sleep. At about the fifteen-minute mark, Woodson tapped on her desk with a pencil and said, "Now you." Ben spoke for about fifteen minutes, and she tapped her pencil and said, "Enough."

She looked at them and begin swinging in her swivel chair.

"These are not happy events, so why should you be happy? Your children seem to be lovely people. Your daughter sounds wonderful. Lovely children are not an accident. If you come to me, we'll try to find out how two such hopelessly mismatched people," she said with deliberate irony, "should have such lovely children. Somewhere lost in here is a better relationship. Do you want to find it?"

"I do," Laura said.

"I like that, a marriage vow," the therapist said. "And you?"

"Yes. I do," Ben said.

''Good. You see me a couple of days a week, and we'll work on it.''

After they left the office, Ben said to Laura:

''I knew once you start with therapy you get hooked in. Another New York couple who can't get by without help.''

''We'll try, right?''

''Right. If we can keep her awake.''

CARL PETERS WANTED THE DETECTIVES to conduct an additional round of questioning on campus. Perhaps someone observed something, overheard something, they had not revealed before. Mallory and Neary went through the laborious process of going back again and asking questions of people they had talked to earlier.

''JIMMY, the police are still asking questions,'' Janna said to him. They had stopped her near her dorm, and she called him immediately. ''They asked me if I remember anything, if you ever said anything about Liz Mason to me.''

''And?''

''I told them what you told me. You went out with her one night and nothing happened between you.''

''Right.''

He wasn't going to reverse himself in the middle of a criminal investigation. He couldn't imagine himself telling her: I said I didn't sleep with her, but I really did, but I said I didn't because I was scared, and I slept with her but I didn't rape her.

''Nothing happened?'' she asked.

''Nothing.''

''If you tell me that, I have to believe you.''

MALLORY WAS EAGER to trap Jimmy Andrews in a lie or an incriminating statement. Hoping to catch him off guard and trying to be casual, he stopped him on a sidewalk on campus and asked if they could have a cup of coffee so he could ask a few questions. Jimmy replied that Mallory was welcome to meet his lawyer for coffee. Jimmy informed MacNeil about this exchange, and MacNeil immediately called Peters.

"This is Brett MacNeil. What are you bothering my client for? We made our deal with you. He came in. He answered what you wanted to know."

"The investigation is proceeding. Other developments have come to light."

"You don't have a case, Mr. Peters. After digging around for months, you have no witnesses, no evidence."

"We'd like to talk to Jimmy Andrews."

"You can't. Let it be, Mr. Peters. You're interfering with this kid's education."

"I'm glad to know you're so educationally minded."

A FEW DAYS LATER, Mallory was sitting in a dormitory lounge with Sandy McDermott.

"I have a few things I'd like to clear up. You said you were at the party on September second with your boyfriend, Rod Wyman?"

"My ex-boyfriend. We broke up over Christmas."

"You were asked last time, and you said you didn't even notice who Jimmy was with that night."

"That's right. I wouldn't have known her then. I know her now."

"How so?"

"From all the stuff going on. I was in the protest. Rod was on the street with those other guys. We broke up because I found out he was seeing other girls. If you ever wondered if you did the right thing, breaking up with somebody, there it was. They were awful."

"So you know Jimmy Andrews?"

"Yes. I used to hang around the house a lot."

"You didn't see him take Liz Mason downstairs during the party?"

"He took her downstairs?" she responded, and Mallory immediately picked up the tone of her voice.

"What's the idea of that room downstairs?"

"They take people down there to make out." She frowned slightly.

"What, Sandy?"

"It was done to me. Some creep last year. Took me down there and tried to rape me."

Calm now, steady and true, Mallory said to himself, knowing he was on the verge of something.

"*In* that room?"

"He didn't get away with it. I was lucky."

"Yes, I'm glad. So someone tried to rape you in that very room?"

"Yes. I think they set it up to help them score. In their little competition."

"How's that?" Mallory asked.

"Rod denied it, but I think they had a competition going."

"A competition?"

"They kept score. Who could screw the most girls per semester."

"Really? That's not very sporting, is it? Did anybody ever tell you that?"

"I overheard little remarks here and there. It wouldn't surprise me."

"What was said that you overheard?"

"Just: What number is that? How many you got? They didn't tell me it was going on, but I was around enough to get the idea."

"Who was part of it?"

"The guys with girlfriends weren't, I don't think."

"The others were?"

"I think."

"Who did you hear taking about this competition?"

"Bill Casley. Jimmy Andrews."

"Jimmy Andrews too?"

"I'm pretty sure he was in with the others."

"Can you be *sure*? Did you hear Jimmy Andrews talking about keeping score?"

"I did. Because that was the time I realized what they were talking about. I thought they were my friends. They shouldn't have thrown things at us and yelled at us. We were just standing up for ourselves."

"I agree."

Mallory thanked Sandy and went to his car and called Neary. She was at headquarters, and he told her he had something. When he arrived, he called out, "Ann, come with me!" and he rushed to Peters' office.

Mallory sat down opposite Peters and waited for Neary. Then he told them:

"Get this. Sandy McDermott used to go with a kid who lives in the house with Jimmy Andrews. She says she was nearly raped in that basement room last year."

"She was?" Peters said.

"There's more. She thinks the boys had a *competition* for how many girls they could screw in a semester. They kept score. *And Jimmy Andrews was part of it.*"

"What?" Peters said, his eyes widening.

"I rest my case," Mallory told them.

PETERS WANTED CORROBORATION of the competition from someone who lived in the house. A likely person to ask was John Hatcher. Mallory and Neary went to the house and stood at the front door facing Hatcher. It was not a good time to talk, he told them, explaining that he was in the middle of writing a paper. Neary said it would take only a little while and that Hatcher had a civic duty to assist in a police investigation. Hatcher responded that he would get back to them in a day or two. John Hatcher was confused about his responsibilities—to a roommate he didn't like, to a freshman girl he didn't know, to his housemates, to ethical behavior.

He left campus to be with his girlfriend. They sat in her room at Hamilton College, discussing his responsibility. He wanted to do the right thing, but he couldn't decide whether to volunteer everything he knew or just answer the questions the police might ask. His girlfriend felt he should tell them what he knew. He couldn't say with certainty that he knew the truth. It was possible some of the stories in the house about scoring were nothing more than harmless bragging. And what was the truth about what happened with Liz Mason? She could have been lying. What if the information he volunteered to the police tipped the scales against Jimmy, who might be innocent?

He called his parents, and they told him essentially the same thing as his girlfriend. He had to be truthful and tell what he knew. John Hatcher was paralyzed. He wanted to be correct and moral, but he didn't want to harm someone unfairly. And he didn't want to undermine his hard-won position as one of the guys. In an exchange with a detective, he could lose his standing and not graduate as one of the guys. He would be a snitch, a sissy. He didn't need his thesaurus to tell him what he would be: he would be a first-class prick.

"WHY DID YOU want to see me?" Elizabeth said to John Hatcher as they sat across from each other at a table in one of the college cafeterias. Elizabeth had been surprised when Jimmy Andrews' roommate asked to meet with her. She had no reason to make distinctions among the people who lived in their house. He had requested a meeting in privacy; she didn't trust him, and they settled on the cafeteria.

"So . . . do they call you Liz?"

"You people call me a lot worse than that."

"I'm not 'you people.'"

"Aren't you?"

"In a house with guys, you get all kinds of guys. We're not just one thing over there."

"I know. Some of you throw eggs, some of you throw condoms."

"I didn't have anything to do with that. I wasn't there."

"If you say so."

"With Jimmy being my roommate, I'm involved more than I'd like to be in his personal life. The police are interested in what I know. I don't know anything about the night in question. You and I met that night—"

"I remember."

"You looked very nice. I thought Jimmy'd found himself a nice girl."

"It's odd to think about it that way, but Jimmy and I were actually a couple for a few hours there, weren't we? Jimmy and Liz. The cutest couple."

"You're too quick for him. Jimmy wouldn't have known what to do with you."

"He found a way."

"I don't mean that."

"I know what you mean."

"Liz, when I first came to Layton, I was worried about how I'd fit in. I'm a pretty good student. My mom and dad are both professors. I was worried I might end up being a grind. So I went out for baseball. I'm a decent player, and I liked the idea of having buddies and being part of the group."

"Great guys."

"What I want to say is, I don't know where in this situation my responsibility is. Is it to the guys, to Jimmy? Is it to you? Is it to some outside model of ethical behavior?"

"You're supposed to be a pretty good student?" she teased. "You sound a little incoherent to me."

"You *are* too fast for Jimmy." Trying to be charming, he said. "Now, if I didn't have a girlfriend . . ."

"You'd take me to a party in The Big Leagues."

"Where did you tell the police Jimmy raped you?"

"In your house."

"In the basement?"

"Yes."

"I see. Did you call out?"

"I did. And you didn't come to rescue me."

"I didn't hear you. I would have come if I'd heard you," he said, so earnestly she was surprised by his emotion.

He fell silent.

"Yes?" she said, more gently.

"Why in the world did you go down there?" His tone was not accusatory; it was closer to poignant.

"The mood of the evening."

"But if you go into a basement room with somebody you've been dancing with, and kissing, and he's been drinking . . . You were drinking too?"

"Some."

"You shouldn't have gone down there."

"I didn't see any crossing guards on the premises."

"No, we haven't posted any lately," he responded. "I still don't know what happened that night. And I still don't know what to do."

"What are you being asked to do?"

"Tell the police the truth. Is there a truth here?"

"Yes, there is."

He lapsed into silence and finally said, "Well . . . I thank you for talking to me."

"Perhaps we'll meet sometime when you're not going through a moral dilemma."

"I'll check my calendar," he said, trying to match her remark, and she smiled.

She rose and he did also, formally shaking her hand. Elizabeth left the cafeteria, and John Hatcher remained to sort out his choices.

As to the crucial question of whether deliberately to volunteer information to the police, he decided he would not. He couldn't explain away Elizabeth Mason's behavior that night. What was she doing going off to the room with

Jimmy? That was an ambiguous element, and he wasn't going to take responsibility for bringing harm to Jimmy or risk the enmity of the guys when something was ambiguous. On the other hand, he would not lie to protect anyone. He would answer all questions that he was asked, and answer them fully and directly. That would be his truth.

# CHAPTER 16

CHEERFULLY OBLIVIOUS to the police investigation of their housemates, the men of The Big Leagues were planning a party. A meeting was called, and the fourteen residents sat around the living room to come up with a theme. Rod Wyman suggested a pro-rape party, but he was hooted down with laughter. Jimmy Andrews was in there, laughing along with the rest, as part of his business-as-usual image. Someone suggested a Dionysian theme, and it was widely supported. John Hatcher sat quietly watching Jimmy, thinking it was like Nero fiddling while Rome burned. Although he had struggled with the issue and come to what he considered the correct response, John Hatcher was feeling apprehensive about what he might reveal to the detectives. The house meeting came to an end. Dionysius prevailed. The guys were going to set out bunches of grapes and walk around in their underwear, wrapped in sheets.

THE DETECTIVES AND the prosecutor were becoming impatient. Two days had passed since John Hatcher declined to be questioned by Mallory. Then Hatcher called police headquarters and said he was prepared to talk if they could meet

271

away from school. Mallory and Neary met him at the
Caldwell Diner at eight P.M. Noticing that the boy was
agitated, Mallory said:

"It's okay. We're not after you. We just want to know
what you can tell us about this rape allegation."

"I'll tell you the truth as I know it," he said, a line he had
rehearsed to give himself confidence.

"You were at the party on September second, and
according to what you told us last time, you were upstairs
most of the night with your girlfriend," Neary said.

"That's right."

"The whole time?"

"At different times I came down to get a beer."

"And you went back upstairs?"

"Yes."

"Then you left?"

"We went out to eat."

"When was that?"

"Eleven or so."

"While you were in the living room, did you see Jimmy
Andrews and Elizabeth Mason together, and were they
dancing and drinking beer?" Mallory asked.

"Yes."

"Do you recall how much beer they drank? The Mason
girl?"

"No."

"Jimmy?"

"He had at least a couple of beers that I gave him."

"A couple? Three, four?"

"Two for sure."

"What did you see involving the two of them?" Mallory
continued.

A direct question, and he was going to answer it.

"They were kissing on the dance floor."

"What kind of kissing—pecking, passionate?" Neary
asked.

"Sort of passionate."

"Anything more than kissing?"

"No."

"And you didn't see them leave?"

"No."

"You didn't hear anything at any time, a girl's cries?"

"No."

"The room downstairs, it's called the Fuck Room, isn't it?" Mallory said.

John was startled to hear that they knew this. He was relieved they weren't hearing it from him.

"Yes."

"Because that's where you take girls to fuck them."

"People have been know to take girls down there."

"To score?"

"Yes."

"And you *keep* score?" Neary asked.

"How's that?"

"There's a competition in your house, and you guys keep score of how many girls you make it with," she said.

John Hatcher was at the moral threshold. He had told himself that he wasn't going to volunteer anything, nor was he going to lie. He tried to balance himself. The detective had not technically asked him a direct question.

"I don't think I can answer that—"

"Do you guys have a competition, and do you keep score of the conquests in the house, the girls you make it with in a semester?" Neary said.

"Yes."

"Are you in the competition?" Mallory asked.

"No."

"Is Jimmy in the competition?"

"No."

The detective sensed he should rephrase the question.

"Was Jimmy in the competition on September second?"

John Hatcher paused. He was aware of the import of the question, but it was a direct question, and he answered.

"Yes," he said softly.

"When did he start keeping score?"

"When the semester started."

"Did he continue?" Neary said.

"At some point he stopped, when he was going with Janna Willis."

"But he *was* in the competition?" Neary asked.

"Yes."

"Definitely?" Mallory said. "He told you he was? You heard it discussed in the house?"

"Yes."

"One of those or both? He told you, you heard it?"

"Both."

"Okay. I think that will do it for now. Is there anything else you'd like to add?" Mallory asked.

"No."

"I appreciate your taking the time," Mallory said. "We'll see you around."

JOHN HATCHER FELT that he had kept faith with morality. He hadn't volunteered information. He had answered everything he was asked. His girlfriend and his parents would approve of his behavior; his roommate was another matter.

When he arrived back at the house, Jimmy was in their room.

"I was just questioned by a detective about Liz Mason's allegation. I decided to tell him nothing that I wasn't directly asked about. They know about the competition, Jimmy."

"You told them that?"

"They knew before they got to me. And our name for the basement—they know that too. Perhaps some sociologist unearthed the local tribal customs."

"It's no big deal," Jimmy said, his palms growing sweaty, his face becoming flushed. "If guys got laid around here, it doesn't prove I raped her."

• • •

JOHN HATCHER WENT into the bathroom to take a shower, and Jimmy left for the pay phone in the street.

"Mr. MacNeil, I'm sorry to bother you at home."

"What's happening now, Jimmy?"

"The detectives were asking more questions around here. They talked to my roommate and somebody else. I don't know who."

"And?"

"There's one other thing that came out. It just proves guys in the house were making it with girls. It doesn't prove anything about the charges against me."

"What?"

"For fun—it was a game, a joke—we kept score of how many girls we made it with over the semester."

"What do you mean, kept score? You wrote it down?"

"We just reported in."

"Explain that to me."

"It was like a little competition—how many girls you made it with."

"You had a competition of how many girls you screwed?"

"As a joke. A college-kid type of thing."

"Jimmy, were you in this?"

"Yes."

"Were you in it when you took Liz Mason to the party?"

"I guess you could say I was."

"So the night you saw her, the night she claims you raped her, you were involved in a competition with your buddies about how many girls you could screw?"

"Mr. MacNeil, she wanted it that night. I didn't do anything the guys around here don't do all the time."

"And you didn't try to force her, to make sure you scored?"

"Not any more than other girls I've made it with."

"What does that mean? Did you force her?"

"You can't always know how far they *really* want to go."

"Was there force, or was there consent?"

"I didn't rape her. What I'm guilty of is picking the wrong goddamn girl to make out with."

"Now we have a sex competition in the picture. Christ, Jimmy! Next time stick to intercollegiate athletics."

THE LAST REVELATIONS, the competition and the Fuck Room, were decisive for the district attorney. The boys had a private room for sex where they took likely candidates, and Jimmy Andrews was part of the competition. If a girl resisted his advances, he might very well have pushed her against her will. Peters congratulated the detectives. Mallory and Neary did not have time to rejoice. A woman on the outskirts of town had been stabbed and claimed her ex-husband was the assailant.

PETERS THOUGHT HE HAD a long shot at a conviction. The case against Jimmy Andrews would be as difficult to win as any date rape case, but he believed the girl. This type of crime usually went unreported and, therefore, unprosecuted. Yet it was common, and Peters saw himself creating a crime deterrent with the case. If it came to trial, he would seek to introduce the competition as motive evidence. He had the doctor and the school psychologist, and taken together, they might add up to something in a courtroom. The crux was the girl and her believability. He had known Martin Reed in New York, and he might use Reed's line, which he had read in the transcript of the college hearing: *she* was the eyewitness to the crime. The easiest and least time-consuming approach would be to avoid a jury trial altogether by convincing the Andrews side that a plea bargain was their best choice. This seemed exceptionally unlikely.

WHILE THE DISTRICT ATTORNEY was doing his calculations, Brett MacNeil was sitting with his colleagues Tom Kelleher and Barbara Malley, discussing the most recent surprise from Jimmy Andrews.

"It's like a piñata. They keep whacking away, and things keep spilling onto the floor," MacNeil said.

MacNeil knew the prosecutor was going to count heavily on the testimony of Elizabeth Mason. But she had been drinking beer under age, she necked with her date in full view, she willingly went to a basement room with him. They needed only one person on the jury who thought the girl was a "hussy," and Jimmy Andrews would go free. In that part of the world, the men might regard the girl as having asked for it. The district attorney probably had enough to bring the case before a grand jury, and if he was any good and the girl was persuasive—and they knew she was from the hearing—the grand jury would probably hand down an indictment. But the defense would definitely win in trial.

"Unless we lose," MacNeil said. "Unless this girl is so completely convincing and sympathetic that they *want* to believe her. There is a chance we could lose."

"Slim," Kelleher said.

"But a chance. If it goes to trial and the tabloids get hold of his background, it's going to make for cute headlines. The Country Club Rapist."

MacNeil received a call that day from the district attorney.

"Mr. MacNeil, good day. It's Carl Peters."

"Yes, Mr. Peters. Calling it off?"

"We have some new information. We'd still like you to bring the boy in for questioning."

"That they had a private room in the house? That some of the boys kept score?" he said defiantly, trying to show the district attorney that he was aware of the new developments and unconcerned. "That's not admissible, and it surely doesn't prove beyond a reasonable doubt that my client raped anyone."

"Will you produce the boy for questioning?"

"I will not. This case isn't going to help your reputation, Mr. Peters. I advise you to drop it."

"We'll just have to go to the next stage. Thank you for your advice, Mr. MacNeil. Do you plan on sending me a bill?"

PETERS WAS CONCERNED about whether the girl would hold up in questioning before a grand jury. He asked her to come in, and Elizabeth answered his questions for over an hour. Peters probed for inconsistencies in her story from her first account, when she had come into headquarters to file a complaint. He found her steady. He judged her an appealing and formidable witness.

"I'm worried about something," Elizabeth said. "If we go to trial and lose, I look like a fool."

He was uncomfortable with her remark. If she wavered on the stand in a courtroom, a skilled defense lawyer—and he suspected the pugnacious Mr. MacNeil was one—would demolish her.

"We can win on rape and he could go to jail. Even for a few months, jail for that smart aleck won't be pleasant. Or we can get them to plead guilty to sexual misconduct or assault charges. Either way, we have a chance of branding him for what he did and sending a message to others."

"Still, it's a risk for me," Elizabeth responded.

"For me too."

He needed to shore up her resolve, so he decided to tell her about the latest disclosures.

"Elizabeth, we found out something that's pretty nasty. The boys in that house, Jimmy very much included, were in a competition. They were keeping a tally of how many girls they had sex with. The room where he brought you . . . they call it the Fuck Room."

"Really?"

"When he took you down there, it was part of a game they were in, and they were keeping score."

"Keeping score?"

"I believe when you resisted . . . in the heat of the

competition, he went ahead and took you anyway. You were going to be his first for the season. He wanted to get off to a fast start.''

She shuddered. ''Doing it and then bragging about it. And keeping score. The bastard. They're all bastards.''

''Exactly,'' he said, pleased with the response he'd elicited.

CARL PETERS INFORMED LAURA and Ben that he was going to take the case before the grand jury and that Elizabeth would be testifying.

''I'm going to try for rape in the first degree and tack on sexual misconduct and assault in the third degree. If I decide rape isn't doable and I let them plea-bargain, that's going to be my decision, and you have to know that going in. This is your daughter, but it becomes the larger community, the law. The case is going to read The State versus James Andrews. Elizabeth's name won't even be on it.''

''How much time would he do?'' Ben asked.

''I'd be pushing for jail time on the rape. He'd do a little or none on a lesser charge.''

''He can't get to laugh at us all.''

''We're of the same mind, Mr. Mason. Now you have to make certain Elizabeth holds herself together.''

To bolster their resolve, insofar as it might have an impact on the girl, he told them about the room and the competition. Peters might as well have dropped a cherry bomb into their living room, the way the reality exploded in their faces. After they spoke to him, on the phone, they sat blinking. They were sickened by the information. Their daughter was a chip in a game. Ben's face went numb at the idea of Elizabeth as a sexual object for indulged young males. He looked at Laura, his adversary during so much of these last weeks. She had covered her face with her hands. She imagined Jimmy Andrews walking into a room where his pals were, making a thumbs-up sign, to score another

one for him. She crossed over to Ben and put her arms out
to him, and he embraced her.

PETERS BROUGHT ELIZABETH in yet again to go over testimony.
Her account contained several points he found troublesome,
and he raised the questions once more. How much did she
drink that night? Was she necking with Jimmy Andrews in
the living room? Did she go voluntarily into the basement
with him? Did she neck with him there? He coached her on
how to answer these to draw a distinction between behavior
common on dates and at college parties—dancing, drinking,
necking—as opposed to rape. Like Martin Reed, who had
coached her on her behavior for the college hearing, Carl
Peters instructed her on how to present herself in the grand
jury room. Keep your head up. Answer in a clear voice.
Make eye contact with the jurors. If you feel as if you are
about to cry, by all means cry.

   He told her what to wear: a simple skirt, sweater, loafers,
no jewelry or makeup. She said she didn't own such shoes,
and Peters told her to go out and buy a pair. Laura and Ben
arrived with Josh, and they went with her to buy shoes. She
was going to be Betty Coed, after all, on orders of the
district attorney.

JOHN HATCHER SHOWED Jimmy a subpoena he had received
and told him he had no choice in the matter. Jimmy
shrugged it off and then went running to his pay phone.
MacNeil was not surprised to hear it was going to a grand
jury. He had expected Peters to make that move. He told
Jimmy to remain calm; this was part of the legal skirmishes
basic to the system. They were not necessarily going to trial.
Even if they went to trial, the prosecution still didn't have a
case. He repeated this in a call to Malcolm, who seemed to
be having difficulty breathing. Malcolm did not tell Penny.
They went to a dance at the club that night, and he did his
fox-trot with a smile.

• • •

THE GRAND JURY was convened in Albany. Peters was going to call John Hatcher, so the competition between the boys could be established. Sandy McDermott would tell about the Fuck Room and testify that she had almost been raped there. His other witnesses were Dr. Thomas Phelan, Jean Philips, and Elizabeth. The witnesses sat on benches in a hallway outside the jury room. John Hatcher was unhappy to be there undergoing further moral adventures. Sandy McDermott, in anticipation of having her sexual experiences scrutinized by jurors, was grim. Dr. Phelan brought some paperwork. Elizabeth sat on a separate bench with Laura, Ben, and Josh. When the grievance board hearing was held, Laura and Ben had chosen not to take Josh because they thought it would be inappropriate. He wanted to be included this time and not left at home as "a little kid." His parents respected his feelings. Josh's presence appeared to be helpful; it gave Elizabeth an opportunity to be the big sister, and she put her arm around his shoulder to calm him in his nervousness.

Jean Philips arrived, greeted the Masons, and said, "You're doing a fine thing, Liz. More girls will come forward now."

"Depending on what happens to me, maybe they won't."

"You can do it," Ben said.

"I've been heavily coached," Elizabeth said to Philips. "Down to my shoes."

"So have I," Philips responded.

THE TWENTY-THREE grand jurors were assembled in a courtroom with an American flag in prominent view. A vote of twelve jurors is needed in order to indict. Grand jury proceedings are secret. Spectators are barred. The defendant is not permitted in the room, nor can other witnesses observe the proceedings. The judge is available but not active. The district attorney is permitted to conduct

AVERY CORMAN

the examination, and any of the jurors can question a witness.

Twelve of the jurors on this day were women, four black, eight white. Five women jurors were over fifty years of age; two of them looked to Peters to be in their sixties. He was uneasy about the older women, who might view a young girl as having "asked for it" in entering a basement room with a male. Of the eleven men, three were black, the rest white. Four of the men were fifty and over, and Peters had similar concerns about them, that they would think of Elizabeth as a "loose" girl. Fewer than half of the jurors appeared to be in white-collar professions.

Peters knew he would be required to overcome a variety of prejudices against Elizabeth in this grand jury room. She was a student at Layton, of a different social class than most of the jurors. She was young, and that alone could make her morals suspect for the older people. The worst combination of prejudices on the part of the jurors would strand him with a rich, privileged, white New York Jew.

On the other hand, he considered her, and thought she would appear to the jurors, an endearing, honest young woman. And she was a rape victim. The other witnesses were secondary. The result was going to turn on Elizabeth Mason's testimony.

The judge charged the jurors to find probable cause to believe a crime was committed and that the accused committed it. Peters began with John Hatcher. He quickly extracted the main points: the competition between the boys, their name for the basement room, and Jimmy Andrews as one of the competitors. Sandy McDermott followed. Under Peters' questioning, she told about entering the room and being nearly raped there. A juror, one of the older women, was interested to know why she went into the room if it was so isolated, and could she claim to have been a near-rape victim if she willingly went down there? Peters was confronted with a preview of a trouble spot in Elizabeth's testimony. Sandy McDermott handled the question well. She stated that people at the party were moving freely through the house and she had no reason to think that it wasn't just another room. Going to a room with somebody, even kissing someone there, was not the same as inviting intercourse, and not the same as rape.

Peters had established the room and the competition. He next brought in Dr. Phelan for the scientific testimony. As he had testified before the college panel, Phelan stated that he found bruises on Elizabeth Mason's neck two days after the rape was alleged to have taken place. These were consistent with bruises he had observed in cases of physical assault. A retired pharmacist among the jurors, a balding man in his late sixties, was given his moment to shine and challenged the doctor. He elicited that Phelan didn't conduct an examination for rape, and a variety of circumstances could have occurred in the intervening time to result in the bruises.

Jean Philips was led by Peters to give her expert's view of Elizabeth, based on treatment and observation. Elizabeth was a rape victim, she said. No pattern of dissembling was detectable. No motivation for fabricating a story was discernible. Elizabeth Mason also helped organize a campus demonstration against rape. The possibility that she was creating a story so that she could reinforce a false presentation of her rape was impossible for the psychologist to believe.

Several unfriendly questions were directed at Philips by the jurors, indicating a resentment on the part of older men required to deal with a younger professional woman.

"How do you know so much fancy stuff?" one of the men asked.

"I went to school for it," she answered.

"Another fancy college girl," he muttered, and several jurors laughed.

Peters did not find it amusing. There was a packet of

prejudices contained in the man's remarks, town-gown, male-female, white collar–blue collar. Elizabeth had better be good, he thought.

She was next. Given last-minute encouragement by her parents, Elizabeth walked into the room. Even though Peters had told her what to expect, she was intimidated by the number of jurors assembled. The twenty-three people who faced her seemed like a small crowd. Peters took her through the night of September 2, the dinner before the party, the party itself, her dancing and necking with Jimmy. She was asked several questions by jurors about details: where was she when they started to dance, who else was in the room, where were his hands when they were dancing, where were hers? Peters led her to the point when, nearly alone in the house, they descended into the basement. From the time when she described her struggle and his entering her, she held her audience with rapt attention.

A couple of the jurors wondered how she could go into a basement room with someone and not be encouraging the other person to think they were going to have sex. She answered much as Sandy McDermott had. There is sexual behavior without intercourse. Not everything sexual is an invitation to rape. She felt a couple of the men undressing her in their imagination. They were looking at her breasts. She was certain that one in particular, a man in his thirties wearing a sports jacket, was imagining what it would be like to be inside her. The strain of being there, in front of so many strangers, her sexuality being openly discussed, began to break her down, and her voice trembled. "He didn't have to rape me. There was a moment when I said no. I screamed. He knew I didn't want to have sex with him. I couldn't have been any clearer. He knew."

Peters guided her through what happened in the aftermath of the rape: the vomiting in the street, the weeping in her dorm, the visit to Dr. Phelan, his examination.

"You were enrolled in a course for voice when you entered Layton, weren't you?" he asked.

"I was," she said.

"Isn't it true that since the nigh
night you say you were choked a
voice and you no longer sing?"

He hadn't asked that question bel
coaching her. Singing was something she h
mind.

"Yes. I stopped singing," she said.

The awfulness of that admission came over her, and her
eyes filled with tears. "By all means cry," Peters had said
to her. She hadn't intended to, and here she was complying,
as if on cue.

When she left the room she imagined that it was not
beyond possibility for the jurors to applaud. This is what I
do, my performance: the girl who was raped. I take it on the
road from college to college. And I have it down. It gets
them every time. My one-woman show.

"Are you okay, honey?" Ben said as she emerged from
the room.

"I was great," she said.

ELIZABETH WAS CONGRATULATED by Peters, which confirmed
her opinion that it had been a performance. He thought the
elements were in place for an indictment. Laura, Ben, Josh,
and Elizabeth went to lunch in a nearby coffee shop and
then returned to the courthouse to wait for a decision. After
an hour and a half spent on the bench in the hallway,
exhausting all the small talk they had among them, they
went outside for air and stood near the courthouse entrance.
Peters came toward them, smiling.

"We did it!" he said. "A three-count indictment. Rape in
the first degree. Sexual misconduct. Assault in the third
degree."

"What do you know?" Ben said.

Peters explained the charges. Rape in the first: a male
engaging in sexual intercourse with a woman by forcible

..n. Sexual misconduct: sexual intercourse with a
...e without consent. Assault in the third degree: intent to
..use physical injury and causing such injury.

"I feel very good about it," Peters said. "I don't think
I'd even entertain a plea bargain."

PETERS INFORMED MACNEIL about the indictment, saying
he was going to be a decent guy. They weren't going to
arrest his client in the dead of the night and drag him
down in handcuffs. They were going to pick him up the
following morning at eleven, and he would appreciate it if
MacNeil didn't complain that the brilliant lad had to be in
school.

"Incidentally, I've decided to go all the way with this. He
doesn't cop a plea," Peters said.

"Sure," MacNeil replied, sparring. "If you don't have a
case, you might as well go all the way with the case you
don't have."

MACNEIL DREADED CALLING the Andrews parents, and he
didn't much want to deal with the boy, either.

"Jimmy, it's Brett MacNeil. I'm sorry to tell you the
grand jury came in against you."

"What?"

"The grand jury system is a joke. It's been debated for
years whether we should even have it."

"There's going to be a trial?"

"Probably. They charged you with rape. And they threw
in a couple of misdemeanors, chickenshit stuff to build it up.
They'll come for you at eleven. I'll be there. We go to the
courthouse, they read the charges against you. The judge
sets bail. I'll talk to your dad about that. You'll walk right
out of the courthouse. And we have a few weeks to file a
motion to dismiss. We'll do that. Either way, we're going to
get you off."

"I guess I should wear a jacket and tie tomorrow."

"Right, Jimmy," MacNeil said, fatigue. "Wear your best clothes."

MacNeil decided to see Jimmy's parents at the Westport rather than call them. He took his partner Barbara Malley with him for balance, to have another woman in the room for the mother's sake. As soon as the lawyers walked in, Malcolm's hands began to shake. Malcolm made everyone drinks, and they sat in the living room. Penny was confused. She didn't know why they were there. Malcolm had never told her about the convening of the grand jury.

"The grand jury handed down an indictment against Jimmy today," MacNeil said. "Ridiculous. It's been said you can get a grand jury to indict a ham sandwich."

"What are you talking about?" Penny said.

MacNeil flashed a look at Malcolm.

"I didn't . . . say anything to her," Malcolm explained.

"The Caldwell district attorney got an indictment," MacNeil explained. "He wants to bring the case to trial. He's playing politics with this thing. An ambitious D.A. from New York stuck in a small town. He's trying to get some publicity for himself. So tomorrow morning at eleven they're going to arrest Jimmy and bring him in for an arraignment."

"Arrest him?" Penny said.

"A formality," Barbara Malley told her. "They'll read the charge, set bail. He'll be back at school for lunch."

"We feel they don't have a prayer in this case," MacNeil stated. "Lack of physical evidence. Lack of witnesses."

"What if we lose?" Penny said.

"We get to file a motion to dismiss. And we'll take that step," Malley answered. "If we go to trial, it's nearly impossible for them to win a date rape case under these circumstances."

"Nearly impossible?" Penny said. "If we lose, Jimmy goes to jail."

There's also plea bargaining. We can make a deal with the D.A. to accept a guilty plea on a misdemeanor, and we can talk about a suspended sentence,'' MacNeil said.

"What if he *is* sentenced?" Malcolm asked. "What do these charges carry?"

"First-time offender. You have to look at a minimum sentence or probation, which is a real possibility."

"But he could go to jail?"

"There are various combinations here. At the very, very worst, I think we're talking months. But this speculation is the worst possible worst-case scenario anyone could imagine."

"Not guilty," Penny said in a strange tone.

MacNeil suggested that Jimmy would experience some initial anxiety, and Malcolm should be there in the morning for the arraignment. MacNeil emphasized that his office was highly skilled in these matters and confident about this case. He wanted them to keep in mind that they had only begun the legal maneuvering.

MacNeil and Barbara Malley left. Penny closed the front door behind her, turned toward the living room, and fainted. She fell to the floor silently. Malcolm watched, in fear and fascination. He had never seen anyone faint before. It was like a towel quietly dropping off a clothesline, slipping down in a heap. He looked at this person on the floor, who at this precise moment could not bear reality. He wanted to say, "I understand. That's good. Sleep." Then he began to react. He slapped her face and she responded slightly. He ran to get water; he filled a pot and tossed the water in her face, and she stirred.

"Jimmy arrested," she said dully.

"Everything's under control," he said.

"I can't go there."

"Yes. Stay back and rest."

Malcolm Andrews thought how nice it would be to be able to do that—rest, sleep, and not think about it or read the papers. It would surely be in the papers. And maybe when you woke up it would all have gone away.

LAURA, BEN, AND JOSH stayed with Elizabeth for a while in her room, but they decided to go back to New York before dinner. None of them were in a mood to celebrate. The occasion was solemn. Jimmy Andrews was going to be arrested for raping and assaulting Elizabeth. You didn't open champagne.

# CHAPTER
# 17

THE *ALBANY TIMES-UNION* carried an item at the bottom of its police blotter column in the local-news section:

## LAYTON STUDENT INDICTED FOR RAPE

James Andrews, 21, a senior at Layton College, was indicted by a grand jury today on three counts, rape, sexual misconduct, and assault, in an alleged attack on another Layton College student. Bail was set at $5,000. After pleading not guilty, the accused returned to class at the college.

According to Carl Peters, the Caldwell District Attorney, Andrews was engaged in a competition with his friends to keep score of their sexual conquests, and a special room was set aside in an off-campus residence, where women were taken for sex.

Defense attorney Brett MacNeil called the indictment a "travesty" and stated, "There is not one shred of evidence against Jimmy Andrews. In the absence of any evidence, any witnesses, or any proof at all of the charges, I am confident Jimmy's innocence will be upheld."

The treatment of the indictment on the front page of the
school newspaper was not nearly as cool in tone.

LAYTON LOVE NEST?
SENIOR ACCUSED OF RAPE

Women lured to a special room in The Big Leagues? A
competition among the men to keep score of the number
of Layton women they sleep with? These were accusa-
tions made by Caldwell District Attorney Carl Peters in
connection with the indictment of Layton tennis star
Jimmy Andrews, accused by a freshman woman of raping
her the first week of the fall semester.
    Are you reading this in the *National Enquirer*?

The *Layton Journal* article continued with quotes by
Peters and MacNeil, which were picked up from the
*Times-Union* piece. Rod Wyman was also quoted: "We're
not rapists. And as we said the other day, 'You don't get
drunk and spread your legs and get to call it rape.'"

ELIZABETH'S NAME had not been mentioned in the newspaper
pieces, but she was now the most prominent student activist
against rape on campus. After the *Layton Journal* piece
appeared, several women nodded affirmatively as she passed,
walking to and from classes, but the cold stares also made
a reappearance. Heading toward her dorm that evening, she
saw Bill Casley leaning against a tree. As she approached
him along the walkway, he started in her direction. Just as
they were about to pass in opposite directions on the
walkway, he lurched and bumped into her, his elbow
smashing into her arm. She gasped with pain.
    "Sorry," he said. "You going to report *me* to the police
too?"

WHEN JIMMY LEFT police headquarters, Brett MacNeil was
reassuring. He told Jimmy and Malcolm that overzealous

prosecutors bring cases to trial all the time that they do not win. He asked them to remember that in a court of law the defendant was given the presumption of innocence and they had to prove a defendant's guilt beyond a reasonable doubt. And the evidence was nonexistent. Jimmy repeated this to Janna and to his friends at the house. But when the article about his indictment appeared and he was publicly exposed as an accused rapist, Jimmy left campus, took a room in a motel outside Caldwell, and cut classes for two days. He was unable to mobilize himself to return to school.

Failing several attempts to reach MacNeil, he spoke to his father, who wasn't aware of anything new on the legal front. Malcolm said an item about the indictment had appeared in the *Westport News*. He told Jimmy, "We have our position here. Your mother has a statement I wrote out for her: 'An opportunistic district attorney is exploiting rapes at the school. They have absolutely no evidence against Jimmy.' That's what we're telling people."

"Great, Dad. You tell them."

Jimmy considered dropping out of Layton for the remainder of the semester. But he was so close to graduating. I can't drop out now and give the satisfaction to that bitch. It isn't fair. They say no, but sometimes they mean yes. They want you to push them, make them. That's where the expression comes from: Did you "make" her? I'm no criminal. It was a misunderstanding.

He went back over the events. At any moment, it could have turned. If he had chosen Holly Robertson and not her roommate. If he had met someone else before he met her. If he had met Janna earlier.

MacNeil called Jimmy at the motel, and Jimmy informed him he was staying away from campus. The lawyer advised him not to convict himself. He said Jimmy should get back to school and behave as normally as possible. In the meantime, he should not talk to reporters, collegiate or professional. For his own comfort, when the weekend came he could spend it away from campus.

Jimmy returned to Layton in the late afternoon, found a note from Janna on his pillow, and went to her dorm. She was working at the desk when he entered her room.

"Jimmy! I've been looking all over for you. Where have you been?"

"Thinking about things."

"I don't understand what's happening."

"An opportunistic district attorney is exploiting rapes here."

"The paper said you had a competition on sleeping with girls? Jimmy, I asked people, and they said it was true."

"We were kidding around. It was nothing."

"Was I in it? Was I one of the girls you kept score of?"

"No, Janna!"

"I don't get any of it. You told me Liz Mason was an unstable person. But I heard the protest she organized was beautifully done. How could she be unstable?"

"She's obsessed, Janna. She is unstable."

"And you said to me you never had sex with her. But I've been asking around, and apparently you told people you did."

"Janna! Why are you talking to people? Don't I have enough detectives in my life!"

"Did you have sex with her, Jimmy?"

"I didn't."

"The police don't believe you. They say you raped her."

"They're police. If they thought well of everybody, they wouldn't be police."

"That is so glib."

"I'm sorry. I'm under a little bit of a strain, you know. Look, I need to get away from this place for a few days. This weekend, let's just get in the car, go somewhere by ourselves."

"I can't. I don't think we should see each other for a while."

"What?"

"I have too many questions in my mind. We need to have a little rest time between us."

"Great, Janna. Some crazy bitch gets after me, and that's when you decide to have a little rest time between us."

"I don't know if she's crazy. And I don't know if she's a bitch. And that's why we have to stop seeing each other."

JIMMY STORMED THROUGH the house, slamming doors. The wonderful Elizabeth Mason had turned his world upside down and cost him his entire senior year.

You walk through the wrong fucking door and standing there is the wrong fucking person and you're totally fucked.

Several people emerged in response to the noise Jimmy was making, thrashing around.

"Janna just broke up with me. One more thing I have to thank Ms. Liz Mason for."

"Would I love to cause her a little grief," Casley said.

"Well, don't rape her," Jimmy advised, and they laughed at his remark.

Bill Casley was particularly incensed by Jimmy's predicament. He had been drawn into the investigation because of Elizabeth Mason. His answers to the detectives' questions, according to his friends, were probably used against Jimmy. He had settled for smacking into her along the walkway. He would have liked to do worse.

Rob Wyman took a slightly more intellectual approach. He regarded the women's complaints in general and Elizabeth Mason's specifically to be derogatory to the men of Layton. He was the author of the chant at the skirmish, and with pride of authorship he had repeated it to the *Layton Journal* reporter.

"The old tactic when somebody says she was raped is for everybody to say they made it with her too. We could do that when Jimmy comes to trial. Say it wasn't rape, that she was trash," Wyman suggested.

"It's perjury," another of the amateur lawyers pointed out. "Count me out."

"We could sully her lily-white reputation," Rod said. "A bunch of us could go over to her dorm and do the chant."

"Call the newspaper," someone suggested.

"Good," Rod said. "They can print what we think of her and what really happened that night."

"I think you guys can understand why it wouldn't be prudent for me to join you," Jimmy said.

"We'll take care of it," Bill Casley said.

They gathered others willing to participate. John Hatcher was not there and would have objected anyway, but they found several men in their house and in the other houses along their row who thought it would be a nice lark and a way of showing support for Jimmy. A suggestion was made to bring some girls along, and a few of the men gathered their girlfriends. Somebody suggested going over to the athletic field; they might recruit some people there. At the field, the group found several players in pickup games who said they would join in.

"We should have a banner, something?" a person called out.

One of the men scurried off, then returned with a hastily made banner that said "Jimmy Andrews is innocent!" which brought a cheer from the crowd. They were ready. The pro-Jimmy force added up to sixteen people, twelve men and four women.

"This is the ad hoc committee to free Jimmy Andrews," Rod Wyman said to the group, and they cheered boisterously. "We don't want to get stopped by campus security, so let's split up and meet at Brewster, where the enemy is encamped."

"What if she's not there?" someone asked.

"We'll make the point anyway. Okay? Let's try it. One finger, we chant: 'Jimmy Andrews is innocent.' Two fingers: 'You don't get drunk and spread your legs/And get to call it rape.' Ready, everybody?"

He held up one finger and they chanted accordingly,

enjoying the solidarity. He held up two fingers for the second chant, and they were getting into the spirit, chanting loudly. They headed for Elizabeth's dorm.

SHE WAS READING in her room when she heard the stir outside her window. Elizabeth pulled open the curtain, and as soon as the crowd saw her, they applauded and yelled for their good luck. In front of the group, someone was holding the banner "Jimmy Andrews is innocent!" They started chanting, "You don't get drunk and spread your legs/And get to call it rape," again and again. Then they chanted, "Jimmy Andrews is innocent." She watched, transfixed. Billy Casley was in the front rank of the crowd, as were a few other people she recognized, housemates of Jimmy Andrews. Women students she had seen on campus were there also. The chanting persisted. She drew the curtain and sat down on the bed, as the chant continued: "You don't get drunk and spread your legs/And get to call it rape." Outside, people who were walking on campus came over to watch, while others from the dorms wandered out to observe. The hecklers added another chant: "Liar, liar, liar, liar," which they alternated with the others.

Sterling rushed into the room.

"Call security," she said. "They have no right!"

Elizabeth went to the window and looked out. At least forty people were present, hecklers and onlookers. Sterling dialed security, complaining of a disturbance.

"I'm going out there," Elizabeth said.

"I don't think you should. Someone might throw something."

Elizabeth took a piece of oak tag left over from her demonstration and with a permanent marker wrote on it: "No still means no." She headed for the door with it, and Sterling went with her.

They stood on the steps of the dorm, held up the banner, and the crowd began to hoot and boo. Others, worked up, seemed angry.

"My name hasn't been in the paper. I would say somebody figured it out," she said archly to Sterling.

Onlookers began to accumulate, and among them were several women who had marched in the rape protest. They came over to stand alongside Elizabeth and Sterling. The crowd's response was to boo and chant loudly. Elizabeth, Sterling, and ten other women who joined them faced the crowd defiantly. The crowd had settled on one chant, and they stayed with it: "Liar, liar, liar, liar!"

Four campus security officers arrived, and after some pushing and shoving the group scattered, people calling out over their shoulders, still chanting as they walked away.

"We protest better than they do," one of the women said, patting Elizabeth on the back.

"It's our demonstration of the week," Elizabeth told them, returning to the room with Sterling. Inside, she collapsed on her bed.

PENNY HAD TO TELL her mother, Elena Fisk, about the indictment, for fear she would hear it from someone else. She could already anticipate her mother's recriminations. You let two sons go wrong. It was that man you married. He doesn't know how to bring up men to take their rightful place because he's never been in that place. Elena had said as much when Mitch went to California. What would she do with this, a criminal indictment? Penny thought that if it was explained properly, her mother might understand. Before she called, she spoke to MacNeil and took notes. Penny told Elena that Jimmy had been accused unjustly of rape. She gave as factual and accurate a presentation as she was capable of and explained the weakness in the prosecution's case.

How dare anybody accuse a fine boy like Jimmy of such a deed, Elena responded. He was so handsome, he didn't have to rape anybody. That was the reaction Penny was looking for. What kind of lawyer had they retained? Elena had not heard of him. You don't get a local lawyer to handle a case like this; you get someone from New York who handles big cases. Why wasn't Penny taking care of that? What was she doing?

Penny said the lawyer and Malcolm were handling matters. Elena was furious with her. She should have been taking action, the way the Captain would have, the way any of the people in the family would have. This is our Jimmy. Elena said she would make some calls to the Captain's old friends and get a lawyer lined up. Penny should go out and buy a new dress and stand tall at the club, because sure as can be, the tongues were going to wag in that town. She should remember that she was a Fisk. She was more the Captain's daughter than she was this man's wife, and she should remember it and act accordingly and that was that.

PENNY STOOD at a table in the living room where she kept a display of the family photographs: pictures of relatives, of Malcolm and her, of the boys. She recalled the evening after Mitch had just dropped out of Princeton. Why couldn't Mitch have taken the time he wanted? Why didn't she stand up to Malcolm? She looked at a picture of Jimmy as a little boy, holding his first tennis racket, and remembered all the lessons and the tournaments.

Penny Andrews conjured an image that captured their marriage for her and made her shudder: Malcolm home from work, carrying bouquets of dead flowers. Malcolm filling their lives with false expectations.

She went to Saks and bought a new dress for the tongue waggers. She would stand up to them. And she was not going to defer to Malcolm, either. He would not cost her another son. He could no longer bring dead flowers to a Fisk.

TO GET OFF CAMPUS, Jimmy went home for the weekend, a weekend he would have liked to spend with Janna, not with his parents. But he needed to get away from that campus, and he didn't want to spend the time alone. He walked into the house and saw his mother for the first time since the indictment. She pressed him to her chest.

"I'm sorry, Mom."

"You didn't do anything bad."

"It was just a misunderstanding."

"We'll get it fixed," she said.

Penny made one of her elaborate dinners, and the table conversation, which she directed, was defense strategy and the strong and weak points of the prosecutor's case.

"You shouldn't be making yourself so tense," Malcolm said.

"I have to be involved. This is our Jimmy."

THE NEXT DAY, all three went to the club. Penny was wearing her new dress. Malcolm and Jimmy played a friendly set, trying to be good-natured on the court to show potential gossipers that everything was okay.

ELENA FISK had obtained the name of a lawyer through the Captain's former colleagues.

"Use him!" she told her daughter. "He handles big criminal cases in New York. Jimmy has to have the best."

Penny contacted the lawyer, and he said he would participate. Rupert Dobbins was a tall and broad-shouldered man in his fifties, with the face of a tough marine and a military crew cut to match. The two defense lawyers knew each other. Dobbins told MacNeil that he had been brought in by Penny Andrews for additional support, and they agreed they would work as a team on the case.

Informed by Penny that she had called in another lawyer, Malcolm was mystified.

"How do you come to do such a thing, on your own, without consulting me?"

"I spoke to my mother. She made some calls and got his name."

"Your mother? We have a good lawyer. *I* got him for us."

"You have to do everything you can."

"This is going to be very costly."

The instant he said it, Malcolm knew that was a mistake. He didn't mean that you scrimp on your son's well-being. It was an instinctive remark, because high-priced lawyers were expensive, and now they had a second and that would be doubly expensive.

"I didn't mean I'd want to save money on Jimmy."

"I have money. I have my own money. We'll pay for the lawyer out of my money," she said coldly.

"That's not necessary."

"Let's not discuss it anymore. He has the best now, which is what he should have."

DOBBINS WENT to Layton to conduct his own investigation, bringing with him two associates from his staff, a man and a woman, both in their early thirties. Dobbins and his colleagues surveyed the surroundings, went through the house and the basement room, and interviewed people in The Big Leagues in a group setting. Dobbins invited Jimmy to his room at the Layton Inn, where all three lawyers questioned him intensively about the events of the night of the alleged rape. Jimmy stayed with his version: the girl was eager for sex, they had sex with her consent.

"Let me see if I have your explanations straight," Dobbins said to him. "She accused you of rape because she was rejected, vindictive, and unbalanced."

"Yes."

"The students you originally told that you had sex with Elizabeth Mason you've now, in effect, untold. You said, 'Strike that. I didn't have sex with her.'"

"More or less."

"The only people to whom you've admitted you did, in fact, have sex with her are your parents, Brett MacNeil, and now us?"

"Yes."

"Some mess, isn't it?"

"It is. Bad luck. Bad timing."

"How so?"

"Getting involved with the wrong girl," Jimmy responded.

"Oh, is that it? You had bad luck in getting involved with the wrong girl, and that's why we're here."

"I've never even had a traffic violation before this. I work with kids in my spare time. I give tennis lessons at a day care center."

"You wouldn't be telling us that to finesse us, would you, about what a moral guy you are?"

"It's a fact, that's all."

"What does giving tennis lessons to kids in a day care center have to do with whether on September second you took a girl into a place called the Fuck Room and, in the midst of a competition with your buddies on how many girls you could score with, did or did not rape her?"

"I'm just saying—"

"I know what you're saying, Jimmy. You had some bad luck."

ON THE QUESTION of whether to place the defendant on the stand, Dobbins decided after the interview that he wouldn't risk having the prosecutor go near this young man. Dobbins was in possession of the core of the case. MacNeil had briefed him. He knew who the key witnesses against Jimmy would be and the extent of the evidence so far revealed against the boy. While he was in Caldwell, he went to see Carl Peters, hoping to overwhelm him with his name and reputation. Peters was not moved. He hadn't tried cases against Dobbins when he was in the Manhattan District Attorney's office, but he had seen name lawyers before.

"This is getting spicy," Peters said on shaking hands with Dobbins and his colleagues.

"I can't see why you're bringing this case," Dobbins told him. "There's nothing here."

"A rape. And a couple of lesser charges," Peters replied.

"We've done a pretty good investigation on our own, and if I were in your seat—"

"Which you're not—"

"I'd pass and save the taxpayers some money."

"I think this kid should do time."

"Why? It was an ordinary sexual exchange between kids on a date."

"But you'd entertain a plea bargain?" Peters said.

"Do you have something in mind?"

"Do you?"

"Misdemeanor with a suspended sentence," Dobbins replied.

"That's not even a slap on the wrist."

"What do you propose?" Dobbins asked.

"I think we'll go to trial. This is going to be a real media event, with you here, Mr. Dobbins. The local press is going to love it. Good day, folks. While you're in town, you might want to visit our new mall."

PENNY ANDREWS received a visit from her older sister, Cynthia, who lived in Darien. Cynthia was the prettiest of the Fisk girls, petite and demure into her fifties. Married to Stuart Harrison, the current chief executive officer of Fisk Electronics, she occupied herself with charity work in Darien. Cynthia was wearing a tailored suit with a little flowered hat. The purpose of her visit was "Jimmy's situation," as she phrased it. She had discussed it with their mother and had read about it in the newspaper. Cynthia felt that nobody from such a fine background and who looked as striking and handsome as Jimmy would have to rape a girl to get sex.

"Stuart said it's crucial that Jimmy doesn't spend even one night in jail."

"We don't intend him to."

"Stuart doesn't think you should accept any arrangement, but you should fight it all the way and win."

"Yes, that's our strategy."

"Jail for a boy like Jimmy would be horrible beyond belief. If just for one night, horrible, the things that could happen, Stuart said. They rape boys."

"I beg your pardon."

"Male rape. Gang rape by men. It's unbelievable. Stuart said they've had cases where a boy is just being detained overnight and in that one night he's raped by the other prisoners. So Jimmy can't go to jail, not even for a short sentence."

Penny felt ill. At her darkest moments, she had thought of Jimmy behind bars, in a ghastly uniform, eating vile institutional food. She hadn't imagined rape.

RUPERT DOBBINS ASKED Malcolm and Penny to meet with him in his office, in the Seagram Building in New York City, to give them his judgment about the case. He regarded the work done by Brett MacNeil as beyond criticism. MacNeil was a solid defense lawyer, and according to Dobbins, the case was being handled in an extremely able manner. "We won't put Jimmy on the stand. We'll let the weakness of their case topple itself. It comes down to two kids on a date. They have to prove his guilt beyond a reasonable doubt, and as MacNeil argued in the college hearing, doubt runs right through this case."

"So it's impossible to lose?" Penny asked.

" 'Impossible' is not a word a lawyer would like. If we go to trial, I'd put our chances of losing virtually at nil."

"But it's still *possible* to lose."

"Penny, he's telling you that it doesn't make sense to think that way."

"Don't tell me what makes sense. I heard that boys like Jimmy, if they go to prison, they could be raped by the other prisoners. Is that true?" she asked Dobbins.

"As your husband said, it really doesn't make sense to think that way, Mrs. Andrews. You're speculating about your son in prison, and I can't see us losing the case."

"You didn't say it was *impossible* to lose. Do they rape

young men like Jimmy in prison? Answer me, Mr. Dobbins.
I'm paying you for your answer.''

"Should we arrive at that most extraordinarily unlikely
point where Jimmy is sentenced, we would make certain it
would be the safest, most comfortable circumstances.''

"Penny, he's not going to jail," Malcolm said.

"Are you in a position to guarantee that?" she challenged.

Dobbins painstakingly went over the defense strategy and
the prosecution's case in an attempt to reassure Penny.
Malcolm was convinced, but the lawyer still was unable to
guarantee Penny that Jimmy could not possibly be found
guilty of one of the charges. Even if the odds were
overwhelmingly in their favor, the possibility *still* existed.
That little baby boy, who grew up to be such a handsome
young man, so unhappy when he came home the other day
and she held him in her arms as she did when he was
little—he could be raped in prison. He could be raped by
someone with AIDS in prison, and he could die.


"COULD I ASK what this is in reference to?" Laura's
secretary said to Penny.

"Would you tell her it's Jimmy Andrews' mother."

Laura came on the line.

"Yes? This is Laura Mason."

"I hope you'll excuse me for calling you at your place of
business. I got your number through the Layton office."

"What is it?"

"Could you meet me for a drink today when you're
finished with work? It's desperately urgent."

"I don't know if I should. I don't know if I want to."

"It's between mothers. Please, Mrs. Mason. I must speak
to you."

Her voice was so desperate that Laura agreed to see her.
They arranged to meet at six-thirty in the Polo Lounge of
the Westbury Hotel.

Penny was seated with a half-finished drink in front of

her when Laura arrived. They shook hands, Laura warily. She ordered a Perrier and leaned back, waiting.

"Mrs. Mason, you're a mother, and I thought you'd be able to understand what I'm going through. Jimmy is not a bad boy. He's had pressure put on him. Much of that is my husband's doing, pushing him to excel. And I suppose to the extent that I went along with it, I'm responsible too."

"Lots of young men have pressure on them today. They don't all rape girls."

"We've brought in another lawyer to defend Jimmy. Rupert Dobbins."

"I've heard of him."

"He said it was extraordinarily unlikely for Jimmy to be found guilty of anything."

"Congratulations to you all."

"The new lawyer is very smart, very able. I asked him whether is was *impossible* to lose. He said 'impossible' was not a word he was comfortable with. So I sit before you as a mother, knowing that it is still within the realm of possibility for Jimmy to go to jail."

"That's what a prosecution is, Mrs. Andrews."

"What*ever* happened between your daughter and my son was a misunderstanding. And because of it, my son Jimmy could die."

"Die?"

The woman had seemed unbalanced at the college hearing. Laura had confirmation of that now.

"The sentencing won't call for the death penalty," Laura said to her.

"I'm talking about AIDS."

"AIDS?"

"In prison, Jimmy runs the risk of being raped. The other prisoners can rape him. One, maybe a gang of them. Lining up to get at this college boy. That's what goes on in prison. Do you know what that does to me, to think of that happening to Jimmy? And if a person who rapes him has AIDS, Jimmy can get AIDS, and he could die."

"You raise terrible possibilities."

"What do you think is a sufficient punishment here? It can't be that."

"No, it can't be."

"My husband doesn't know I'm here. The lawyers don't. This is between us. I beg you to use your influence to have the charges against Jimmy dropped. I thought this out. I know how it can work. Your daughter can change her mind about the testimony. She can say that she doesn't remember too well what happened. Without her, there's no case against Jimmy. That's all she has to do, not remember."

"You want her to lie?"

"It's not lying. It's just becoming vague about the details." She cleared her throat in nervousness. "Mrs. Mason, I thought a financial compensation would be in order. I would be willing to write you a check for twenty thousand dollars."

"I beg your pardon?"

"Should it be more?"

"Do you think this is about money?" Laura said.

"I wasn't presuming that it was. I thought merely as compensation for your troubles and your expense—"

"First of all—and I'm repeating what the district attorney told us—this isn't even Elizabeth any longer. This case is The State versus James Andrews. There's a larger element here."

"Will you consider it? Please. If the money was an insult, I'm sorry. Let me just appeal to you then as a parent. If our situation were reversed, and the possibility existed of what could happen to Jimmy happening to your child, wouldn't you want the other family to find the compassion to save your child?"

"I don't know what to say to you, Mrs. Andrews. It isn't even my decision to make."

BEN CYNICALLY SUGGESTED that Penny Andrews was not operating as a sole agent, that she had been put up to it by

the defense team. Laura disagreed. Penny Andrews' appeal
had been so fervent and the money offering so clumsy, she
seemed thoroughly believable.

"I think we're obliged to tell Elizabeth about this,"
Laura said.

"Why?"

"These are the implications of the trial. It involves her."

ELIZABETH WAS SHOCKED when she heard of Penny Andrews'
conversation with her mother.

"I've never thought of Jimmy being raped," she said.

"I don't think it's a legitimate concern," Ben said. "He
wouldn't end up in a tough prison."

"She was offering twenty thousand dollars?"

"Everything has a price," Ben said.

"There's not any part of this I don't hate," Elizabeth said
to them.

THE NEWS COVERAGE in the college newspaper—articles about
the protest, the indictment, and the scene outside Elizabeth's
dorm—were creating repercussions among alumni and parents. Many of these people received the newspaper and
demanded to know what was going on at Layton. President
Baker assured callers that the campus was safe and the boy
who was indicted represented an isolated case. Furthermore,
he was innocent until proven guilty. Some callers advocated
curfews, bed checks, more police. Others were questioning
the entire fabric of male-female relationships on the campus.

Baker and his aide Morgan Warner didn't want to look at
one more news report that reflected unfavorably on the
college. The indictment of the Andrews boy was a time
bomb. As the case proceeded, there would be more publicity
and more attention focused on rape at Layton. Pressed to
make use of his diplomatic skills, Baker told Warner:

"If campus rape is a national problem, and we as a
college lead the way on rape education, we can turn the

image around for Layton. We become the leader among colleges.''

"That has a nice feeling to it, Hudson. We don't get singled out for rape if it's endemic to college life, but we do get credit for taking a stand.''

"So where is that Jean Philips with her rape colloquium? What we have to do is embellish it. Do it with a flourish.''

JEAN PHILIPS had been working in an orderly manner, assembling a student panel that would represent various points of view. Baker did not want to wait any longer.

"We'd like to do it early next week, Jean. Tuesday afternoon would be good, so we can make the Wednesday papers and local television.''

"They don't usually cover our programs—''

"This is going to be a significant event at Layton. Mandatory attendance for all students. Mandatory for all members of the faculty. All classes canceled.''

"All classes canceled?''

"And that rape protest of the women that was disrupted. I'd like you to arrange to have that brought right *into* the theater.''

"Really?''

"Yes. We're going to be in the forefront of rape education here at Layton,'' he said, as though that was what he had always had in mind.

THE LAYTON THEATER was filled; faculty and administration members occupied a section on the right-hand side of the auditorium, television crews from the local stations and news reporters were in place in front of the stage. Jean Philips led out the panel members and called for quiet, and after a while the restless audience became calm.

"In America every six minutes a woman is raped,'' she said. "In a survey of college campuses, the number of date rapes was shockingly high. It's a national crisis, and it's our crisis.''

The student panel on stage consisted of three men and three women, including Sterling May and Rod Wyman. After they exchanged views for a while, the discussion was opened to the audience at large. People talked about the pressures on them in sexual matters, the elusiveness of clear messages about sex, sexism, sex in the time of AIDS. The discussion lasted for an hour and a half. People were engaged by the subject and concerned.

Philips then signaled to the rear of the auditorium, where Elizabeth, Donna, Candace, and about forty women who had volunteered to be in the demonstration were ready to march down the aisles. They carried the masks. People were in place to mime the tableaux of sexual violence. Sarah's music would be heard over the sound system.

There were three nonstudents in the group. These were women Jean Philips had contacted, who had agreed to participate. Each of these women, former Layton students, had been raped while at the school. When they reversed their masks, the signs would read: "I was raped at Layton." Elizabeth and two current Layton students also carried these signs.

The students in the audience had been treating the event with seriousness. With that mood prevailing, as the music played and the demonstrators made their way down the aisles, stopping for the tableaux and reversing the signs, the audience began to applaud. The applause continued as they made their way onto the stage and faced the audience.

At Elizabeth's signal, the music stopped. The audience became quiet as, in silence, one by one, the rape victims, who were in the front of the group on stage, began to reverse the masks, revealing the words "I was raped at Layton." They then lowered the signs so their faces were in full view. This confession that was also an accusation froze the audience. The rape victims were staring out, in some instances finding the very person in the audience who had raped them and looking directly at the rapist. Men in the audience were turning away, gazing at their feet, at the ceiling. Elizabeth located Jimmy and looked right at him. He looked away.

The six women who had been raped held that stance for about a minute. The plan was for the women, on signal, to reverse the signs and the entire procession to exit from the auditorium. Suddenly, unplanned, a woman rose from the audience and deliberately made her way toward the stage, to take her place alongside the women who had been raped. A moment later, another woman rose and came forward. And another. It was like a religious revival meeting. The audience was watching transfixed as rape victims were coming forward to announce publicly that they, too, had been raped. One of the former students handed the sign ''I was raped at Layton'' to a woman who came up on stage, and now she held it before her. Others handed over their signs to the new women joining the demonstration. Some of the women were crying, others were rigid with defiance.

They stood for a few moments more, a row of eleven women who had been raped at Layton College. Elizabeth gestured for the music to resume, and the marchers made their way out of the auditorium, the audience silent, stunned by the power of the testimony.

# CHAPTER
# 18

THE "LAYTON RAPE AWARENESS COLLOQUIUM" was the lead piece in the *New York Times* Sunday wrap-up of college activities, and since the *Times* now featured a national edition, the suddenly enlightened position of the college on the subject of rape was news across the country. The piece contained a statement from the rape awareness pioneer Dr. Hudson Baker, calling for all colleges to follow Layton's lead. He outlined the innovations at Layton. A Rape Awareness Colloquium would be a mandatory event for all students at the commencement of each fall semester. A course on human sexuality, with special emphasis on rape, would become a freshman requirement. A new psychologist would be added to the Layton staff for counseling and to administer workshops and seminars on male-female relations. The campus security force would be increased, and with the cooperation of the local police, the sale of alcohol to students would be closely monitored.

Coverage of the colloquium was shown on the area television news programs, and a large article, with a photograph of the marchers in the auditorium, was page one of the local section in the *Albany Times-Union*. The colloquium and the

changes at Layton were the subject of an entire issue of the
*Layton Journal*. Baker was now inundated with congratulations on his responsible policy. The diplomat had managed to take a public relations crisis and convert it into high
praise from parents and alumni, renewing the college's
fund-raising capability.

The news about Layton also had a positive effect on
many of the students. They were pleased that the college
they attended was being singled out for its wise course of
action and that they themselves had been favorably treated
in the news pieces for their behavior at the colloquium.
Elizabeth felt a change in the way she was regarded after
that evening.

Rod Wyman, as much an adversary as she could imagine
with his vicious chant, approached her in front of the dorm
and said:

"It went well."

"Yes, it did."

"I think both sides learned something from it," he told
her, taking credit for his own participation.

"I think that's true."

"Well, see you around," he said with an actual smile.

Janna Willis came up to her in the library.

"Excuse me. I used to go with Jimmy."

"Yes, I know."

"I don't know what happened between the two of you,
but I just wanted to say I was very moved by the event in the
theater."

"Thank you."

"Jimmy has some good qualities, you know."

"It's hard to remember."

People she didn't know greeted her as she moved back
and forth between classes and the dorm. Those she did know
made a special point of saying hello, chatting with her.
Elizabeth felt like an athlete who makes a winning score in
the big game.

• • •

LAURA AND BEN were overjoyed by these developments. But on the Andrews side, the news coverage of the colloquium and of the new measures instituted by the college troubled the defense lawyers. They did not need the college administration publicly acknowledging a rape problem on campus. But Dobbins and MacNeil reassured the Andrewses, saying that nothing had altered the evidence in the case or produced any new evidence against Jimmy. However, the Andrews family knew what was appearing in the press.

ELIZABETH SAW Jimmy Andrews from across the campus one afternoon. It was raining, and he was walking head down, slightly hunched over. She couldn't tell if he looked that way because of the weather or because of his emotional circumstance. Elizabeth, who had once walked this campus avoiding people's eyes, stopped to watch him, fascinated at the way their styles had become reversed.

PENNY ANDREWS MOVED the money. She took it out of a bank account she kept separately from the funds she shared with Malcolm. It was her money, an inheritance from the Captain, and she placed it in a separate checking account. What price would you place on your son's living a normal life, being a whole person? She wrote a check for twenty thousand dollars, prepared to pay more if they wanted more.

Dear Mrs. Mason:
I am desperate. That my son might go to prison, even for the shortest time, is an unbearable thought. I realize you did not pursue this because you were seeking money. The money is only to help compensate your daughter, your family, for your difficulties in this matter. Please, please, have her change her testimony.

Very truly yours,

Laura and Ben brought the letter and the check to their next session with Angela Woodson. They were continuing to see the family therapist once a week now. Woodson believed that although they were beginning to get back to a level of kindness toward each other, they should try to understand how they had drifted apart, to avoid a repeat of the situation.

"Separation from your daughter is a major part of your problems," Woodson told them. "Difficult as it is, you can't impose your experience on her. You have to let go. She's the one who must decide about this."

ELIZABETH WAS STRUGGLING with this very issue. She gathered her friends in her room and showed them the letter, which had been forwarded to her by her parents. They all dismissed it as absurd and insulting to think she could be bought.

"There's not any part of this I don't hate," she had said to her parents. She didn't want to go through a trial. She wanted to be done with it. Taking precedence over everything for her was the sense that she and her allies had triumphed on a larger scale than any specific punishment for Jimmy Andrews. Requiring him to stand trial seemed irrelevant to her now.

"We got the administration to stand on their heads," she told her friends. "We got enemies to be on our side. What else is there to win?"

"I suppose you could let him off. But if he 'goes up the river,' he could always sell his story to the movies," Donna joked. "We haven't had a good, raunchy prison movie in a while."

"We did win," Sterling said. "It was amazing to feel that quiet in the theater when the women came up on stage."

"I have my justice," Elizabeth said. "I have that event. I have Baker practically carrying a 'No Means No' banner. What more do I need?"

"So let it be over," Sterling said, and the others agreed.

"There it is," Elizabeth said. "We won."

• • •

RIDING THE WAVE of this endorsement by her friends, Elizabeth went to see the district attorney in his office. Elizabeth announced to Carl Peters that after serious reflection, she wanted to drop the charge against Jimmy Andrews. He exploded.

"What are you, the white Tawana Brawley?"

"I don't want to be a witness. I don't want Jimmy charged."

"He *has been* charged. A grand jury indicted him."

"The charge can be dropped, can't it?"

"Look, you came in here with your parents. You said you were raped, and we investigated. It was a difficult investigation, because you stupidly destroyed all the evidence. But we went ahead. We spent many hours questioning people, analyzing the case. And we broke the case. *You* said you were raped, and *I* believed you."

"You can still believe me."

"Why do you think I decided to prosecute? Because a crime was committed! And the person who committed it was walking around!"

"But justice was done. When Jimmy was indicted, we were able to have a big event at the college, and the administration came around to where they're totally changing the way they deal with rape, and that's real justice."

"That's not justice from where I sit. I'm obliged to see that criminal acts are punished. So that little girls, even if they've had a couple of beers when they shouldn't," he said fiercely, "even if they neck with guys and rub up against them, don't get raped."

"Mr. Peters, I already won everything there is to win."

"Wrong. You lost. Because he rapes you, nothing happens to him, and he can do it again."

"I don't think he would."

"Oh, in addition to being judge and jury, you're the court-appointed psychiatrist. He gets away with it. And you've *announced* that somebody can rape a girl and get away with it.''

''I think, in the light of what's happened since then, people would understand.''

''Do you? And is his family going to understand? And his lawyer? They can say you falsely accused him. They can come after you and file charges against you.''

''I guess I'll have to take that chance. I can't, for myself, go on with this.''

''Young lady, I'm not prepared to allow you to manipulate me and my office. You have testified under oath to a grand jury. If you do not agree to appear as a witness for the prosecution, with the same certainty about this crime that you expressed to me and to the grand jury, I will personally see that *you* are brought to trial, for perjury,'' he threatened.

SHE WAS SUPPOSED to hand in an English paper on Monday morning. She couldn't deal with it. She was worried, unable to think clearly. She called her parents and said she was coming home for the weekend. Elizabeth made a crash landing into her parents' living room. She talked in a rush, telling them everything: her quandary, her fears, her feeling that she had already won her victory. Both Laura and Ben were able to extract the lead from the story: Elizabeth didn't want to go to trial. She didn't want to pursue it any further, and Laura and Ben were, at heart, relieved.

MARTIN REED WAS consulted about the legal implications. Reed thought the Andrews side would negotiate and not press charges against her. As for Peters' perjury threat, he explained that not agreeing to appear with the same certainty about a crime is not perjury; testifying materially differently is. He had known Carl Peters in New York and said he would speak to him. He reached Peters the following day.

''Hello, Marty. How have you been?'' Peters said.

''Good. How are you doing up there?''

"I don't get a chance to go against you, but it's interesting from time to time."

"Carl, I represent Elizabeth Mason."

"Yes, I saw that."

"She's a fine girl."

"And an excellent witness. I have a shot against the Andrews kid. Long odds, but you never know."

"She's been through the mill already. She wants out, Carl. Let her be."

"This case is a crime deterrent," he said. "The kid's not a conventional criminal. Rapes like this happen all the time, and it's going to have an impact if I win."

"From what the father tells me, the girl already won some big concessions at the college."

"I couldn't care less about the college, Marty."

"It's something you have to consider. Because of what she did, they won't have as many rapes over there. Come on, Carl, give her some peace. Let her out of it."

"Her testimony was not given under duress."

"I can coach her through this, and you know it. She goes on the stand, she keeps faith with her prior testimony, but there are little lapses. Nothing substantial to invite perjury; just enough for Dobbins to destroy her."

"If she's a person of such high standards, she should testify for the greater good."

"She's a little fish, Carl. Throw her back."

"I'm not so eager. I'm going to talk to her again."

ELIZABETH WAS ASKED by Peters to come to his office. She brought news clippings with her of the events at Layton, to convince the district attorney that something important had been accomplished without a trial. She was concerned that if the case went to trial and Jimmy won, it would be disastrous for their side. A claim could be made by the hecklers at Layton that the rape demonstrators based their position on a lie, and that if Jimmy was innocent, so were the others.

Elizabeth sat in the waiting area, clutching the folder containing the news clippings as if it were a talisman.

While she was waiting to go in, Mallory and Neary came out of Peters' office and saw her sitting there. They both reacted similarly, with a nod of recognition that did not contain much warmth.

"Hello," Elizabeth said.

"Why did you change your mind?" Mallory asked her bluntly. "A lot of hard work went into this case."

"I know. I appreciate what you've done."

"It's an odd way of showing it, letting him walk," he said.

"He committed a crime," Neary added.

"But he's not really getting away with it."

She offered the clippings in the hope the two detectives would be convinced.

"She has her own press file," Mallory said.

They looked through the clippings quickly.

"This was a victory," Elizabeth said. "And it wouldn't have happened without your investigation and then Mr. Peters' getting the indictment."

"Does this satisfy you?" Mallory said, handing back the clippings. "Do you really consider this justice?"

"Yes, I do."

"I guess you do. Well, we're not the ones you have to convince," Mallory told her.

About fifteen minutes later, Peters came out and gestured for her to take a seat in his office.

"So have you had a change of heart since our last conversation?"

"No. But I brought these. They show how much was accomplished without a trial."

He looked through the clippings cursorily.

"And?"

"This was a college where they didn't even want to hear about rape. It's all changed. I just told that to the detectives, that everybody's work helped."

"What we're upholding here is the law. Men rape women and they get away with it. The women don't report it. Or the cases don't stand up. Jimmy Andrews is every casual rapist. If I can successfully prosecute this case, then everybody, not just in your little domain, is on notice about rape."

"If he *wins* the trial, what we got from the college is lost. The boys can get to say he was innocent all the time, and the others were too. It gives them an out. They shouldn't have that. They shouldn't rape us."

"We both want the same thing."

"But I won. It's over. Let us have this victory and let it end. Please let it be over."

He looked at her carefully. The phone rang and he answered it, a crisis about a missing witness on another matter. He cupped the phone and said, "We'll talk some more," dismissing Elizabeth.

A FEW DAYS LATER, in a case Peters had been pursuing for months, the real estate developer of the Caldwell shopping mall agreed to testify that he paid kickbacks to the mayor of Caldwell and two members of the town board in exchange for preferential zoning treatment and tax abatements. The same week, a bartender in a roadside restaurant was shot and killed by an an off-duty security guard. Peters had two major cases to administer. In the Andrews case he was dealing with a long shot and a suddenly recalcitrant key witness. He decided to clear away *State v. James Andrews* and concentrate on the other matters. Peters informed Brett MacNeil that he was not going ahead with the trial. He didn't want any residue from the case costing him more time, and he advised MacNeil not to file countercharges against the girl, implying that her people might change their minds. He also strongly advised MacNeil not to join with Dobbins in calling any self-congratulatory press conferences.

• • •

Jimmy learned about the district attorney's decision from MacNeil, who then called Penny and Malcolm. They rushed to speak to Jimmy.

"I knew you were innocent!" Malcolm proclaimed.

"Right, Dad," Jimmy said softly.

"Praise God for this, Jimmy," Penny said. "You're a good boy."

"Thank you for saying that, Mom."

"Could you come home this weekend, Jimmy? Or can we come there? I have to see you."

"I'll come home."

Malcolm went to the club that night with the news. He wasn't going to run around shouting it. Better the nonchalant approach, that it never had been a cause for alarm. He positioned himself at the bar and, making sure it could be heard by a couple of the club members, said to the bartender:

"By the way, Jimmy was totally exonerated on that problem at school."

"That's great, Mr. Andrews."

"Congratulations," one of the men said.

"Thanks, but it's not a reason for congratulations, actually. He was always innocent. They never had a case against him."

At The Big Leagues, Bill Casley and the guys let out a loud cheer when Jimmy announced in the living room to the group at large that the charges had been dropped.

"We've got to throw a party," Casley said.

People agreed; an excuse for a party was always welcome.

"Do you really think that's appropriate?" John Hatcher said sharply, looking directly at Jimmy.

"Forget a party," Jimmy said. "Let's just have a beer, guys, and put it behind us."

"Right," John Hatcher responded. "I mean, Jimmy's not Nelson Mandela."

• • •

LAURA AND BEN SPOKE to Elizabeth, all of them overjoyed that it was not going to trial.

"It's finished legally," Laura said to Ben after the call. "Let it be finished emotionally."

"I'll try," he said.

"I will too."

Elizabeth wanted to be with them and took the bus to New York the next Saturday. As she entered the house, Laura and Ben came to her, put their arms around her. Elizabeth started to cry in release. Josh entered the room and the parents extended their arms to hug him too, the four of them holding on to each other. They went to dinner at a Chinese restaurant that night, and they talked about the end of the case, but then they moved on to discuss movies, and Josh talked about the coming baseball season. That was the celebration, a celebration of normalcy, a time when they were together again as they once had been.

ELIZABETH, SETH, DONNA, STERLING, AND CANDACE went out for pizza for their celebration. Over dinner, they decided that they were going to apply for off-campus housing together for the following year; they would rent a house and call it "The Layton Five."

PENNY MADE A bountiful meal for Jimmy's appearance, a holiday dinner.

"Thank God this is done with," Penny said, raising her wineglass in a toast.

"Right," Jimmy agreed. "Now I'm just looking forward to a strong season on the court."

Malcolm offered his own interpretation of the events.

"This may not necessarily be done with. That girl slandered Jimmy. She falsely accused him of a crime. MacNeil said Peters doesn't want us to raise a counter-charge, but that's for Peters' convenience."

"You want to file a charge against *her*?" Jimmy said.

"These are not poor people. They sent their girl to Layton. We should sue the pants off them."

"We don't need the money," Penny said bluntly.

"We'd be righting a wrong. Jimmy was wronged."

"I say drop it. He's home. He's safe," Penny told him.

"I don't happen to agree with you. I'm going to look into it. Perhaps get another lawyer, someone who'll be more disposed to take this case on. People like that shouldn't be allowed to drag people like us into the dirt."

"Drop it, Dad."

"This isn't entirely your decision, Jimmy," he said.

"They'll win, for Chrissake. Stay away from them."

"In a court of law—" Malcolm continued.

"Let me just play some tennis. That's what I was *brought up to do*, wasn't I?"

FOR SEVERAL DAYS, Penny Andrews phoned her bank to find out if a check had cleared in a large amount. Malcolm could go to the club and accept the greetings of well-wishers and say to them that Jimmy was innocent all along. But Penny knew it was she who had influenced the girl's reluctance to testify, with good, reliable money—old money. Penny Andrews stared in surprise when one morning she opened an envelope mailed to her by Laura Mason and found the check inside, torn in half.

AS THE SEMESTER CONTINUED, Elizabeth worked on her courses, spent time with her friends, and joined a student committee to organize the rape colloquium that would begin the fall term. She asked to be HIV tested and was relieved when the result came back negative. The semester passed without incident. But her bad dreams did not disappear, sometimes frightening her out of sleep. Figures would hover over her, obliterating her. And when she walked home at night she was always wary. And when young men expressed interest in her, she was distant. She would have liked to have someone hold her, but it seemed too complicated.

• • •

For the *Layton Journal*'s final issue of the year, Dr. Baker issued a statement. He bade farewell to the seniors, looked forward to the return of the underclassmen, and listed, among the year's accomplishments, ''Layton's new awareness about rape.'' He also announced a new acting dean of students, Jean Philips, who would be replacing William Harlan.

The people in The Big Leagues were preparing to leave. Jimmy and John Hatcher were in their room, packing.

''I don't know why you had to give me such a hard time,'' Jimmy said to him. ''When you come right down to it, I won the hearing. I won with the police.''

''You didn't win anything. You got away with something.''

''You weren't in the room with us that night. You don't know what happened.''

''I can figure it out. Remember you told me she was crazy? Liz Mason turned out to be a *student leader*.''

''And she screwed up my whole year with her politics.''

''Oh, now this was a political thing? Jimmy, stop shitting me. I'd have to keep your stories on my computer to keep track of them all. You raped her, and you got away with it.''

''I didn't do anything different from what I've done before and you've done before and a lot of guys around here have done before.''

''Speak for yourself.''

''She was coming on to me, she was all over me, I thought she wanted to be pushed, and I pushed her. That's a misunderstanding. That's not rape. And no court would ever call it rape, according to some very high-priced lawyers.''

''I'm not a lawyer. But I know the rules. And you went too far, Jimmy. You crossed a line.''

''What I didn't need this year was a preachy, tight-assed

roommate. I'm glad to be getting out of here. This whole year's been bad luck and bad times.''

"Bad luck? You asshole, you were lucky.''

HIS NEED TO justify himself before he left the place was frustrated by John Hatcher, so he took his plea to the court of last resort.

"It's me," he said, standing in Elizabeth's doorway.

"What do you know?''

"I've come to say goodbye," he said.

"Goodbye," she said curtly.

"May I come in?''

"Oh, you want to say more than goodbye.''

"Please . . .''

"Only if you leave the door open.''

He entered, and she did not offer him a place to sit, indicating that whatever he wanted to say had better be brief.

"I figured we're never going to see each other again," he told her.

"That's a reasonable assumption.''

"Well, this year has not been the greatest for me," he said.

"My sympathies.''

"I guess it wasn't what you had in mind, either.''

"No, this wasn't in the Layton bulletin.''

"It's been a pretty rough experience for both of us. And I'd like the slate to be wiped clean between us. I came to apologize to you.''

"Oh?''

"I really regret we had such a misunderstanding. And I wish the rest of your college years will be a whole lot happier.''

"Misunderstanding? There was no misunderstanding. There was a rape. Don't you get it?''

"Sometimes you can't tell how much a girl wants to be pushed . . . ," he said, still trying to sell that idea.

"You don't get it. Not even now. Jimmy, the only reason you're not going on trial is because *I* let you off!"

She studied him. He was unrepentant and unconscious. She realized that to spend any more time concerned with such a person was to make him more important than he was entitled to be.

"All right, Jimmy, enough of this. It's a clean slate. Now get out of my life."

THAT WAS THE last time Elizabeth Mason and Jimmy Andrews saw each other. The following semester, Holly Robertson told her she had heard Jimmy was playing on the tennis circuit. He hadn't won anything major, and he hadn't won anything minor. Holly also said that Jimmy's parents had separated and were getting a divorce.

ON THE FINAL DAY of her freshman year, Laura and Ben drove up and Elizabeth gathered her belongings and they took her home. That evening, she went over to her friend Sarah's house and asked her to take out some sheet music. Sarah played, and Elizabeth started to sing.

AVERY CORMAN is the author of the novels *Oh, God!*, *Kramer vs. Kramer, The Old Neighborhood,* and *50.* He lives in New York City.

*New York Times* **bestselling author of**
*The Accidental Tourist* and *Breathing Lessons*

# ANNE
# TYLER

"To read a novel by Anne Tyler is to fall in
love!" —*People Magazine*

Critics have praised her fine gift for characterization and her skill at blending touching insight and
powerful emotions to create superb entertainment.

__The Accidental Tourist            0-425-09291-7/$5.95
__Breathing Lessons                 0-425-11774-X/$5.95

**For Visa, MasterCard and American Express
orders ($10 minimum) call: 1-800-631-8571**

**Check book(s). Fill out coupon. Send to:**
**BERKLEY PUBLISHING GROUP**
390 Murray Hill Pkwy., Dept. B
East Rutherford, NJ 07073

NAME_____

ADDRESS_____

CITY_____

STATE_____ ZIP_____

**PLEASE ALLOW 6 WEEKS FOR DELIVERY.**
**PRICES ARE SUBJECT TO CHANGE**
**WITHOUT NOTICE.**

**POSTAGE AND HANDLING:**
$1.50 for one book, 50¢ for each ad-
ditional. Do not exceed $4.50.

**BOOK TOTAL**                    $_____

**POSTAGE & HANDLING**           $_____

**APPLICABLE SALES TAX**         $_____
(CA, NJ, NY, PA)

**TOTAL AMOUNT DUE**             $_____

**PAYABLE IN US FUNDS.**
(No cash orders accepted.)

210a

FIC
COR        Corman, Avery.
                Prized possessions
           :

ORISKANY HIGH SCHOOL LIBRARY
ORISKANY, NEW YORK  13424

GAYLORD M2